Jane is a coffee, chocolate and red wine lover, and a late-night writer of compelling, passionate, and emotionally charged fiction.

and a coffee, chocolate and red wine lovers, and a late-night
+ chocoholic) has time and time again only emerged

After You Fell

J. S. LARK

OneMoreChapter

One More Chapter
a division of HarperCollins*Publishers*
The News Building
1 London Bridge Street
London SE1 9GF

www.harpercollins.co.uk

This paperback edition 2020

First published in Great Britain in ebook format by HarperCollins*Publishers* 2020

A catalogue record for this book
is available from the British Library

ISBN: 9780008366148

This novel is entirely a work of fiction.
The names, characters and incidents portrayed in it are
the work of the author's imagination. Any resemblance to
actual persons, living or dead, events or localities is
entirely coincidental.

Set in Birka by Palimpsest Book Production Limited, Falkirk, Stirlingshire

Printed and bound in Great Britain by CPI Group (UK) Ltd,
Croydon CR0 4YY

This book is dedicated to an old and deeply missed friend from my school days, Caroline Wentworth; you passed on too soon.

LOUISE

Chapter 1

20 minutes after the fall.

'Is there a heartbeat?'

Something presses into my neck.

'Barely and it is weakening.'

A gurgling rumble struggles against the pressure on my throat.

'Get back. Stay back, please.' A distant, dominant voice.

There are lots of people here, talking in different tones. Some whispering.

'Have some respect. The medical team need space. A woman is injured. This is not a circus. Move on.'

'She's losing a lot of blood.'

'I'll treat her head injury, you find out what else is going on.'

Hands touch my head and leg.

'This is a nasty break.'

Another breath drags into my lungs. My eyes are open but I can't see.

'How bad is it? The woman's husband is in the car park. He's asking.' Another voice.

'It's bad. We'll be lucky if she's alive when we reach the hospital. Cross your fingers or pray, whichever is your thing.'

'I'll keep her breathing.' A mask presses down and the air is cleaner and colder but the pain of breathing is an excruciating shout.

'Give her some morphine and get a splint for her leg.'

Where is he?

The air chokes me, as if I am a mile underwater, the weight filling up and crushing my lungs from the inside out.

'Her airway is constricted. Get me a scalpel. I'll try a tracheostomy.'

'She has broken ribs. She may have punctured both lungs.'

I try to speak. My lips will not say a word.

The world is white.

'Her pulse is fading.'

A siren wails in the distance as the white gradually darkens and becomes black.

Chapter 2

50 minutes before the fall.

'Don't touch me!' An urge for flight darts into my legs and I step back; every muscle in my body is quivering, exhausted by the fight.

I imagine the feel of pavement under my feet. I am running – running and running.

'You're upsetting the children. All you think about is yourself. Your baby is crying in there!' His hand thrusts out, gesturing in a circular motion directing my eyes to the noise coming from the kitchen.

The sound tears at my heart and rips through my head.

'I can't cope with her.' *Or you.* I don't want to hear the screams any more. *Let me leave.*

'You wanted her.' His pitch drops, accusing me of betrayal. 'You promised you would try.'

'I tried. I can't do it.' *I can't cope with the look in your eyes.* I failed. But it is not just me. We have failed.

His clenched fist lifts and hovers an inch from my face. One day he'll break, then he'll hit me or put his hands around my neck.

'I can't help it.' The words leave my throat in a whisper because he's too close.

'You have to help it. I can't deal with you and if I can't then the children don't stand a chance.' His hand opens.

I think he's going to slap me.

There's no loyalty between us any more. No love. No hope. Nothing except anger and arguments.

His hand drops, but he snarls in my face, sounding like an attacking wolf. Then he turns away in a sudden movement, lifting his arm again and striking a fist into the wall.

His mother's favourite blue and white china vase, an antique on the bookshelf near him, wobbles as if touched by the strength of his anger. Then it falls on the parquet floor, shattering with a sharp sound that breaks our argument. Stop.

His mother found that vase at a car boot sale. She bought it for next to nothing. She was so proud of it. But she is proud of her son too.

He shakes out the hand he's hurt, ignoring the ruined vase.

'Mum ...' Our son stands in the centre of the open doorway, his beautiful face distorted in an expression of fear.

'I'm all right, love. We are both all right. Daddy is just having a tantrum.'

He thrusts a glare over his shoulder with the toss of a dagger, then walks out of the room, herding our son out of the way.

I pull the mobile from the back pocket of my jeans. It drops on the floor with a clatter because my fingers are shaking even harder now the adrenalin is ebbing away.

The phone lies there, looking up at me with a fresh crack across the screen, another testimony of our failure.

Bile rises in my throat, a bitter taste that wants me to be sick. I bend to pick up the phone. I can't remember when I last ate.

The desire to hear my mother's voice screams as loudly as my child.

I bring up my recent calls, and touch the icon saying 'Mum'.

The phone rings twice before she answers. 'Hello, love.'

'Mum.' Help me.

'Yes, darling.'

I sniff back the tears before they run from my nose as well as my eyes.

'Are you all right?'

'No. We argued.'

'Again.' A tut echoes from the phone.

We haven't made it through a single day without arguing this year.

A tear drips from my chin, falling to leave a tiny puddle on the floor that will run into a crack between the blocks of wood. The story of my marriage is shouting, shattered china, cracked glass and puddles of tears.

I swipe other tears away with the heel of a shaking palm. But tears trickle from my nose. I wipe them on the back of my hand. 'He doesn't love me. None of them do.'

'The children do.'

'No. They hate me. They blame me because he does.'

'The children love you. Shall we come over to see you? Would that calm the argument?'

'Do you think he'll leave? Do you think he'll take the children?'

'No.'

'He can't stand to be in a room with me.' Our marriage is cracked down the middle, as if the earth between us has been torn open in an earthquake and his position is on the other side of the ravine, with a glowering expression of judgement. I have tried to reach out. But I can't reach him. He has other women because I do not want him to touch me like that. But I still want to be hugged sometimes. Those moments never happen. He doesn't even kiss my cheek.

'We'll come and talk to him.'

'Mum, you can't. It will cause more trouble.'

'I can't leave you this upset. We'll be there in twenty minutes.'

At least if they came they would be here for the children.

His parents have gone out for the day. They turn their backs on our rows.

'All right. But I'm going out, Mum. I need to get away from the house. I love you. Look after the children when you get here.'

'I love you too, darling. We'll see you soon.'

'Goodbye, Mum.'

'Goodbye, dear.'

I step over the broken china, to look for paper and a pen in the drawer of the television stand and write a note telling him where I am going. To stop him being angry when he discovers that I have gone.

The note left beside the television, and the china and my tears left on the floor, I push down the door handle to get out.

The patio door glides open with a whisper, keeping my departure a secret. He will not know I have gone for a while. I'll use the back gate into the alley beside the house.

The sound of a lawnmower cutting grass in a nearby garden enters the living room. The breeze carries the scent of freshly cut grass and the sweet perfume of the mauve wisteria flowers that dangle from the plant above the door.

The note I left by the TV blows off the side and flutters to the floor.

HELEN

Chapter 3

3 days after the fall.

There's a rhythmic electronic beeping near my left ear. It echoes back from bare walls.

The thin elastic cord holding the mask over my nose and mouth scratches at the top of my ear. I turn my head, twisting my neck to look at the machines. The air inside the mask is warm and moist with condensation that tells me I have been lying here with this mask on for some time.

A soft whistle plays out from the oxygen cylinder near the bed.

A bank of tubes that are connected to my neck rattle with a plastic pitch as I look over at the open door.

I am alone in the clinically all-white room with the machines.

The urge to touch the wound lifts my hand and drags the black cable hanging from the finger-clip over the greying-white cotton blanket.

The clip is sending messages to one of the machines beside me, measuring the oxygen level in my blood.

It feels as though a weight is hanging from my wrist, the pressure of gravity drains so much energy from me with the tiniest movement – I am used to that feeling. But a pulse thumps through the crook of my elbow – that is a new sensation.

Pump-pump.

Pump-pump.

The rhythm of a drumbeat is everywhere inside me and it is repeating on the monitor.

Bleep-bleep.

Bleep-bleep.

The oxygen travels deep into my lungs, releasing energy that says something is coming.

You are going to be strong.

The feeling speaks.

Nothing else tells me a ghost is here and I do not usually hear them talk, I just know when they're near.

It might be my belief speaking.

I breathe out, and listen to the throb of sound in my ears. That is the heart calling to me. The rhythm of it tingles all the way down to my fingertips.

A hum rumbles in my nerves. I saw bees on a honeycomb once, when they had been pulled out of a hive. When my nerves hum like this, I see the shimmering silver wings of the bees as they work and dance to tell the others where to go.

Angels dance, in spheres of light, to tell others which way to go.

I can't feel the wound, only the soft dressings that cover where the incision was made.

Beneath the sheet and blanket is a rash of sensors, scattered over my chest, their information conducting the rhythms on the machines.

A thin plastic tube shakes as I move my hand down; the tube dangles from the clear bag, dripping fluid into my arm.

A man slid the long needle for the tube under my skin while someone on the other side of me counted down from ten. I can't remember anything else from then until now.

Voices chatter from somewhere outside the room. Things move and footsteps squeak across the tiled floor. The sound of one set of soft-soled shoes comes closer.

'Helen?'

The owner of the unknown voice is at the doorway into the room. A nurse with dark hair scraped back into a high ponytail, wearing a pale blue pyjama uniform. She has a bright smile, with white teeth that look chemically treated.

'Hello.' The word scrapes my throat as though my voice hasn't been used for a year.

The nurse's smile widens as she comes closer and touches my hand.

Her hand is cold.

'Hello. I am Mandy. I haven't had the privilege before, but I am glad to meet you at the point you'll be getting better.' She turns away, looking at the monitors.

'What time is it?'

'Eleven, and it's Saturday. We kept you unconscious for a while after the operation to give your body chance to rest.'

'Is everything okay?'

She smiles again, more reassuring than any words could give, before looking at the bag of slowly dripping liquid. 'Everything is fine and your brother is waiting outside. He'd like to come in and see you if you are up to a visit?'

'Is he alone?'

'Yes.'

A ripple of pleasure skims through my body. He chose to stay here with me. 'Please.'

'He's been here a lot.'

A smile pulls at my lips. A smile that has risen all the way up through my body, right from my toes to my lips.

When the nurse leaves, my fingers curl and press into the crisply starched sheet. I check that my toes move, brushing them against the weight of the sheet and blanket.

The machine's rhythm carries on with its sharp bleep declaring the pace of my heart. My heart now; someone else's heart before.

But mine now.

The pulse resonates in my fingertips, toes and ears. It is a strange feeling – an extreme, unreal feeling – to have a heart that works.

A sphere of light shimmers at the corner of the room. Near the ceiling.

I look at the open door, waiting for him to come.

Pump-pump. Pump-pump.

The sphere flies in front of my vision, across the open door. But it stays in the room with me.

I am in a hospital. It doesn't surprise me that there are spirits. But I do not want to engage with them here. They will have experienced pain here. I have known enough of my own pain, I don't want to know theirs.

Another breath runs out of my lungs, in a smooth, easy, pain-less motion.

I am used to a lack of energy that doesn't give me the strength to breathe. A week ago, my heart lurched in a beat when I breathed in but barely moved when I breathed out.

'Hello, you.'

'Simon.' The excitement in my recognition is muffled by the mask but my hand stretches out, in the way I would have reached out and wrapped my arms about his neck if I could.

His footsteps are heavier than the nurses, hard leather soles that I am used to hearing on tiled hospital floors.

'How are you feeling?' He lifts the mask off my nose and moves it down to balance on my chin so he can kiss my cheek. Extra pulses shoot from my new heart.

'Tired. But amazing, and thirsty.'

'You can give her some water?' The nurse is standing by the open door.

I nod at Simon, ignoring her. The pillowcase feels coarse and my hair dirty.

He's all I have. Him and his children.

I want my own children, though, not just to borrow his.

Another ripple of emotion flows through my prone body.

I have the heart I have been waiting for. But I no longer have Dan.

We had talked about adoption.

Now I have a healthy heart, now I can have children, and Dan is not here.

Pump-pump. Pump-pump.

The heart moves in my chest, squeezing out and pulling in the blood – its pulse striking its rhythm in every artery like the tune of a ticking clock in an empty house. It is so strong it feels as if the heart will beat its way out of my body.

It can't. It is trapped inside me now. Attached, so its movement keeps me alive.

There is someone here, though.

Someone with me.

Someone who is no longer alive.

The weight and density of their spirit is filling the space in the small room, making the atmosphere close. As if I am standing in a large crowd and too many people are breathing the same air.

The owner of the heart?

The straw Simon holds to my mouth scrapes my lip.

I have been breathing slowly for months, sitting in a bed or a chair, doing nothing, trying not to tire out my heart; preserving my life second by second and hoping that a heart would be found. The longing for children kept me going even when my old heart cracked open and oozed pain like the leaking yolk of a soft-boiled egg.

I can have the children I want now.

Thank you. I say the words to the soul that's hovering around me. If it is you: thank you.

This operation is a beginning. Today is the start of a new life for me. But it was the end of theirs.

The water is deliciously cool. It tastes far too nice to be water. I can feel it inside my throat as I swallow almost as much as I can feel the beat of the heart in my chest.

Simon is the one that kept me alive when I was young. He gave me reason after reason to fight on with unconditional love as wide as an ocean. I want to give all the love that he's taught me to my children.

He takes the cup away and puts it down.

I lift a hand, asking him to hold it.

His hand strokes over my hair, the touch stirring strands that are matted. His hand falls, wraps around mine and holds tight. 'You're going to be okay.'

I nod. I know.

A cartoon-like sparkle catches in his right eye, the white light in the room reflecting on the sheen of tears. The aura around him is sunshine, orange and yellow, and the orb is hovering behind him.

But the orb is not the owner of the heart.

The weight of exhaustion suddenly presses like large hands

on my chest, pushing me down and submerging me in a swamp of fatigue. I can't stay awake any more.

A memory of Simon and me curled up tight together as children hovers.

The bleep echoing my heartbeat slows.

Chapter 4

2 weeks and 3 days after the fall.

'Come on, then. Hurry up. There are people waiting to greet you,' Simon shouts over his shoulder as he walks ahead with the small suitcase I have brought back from the hospital.

I am walking much quicker than I had on the way out to his car after we had the call saying a heart was available. But there is a sharp pulling in my chest that means I do not rush. It is from the surgery, though, not weakness. I still have that celebrating hard pump of blood, like the vibration of a chiming bell ringing in every artery and vein, yelling out that one day soon I am going to be entirely better. *Hear ye. Hear ye. Helen Matthews is well.*

My brain is diagnosing the level of my health like a Fitbit measuring every sensation – each out breath and every moment a muscle or tendon moves. I do not want to reject this heart.

The front door opens.

'Hello.' Miriam, Mim, waves as she steps out. 'It is good to see you with colour in your cheeks.' The colours around her are muddy browns and greens. It is a spiteful aura.

'Auntie Helen!' Kevin and Liam squeeze past their mother's legs and run to me.

'Remember what I said,' Simon calls. 'Be careful with your aunt, she's recovering.'

I lift my hands, encouraging the twins to grasp one each. 'As long as you don't pull I'll be fine.' They are used to Auntie Helen's frailty.

A picture runs through my mind, a memory that doesn't belong to me. I am running along a beach, holding the hand of a small girl and jumping the shallow waves that roll onto the sand. I know the girl is my daughter, but I do not know how I know.

I want a daughter first. If I can pick.

'Welcome home.' Mim's arms wrap around my neck and she kisses my cheek. I do not mirror the embrace; the boys have possession of my hands. 'We have a celebration tea planned—'

'With fizzy orange!'

'And ice cream!' the boys add as their hands slip out of mine in unison. They run into the house bursting with the constant excitement of four-year-olds.

'And pizza. Sorry, it's more their party than yours,' Mim whispers.

I don't mind. If the boys are happy, I'm happy.

I have been guilty of spoiling Simon's boys as if they are mine since they were born. They are a relief for the craving in my womb.

Dan hated me talking about children. He always said he wanted children, but then changed his mind two years ago.

'Don't go on about children, you can't have them, you are too ill, stop talking about babies, even if we adopt how are you going to look after a child?'

Every time he said words like that there was another sharp pin stabbing into the voodoo effigy of me, the effigy it felt as if he held in his hand.

Then he told me, 'I don't love you any more. You have to go,' driving a kitchen knife into my sick heart and making it shatter.

He moved his pregnant mistress in a week after Simon had loaded up the car with the boxes, bags and cases packed full of my half of our life together.

Every day, since the day I moved out of the flat, was a day to endure – surviving long enough to get this heart.

That was the end.

Now I have the heart.

This is the beginning.

It whispers to me all the time. The heart.

A coverall smile gathers up my expression as I walk into the house behind Mim; the smile I have given everyone who has asked how I feel over the years.

Simon's hand touches my waist as he leans to put the case on the floor near the stairs in the hall. 'Welcome home. I'll take your case up after we've eaten.'

'Thank you.' The children and Mim are in the kitchen already. I turn, stretching up to wrap my arms around his neck. It pulls my chest. I hold on tight and pull him down a little.

He is six years older and six inches taller. I have stretched up to hold him for as long as I can remember.

His arms slide around my middle to return the hug. I kiss his cheek. He kisses mine. The world is perfect for a moment.

'You'll be all right.'

I nod as I let go, my cheek pricked by the hairs of his short beard. 'I know I will. I'm excited.'

Excited because I know that one day soon I am going to start my own family.

Colour creeps up from his neck into his cheeks. The pink tint in Simon's skin when he or I mention anything that might refer to Dan keeps telling me Simon feels guilty. Dan was, is, his friend.

Simon introduced Dan to me in my first year at college. Dan asked me out that day. But how we ended is not Simon's fault and Simon took me in, looking after me for the last few months. Just as he did when we were children.

This man, my brother, is the perfect man. Mim is lucky.

'Daddy. Auntie Helen. Hurry up. We're hungry!' The children shout from the kitchen as the mouth-watering smell of melted cheese and pepperoni wafts into the hall.

Simon smiles. There is a look in his eyes that I have seen for as long as I can remember. I see this look in my mind's eye every night before I go to sleep. The expression says 'I love you' with no need for words.

I see that look from a young boy, and I am standing in another hall, in another house, and the boy ... I don't know him.

Will he be my child?

Am I connecting with spirits from the future now as well as the past?

'You first.' Simon's hand lifts. 'It's your coming-home party. But go on up to bed if you start feeling too ill.'

'Yes, Dad.'

A low laugh follows my movement.

A muffled ringtone vibrates through the fabric of my suitcase behind us. I turn back, pointing. 'My phone.'

'I'll get it.' Simon turns, bends to release the zip on the suitcase, takes out the phone and looks at the caller ID. 'It's Chloe.' He puts the phone in my outstretched palm just as the ringing stops. 'I'll call her back after we've eaten.' I slip the phone into the back pocket of my jeans.

'She can come over if you want her to.'

'Tomorrow. I'm too tired tonight.'

'Whenever suits the two of you.'

Chapter 5

3 weeks and 1 day after the fall.

The radio plays from its position at the end of the kitchen work surface; talking and singing to me as I skim through the internet pages, sliding the stories up on the small screen of my phone.

Even little things like this, like being able to concentrate on anything in the world outside my head, was hard in the years that illness stole my life. In the end, all I had the energy to do was sit in a chair and watch television and it was hard to even concentrate on that.

It is impossible for other people to imagine what it's like to be trapped in a body that can't do anything. My thoughts were busy controlling my breaths and cluttered with weakness, while pain constantly screamed, even through the fog of pain-killers.

I thought about suicide when Dan and I split up. But whilst there was still a chance of being able to live properly with someone else's heart, I held onto that cliff edge of hope for months. Living for when the time came.

The time is now, and ever since I have come back to Simon's I've been feeling like a sprinter in the starting blocks waiting for the gun to go off. And when it does, I am going to run so hard and fast, just because I can.

Pump-pump. Pump-pump.

The sound of my heart continually talks to me. The blood thrusting through my body, making all my senses alert.

I can read today, I can read and soak up information like a sponge dropped into water, and at the same time I am listening to music.

The pulse of my heartbeat follows the baseline of the song on the radio – expressing its power.

If I could see my own aura, would it have changed? Would I now have some of the aura of the person whose body is muddled up with mine?

I still feel them. If it is them. I feel someone here. Someone who came back from the hospital with me. I think they're trying to press their emotions into my heart, but it is just a pressure in my bloodstream that I do not understand.

A repeated knock rattles the thin glass in the back door; double glazing is still on Simon and Mim's to do list in their 1920s terrace.

Before I respond the door handle twists. 'Hello.'

'Chloe.' I stand up. 'You made me jump.' But I knew she was coming to make me lunch.

She smiles with the captivating look that made me fall for her friendship when I was sixteen. Before then my friendships had been brief play-dates and playground-mates. The foster homes and hospitals Simon and I had travelled around on a never-ending roller coaster meant I didn't attach myself to people because in days or weeks we would move on.

I had not let proper friendships form until I had obtained control over my own life. Dan and Chloe came along at the same time; friends arriving like red London buses. They had become as important to me as extra limbs after only a few weeks.

Dan told me I was needy, that I had desperately been waiting for friends, and when I had found them I clung on.

I told him that if he'd had a childhood like mine and Simon's he would know the value of loyalty and people who care about you.

Dan had not valued me.

Chloe's dark hair tickles my ear as she holds me and I hold her. She values my friendship as much as I value hers. I have Chloe as well as Simon and the boys.

The scent of the perfume she always wears calms me immediately.

'You look so well.' Chloe's voice is deep, sexy; it draws attention to everything she says. It made me gravitate towards her. It makes men gravitate towards her. When we were younger and I was well enough to go out there was always a pack of men around her by the end of the night.

Chloe's aura is golden; it is shades of yellow, orange and amber.

Her hands stay on my shoulders. 'Your skin is a decent colour for the first time in years.'

'Thank you. I think.'

She laughs as her hands fall away. 'Tea?'

'Yes, please.'

A smile tumbles over her shoulder in my direction. 'I am going to put sugar in it; you need to put some weight on now you're well.'

'I hate sugar in tea.'

'I don't care what you want. You're doing what is good for you. What do you want to eat?'

'There's a tin of soup in the top of that cupboard.' I point at the cupboard then grip the table so I can ease into the chair and avoid pulling the stitches in my chest.

'Are you in pain?'

I didn't notice her looking at me. 'A little.'

'Is it time to take your tablets?'

'Probably.' I move to get up but she lifts a hand.

'Stay seated, I'll get them, and I'll heat up the soup after we have drunk the tea.'

'Thank you.'

'No need for thanks. I want you better.' Her voice bounces off the blue tiles behind the sink in the moment before the tap turns on. 'People say the world can be put right with a cup of tea but I think a new heart wins. What does it feel like?' The pitch of her voice rises so I can hear her over the water running into the kettle.

'Life-saving.' A laugh stutters from my throat. Then I add, 'Strange. I'm certain no one else is as conscious of their heart beating. It's as if someone is making a heartbeat sound in my ear all the time, and it feels like it's jolting me.'

Chloe faces me and leans back against the wooden work surface while the kettle heats. 'I can't imagine having a piece of someone else inside me. It must be weird. Especially when you know how quickly that heart moved from beating inside someone else to you.'

I glance down at my phone; the screen is black. 'Yes.' The rhythm beats harder, and so constantly it is like someone relentlessly banging on a door to obtain my attention.

'It has someone else's DNA.' There's a teasing note in Chloe's voice. 'I wonder if it's changed your DNA. Then if you did that Ancestry DNA thing they might connect you.'

She doesn't know I can feel spirits.

I never talk about my sixth sense.

The doctors in the hospital taught me, with electrical shocks to the brain, that people do not believe in a sixth sense. Everyone else thinks it is a symptom of bipolar. Imagined. Not Real.

It is real.

Those of us who have a sixth sense know it is real.

But I have never met anyone who can see and feel the things that I do, because I never tell.

A shiver runs through my spine, a ghost passing through me. The owner of my new heart passing through me?

No. I am sure their spirit is in the heart, inside me.

Steam erupts from the kettle behind Chloe as it clicks off.

She turns and pours the water into the mugs, then fetches the milk from the fridge. 'I think a heart being transplanted is stranger than a lung or a liver because, okay, everyone knows that there aren't any thoughts or knowledge in the heart—' the spoon clinks against the edge of the china cup as she stirs in sugar, moving the spoon round and round '—but you feel emotion in your heart, don't you?' She looks over her shoulder at me.

I nod. Because of course it's true. My last year has made that very clear – the pain in my emotionally broken heart has been worse than the pain of illness at times.

I was isolated as a child. Cut off from others by illness and homelessness. Isolated by a mind that did not function like other people's. Dan isolated me again. He kept our friends, home and possessions.

I arrived at Simon's with only a few boxes of personal things and my clothes. I have been shut away in a room here ever since, too ill to go out, waiting for another chance to live.

The soul that has given me this heart has given me that chance.

Chloe throws a teabag into the pedal bin; the lid chimes as it drops. 'My heart feels tighter when I'm angry.' She returns to fish the teabag out from the other cup and keeps talking as she takes that over to toss it in the bin. 'And soft and squidgy, like marshmallow, when I'm falling for a man.'

The teaspoon drops in the sink. She picks up the mugs and turns with a handle held in either hand. 'I wonder what your heart felt before it came to you?' The mugs clunk down on the wooden table and the tea spills slightly.

The paper towel is in my reach. I pull some off and wipe up the spill as she fetches the bottle and packets of my pills and a small glass of water to wash them down.

'Thank you.'

She chooses the chair opposite me, sits, and pulls her mug close, embracing it with both hands. Her eyes are glossy with an expression of excitement. She loves a good gossip. 'What do you think?'

'I hope it suffered a lot less pain than mine.' The conversation is sparking more shivers up and down my spine.

I reach for the bottle. The pills rattle. The lid is stiff but after a second it opens and I tip out two small white pills. With those pills cradled in my palm, I pick up one of the packets.

I always lay pills out in a row before I take them.

I have more medication to take than I did before the operation. What does this heart make of all this prescribed poison? Drugs that make the natural defences of my body impotent, drugs that silence the cry of pain, antibiotics that fight the bad bugs and emotion-controlling pills.

'Hearts spend most of their time in pain in my experience,

and I'm not talking about malfunctioning hearts. Although perhaps I am because my pain was mostly caused by Mum's and Dad's malfunctioning hearts.'

'The inability to put you and Simon first was in their heads.'

Simon thinks our mum had bipolar too. 'Wherever their motivation came from it permanently hurts my heart to remember how they deserted us. A sick child didn't fit in with their hippy lifestyle. They couldn't be tied to the proximity of hospitals.' I pick up a pill and sip the water to wash it down.

The feelings of loss and loneliness are in me again, and, as Chloe said, they grasp the heart and squeeze it until it hurts.

The need for love in humans is a terrible thing. It destroys people. It has tried to destroy me lots of times. I need others. I need to belong. I need to be wanted. I need to be needed.

Chloe's hand reaches out and brushes the back of mine as I take the next pill. Then there's a smile that sweeps everything away. 'And then Dan the bastard ...' she says in a low voice.

We laugh, but my new heart clenches again in response to the memory of the brutal way he betrayed me.

I swallow another pill, sensing the irony of the bitter pills of fate that I have swallowed in my life. I was even too sick to cry over Dan's disloyalty. If I had cried it would have exhausted my heart and so I had to control my heartbreak to stay alive. Isolated in a room, living from breath to breath, not day to day.

'Have you heard from him?' Chloe's voice has a cautious cadence because she knows I have no desire to hear anything about him. But maybe she thinks he will send some good wishes.

I take more pills without answering for a moment. Then look into her eyes. 'No.' My answer is in the flattest tone. I take the last pill and drink the last of the water.

'Does he know about your operation?'

I wrap my hands around the warm mug, lacing my fingers together on the far side. 'I should think so. Simon must have mentioned it or, if not him, then someone else.'

Dan and I were us for so long all his friends were mine too. But I haven't spoken to any of them since we split. It was too embarrassing to face the truth and the truth was being flaunted in front of their faces by Dan. They know the other woman, when the baby is due and how happy the two of them are. I do not want to know any of that. I let him have our mutual friends as part of the separation.

'How are you going to spend your time while you are recovering? You need to do something different.'

'I might order a jigsaw puzzle.'

'You party animal.'

'Maybe I'll take up Tai Chi. There are YouTube videos.'

She nods, smiling, because she knows I am not considering anything.

My thoughts spin. I see Dan in the days I was convinced I was loved by him. So many moments when I believed we were happy. Those days have all been burned to a pile of ashes.

This heart felt the same before it was put inside me. I can sense it. As if the previous owner is sitting where I am. Sitting inside me.

I hear children laughing, then children crying. My future children or this soul's?

'We can go for a short walk every day next week. Then the week after we can walk farther and so on, until you are well on the mend. It won't be long ...'

'I know it won't.' Before I can be me.

I push the ghost aside and smile.

Chloe reaches out. I reach out too and we clasp hands.

Her hand is warm from the heat of the hot tea in her mug.

'The NHS will send letters for people who have received donated organs, so you can say thank you to the family. Did you know that?'

'No.'

'The nurses will probably tell you. But I looked it up.' She lets go of my hand and twists to take the phone out from the back pocket of her jeans, then concentrates on that as I sip my tea.

Every sensation seems to be more intense; even drinking tea is improved by a healthy heart.

She looks up. 'Here.' She holds out her phone, tilting it to show me the screen. I take the phone and look at the NHS leaflet. It says what she has just told me – I can write to the person's family and say thank you. It encourages me to do that. But I can't tell them my name.

'Do you think you'll do that?' Chloe asks.

I hand back the phone and sense someone else reaching out with me. I can't explain the feeling. If I could describe it better perhaps others might believe in a sixth sense. 'Probably. I would like to say thank you.'

If I write, I will tell the family that I can have children now. The soul inside my heart has given me that chance.

When I hold the front door open just under an hour later, standing on the doorstep and waving to Chloe, before she turns the corner at the end of the street, the spirit is whispering. I can't understand the words but the sound surrounds me.

Perhaps the spirit wants me to contact their family before they pass on?

I shut the door. The silence in the house is deafening – as though silence is the loudest noise.

Chloe turned the radio off when we were talking. I like sound.

I smile as I turn the radio on, because I recognise how quickly I walked along the hall.

A dance song is playing, the bass beat stirs my shoulders into a little shake. The zip of stitches in my chest shoots a sharp pain through my torso that makes me wince. But I smile at the same time. 'Enough of that for now, but soon I'll be able to do everything.' That is what I'll write about in my thank you card, about the chance of children and dancing.

A buzz hums in my blood, drowning out the beat of the heart. Excitement is a dance rhythm of its own.

I sit at the kitchen table and pull over my laptop. Then open my phone and look at the list of links in my search of obituaries.

Who did this heart come from?

What has it felt before?

What life has it known?

The whispering intensifies, but it is still too muffled to work out any words.

The soul wants me to know who it is. I know that.

Chapter 6

3 weeks and 2 days after the fall.

'Tea.' The shout comes through the glossy white bedroom door.

'Come in,' I shout to Simon as I click to close the laptop's browser window. The laptop's lid snaps down like a crocodile's bite as the door opens. I put the laptop aside on the bed next to me and adjust the pillows I am leaning on, as he puts a mug of tea down on the bedside chest.

The smell of hot tea says good morning and stirs up a *déjà vu* moment that makes a feeling of safety clasp at my heart.

'Has Chloe confirmed she's coming in to make you lunch today?'

'Yes.'

'Good. I know we can make you a sandwich ahead of time, but I'll worry if you are here all day on your own.'

'I'm fine. I managed before the operation.'

'With difficulty.'

'I know, but I'm getting better every day.'

A smile pulls at his lips and his hand lifts and runs over my hair. It's a gesture that's most common when he's with the boys now. But it's a gesture I have known for as long as I can remember.

I think Simon has always felt like a father to me and I have always looked up to him. We are not a normal brother and sister. But who would be normal after our childhood?

The bed dips as he sits on the edge. He holds my hand. 'Your eyes have dark circles. Did you sleep?'

'Not much. I'm too excited.' I smile. 'And thank you for pointing out I have bags under my eyes.'

His eyes open wider and his eyebrows lift as he squeezes my hand but he doesn't answer my comment. 'Where are your tablets?'

'Downstairs in the cupboard. But it's not because of that. Everything has changed – anyone would be excited.' It is not a bipolar episode.

'I know. But you can take your tablets with the tea.' He squeezes my hand again then lets go and stands up. 'I'll be back in a minute.'

'Okay.'

I rest back on the pillows, looking at the plain ceiling, remembering the bumpy or swirly Artex ceilings I stared at when I was younger. Patterns on the ceiling or in the curtains became mythical creatures. Fairies. Trolls. Unicorns. Dragons. There is no fictional image in Simon's smooth replastered ceiling.

'Pills.' He walks into the room rattling the bottle like a maraca. His other hand holds out the packets. 'Here.'

'Thank you.'

He's left the door open and the noise of the boys talking to Mim at the breakfast table downstairs flows in.

'What will you do today?'

A shrug lifts my shoulders.

He sits on the edge of the bed again. Many hours of our

relationship have been spent in this position on hospital, hostel, foster or children's homes' beds.

'What were you looking at on the laptop?'

'Nothing really.'

A smile. He knows me too well. 'Binge watch a boxset to stop yourself from becoming impatient with the immobility. It will stop you getting obsessed with something unhealthy.'

'I'll be mobile soon, so I have a reason to be impatient.' I lean forward and hold his hand. 'And as soon as I am mobile I won't have time to become unhealthily obsessed with anything. I'll be too busy being healthy.'

A deep-pitched laugh rumbles low in his throat. 'The boys have some video games you could play?'

'For four-year-olds. No, thank you.'

His hand slides out of mine. 'I'd better get off to work.' He stands.

I reach up, encouraging him to lean down for a hug.

He kisses my cheek as I kiss his. 'Have a good day.'

'You too.'

'Oh, I will.' I smile.

He strokes my cheek.

When the door shuts behind him, I open the laptop again. All the pages I have been looking at are open browser tabs: obituaries posted by local and national papers.

I click on the picture of a middle-aged, middle-weight man with a receding hairline at his temples.

I am reading the obituaries of the people who died on the day of my operation, or the day before it.

The man lived in a small town in Wales, not far from Cardiff. How far would they move a heart around the country?

I click the back arrow and return to the column of names

and faces, then click on the next picture. It is a younger man with thick short ginger hair and a beard. Rory Smith. He'd died after a motorcycle accident. I click the back arrow.

It is surprising how many people die in one day.

The mug of tea and the tablets are still beside me.

I click on the story of another dead person and read as I pick up the bottle and tip two little white pills onto the plain powder-blue duvet cover. I swap that bottle for a packet and push out a pill from the foil. I keep popping out different tablets until there is a line of pills in front of me.

I take the tablets one by one with my tea and click on another dead face.

Chapter 7

4 weeks and 5 days after the fall.

A tap hits the glass in the back door. It's Chloe.

'Come in.' I touch the screen to close the notes on my phone and minimise the browser on the laptop.

The door is already opening.

I stand, turn and shut the lid of the laptop behind me. 'Hello.' I smile; not at Chloe but because I moved quickly.

My movement slipped from first to third gear with ease and everything I notice like that makes me smile. The operation scar doesn't pull very much any more and I hardly notice my heart beating.

'I bought us a treat for lunch.' She raises a thin white plastic carrier bag that is hanging from her right hand. 'I went to the deli and bought one of their quiches and a selection of salads.' She places the bag on the table.

'Thank you. I'm getting a bit bored of soup.'

'Me too.'

I smile when I sit down but the expression feels awkward. Guilt is a sharp pang in my stomach. It is because I hid the images on my laptop screen. But I have to keep my morbid search secret because no one else will understand. Or believe me. I can't tell them the spirit of the person my heart came from wants me to find their family.

Chloe delves into the opaque carrier bag and begins unloading it. 'What have you been up to today?'

'Not much. I didn't get out of bed until eleven, then I had a bath. I haven't been downstairs long.'

'You sound so much better already.'

'I feel it, but there is a long way to go.'

'How many weeks is it before you'll be able to work?' She takes the plates out of a cupboard while she talks.

I can probably pick up plates now but the consultant told me not to lift anything for six weeks and I am following every piece of guidance religiously.

'Three months, if I go back into childcare.'

'It's hardly any time, really. New heart. New life. New work opportunities.' She turns with the plates in her hand. 'It's astonishing—' the plates clunk on the table '—what they can do now.' She smiles before turning away. 'I've been reading stories about people who have connected with their donors.' She delves into the drawer for knives and forks, rattling the cutlery. 'Do you want a hot drink? Tea? Coffee?'

'I'm fine with water.'

The cutlery clatters onto the table, probably scratching the already scarred wood. But it is a young family's table with rough-and-ready boys. She takes glasses out of the cupboard. 'So anyway, I was telling you about the stories I've read.'

'Yes.' Her thoughts have been turning in the same direction as mine.

'A woman in one of those true-stories-from-the-readers magazines said ...' the water runs, hitting the bottom of the sink and drowning her words; I listen harder '... she wrote a thank-you letter.' The sound of the water changes to a dribble as Chloe tests to see if it is running cold enough to be fresh. 'She was younger than you.' The water runs into a glass as Chloe glances over her shoulder. 'Her kidney had come from an older woman and the family she contacted were the donor's children.'

The tap turns off, then Chloe turns around with a glass in either hand. 'The family wrote back to her, a brother and sister. It was the sister who really wanted to make contact. The brother wasn't very interested.' Chloe sits at the table, looking me in the eyes as she slides a glass towards me. 'But the sister gives this woman her contact information and they write back and forth. Then the sister suggests they meet.'

The sip of cold water grasps at my throat and a shiver runs down my spine.

'She persuaded the brother to go along to keep her company. But when the brother and woman met, they got on really well. To cut a long story short they fell for each other and married. Don't you think that's odd?'

'But it's the sort of sensational story that sells those magazines, isn't it?'

Chloe picks up a large knife and pulls the quiche towards her. 'How much do you want?'

'Just a small piece.'

'There's another story. It was on one of the morning TV programmes. It was a mother who lost her teenage daughter. She had donated lots of different organs.' Chloe slid a plate over to me.

I reach for the spoon to delve into the tub of coleslaw and green salad.

'The mother had half a dozen thank-you letters and she replied to them all. Now all those people meet at least once a year. They're all friends.'

'Really? I can't imagine all those people with elements of one person.' I don't want to know if other people have a part of the person I received my heart from. Possessiveness pulses into my blood. I am tied to this person. It is a strange connection to have with someone. But the heart was a gift given to me. That is what I feel from the presence of the person I think this heart once belonged to – that they chose me.

'There's another story,' Chloe carries on between mouthfuls of lunch. 'An older woman had a transplant. The donor's daughter is a single parent with six children. The older woman had no family and so she became a surrogate mother and grandmother.' Chloe looks at me with an expression that asks for a reaction.

'What are you saying? That I should write a thank-you card to the donor's family solely to acquire a parent or a husband?' She knows me too well; she knows I'll be thinking about the owner of this heart's previous relationships and be jealous of any love, even though she doesn't know I speak to spirits.

'You never know.' She smiles, unreleased laughter dancing in her eyes.

I smile too, but in that moment of shared amusement an immediate decision thrusts its way up my throat and into my mouth. An urge to tell her my secret is so strong my lips can't close on the words. 'I have been trying to work out whose heart it is.' The statement slips out like a slippery fish. But now it is told I can't pull it back. I fill my mouth with quiche so I will not say more.

'Pardon?'

'It's just something to do.' It's an attempt to pull the words back but I can see her mind chewing on them as her gaze reaches beyond me.

I shouldn't have said anything. She knows I can obsess over things at times. She is thinking about that.

This is nothing to do with bipolar, but I can't tell her why I know that because she will think that I am crazy anyway if I tell her.

Her eyes refocus on me. On my face. On my eyes. 'How are you trying to work it out?' She's looking at me with the odd expression that Simon's face twists into when he is asking himself, is she having an episode?

My cutlery clatters onto the plate and I reach for my phone. I touch it so the screen shows and tilt the phone in her direction to show her the list of names and websites. 'I'm looking at the people who died the day of my operation or the day before. I was bored, and it was something interesting to do. You were the one who raised the subject.'

'I know I said write to the family, but looking up dead people is a bit odd, Helen.'

'The family might not write back, and I want to know who owned the heart.' Who is inside me, whispering and thumping for attention?

She takes the phone and looks. 'You know we agreed I would warn you if you do anything strange? Well, this is strange.'

I shake my head, certain there are wrinkles on my nose as my face expresses a violent rejection of that idea. 'No.' This is not about bipolar. 'Wouldn't you want to know?' I throw across the table as I pick up my cutlery. Surely someone with no sixth sense would want to know too?

'Now I think about it I might definitely not want to know.' She laughs as I swallow another mouthful of quiche. Her expression twists from one look to another over the irony of having just talked about people who have done the opposite. 'But this is too morbid, searching for the person.' She puts the phone down on the table. 'You should think about the future, not the past.'

'I am.'

'Have you taken your tablets?'

'You are as bad as Simon. I appreciate you buying me lunch, but you don't need to mother me. And my tablets are in my room upstairs.'

'I'll fetch them when we finish eating.'

'Thank you.'

'Are you going to write a letter and stop searching obituaries?' Chloe says as she steps out of the front door.

We haven't talked about the donor for the last half an hour, but the conversational leap backwards doesn't surprise me. It proves I shouldn't talk about it. 'I'll speak to a nurse when I go in for the next check-up.'

'Take a thank-you card with you – they can pass it on. But leave it at that.' Her arms settle on my shoulders and wrap around my neck like the wings of a mother hen. A firm kiss is pressed on my cheek; a kiss that says, promise me. 'Take care of yourself,' she says near my ear as she lets me go. 'Do not obsess over the donor.'

I smile as her hold slips away. 'I'll see you tomorrow.'

'Yes.' The door bangs. I shut it too hard. I don't know my own strength now; there is so much energy humming in my limbs. It makes my body want to bounce with the rhythm of life. I am going to start walking at lunchtime next week, with Chloe for a crutch until I build up my stamina and feel confident going outside alone.

Ready. Steady. Go.

A starter gun fires in my head.

I return to my place at the kitchen table, open the laptop and expand the browser. All the recent links I have added to my favourites are open. Each tab tells me something about someone on the list on my phone.

The faces stare at me.

I have been waiting for the spirit to whisper when they see themselves, to draw me to one of these people. I haven't felt them speak clearly. But I am ignoring the men. The sense I have of someone moving in my body is a sense of someone light, thin, and the whisper is not a deep tone.

I open the fourth tab.

Louise Lovett.

I like her the most.

I like her wide smile. Her eyes glow as she looks directly into the camera expressing the emotions of a life that lacks nothing.

I feel as if she's looking at me; asking me something with her eyes.

A sensation, like catching the breeze from someone's outbreath, whispers through me.

She's very young in the picture. Early twenties ... She was thirty-two the day she died. Her obituary doesn't say much. It was published on a regional press website, written for the benefit of local people.

"Thank you to everyone who joined us in celebrating the life of our beautiful daughter Louise at Christ Church, Old Town in Swindon. We miss her. She has been taken from the world far too soon."

The obituary stands out because it doesn't say anything about her life. It seems as if the parent who wrote it could not bring themselves to mention any more, as if they can't cope with the words.

I open a new tab, click on the search engine and type 'Louise Lovett'.

The third link down reads '*Louise Lovett Profiles | Facebook*'. I click on the link and then there are more faces to look through. I increase the zoom on the screen so the pictures are clearer and easier to scan for Louise's face. She's there, three web pages in. The picture is the one used on the paper's website. When I go into her profile there's the picture I know and a solid black header that tells me her profile is private.

All the posts beneath the black header are viral videos that she's shared.

The last post is months old.

I save the webpage to my favourites and go back to the original search results.

The heart is thumping hard. Bump-bump. Bump-bump. It is so strong it might be someone putting all their strength into thumping their shoulder against a door to break it down.

Is Louise telling me that this is her?

The list continues to lead to social media sites. '*Louise Lovett Profiles | LinkedIn*'. '*Louise Lovett | Twitter*'.

Then, '*Woman dies in fall from a Swindon car park.*' The words underneath the headline read, '*The South Western Ambulance Service NHS Foundation Trust spokesman said: "We were called to the scene of the incident at 1349 responding to reports that a woman had fallen from the top floor of the car park. We sent one ambulance crew and a duty officer. Sadly, a woman in her 30s was pronounced dead before …*'

I open the link and a news screen full of colourful adverts pops up, denying the morbid subject of the article. The article consists of four short paragraphs. It says that there is no known reason for the woman's fall, talks about the ambulance crew's attempt to save her and mentions that there is no statement from the woman's family.

The date the story was posted is the day that Louise Lovett died. She died in Swindon. She died after a horrific fall.

The laptop snaps when I shut it as the heart lurches, as though it skipped a beat.

She is inside me. I know she is.

Chapter 8

5 weeks and 6 days after the fall.

My hands slide into the back-pockets of my jeans in a self-comforting uncertain gesture. This is the first day I have been outdoors on my own and I've come a long way from the house.

The sky is a blanket of writhing, murky, grey clouds that promise rain but it's a warm day.

I haven't brought a coat with me. I didn't think to look at the weather forecast. I have spent so many years trapped inside buildings, sick, entirely unaware of what was happening outside, weather is not something I think about.

But I have set up my vigil in the car park of the Baptist Church, and the door into the porch has been left wide open. There are cars parked here. There must be people inside.

A movement catches the edge of my vision. Someone has turned the corner at the end of the street. A woman with a pushchair.

I look back at the house on the opposite side of the road.

I stared at the image of that 1950s house for days online, until I found it.

But it is Louise's parents I want to see, not their house. Where are they?

The woman with the pushchair walks past the house.

There is a car on the crescent drive, in front of the post-box-red garage doors. I saw that car in a picture. I recognise the registration number.

The red front door is partially obscured by a semi-circular flower bed packed with white roses in full bloom. The scent of the roses, myrrh, is so thick it carries to this side of the street.

My fingers curl into fists in the back pockets of my jeans.

I have been waiting for nearly an hour.

I am sure they're in the house.

A large, warm drop of rain falls on my forehead, another drop falls on my hair, a third leaves a damp spot on my shoulder in a final warning. Then the rain comes down in a harsh rush, hammering on my head, hitting my shoulders and soaking through my T-shirt in seconds.

I run for the sanctuary of the church entrance.

When I am under cover, I slide the rucksack off my shoulder, let it drop onto the tiled floor and turn to watch the rain.

It is the heaviest rainfall I remember.

I reach out a hand to catch the large, warm drops of water. I have spent years hiding from rain; hiding from life. I do not have to hide any more. I am not weak. I do not need to be afraid of consequences.

My arms open wide, I take another step forward, closing my lips and eyes and tipping back my head so the rain runs over my face. I don't remember feeling rain before.

I love it.

Why do people complain about rain? It feels beautiful.

The darkness behind my eyelids lets me focus on the sensations of the water soaking through my hair and clothes.

I am alive – living.

'We need to hurry.'

I open my eyes and look over the road. The front door is open and a man has stepped out.

I take a step, pulled forward by emotions I can only describe as longing. I am not sure if the emotions are mine or Louise's.

I stand at the edge of the car park, under the trembling green canopy of a large conker tree.

A woman steps out of the front door and hurries to reach the passenger side of the car.

I'm not sure it's them. I can't see them properly. The roses are in the way and they're using an umbrella.

The rain stops as quickly as it started just as the woman pulls the car door open and ducks inside.

Rain is dripping from my fingertips onto the tarmac.

The man walks around the front of the car to the driver's door, his face covered by the umbrella as he lowers it.

Heavy, colder drops of water drip off the leaves of the tree onto my hair and shoulders.

He opens the car door, his back turned to me, and collapses the umbrella.

Cars travel along the road, passing between us. The cars are noisier now their tyres run over the wet tarmac, the surface water flicking up behind the wheels.

They are both in the car. I see the movement of his arm as he turns the key in the ignition, then he looks at the woman.

It's them.

I step forward again, trying to see better, to read their lips, to know what they are saying to one another.

Hours of research have brought me here.

It is the half-circle flower bed full of white roses that convinced me this is the house I saw. The roses were in bloom in the picture on Facebook.

There was one clue a long way down in the stream of posts under Louise Lovett's profile. A public post from someone else. *'Happy birthday my darling daughter.'* The picture beneath the words contained an older man and woman holding up a glinting happy birthday banner with two grinning, young blond children.

My heart knew the children. Emotion wrapped around the heart and pulled tight, like yellow ribbons tied around the trunk of an old oak tree, with loose ends waving in the breeze – holding onto memories.

The post was published by Robert Dowling. Robert Dowling wrote the word 'daughter'.

His Facebook account is not private and he posts everything. He checks into coffee shops, cinemas, restaurants and parks.

He lives in Swindon. Louise Lovett died in Swindon. They could have transported her heart to London within two hours of her death. I am sure it's her heart.

Louise Lovett's funeral took place in an Anglican church half a mile from here.

There is a picture on Robert's Facebook page that pointed me to this side of Swindon too. In that picture, he is reaching out, holding the top of a Christmas tree, in a posture that asks questions of the onlookers. Is this the one? Are the branches even? The onlookers in the picture are the two blond children. But the thing that stood out to me in the post was the sign in the background. *Waitrose Wichelstowe.*

I have become a detective. I've spent all my hours, when alone, looking at the places Robert Dowling has been to, working out where he lives. There's a map of Swindon in a drawer in my bedroom with dots marking in blue Biro the places Robert checks into and posts from. There's a cluster of blue dots around this church.

There are three parks he visits near here: Queens Park, The

Lawns and Coate Water Country Park. When he goes to the cinema, McDonald's or Frankie & Benny's it is always in the Greenbridge Retail Park, which is less than ten minutes by car. He uses shops in Old Town, a few minutes in the other direction, and takes the children to the library and the museum there.

It was a guess that he lives somewhere in the middle of these places.

Hours of my time have been consumed dragging a yellow man over street maps on the tip of the cursor, turning the camera from angle to angle, searching for the flower bed his wife stood in front of. Her raised hand was covered by a muddy gardening glove and the smear of mud marking her nose said she was weeding and had wiped her face. It was a moment of very normal life preserved forever.

The car is facing me. The man is looking right and left, waiting for a chance to turn but cars are passing. He looks at me through a brief gap in the passing traffic.

It is Robert Dowling.

My heart bursts, rushing into a rhythm of excitement that does not feel as if it is my emotion.

Is he wondering why I am staring?

My hand lifts unconsciously as if to wave.

She wants me to speak. Louise. She is trying to push words out of my mouth, to form them with my lips and tongue. But I still can't hear her voice clearly.

He looks left, right and left again then steers the car out into the road.

His aura, and his wife's, are shades of red from a deep blushing pink on to scarlet and the darkest claret.

Chapter 9

13.21.

The man sitting diagonally across the table from me is playing loud music. It would be better if I could hear the song, but all I hear is the thud of the rhythm. The same rhythm my heart is playing.

I want to forget about the rhythm. Forget that the heart is not really mine. The heart separates itself from me when it does this, as if the rhythm is from a music speaker, not from within me.

The edge of the table rubs my forearms. I am trying to play a game on my phone to distract my mind, but my concentration is constantly broken by that man's music.

A suited-man in the seat beside me coughs loudly as though the music is annoying him too.

The woman opposite, who has been clicking away on her laptop ever since I boarded the train in Swindon, looks up from the screen and glances at the music player.

A vibration rumbles through my fingers.

My phone. The screen says, 'Chloe'.

I lean against the window and answer, jamming myself into the corner and pushing the phone hard against my ear so Chloe's voice will not seep out to others. 'Hello.'

'How are you?'

'Fine.'

'I'm checking in because you haven't rung me.'

It's only been three days. I smile, for her benefit, even though she can't see. 'Sorry.' I have been busy, trying to speak for a ghost.

'I rang Simon last night when you didn't answer. He said you had an interview in Swindon today.'

'I did. It's just finished. I'm on my way back.'

'How did it go?'

'Good. I think.'

'In Swindon, though?'

'Yes.'

Her breath slips into a sigh. 'What was the school like?'

'Nice.'

'Don't go on about it, then.'

An amused sound like the start of a giggle escapes from my throat. I close my lips and it becomes a choked cough. 'I'm on the train,' I whisper.

Sounds of amusement rumble from her throat. Her dirty laugh, as Dan used to say. 'Now I have to think of something to make you blush.'

My next amused sound escapes.

The woman on the laptop glances at me.

'Have you had a letter from the donor's family yet?' She's asked me the question three times before. It makes me smile because she keeps asking, despite denying that she would want to know.

'No.' I have seen them.

'There's still time.'

Another vibration ripples through my hand. I hold the phone away, looking at the screen. It's a news headline from the paper that ran Louise's story and published her obituary. I put the phone back to my ear.

'... getting together,' Chloe is saying.

'Sorry, I didn't hear.'

'When are we getting together for our first night out? We can go out for a meal and fatten you up some more.'

It would be the first time we have been out properly in over two years. 'Okay. When's good for you?'

'Next week. Thursday? But shall I come over for lunch tomorrow so you can tell me more about the job you went for?'

'All right, Thursday. And you are welcome to come for lunch.' Although I have no idea what I can say about the job.

'Okay. See you tomorrow, then.'

'Yes, see you then.'

She ends the call.

I look through the window and smile into the distance.

A crackling announcement from the tannoy system says the train is approaching Didcot.

The man diagonally across from me takes his earphones out. I still can't work the song out. He stands up and pulls a bag down from the overheard luggage rack, flashing a line of skinny waist and the top of his red designer underwear.

I look down at my phone and touch it to open the news story. *The parents of the woman who fell from a Swindon car park are calling for witnesses.*

I touch the link as the train slows.

Louise's parents have been on a local radio station asking for people to come forward if they saw Louise on the day she died.

The train draws into the station. The music player walks away.

I open Facebook on my phone and look at Robert Dowling's account. His profile image is a picture of him and his wife. They must have been leaving to do that interview when I saw them. They still care about their daughter. She's dead and they will not let her go. They're the parents I dreamed of as a child.

An empty sensation swells inside me, just below my ribs, deep in my stomach. A space for love, that was supposed to have been filled by my parents. It is parent-shaped. Neither Simon nor Dan ever filled that gap. My parents left it empty. Instead of having love to warm me like a radiator, exuding a sense of safety from the inside out, there is a cold vacuum in me. A black hole, pulling at everything, dragging my consciousness back to the things I have missed out on because they went away.

At times in my life that black hole eats me alive.

If I had parents like Louise's how different would my life have been?

My thumb slides over the screen on my phone, scrolling through happy family pictures.

There are lots of pictures of the blond children.

Why did Louise fall from that car park?

The friend button stares at me in the way Robert Dowling did through the car's windscreen. I touch it to send a request. I want to help them.

'How did the interview go?' Simon hands me a pile of knives and forks.

This time of the evening, when Simon has just walked through the door, the house has the activity of a trout pond at feeding time, there is such a rush to get the tea on the table.

'I like doing the cutlery.' Liam grasps the sharp ends and pulls the knives and forks out of my hand.

'Careful, you'll cut yourself,' Mim warns.

'I can carry the plates.' Kevin bounces over to take them from

Mim. Then braces them on his forearms, to carry them safely.

'Thank you,' Mim acknowledges as the pile of china wobbles.

'The interview, Helen ...' Simon pushes at me.

I glance over with no excuse left to avoid the conversation. 'It went all right.'

'I'm not sure you're ready to go back to work, though. I think you should wait.' He's running cold water to fill a plastic jug to put on the table. 'You don't need to worry about getting back to work. There's no hurry.'

I turn to the cupboard to fetch plastic cups for the children. He couldn't have said anything better. 'I'm not worried. If I get a job I wouldn't start until January, for the spring term.'

'Good. We like you staying here.'

The boys are climbing onto their chairs. They lift their knives and forks upright in an impatient gesture. I reach over and put down their cups. Simon walks around to fill their cups.

'But I am excited about getting back to work.' Just busy doing something else. 'This just wasn't the right job.'

Simon sits down as I turn to get three glasses.

Mim puts a dish full of steaming cottage pie on the table as I put down our glasses for Simon to fill.

Mim and Simon share a look that communicates something.

The smell of the cheese that has melted into the mashed potato stirs my appetite.

When I sit down, an image of the children from Robert Dowling's Facebook posts comes into my head. An image of them sitting around a table. It is one of Louise's memories. She can't make me hear her words; but she sometimes succeeds in making me see her past.

What's the conversation at their dinner table tonight? They must all miss Louise, and I know she misses them.

Her sadness pulls at me like the flow of an outgoing tide that drags all the sand out from around my feet, sucking at my legs and trying to pull me out with the tide. I am no-longer hungry.

Emotions and visions are connecting me to Louise with a slowly firming knot – like a lace being pulled as I walk, gradually tightening an accidental knot that's formed itself in the place where a bow has been. If I want to untie it, I'll struggle now.

Mim passes Simon the spoon to dish up.

'Hold up your plate, Helen,' he says.

I lift the plate so he can fill it. 'Stop. That's enough.'

He's not looking at me but telling Mim about his day at work. I put my plate down. The serving spoon falls against the rim of the pot as she tells him something about her day too. There is nothing to be said about my day. I fill up my fork and blow on the steaming meat and potato to cool it.

I force myself to eat four mouthfuls, then set the knife and fork to rest on the edge of the plate and push the plate away by a couple of centimetres. 'I'm not hungry tonight. I think I'm going to go to bed.'

Simon looks from Mim to me. 'Did you do too much today? It was—'

'I'm fine. I promise. Just tired. Everyone gets tired occasionally.'

A slight frown creases his forehead, making several rows of long thin lines. He looks about ten years younger than he is until the moment he frowns and those wrinkles show.

I take my plate away and scrape the leftovers into the bin. It's a waste. The lid of the pedal bin falls with a sharp ring. When I turn around Simon is looking at me. I smile, widely, probably overdoing the happy show, walk over, bend down and wrap my arms around his neck. The movement makes the scar on my chest pull but it doesn't hurt much. 'I love you,' I say quietly against his ear; they are words that are just for his ears. He pats my shoulder as I pull away.

'Goodnight,' I say to Mim.

I walk around the table and kiss Liam on the top of his head, then Kevin on the top of his head.

My laptop is in the living room. I stop to pick it up so I can take it upstairs. I'm going to bed to look up Robert Dowling's interview. It will be on the iPlayer Radio.

'Simon ...' Mim's voice reaches from the kitchen behind me, with a tone of warning; the tone that comes before the boys get a 'ten seconds to do something' countdown.

'Don't,' is his answer; a full stop that ends a conversation that never began, and then there is no sound except the scraping of cutlery on plates.

I listen to the interview in the dark, in bed, with an earphone in my left ear, my head sinking into the pillow. The cotton releases the smell of Mim's lavender-scented washing conditioner. It is a smell of safety. My whole body calls this bed mine but it is Simon's and Mim's spare bed, for guests, not a permanent place for me.

I have no home.

Nowhere that I can call mine. I think it makes it worse that the only place I have ever thought of as mine is now Dan's and his new woman's. But I couldn't be the one who kept the flat because I was too ill to live in it alone.

If I'd had parents, I would have had a home to always go back to. A home like Louise's, with a flower bed full of scented roses, and parents who loved her. There's that vacuum again.

The emotion in me is envy. It is my emotion. Louise had what I always wanted.

When the vacuum sucks everything away this is what's left:

darkness. Envy. Anger. Pain. These are the emotions that can take over when bipolar slips into what people call manic depression.

The Dowlings' radio interview is eleven minutes long. They talk for four minutes then there is a break for a song and another seven minutes.

I want to help. I wish I had something I could say that would help. Their love for Louise flows in the cadence of their voices. There is a moment when Robert says something to his wife, Patricia. '*I know, Pat, I feel that way too.*' I imagine him holding her hand as she makes a sound, a slight acknowledgement that says she is reassured.

An ache presses through my heart, as it makes itself heard, in a gentle rhythm as I listen to the Dowlings again.

Louise's sadness becomes a lead weight in my chest and there's a tension in my throat; she wants to cry.

If I were her, I would be crying.

I want to know love like that.

In Louise's body, while she was alive, I think this heart would have clasped tight with love when she heard these voices.

The Dowlings mean everything to one another and Louise must have been enveloped in that love too.

When I was young, I imagined myself in a happy sitcom family. But Louise's family are painting a new mental picture of what life would have been like with parents. What her life was like. What mine could have been like – still might be like.

I look up the one image of Louise that I have access to and play the recording from the beginning, listening for her voice inside me. I can't hear the words but I hear her: a whisper that's out of reach.

I want to hear her. I want to understand what she's saying. I want to understand what she wants me to do.

Chapter 10

6 weeks and 1 day after the fall.

When I leave the railway station, a strong breeze sweeps at me like a broom trying to push me back through the sliding doors.

An answering shiver rattles through my body, up my spine and into my shoulders.

When I dressed this morning, I chose a thin jumper, not thick enough to keep out the cold. I haven't mastered the forecasting skills required for being outside in the British weather, and the chill in the air is a reminder that in just over two weeks it will officially be autumn.

But perhaps the shiver came from the sense I have that Louise is watching me walking the streets of Swindon – a someone-has-just-walked-over-my-grave sort of shiver.

Her spirit feels more active today. Louder. My heart is pulsing hard and there is a hum of energy in my blood that is making her undeterminable whispers stronger. It is like having someone fidgeting impatiently in my body.

The crossing that is in front of me will take me to the shopping area.

There are tall buildings all around the station but the multi-storey car park is farther away.

Other people who disembarked from the 11.27 train cross the road beside me while the green walking man counts down. The knowing pace of the man in front of me leads me in the right direction, across paved pedestrian areas.

The shopping area is busier than I expected. It will be even busier in fifteen minutes when the office-workers spill out of the high buildings, like ants from an aggravated nest, to buy lunch.

A young boy who is close by complains to his mother. 'Get in the pushchair!' she yells, provoking a tirade of screams.

Blustery breezes stir up children. They want to run. Children in a playground are like birds when they play on a strong breeze. There is excitement and expectation in the air of a good breeze.

A young woman sweeps past on a skateboard, putting one foot down to push the skateboard on as she cuts in front of me. She weaves quickly through the people ahead. My gaze follows her until she disappears into the crowd. Then I see it.

The car park is a looming shadow stealing the sunlight from the street farther on; a concrete mass that peers over the top of the shops in the structure of a layer cake.

This is the street that Louise fell into.

At the top of the car park there is a wall. Somehow Louise fell over the top of that wall.

The sky is an innocent, denying blue today. Nothing happened up here, it tries to say.

But something did.

Picture after picture of this street and that car park are in my head. The images I have studied on my laptop in the last two days.

What happened, Louise?

I think she knows I have come here to find out. I think this is what she wants me to do.

The flow of people carries on into the town. A fast-running river of humanity.

I am looking for the narrow alley I have seen on Google Earth images that runs between two of the shops, to a pedestrian entrance at the side of the car park.

Three woman cross the pavement in front of me, from one shop to another. I stop to let them pass.

There is another skateboarder ahead, using a metal bicycle stand as an obstacle to perform tricks. The stand is outside a shop door that I have stared at in news articles.

It is the door.

The shop.

Louise fell onto this pavement, in that place.

I do not walk on. I can't move. My feet are stone. The ground is thick mud to be waded through and my trainers are stuck in the sludge.

There is no mark, no rusty iron-looking bloodstain to say she was here. Nothing. It is as if the fall that ended her life, and began mine, did not happen. The sky, the car park and pavement all cry out. It was not me! Nothing happened here!

But something very wrong happened here. Women don't just fall over car-park walls.

This heart must have pumped the blood through her broken body while she lay here.

The alley I have been looking for is on the left: a metre-and-half-wide rabbit-hole.

The block paving carpeting most of the town centre doesn't reach into the shadowy environment of the alley. This area of

Swindon, that's hiding behind the shops, must have been built in the 1970s concrete explosion.

No one else is walking through here but there's a man sitting on the floor a few metres ahead, on a filthy sleeping bag, with a dog; both have their legs stretched out. The man's back rests against the wall, his hand repeatedly stroking the dog that's lying flat beside him.

The man's dirt-stained jeans are torn and fraying at the knees.

The dog is a small crossbreed that must include some sort of terrier DNA. Its brown eyes look at me, without any movement of its head.

There's a presence around the man, more than in his brown-shaded aura, that says he's given up hope of being anywhere else but on the street.

Three takeaway coffee cups stand beside the dog. I presume they're empty and probably left there to say he doesn't want gifts of coffee, just money. But money for what? He needs to feed the dog as well as himself and most hostels will not feed the dog.

I have change in my pocket, left over from buying a coffee at Paddington Station.

The dog's gaze follows my approach.

I hold out the coins even though the man hasn't asked for money.

He looks at me; the bit of his face I can see between hair and beard is tanned, leathery skin, tainted by a difficult life spent mostly outdoors.

A shaky hand lifts, palm open, outstretched. 'Thanks.' A Special Brew beer can is tucked beside his hip; it is hidden when his arm lowers.

'You're welcome. Do you always sit here?'

'Unless the police move me on.' His fingers have fisted around the precious coins.

'Were you here the day a woman fell from the car park a few weeks ago?'

'No, love. I never saw anythin'. Did you know 'er? Don't y'u think the police did their job?'

'I – I just wondered.'

'Well, I never saw 'er. I wasn't 'ere at the time.'

'Okay. Thank you anyway.' I walk on because there's nothing else to say.

The air in the side entrance for the car park smells of mildew. I grip the cold metal handrail, which is covered in peeling green paint, and climb the steps. The doors into the parking floors have blue paint that is scarred by numerous initials carved into the wood. Just above the door to the second floor the smell of stale urine taints the air.

The steps are made of bare concrete and the outer wall is constructed with green-painted metal bars that I can see between. The man in the alley is sifting through the coins.

Did Louise climb these steps that day?

The higher I climb, the more I have a sense of her in my chest.

My heart, her heart, is racing with that heavy pulse that I can't ignore. *Listen. Listen. Listen.*

I know she wants to tell me something, or persuade me to tell someone else something.

At the top I push the scarred blue door wide and step out on the top floor. I expect to walk into sunshine, but the horizon is grey now.

There are about a dozen cars sprinkled across the space but no one else is up here.

What a place to die. Why was Louise here? Was she alone?

A full rainbow appears, arching over the buildings on the other side of the town.

The side of the car park that hangs over the shops slightly is only a few metres away from the stairwell. The shop Louise fell in front of is under the corner there.

I try to hear Louise's voice as I walk to the corner where I know she stood. But I can't make out any words. 'What happened?'

Beyond the rainbow, the horizon is blurred by the rainstorm.

The wall is bare, rough concrete, like the rest of the car park. I imagined the wall would be waist-high but the top of the wall is chest height.

Louise could not have fallen accidentally; she must have been picked up, or climbed up.

My elbows rest on the wall as I look down. Even on my toes I can only just see the shops on the far side of the pedestrian area.

A breeze tosses the hair away from my face and makes it dance as the air sweeps up from below.

I want to see what Louise would have seen that day. I feel as though I should know why she was here. I'm hoping that being here will increase the connection I have with her. I look for images in my memory, memories that are not mine, but I can't find them.

My hands press on the wall and I scrape the toes of my trainers as I scramble and pull myself up. The rough concrete catches at strands of the fine wool in my jumper and scuffs my jeans while I manoeuvre my legs so I can sit on the wall with a leg dangling either side.

The area below is flooded with people walking into the town centre.

I have never been afraid of heights. Living with a weak heart that threatened to kill me any day meant nothing else scared me as a child. I was always reckless and careless, rather than cautious. I was either in hospital or pushing the boundaries and packing in as much enjoyment as possible before the next time.

But my periods of enjoyment were manic. Out of control at times, as I tried to fill up the vacuum in me. I was scared and lonely for large parts of my life, even with Simon as a surrogate father, in his school and college days. He was so much older and there were times when I wanted him, and he wasn't in reach.

What about Louise? Was she scared that day?

Surely someone must have been here with her? The wall is too high for it to have been an accident. Someone must know how she fell.

I look down and see a vivid image of her broken body lying on the pavement. Louise would have realised she was falling and, in the next moment, hit the ground.

I look up at the rainbow and the haze of the rain in the distance.

The only reason Louise would have been here alone was if she had chosen to fall. Which means this heart must have been unbearably sad. But I know sadness can drag people down into the strong undercurrents of a black, thrashing sea.

The rainbow is brighter now, defying the dark grey behind it. I don't want to think of Louise broken on the floor down there. 'I will think of the hope you are giving me.' Even though I can't hear her, perhaps she can hear me, and she must know how grateful I am.

The wooden skateboard scrapes on the metal of the cycle rack, pulling my gaze down to the youth practising his tricks.

I see a free runner when I look back at the tops of the high buildings; I see bravery and body strength to balance, watching an imaginary me jump along the tops of the buildings. Me. A *Marvel* superhero making this world mine. If I weren't ill, I might have become someone with that much freedom. Not a superhero, obviously. But unrestrained. That was the good thing about my bipolar: it made me vibrant at times, capable of anything.

I will not be a free runner now, but Louise's gift means I will be able to do other things to set this heart on fire with adrenalin.

The colours of the rainbow fade.

A girl's laugh rises from somewhere in the lower levels of the car park and a mother's sing-song voice responds.

A child – that is what I want to set this heart on fire. I just want to fill this heart with love. To fill the hole in me.

A sadness that is overwhelming pushes through my chest, forcing its way in. I think it is Louise's sadness. I don't feel sad.

Perhaps I have made her think about her children. They're orphans now. Like me. But not like me, because they have grandparents.

'Why were you here, Louise?' The words are swept away on the breeze, without answer. She had parents who loved her, and children.

'How did you fall? You can't have wanted to leave your children.'

The long grey smudge of rain is moving past Swindon, along the outskirts, over the distant hills, blown by the wind higher up in the atmosphere.

I swing my leg over and drop down onto the tarmac.

There is somewhere else I want to go before I catch the train back to London.

There's space on a park bench next to a young woman. I perch on the edge because there's a missing piece of wood in the seat.

The heels of my shoes tap a quick beat on the pavement. It

is a nervous habit that I have had for as long as I remember – 'You have a twitchy leg,' Simon used to say when we were sitting in waiting areas for whoever would collect us next.

There is dust from the wall on my jeans. I brush it off.

The woman is looking at two young boys who are feeding the ducks. A swan is hissing at the boys to persuade them to drop their bread. They throw the bread into the lake and run to the woman beside me, shouting at the swan, 'Go away.'

There's a picture of the blond children feeding ducks in this park. Perhaps Louise walked along this path to reach the car park?

Perhaps Robert and Pat walk here with the children.

Louise tells me that they do, without words; it is just a knowledge that I seem to have always had. I look along the path as if I'll see them. She wants me to see them.

The path wraps around one edge of the lake.

They're not here.

On the other side of the park there's a grass area where they might be. I can't leave the park without looking.

I get up and walk around to look.

They're not there.

On the way to the railway station, thoughts spin in my head. They distort and jump like a vintage LP. Louise could not have fallen accidentally. But why would she have chosen to die when she had children who love her?

Was it murder?

Are the police investigating her death?

I stand on the station platform, looking along the track for the train to appear, with one question in my mind, which escapes my lips. 'Do I have your heart for a reason?' I want her to answer. 'Tell me.'

I won't know unless she answers.

Was I chosen or found?

Pump-pump.

Pump-pump.

The same banging but no answers.

Why won't she put the answer in my mind?

'Did you leave a space for me to take?' Is that it?

She has nothing to say about her death, so is she looking for me to step in and fill the gap she's left in the children's and her parents' lives?

Chapter 11

21.35.

'Are you decent?' Simon's call resonates through the bedroom door.

'Yes.'

The door opens in a hesitant way that says he has come to be a father, not a brother.

I smile as I say, 'Yes,' again, in a tone that adds, go on, then, speak up. I move my leg so he can sit on the edge of the bed.

He holds out the stack of medicine packets. I left them on the kitchen work surface. I should've put them in the cupboard away from the boys.

'Thanks.' I take them and put them on the short chest of drawers beside the bed.

'You okay?' There's an undercurrent in the enquiry.

'Yes.' Why?

'You've been disappearing a lot lately.'

'I went to Swindon to find out about another job. I told you.'

'I know what you told me, after agreeing you weren't ready to go back to work. But it's not just that you are disappearing physically, you're disappearing into yourself a lot. Even when you're with the boys, you go silent at times when they're talking to you. And why are you so determined to look for jobs in Swindon?'

'Because I'm well enough to live alone and I can afford somewhere in Swindon if I find a job. I've had a heart transplant, Simon. I have a lot to think about. I can do things I haven't been able to do for years. I'm thinking about what I want to do with my life.'

A smile touches the corners of his lips before a sigh leaves his throat, then he breathes in. 'Let me know if I can help.'

'I am the only one who can decide.'

His lips purse and he leans to one side to reach into his trouser pocket then pulls out a brown plastic bottle. 'The tablets for your bipolar.'

'Don't tell me you've been counting the pills to see if I'm taking them? You weren't there to count my tablets when I lived with Dan.'

'I know.'

I snatch the bottle, rattling the pills. 'I am taking them.'

'Good.'

'And I'm not taking one in front of you because I've already taken one.'

'All right. I believe you. I care about you, that's the only reason I interfere. The last thing you need is to be sectioned now.'

'Thank you for reminding me about one of the worst times in my life. That's the last thing I want to think about now.'

'I know. But you are so physically healthy I want to make sure you are thinking about your mental health, too.'

'I am. You don't need to lecture me. I don't want to be unwell.' I think this lecture was spurred on by Mim. She's been watching me with increased intensity.

My bipolar frightens Mim. She's scared of it – of what the illness might do if it takes control of me. The obsessions, envy and anger.

A deep-pitched laugh ripples from his throat. 'I know. Sorry. Sometimes I can't help myself.'

There's only one thing to do: stick out my tongue, in the childish gesture that was a favourite of mine when I was small and he was overbearing.

He mimics the gesture: a grown man sticking his tongue out in answer.

This is why we are special, because we still connect with one another as a brother and sister as though the years of pain growing up have not occurred. Perhaps because we had already grown up when we were still so young. Perhaps because he shares the same parents-shaped hole. The same journey of pain and isolation.

The moment takes me back through the years to the hours we spent in foster homes when we retired to the shared bedroom he insisted on, to the place where it was just us. The place where I was wholly understood and we clung to each other because there was never anyone else to rely on.

The bipolar medicine bottle is left on the bed as he stands.

I grasp his hand, holding it tight and saying nothing because we do not need to speak to say things.

His fingers squeeze mine, telling me the things I know about what he feels for me.

When his hand slips out of mine it is always a conscious decision on my part to let him go to Mim and the boys. I learned to let go of him a long time ago. But when I want him back, he always comes.

'Goodnight.' His baritone rings around the room.

'Goodnight. I love you.'

'I love you too.'

Chapter 12

6 weeks and 2 days after the fall.

Chiming bells ring close to my ear. My hand reaches out on autopilot to find my phone on the chest of drawers. My brain is heavy and clogged with the dulling interference of prescription drugs. The sound rings out again. I look at the clock on the bedside chest by my phone. The vivid green numbers tick over to 9:14. Simon and Mim will have left with the children. It will be a message from Chloe.

I pick up the phone, squinting through tired eyes. It's not a message. It's a Facebook notification telling me that Robert Dowling has accepted my friend request.

Life rushes into my brain, as though a switch has turned my body on.

I want to post a thank you on his wall, for making friends.

But if I do that I'll stand out and perhaps he hasn't realised he doesn't know me.

I am a similar age to Louise – he might have assumed I was a friend of hers.

It makes more sense to be cautious, stay quiet and remain an observer of his life – of Louise's old life.

My legs bend under the duvet. My arm embraces my knees

as his Facebook page opens on the small screen of my phone. Picture after picture slides past under my thumb. Most of them are of the children, lots more than those on his public posts. The other pictures are dated before Louise's death, and posted privately by her.

I scroll back through time, just over a year, then stop on something unusual. The children are with a blond man. The girl's bottom is balancing on his forearm, her fingers clinging to the back of his neck in a way that says she is used to the position. The man's other hand is on the boy's head and that too looks like a frequent gesture that is well known by the boy.

I can't see the man's face. He's looking away from the camera at a door that must lead out of the room. Only the girl is looking at the camera, waving with her free hand.

The text above the image says, '*Louise Lovett, Alex has picked up the children and is on his way.*' The post is marked as just for friends, but it reads as a message that is just for Robert's daughter.

Alex.

The man's hair is a riot of messy curls like the boy's. The same curls are looser in the girl's longer hair. Louise did not have curly hair.

Was she married when she died?

It is obvious she married at some point because her surname was different from her parents' but this is the first hint of a partner being involved in her life.

The man's left hand is hidden. I can't see if he's wearing a ring. But even if she was married a year ago she might have been divorced or separated by the time she died.

I want to know more about this. Frustration grips at me, more a feeling in my stomach than my heart, a feeling that is my desire, not Louise's.

I open Google on my phone and type, 'Alexander Lovett'. Frustration switches to urgency that might be Louise's.

The surname is worth a try.

Images of the children flood my head as the heart pulses faster.

The usual social media search links come up. But there's something different amongst the links; the word photographer appears again and again. I click to the second page of links and '*Alexander Lovett photographer*' appears in the text under nearly every link.

'*Alexander Lovett on The Perfect Image*', one of the links says in the heading. It is posted on a country-living magazine website. I click on that. The article is full of beautiful images of the city of Bath. The back arrow returns me to the search results. I want to find his business link.

www.AlexanderLovettPhotography.co.uk.

Click.

The website displays a clean-edged contemporary style. The Instagram link takes me to post after post of pictures of beautiful places, people and nature. There are no pictures of him or anything personal.

I go back and click the Facebook link to a business page that I *Like* before scanning through the same professional images. There's nothing personal on here either.

I want a picture of him so I can tell if this photographer is the father of Louise's children.

There is an *About us* tab on the website. Click.

The Team, it says at the top of the page, and beneath the heading, centre screen, there is a picture of Alex Lovett. He has tight curls in his blond hair.

He's looking into the camera lens in a way that communicates with the person behind the camera. His eyes, which I imagine are blue in some lights but are pale ice-grey in this image, are bright and full of an expression that tells me a moment after the camera has clicked he's spoken.

I feel as if Louise is staring at him through my eyes. The energy in my heartbeat has stalled as she stares, the pulse weakening.

He's remarkable. The sort of man I would look at if I walked past him in the street. The sort of man any woman who liked men would look at if they walked past him in a street.

Very little is written beneath his image, just information about his professional capability and achievements.

Louise lived with this man. If not at the point she died, for years at least, because they had children.

There is a *Contact us* tab at the bottom of the webpage.

The studio address is in the city of Bath. By train, Bath is about half an hour further on from Swindon.

The business is a limited company; it will be registered with Companies House. The registration might record Alex's home address.

The site shows a correspondence address in Bath that is different from the studio's address.

The phone drops out of my hand onto the duvet. Instead I pick up the laptop. This needs a bigger screen and Google Earth. As the lid lifts the screen comes to life. I glance over to get the address and type it in.

It looks like a residential street.

I drag the yellow Plasticine-like man, that reminds me of *Morph*, over the screen, waving his legs, and put him down in the street then turn the camera to the houses. It is a house. Definitely. Not an office. I move the camera shot looking at the numbers on the doors. When I find number twenty-two, it shows curtains in the windows, a vase and other ornaments on the windowsills. The house looks lived in, not worked in.

Is this where Louise lived with the children? Perhaps she was inside this house when the Google' street pictures were taken.

The Companies House information on my phone shows Alex Lovett's age. He is four years older than me. His birthday is the same month as mine, but I am Aquarius and he's Pisces.

My legs cross underneath the laptop as my heart jumps with excitement. My excitement, at the success.

This is a breakthrough.

Chapter 13

12.53.

The glossy white door with the fox-head knocker and the brass number twenty-two is in front of me, staring at me from across the street.

The only difference in the view I am looking at, compared to the day *Google's* street view captured this image, is that there are no flowers planted in the boxes attached to the railings in front of the house. In the *Google* image, this house has full flowerboxes bursting with scarlet-red pelargoniums, white euphorbia and trailing ivy. But now, they have all gone.

I think this is the door that Louise Lovett walked in and out of day after day. The door to her home.

I feel as though she's holding her breath, waiting and watching inside me, with fear and hope. I know she wants me to be here, but I do not know what she wants me to do.

I lean back against the cast-iron Georgian railing that edges the park on the opposite side of the street from the house. The action crushes the rucksack hanging from my shoulder. The rucksack contains a raincoat and umbrella. But today the rain has stayed away.

The five-foot-high iron bars of the railings are topped by

pointed fleur-de-lys shapes and so my head rests against a sharp cold fleur-de-lys design. One foot lifts to settle on the stone that the ironwork is embedded in.

This is an old street. In the park behind me are half a dozen plane trees with broad shady canopies and thick trunks over a metre in diameter. The trees must have been planted around the time the houses were built. The park was made to be a garden for the rich who lived in these houses in the eighteenth and nineteenth centuries. The people who live here today must appreciate it even more because there's a road behind them, and a supermarket beyond that.

I glance at the watch on my wrist then look back at the door, breathe in then exhale slowly. I have been standing here for twenty-two minutes and there's been no movement in the house.

The street has a dead end, so even though on the other side of the park there's a noisy main road, here there are no people or traffic, just parked cars and closed front doors.

My foot slips off the stone and I walk forward with a sudden urge to respond. It's not a choice to move, it's a need. Louise's impatience, not mine.

I cross the road, mount the pavement, walk up to the door and grip the doorknocker. The brass fox-head drops onto the metal plaque with a heavy clang. I lift and drop it again.

I need to know if there's life in this house — if the children are here.

Louise wants whatever she has brought me here for to begin.

The button of a modern doorbell is on the doorframe on the left, as though it's hidden to prevent it spoiling the appearance of the frontage. I press that, holding it down for seconds. The property is five floors tall, including the windows of a cellar in the area behind the railings.

I step back so I can look at the windows, trying to see someone moving in the house.

One thing is obvious about Alex Lovett: he has a good amount of money; he must do otherwise he would not be able to afford to live in this property.

Noisy footsteps echo beyond the door with the hollow sound of wood.

Someone is running down bare wooden stairs.

I step forward as a chain rattles on the inside of the door. There's a scrape of metal. I imagine a door-chain being slotted into its holder to prevent the door from being pushed fully open.

When the door opens, the face of a young woman peers through the gap. 'We don't buy anything at the door ...'

There are high-pitched shouts and small feet running in a room upstairs. There are children in the house somewhere.

The sound of them breathes emotion through my heart, as though Louise's lips have pursed and blown a kiss, as gentle as a blow on the sails of a paper boat.

My children, a voice in my head declares.

I smile in a way that tries to reassure. 'Is Alexander Lovett in?' I don't know what I will say if he is in. But the one thing I do know is that Louise wants me to find a way into this house. This family.

The thought sends a sharp pain through my middle.

My black hole stirs, like a waking dragon. Opportunity and hope are being absorbed. It consumes every thought other than those that focus on the children.

A family here have a space for me, and I have a space for them. It is a jigsaw puzzle left on a table waiting to be completed with the last piece.

The last piece is me.

'He's at work. Can I take a message?'

'No. I'll contact him at the studio.' I don't give her a chance to answer. I don't want to hear her try to put me off the idea. I know what I need to know from this house. The children are here and I need to find a way into their home.

I walk back to the centre of Bath caught up in a dream, the rhythm of my heart setting the pace as I stride through streets packed with tourists. People bump my shoulder or legs with their shopping bags.

Alex's studio is on the other side of the city centre, in a side street near the Holburne Museum.

Once I'm on the other side of Pulteney Bridge, the density of tourists dissipates and the road widens into a broad avenue of high, pale-stone terraced houses. There is a fountain in the middle of the road. I turn left there and look at the numbers on the buildings.

My fingers grasp the shoulder strap of my rucksack as I walk to the studio's front door. My legs and arms are shaky. I'm nervous, but I will not run from this.

There are three polished brass plaques inscribed with the names of different companies that have separate intercom systems.

I press the intercom for Alexander Lovett Photographic Services and Studio Ltd.

'Hello, can I take your name?' A female voice crackles through the speaker.

'Helen Jones,' I lie.

'Are we expecting you? You're not on the list.'

'No, I'd like to make an appointment.'

'People usually ring to make an appointment.'

'I want to see Alex Lovett. Is he there?'

'No. Alex is working in London today, but I can help. Come in.' There's a buzz, then a click.

I push the heavy door. It opens.

The doors on the first and second floor are for the other businesses. On the third-floor there is another brass plaque for Alexander Lovett's studio.

The door opens into a reception area, with brown leather seating and photography lining the burgundy walls.

A woman, who I presume is the person I spoke to through the intercom, is sitting behind a curved dark wood desk. 'How can I help you?' She is tapping the end of her pen on the desk.

The strap of the rucksack cuts into my palm as I grip it tighter. 'I'd like to talk to Alex about photography for a wedding.' The second lie slips out easily, although I might be blushing.

She's his gatekeeper.

The pen is raised like a spear as she stands on guard. She'll send me away if she doesn't think I have a good reason to meet him.

He is the gatekeeper for the children.

She smiles; a customer-service smile. 'Alex rarely gets involved with weddings. I can put you down to talk to one of the others? They're all very good. I can show you their portfolios if you would like to choose someone?'

'It's not my wedding.' I sit down in the chair on the opposite side of her desk, my jeans sliding on the leather seat. I am under-dressed, in jeans and canvas daps. 'I'm a wedding planner and I have a large society wedding scheduled for next year. I want the best photographer. These shots will be on the mantel-pieces of stately homes for generations.'

A dubious gleam twinkles in her eyes. She judged my clothes when I was standing and now she's judging my scarce make-up and un-kempt hair and she knows I've lied. I don't look wealthy enough to be a society wedding planner. I would be dressed in a figure embracing, tailored, deisgner suit and I would not have even come in person, I would have rung first.

Anger overrides the nervousness. I square my shoulders and the lies become even easier to say. 'No one else will do. That is why I have come in person, to express how important this event is. The bride's family won't accept one of his assistants.'

She stares at my face while she decides what to do. 'Okay, I can book you in for a quick chat with him, say an initial quarter-hour, and he can make a decision if he wants to do it or not. But I'm not promising. Alex is in demand.'

'Yes, I'm aware.'

She flicks through pages in a paper diary, the sweeping sound of the paper stirring the air in the small waiting room. 'His diary is full for weeks,' she adds as she continues looking. 'Ah. Here's a small slot. Four weeks' time. He won't charge you for a first appointment.' Her gaze drops down as she reaches for a card and writes the time and date on it. Then she looks at me. 'Here.' She holds out the card.

'Thank you.' I stand again, re-exposing my jeans that are faded from over-washing, not fashionably bleached, and the jumper that has pulls in the threads where it caught on the wall in the car park in Swindon.

'Goodbye,' I say to fill an awkward moment.

I am given another bland customer-service smile. 'Good—'

I shut the door on her last syllable.

Chapter 14

6 weeks and 5 days after the fall.

The lies I have been telling Chloe over lunch are becoming as thick as pea soup; if I'm not careful they will become so thick and deep the pea soup will drop on my head in a smothering, embarrassing slime. But she keeps asking questions, wanting me to expand on the details I'm making up.

Louise's urgency is in me; it has been racing through my blood for hours. Her energy pushes the lies from my mouth. I feel like the friend of a bully. I can't hear her words, but I feel her pressuring me. Rushing me. She doesn't want me to be here with Chloe. She thinks this is wasting time. But even though I have her heart, she doesn't own my mind and body.

Whereabouts was the job in Bath? Chloe's questions go on and on. How big is the school? What are the staff like? What are the class sizes? Have I looked at places to live near there? Can I really afford a place on my own?

I won't remember what I've said if she asks me to repeat anything later. I'll tell her I didn't get the job as soon as I can.

I want to change the subject but it's hard to find a moment in the rush of her incessant questioning.

'I can't imagine you leaving London,' she says eventually, 'or living alone.' She doesn't want me to get the made-up job anyway.

Chloe and Simon are too used to my dependency on them. I must break that. I want the freedom I have access to. 'I'm well now. I don't need people to be there for me all the time. I know how to wash myself,' I joke.

She smirks.

'I can even wash my clothes now; I can pick up the washing basket and fill the machine. I can polish my shoes too and, guess what, I can lift a spoon to my mouth.' I laugh.

She shakes her head. 'You're not funny. I can't help being nervous for you.'

'If I decide to move to somewhere in that direction it's only a short train journey away, and I'm not nervous.' I am eager and excited – but those emotions are merged with Louise's impatience.

Chloe's lips twist and her nose twitches. She's worried because ever since I've known her I have been ill to some degree.

I can feel the difference Louise's heart pulses into every cell in my body. Chloe can't. It will take her and Simon longer to know how different my life is now.

'What if I promise you will be the first to know if I feel unwell? And if I do feel ill I'll hand in my notice and move back to London.'

Chloe gives me one of her broad smiles that throws good cheer out. 'I'll take that promise and I'll hold you to it.'

I hold out a hand to shake on it. 'Deal.'

'Deal.' Her hand takes mine, warming it as her fingers wrap around and hold on securely.

We hug each other in the entrance hall of the underground station, then say goodbye, before I descend on one set of escalators and she disappears into the tiled tunnel leading to another Tube line.

It's 5.45 and busy; teeming with commuters who rush and push past me with no courtesy, just a need to carry on with the next part of their getting-home journey.

I shuffle along in the herd of people navigating the London rush hour, manoeuvring down the narrow escalator and then finding a carriage to squeeze into, like cattle packed into a pen. I stare out of the windows that show me nothing but the black tunnel we are speeding through. But that's better than looking at the armpit of the man who's hanging onto a ceiling bar an inch away.

There's something strange in the reflections formed on the windows, with the blackened tunnel wall beyond them – a blurred figure. A woman who seems to be looking at me.

I look over my shoulder; the woman isn't there. It is just the man's arm and chest.

When I look back at the window, the woman has gone.

I want to get home. I love seeing Chloe, but today feels like a wasted day. I've been trying to find out the name of the young woman I met at the house yesterday. I think she's the children's nanny, but Alex doesn't have any personal social media accounts and as far as I can tell the nanny hasn't liked or followed his business accounts.

When I walk through the back door into the kitchen, Mim is straining the water from a saucepan of peas.

She glances over her shoulder. 'Hello.'

'Hello.'

'Did you have a good afternoon?' She puts the saucepan down, but there's an odd stiffness in the movement that hints at the fact she feels uncomfortable.

I smile, slightly. 'Yes. Thank you. Can I do anything?' Maybe it's because I could do more to help, and she's fed up of me being as much work as a child. I should help with the cooking and looking after the boys now that I can. I've taken more than my share of Simon's concern and money over the years. The boys are in a play club all day at the moment until the school holidays end but perhaps I could entertain them in the evening and put them to bed. It would be nice to join in with the children's bedtime routine – be the one to read their goodnight story.

'Everything's done, I'm just dishing up. But you can call the boys and Simon and tell the boys to wash their hands.'

'Kevin. Liam. Simon,' I shout as I walk across the room, directing my voice through the door on the far side.

Simon leans his head around the door frame within a second, holding onto the frame on the far side. 'No need to shout, we're here.' His words are punctuated with a grin.

'The boys need to wash their hands.'

'They've already gone to do it. They smelled the sausages.'

An emotional urge that's not a thought-out decision makes me walk towards him. He knows why without me speaking. He lifts his arms, waiting for me to wrap my arms around his middle and hold on. This is the black hole speaking.

His arms fall onto my shoulders to embrace me and he presses a kiss on my temple. Then he lets go and moves on, talking to Mim as he walks around me.

This is his life. His family. I want my own. That's all I want to do with this new heart. I don't want a job. I want a family.

A cry, or something more like a wail, a scream of longing, rips through my head. It is the loudest sound that I have heard in Louise's voice.

The anger in her impatience is making her spirit stronger.

My hands slide into the back pockets of my jeans, restraining the thoughts in my head, to stop them from slipping out of my mouth. I see Louise's children in my mind, not her memories, but images of them from the pictures on Robert Dowling's Facebook page.

Simon would call my thoughts abnormal. He would say I shouldn't let myself become emotionally attached to the children of the woman I think donated my heart. But I can't help myself. I already am.

It feels right.

That I have her heart.

That I know where her children are.

That I know where her parents are.

But without being able to understand what it feels like to have a sixth sense, to feel Louise's emotions, Simon, like Chloe, will think I am going mad.

Since I was sectioned and diagnosed at fourteen, Simon's favourite phrase has been, 'You do not have a sixth sense, you have bipolar.' He's never believed.

It's better that I don't tell him or Chloe anything.

It's better to lie.

I won't be able to get closer to Louise's family if I tell the truth.

'Have you heard about that job today, Helen?' Simon asks when we are sitting around the dinner table.

'I didn't get it.' I accept a plate of sausages, mashed potatoes, peas and dark thick gravy from Mim.

'Why?' Simon says. 'Not that I'm complaining about that.' He takes his plate.

'I didn't ask why, but I think working with a class of primary school children might be too much for a little while anyway.

I'm well enough to look after a couple of children so I think I'm going to look for a nanny job instead.'

Simon's lips purse as he picks up his knife and fork, his eyebrows quirking in that paternal expression.

'What's wrong with that?'

'Simon,' Mim protests, on my behalf. Or perhaps hers, if she wants me out of their house.

'Nothing. Not really. I agree it's a better idea to take that step first. I just don't like the thought of you living with strangers ...'

'I didn't say I would live in. Although it would be good if I could.' My heart claps its hands and taps its heels at the idea of living in. Because I do not want to be anybody's nanny, I want to be Alex Lovett's nanny. I want to look after Louise's children, and if I can live in the house ...

My heartbeat skips.

Chapter 15

7 weeks and 3 days after the fall.

The coffee inside the takeaway cup resting on my knee is cold. I've been sitting on this old iron park bench for nearly two hours.

I'll have to go soon. Simon and Mim will be back from her parents' in three hours. Simon will question me if I get home too long after them. He expects me to be there when they walk through the door.

The only movement in the house on the far side of the park has been a single view of the nanny; she walked past a window on the right-hand side on the first floor. I haven't seen anyone else. Sitting here has shown me nothing. But I'm closer to the children and my heart feels happier.

I think there's an entrance to the cellar of Alex Lovett's house on the other side of the park. A door cuts through the wall beneath the iron railing that's topped by the Fleur de Lys. The ground of the park drops into a ditch that is more than a metre below the street level, and there's a row of short doors in the wall supporting the street; one for each house. Those doors were probably used for deliveries for things like coal, blocks of ice or bags of flour years ago. Today, though, they must still provide access, through a tunnel under the road, to the basement floor of the houses.

I stand, only because my bottom and legs are numb from sitting here so long. I walk to the left, because when I turn at the corner I'll be able to look at the house for the longest period of time.

There's so little activity in the house, I think Alex has taken the children out.

It is Saturday.

I throw the cup of cold coffee in a rubbish bin.

Frustration grips as a pain in my stomach again – right in the middle of me. I want to see the children. The frustration starts to bubble, like fizz rising in lemonade, but it feels as if in a moment it is going to boil like water that tries to jump out of a saucepan.

They are my children, a voice says – a voice that might be Louise's.

She's frustrated too.

I walk across the park in the direction of the house, listening again for Louise's voice, but nothing else is said.

A knocker rattles, announcing that a door is opening. Conversation tumbles into the street.

It is Alex Lovett's front door. Children's voices carry on the air and they come out into the street.

I walk down the slope, into the valley at the edge of the park, towards the wall, towards the house.

'Granny,' the boy says, looking at a woman I do not know. She's past middle age. There's an older man with the children too. I haven't seen either adult in Facebook posts.

I guess they're Alex's parents.

The door closes without an appearance from Alex.

It is less than two months since Louise died.

They need their father.

Their mother.

He should be with the children.

I walk up to the railing, and hold the bottom of the metal rails, watching from my rat's-eye-view, as they walk off along the street.

Chapter 16

7 weeks and 6 days after the fall.

The edge of the plastic lid scratches my lip, then the coffee burns the roof of my mouth. I move the cup away, flinching.

I am trying to look like a casual occupant of the park bench. Day by day I am claiming this bench as mine.

It is the perfect place to watch Alex's house from.

He usually leaves the house at 8.20 to walk the boy to a holiday club. I followed them the first day I'd come here early, but I can't follow them every day because it will be too obvious. He holds the girl's hand but the boy keeps a little distant and tucks his thumbs inside the shoulder straps of his backpack denying any chance of contact with his father.

Alex returns at 8.50, with his daughter. They go back inside the house and then at 9.00 the door opens again, and he comes out with keys rattling in his hand as he either walks off down the street or goes to a large Range Rover.

I do not know what time he comes home after work. It is too late for me to stay and watch.

The door opens now, following the same routine.

I put the cup up against my lip and hold up my phone as though I am looking at the screen and look beyond it.

The curls in Alex's hair are disordered, untidy in a way that suggests his hair has not seen a comb or had a cut for weeks. He's not shaven either and the growth of blond hair on his chin denies any thought of grooming. The shirt he's wearing is rumpled.

Watching him is fascinating, like studying an animal. I hear David Attenborough narrating the family's movements in my head.

I need to understand Alex's life if I'm going to work out a way to become a part of the children's lives. I need to spot a weakness – a door that's been accidentally left open, that I'll be able to push my way through.

The girl holds onto his hand, which hangs loose. Alex looks back into the house and calls for the boy, who squeezes past his dad and sister and runs ahead.

Louise's heart pulses with a rush of emotion every day when I see them come out through the door.

'Wait for us!' Alex's call stretches across the park that contains me and two people with their dogs.

His aura's strange. I have never seen anything so dark before; it is greys, black in places, like a terrible storm wrapping about him.

Alex and the children disappear around a corner.

I drink the cooling coffee and look through Robert Dowling's pictures on Facebook while I wait.

My life is now paused and played on Alex's command.

It's cold today; my free hand slides into the pocket of my coat. There are several used train tickets and the one I need to get home in my pocket. The price of a ticket is extortionate at this time of day.

I have savings: a lump sum put away when Dan told me to get out of the flat; a pay-off for all the jointly purchased white goods and furniture I left behind, and the half of the deposit I lost. But I can't afford to travel backwards and forwards to Bath every day for long.

You are getting obsessed, Simon's voice whispers through my head.

I can become an addict of anything, because of bipolar. It is like a gambling addiction, or drug abuse – I can't stop once I have started believing something. My mind becomes fixated.

This is strange, Chloe's voice tells me.

It is strange. I know it is. But being given someone else's heart is strange, especially when that woman steps into your body and tells you to find her family. But this is real. And the house is the jigsaw puzzle that's waiting for me to step into place and complete it.

I owe this to Louise and I want it for me.

The distant sound of conversation pulls my attention back to the corner that Alex and his daughter appear from. She is half running, taking four or five steps with her short legs compared to his two strides. He's rushing today.

He opens the front door of his house with the key, but doesn't close the door after he's taken the girl inside. Then after a moment of some sort of exchange behind the half-closed door he reappears.

When he walks away from the door the headlights of the Range Rover flash as the car doors unlock.

I wait until he's in the car and pulling away from the kerb, then stand.

Once he's gone I usually go somewhere to eat breakfast. Then I come back.

There's the rattle of a doorknocker that has a looser sound than anyone else's. I look back to see the front wheels of a pushchair appear from Alex's house.

The third child will be in that pushchair.

I have only seen the youngest child in a few of Robert Dowling's pictures.

The nanny steers the pushchair over the threshold, then looks back and says something to the girl who follows.

I think the girl is three years old. She captures my attention more than the others. She's so small and pretty. I have always wanted a girl and she's my dream child. My hands want to reach out for her every time I see her. That's Louise's desire too, but I know my own feelings are the same, not just hers.

I feel as if Louise would simply pick the children up and run.

I can't do that; I would not be able to keep them. And I want to keep them. I want to make them mine.

The girl holds onto the pushchair as the nanny locks the door.

The nanny turns the pushchair in my direction, to cross the street.

For the second time, someone is looking at me looking at them.

Perhaps she's come out of the house to investigate me – the strange woman who has started sitting in the park every day, staring at their windows.

The little girl speaks and the nanny looks down.

A dummy rolls across the tarmac. The little girl picks it up and holds it out. They are in the middle of the street. The noise of the traffic on the busy road behind me feels like a threat but they are in a street with a dead end; the traffic is not near her.

The nanny takes the dummy, wipes it on her top then gives the dummy back to the child.

I am not OCD about cleanliness but I am qualified to look after children and the five-second rule doesn't apply to children who have barely started developing their immunity.

I start walking as the nanny tips the buggy back so it can get over the kerb on this side of the street. Called into action by her ineptitude.

Louise and I are on the same page. I may not want to take the children, but I want to get rid of that nanny. The children need me; Louise and I know that.

People who do not look after children properly do not deserve to have them.

They walk along the path on the other side of the park's railing.

I walk in the same direction, towards the park's exit.

The woman looks to be in her late teens or early twenties. Too young.

The small girl is on the far side of the pushchair so I can't see her. I want to see her.

I walk quicker to get ahead of them. I can see the girl's expression is compliant as she looks at the pavement, silent.

The colours in her aura have faded, as sadness dances around her. Children often have splashes of colour, not layers. She has a cloud that is blended to a point it is hard to pick out the different shades.

The girl's sadness lances through me, cutting into the flesh of my heart with a quick thrust. Things are not right in that house.

I want to help the children. I know what it is like to grow up without a mother. They must be feeling broken. Black holes will be forming, stealing all their happiness.

They need me.

I am so glad you brought me here, Louise. Thank you. I know you are right.

The park's exit is at the tip of its triangle shape. The path I am walking on and the path they are walking on brings us closer.

The nanny looks at the main road.

I pretend to look at my phone as I walk, and laugh, as though

I have seen something funny, then lift the phone to aim the camera. Tap. Tap. Tap. It will not be the best picture, the nanny is side on, but it is something for me to use to help me find her on social media.

The distance between us becomes a few paces.

I grip one of the fleur-de-lys at the corner of the iron railing for a second as I walk out while she takes the last few steps. I think she's going to walk on along the pavement, so I wait, to let her pass, but she turns the pushchair into the park.

An intense urge begs me to bend down and touch the little girl's head. To run my fingers through her curls. To touch her shoulder, reach for her hand and help her run. But all I do is smile at the woman I hate and step out of the way.

She walks past me with no acknowledgement as though I am nothing.

I think she's going to the playground in the farthest corner of the park.

I want to walk along the path by the railing, so I can keep watching them. But that would be too obvious.

I press the button for the pedestrian crossing, stop the traffic and walk away.

I turn the key and open Simon and Mim's door long before they will be home. Simon will not know I have been out today.

When Simon comes in the back door, I am lifting a fish pie with a golden, crispy mashed-potato top out of the oven. A steamy smoked-cod smell fills the room. I made the pie before Mim got home with the boys and I'm proud of it. No one would call me a cook. Dan and I lived on ready meals, but that was out of necessity in the last years of my incapability. This pie is a triumph over a fate that tried to kill me.

Louise changed that fate.

Perhaps she was a good cook?

I know that today has spurred me into wanting to play happy families with her children. All I can think about is looking after them. My head is running through the images of my life with them. They are not Louise's memories, they're my hopes.

Simon smiles at me as I straighten up, put the hot dish on top of the oven and push the oven door shut with my toes.

His gaze moves to Mim and the boys, who are sitting around the table. 'Hello,' he says as the boys scramble to say good evening, their chairs scraping on the floor.

Their arms wrap around his legs.

I see Louise's children greeting me like that.

He slides the rucksack he uses for work off his shoulder and unzips it, looking at me again and deploying the grin the boys have inherited from him.

He pulls a magazine out of his bag and holds it out. 'For you.'

A copy of *The Lady* hovers in front of me.

I pull off the blue striped oven mitts and drop them down beside the pie dish.

'I agree.' His voice lifts with conviction. 'You should find a nanny job, but you don't have to take one that will be too much hard work. If you are going to get a job go for the best position, somewhere they will not expect you to do the cleaning and the cooking too.'

I take the magazine.

But I do not want to be anyone's nanny. I want to be Alex Lovett's nanny.

I just need to get rid of the useless girl he has now.

Chapter 17

9 weeks and 4 days after the fall.

My hand is in my jeans pocket gripping the key for the front door of the house I rent a room in.

The church bells are ringing from two different directions but otherwise the streets are quiet.

There's something unique about the city of Bath. Perhaps it's because the city centre is so much smaller than London and the size develops a sense of intimacy.

I run slightly, in a jog, along the pavement of the last street until the point it meets the main road, then I slow to a walk.

The excitement is buzzing in my ears. Fizzing words and thoughts through my head. I can't believe I am here. Out in the world on my own and focusing on a future that I can see clearly. I just need to work out how to get from this to that. I have spent all night trying to think of a plan.

But with Louise's help, I will come up with a way. I'll get into the house somehow.

It is the first time I have come here on a Sunday. Only a couple of cars pass by on the main road.

Most people are still in bed, eating breakfast, drinking coffee and reading papers.

Jive music tumbles out from the old railway station near the crossing that is now used as an antique market. The music calls to the few of us who have risen early, pulling passers-by inside. I am not drawn.

The railing-imprisoned park is opposite.

I ought to have a reason to sit in there, though. I haven't bought a coffee yet. I rushed, because I was so glad to be able to walk out of a door and come straight here.

I turn back towards the music and the open door. There will be somewhere inside that sells takeaway coffee.

The small door leading into the under-cover market is deceptive; inside it is a huge space with a towering vaulted glass ceiling, held in place by a backbone of wrought-iron arches.

The scattering of antiques stalls is belittled by the architecture and there are scarce customers; it is mainly the stallholders talking to each other as they eat rolls bursting with bacon.

A freshly ground coffee aroma wafts from the far end where the stallholders must have bought their rolls.

When I leave the market the coffee in the cup is so hot it burns my hand through the insulated cardboard. I cross the road, hurry into the park and rush for my bench, then put the cup down on the seat beside me, claiming the bench.

All the pressure and excitement of the last few days slips away on my outbreath.

I have lied so many times to Simon and Chloe my mythical life is a tangled ball of yarn that could unravel at any moment. They think I start a job here on Monday, but I have been vague about the family and the address so they can never try to find where they think I work.

I don't like having so many secrets between me and them, but Louise and her family come first now. They must come first.

This is a place that's been prepared for me. She's chosen me to fill the gap in her family, to love her children.

This is my job.

I am starting to feel as if the reason for my life since birth was to be ready to fill her space. Left alone by my parents so that I would want hers. Born with a faulty heart so that I would need hers. Prevented from having children so that I can love hers.

But I know that can't be true.

I am renting a room in a woman's house. I spotted it for rent only a few streets away on SpareRoom and rushed to move because I didn't want to lose the chance.

I have moved to Bath, and I am going to sit here and live on the last of my savings until I find a way to be with the children.

I am due to meet Alex in just over a week, for the fake appointment. I'll need to create more lies then. But I am becoming a very good liar, with Louise as my cheerleader, pushing all these shameless tall tales out of my lips. But if lying means I can have what I want, I am happy to lie.

The rungs of the chilly metal seat press into the backs of my thighs. The cold creeping through my jeans.

I take my phone out of my back pocket but I don't look at it, I look in through the first-floor windows of Alex's house. Into his living room.

I came last night and saw Alex walk across the room when there was a light on. I couldn't see very much, but I saw enough to know it's the living room.

If Alex or the nanny see me, I imagine they barely notice me. I am probably just *the woman who sits in the park*.

The phone shivers in my hand. The single vibration of a message from Chloe.

'Good morning. What's life like in Bath?'

'Nice. Laid-back.' I reply via WhatsApp.

'At least you're only a short train journey away. If you'd moved farther away I would have hated you.'

'I promise we'll see each other—' my thumb stops, hesitating over the letters when I hear the familiar rattle of a doorknocker '—often,' I type and send without looking back down.

I leave the phone resting in my lap and take a sip of coffee that scalds my tongue.

A woman with long pitch-black hair has stepped out of the house and turned back to face Alex, who is standing in the doorway.

She's wearing a sequin-covered black mini dress and high heels – nothing else. No jumper. No coat.

The sequins catch the sunlight. She wobbles slightly, balancing on killer thin black patent stilettos. She's gripping a small evening bag with both hands.

I get up and start walking over the grassy mound that dominates the middle of the park, sliding my phone into my back pocket and gripping the coffee cup tightly in the other hand, walking across the grass towards the house.

I want to hear what they're saying.

The chaotic curls that define the children's hair suggest Alex has just got out of bed.

'That's okay. But call me. If you want to,' the woman says in a high flirting tone that belongs in a bar, not on the doorstep of a posh street.

'I did say it was a one-off ...'

One hand brushes her hair back. 'Yes.'

If Alex looks across her shoulder he will look at me.

'But thank you for last night.' His hand is holding the door, telling her without words he wants to close it.

He's wearing the same loose grey jeans I saw him wearing

through the living-room window last night, and they look like
the ones he wore to work on Friday. His T-shirt is creased – as
if it has just been picked up off a bedroom floor, but his clothes
are always creased. Today, though, his feet are bare as if he's
dressed quickly, solely to say goodbye to this woman; as if they
have got up together and he's only dressed to walk her downstairs.

I doubt there was even a stop for breakfast, his body language
is so keen to dispose of her.

The woman takes a single step back. 'It was my pleasure.' The
clutch bag is moved awkwardly from one hand to the other as
she turns away and the door bangs shut, rattling the doorknocker
again.

She walks a few paces then stops, fumbling with the catch
on her bag. She takes out a cigarette and a lighter, lights it, before
carrying on with her walk of shame.

It is obvious what went on in that house last night.

Louise's spirit lurches, with the leap of a panther racing into
my heart. If she had the ability to control my body she would
make me run, and make me scratch out that woman's eyes.

Vengeance becomes a pressing emotion on the back of my
tongue, as Louise tries to shout abusive words through my lips.

I don't care about the woman. He can sleep with whoever he
wants to.

But it's a quick bounce-back for a man whose wife has only
recently died.

Louise screams in my ears, trying to focus my attention on
her anger. She wants me to feel it.

Did he love Louise?

It's less than three months since she died in a horrific way.
And that was clearly a one-night stand.

A tremor of disgust twists in my stomach. What if the woman is a dangerous bunny-boiler?

Are the children in there? I don't care about Alex or that woman, but the children ...

From the level of anger welling up inside me, I know Louise cared about Alex, though.

Dan let me down.

What about Alex? Has he done this before?

Are most men unable to keep their dicks in their trousers?

Is this why Louise jumped from the car park? Because he's a cheating bastard.

Now I am angry. I'd like to see revenge dished out on every man who is like Dan. Telling shallow lies about love. Setting up a false shop window about what life would be like with them – from happy ever after to *The Little Shop of Horrors*.

What if Alex created a family with her and then betrayed her? *Bastard.*

I need to get inside that house and save the children from him, not just his nanny.

I walk forward and stand on the edge of the mound, the steep slope dropping away in front of me, down to the wall with the doors for the passages that run under the road.

It is like an ancient moat, a boundary defending the houses on the far side.

Louise is willing me into that house. She's working in my mind as well as my heart, trying to help me think of a plan. I listen, waiting for the words and ideas she is trying to put there, but I can't hear them.

'Is this why you gave me your heart? Because you know I'll rescue the children, and get them away from him?'

REVENGE VERSUS LOVE

Chapter 18

9 weeks and 5 days after the fall. Day 1,
after I saw that woman.

I thrust my fist into the pillow again and lie back down. The pillow feels like a lump of cement tonight even though it is stuffed full of soft downy feathers and releases the aroma of lavender.

I can't stop thinking. I can't stop seeing that fucking woman. *Slut.*

Louise is so angry her thoughts fizz amongst mine, spitting out from a shaken champagne bottle, and she keeps shaking the bottle; she will not let the anger die.

I thought Louise had a perfect life. Perfect parents. Perfect children. A handsome, wealthy husband. A perfect family.

That was the façade. Behind the scenes Alex was a bastard; that's what she's been trying to tell me.

Just like Dan pretending for months with me, while he made another woman pregnant.

Louise and Alex's marriage produced three beautiful children, but at some point it became loveless. Heartless.

I can feel the embarrassment, pain and loss of Alex's betrayal oozing like a picked scab – as deeply as I feel my own because of Dan's. The pain is gathering up in me, in an increasing avalanche, tumbling through my thoughts. Every time I try to sleep, my mind returns me to children's homes, and hospitals, or sitting in restaurants listening to Dan gush about a love that in the end had no roots.

Alex's affections are not only as shallow as Dan's, they are as shallow as my father's and mother's.

I think Louise is telling me there were other women before she died, but even if I am wrong and he didn't have sex with other women, he can't have loved Louise properly. People who love you do not have sex with a stranger three months after you've died.

Louise is loved by her parents, and her children must miss her. But their father ...

I am scared now. If his love is that shallow, what might happen to the children?

They need a nanny to look after them and love them as strongly as Louise loved them.

I will love them that much. I will be their mother – if I can get into the house.

I roll over and look at the clock. 3:04. I might as well give up trying to sleep. Maybe if I do something for a while Louise will press an idea into my mind.

I touch the light stand to turn the bedside light on, sit up, pulling the cushion that was on the side of the bed behind me and reach for my laptop.

Robert Dowling's Facebook page appears as I open the laptop; the last thing that I looked at.

Is Robert Dowling friends with Alex's nanny? I have glanced through his friends' faces before, but now I have the picture on my phone to compare with.

Forty minutes later, I can say for certain that she's not among his Facebook friends.

It was always an unlikely hope. A nanny who shares her social life with her employer's father-in-law would be rare.

The Facebook pages that Robert Dowling likes include Alex's business page. I click through to it because I'm still not tired.

If I were working for someone I would take an interest in their business.

About the thirtieth post down, a familiar face appears in a small icon in the comments.

The date of the post is five months ago. Before Louise died.

I click on the image to enlarge it. It is her. The nanny.

She posted a thumbs-up emoji in the comment stream under a picture.

Her name is Susie Brooke.

One click from the tip of my forefinger and I can see Susie Brooke's Facebook page. It's private. There is just one profile picture of her, a black screen header and a few shared posts from a music band.

I do not send her a friend request. There's no point. Younger people are generally more savvy and judgemental about who they befriend online. She would see that she doesn't know me and wonder why the woman who sits in the park has sent her a friend request in the middle of the night. Then she'd wonder how I know her name.

One thing the page does show me, that I didn't know, is that she isn't employed directly by Alex. Her employer is listed as an agency.

I open another search engine tab and type in Shearing and Smith Recruitment Agency. The company specialises in childcare and other household staff.

The name Susan Brooke goes into another search tab. It is a common name. I open Twitter and trawl through accounts with her picture on my phone to compare. Not one Susie Brooke looks like her.

I open Instagram to search there, scanning through face after face. I want to find images that will not be blocked. Images that will tell me how to get rid of her.

There. I see her.

My fingertip taps the screen by her image as I look from that to my phone. It is her. It's a different picture from the one she used on Facebook but it's her and the account isn't private.

The posts open a door into her life. Places she goes to most, where she drinks, where she eats; and her friends are there, in pictures and comments. Patterns emerge as I scroll through the months. A pub, in Bath, where they all meet up. A nightclub in Bristol that she visits at least once a month. A park she takes the children to more than anywhere else.

The music band that was in her Facebook posts appears several times, and lots of those pictures are group selfies, including Susie. She is either a fan or a friend.

Another internet tab and another search takes me to the band's Facebook page. They're a local, unsigned band made up of young men – they have 4328 likes on the page and Susie is one of their followers.

They play a lot of gigs in and around Bath. Susie's profile image appears in nearly all the comment streams and she *hearts* everything they post.

When I compare Susie's Instagram posts with the dates and venues the band have performed at, every date aligns with a picture on Susie's stream.

The floorboards on the landing creak, with the sound of soft, careful steps. Click. Electric light fills the thin gap around the bedroom door. A different sort of light is seeping through the blind covering the window.

I look at the clock. 5:19.

The floorboards continue creaking and I hear a door. The bathroom door.

I close the lid of the laptop, leaving all the tabs open, put it down and turn off the bedside light.

The toilet flushes, the bathroom door opens again and then there are more creaks as my landlady, Pippa, walks back along the landing.

I try to sleep but my mind will not stop spinning with ideas and plans.

Louise is excited. My heart is kicking. She thinks we have taken another step.

Chapter 19

10 weeks after the fall.

My jeans are absorbing the morning-chill from the cast-iron bench. I fidget, crossing and uncrossing my legs, and take a sip from the takeaway coffee cup.

The coffee is nearly cold.

Kevin and Liam started school today. They were restless with excitement when I spoke to them on the phone last night.

Alex and the children left the house early. They came out of the house at 8.10 and Alex has been away from the house for thirty minutes.

I was lucky I saw them leave. I came here early to try to see them through the windows. Ten minutes later and I might have passed them in the street.

I want another cup of coffee and I am hungry, but if I move I might miss seeing the girl return.

The heels of my boots tap on the ground.

I should be tired, I have not slept for two nights, but my body is full of energy, my mind constantly buzzing, like a wasps' nest, with a dozen wasps continually flying in and out; ideas and thoughts about how I can get into that house.

I know the route is through the nanny. She needs to be disposed of. Louise and I just need to work out how.

'Daddy.' The high-pitched call comes from the corner. The girl is stretching up her open hand, trying to show him something on her palm. He stops after a few paces and looks, bending down, as he holds her hand, his tangled hair falling forward. He says something to her then she lifts whatever it is off and turns to put it down on the leaf of a weed that's growing at the edge of the pavement.

He brushes his hair back as he straightens up and holds out his hand to her.

She takes the offered hand and they walk on.

Where were the children when that slut was in the house? I don't think they were there. He sent them away so that he could have a one-night stand.

Shallow, pathetic love.

But at least he protected the children from it.

He takes the key out of his back pocket and opens the door.

When the door closes, I look at my watch. 8.48.

I stand.

I'll buy another coffee and something for breakfast then come back. I don't care about seeing Alex leave. I don't need to know any more about him. I am meant to be meeting him at the studio today but I'm not going to go. Talking to him and telling him lies will make it impossible to find a way into the lives of the children.

As I walk across the grass, towards the park exit, I look at Instagram, head down, absent-mindedly scanning through posts.

There are three other people in the park this morning, walking dogs: a yapping Jack Russell, an Alsatian walking on its lead with its head up in a position that says it thinks it owns the park and a very attractive-looking Dalmatian. I pass another dog-walker, with a Westie, coming through the park entrance as I walk out.

I press the pedestrian-crossing button to cross the main road then look down at the screen on my phone. Then change my mind; there's a Boston Tea Party café, between the place I live and here; the smell of cooking bacon that came from their extractor fan smelt gorgeous this morning. I'll eat there and it'll be easier to get there if I walk up the hill and across. I turn, looking up as I move, and nearly bump into a man.

Him.

Alex.

My heart leaps, jumping as I stop. Shock.

Louise is here, her words trying to form on my tongue. A stream of abuse.

My phone is in my hand, and the image on it is of his daughters playing in the park.

'Sorry.' His hand lifts, brushing back his hair, and his fingers catch in the curls as he dodges past me.

My head turns, my gaze following him as the crossing lights change and he walks over the road.

His hair looks so knotty it can't have been combed for days. His hand slides into the front pocket of pale jeans as he walks: pale denim with a large light brown stain on the front of his thigh, probably from a spilt coffee. The jeans have been washed since, but the stain has not come out.

His jaw glistens in the early sunlight as he turns to walk around the corner on the other side of the road. He hasn't shaved, and it doesn't look like a carefully crafted designer six-o'clock-shadow, it looks like unkempt laziness.

A vindictive feeling sets like concrete as I smile and walk on. If I *were* a wedding planner for a wealthy couple I would not be impressed by Alex Lovett.

The children need me.

Chapter 20

11 weeks and 3 days after the fall.

I have never sat in a pub on my own before. It's obvious I'm alone, too, because this is a small pub.

My fingers are wrapped around a pint of locally brewed pale ale, as I watch the three young men I've been tracking on the band's Facebook page set up their equipment.

The drummer is putting his kit together; he arrived later than the others. Another man is tuning an electric guitar that's slung around his neck. The third man is setting up the sound system they carried in with them.

The door into the pub opens. I look. I want people to assume I'm waiting for someone.

I am waiting for one person. Susie Brooke.

But it's not her who walks in.

I lean back against the wall, hiding in the corner, cross-legged, with an arm resting on my handbag and the pint glass held firm.

I chose the corner table because I can see the whole bar from here, and if it gets busy later I'm by the toilets, so I can see Susie go in there and follow if I want to.

Susie hasn't missed any of the band's gigs; I am sure she'll come tonight. I think she's dating one of the men in the band, or fancies one of them. Her comments on their page are always gushing.

The band's name on the front of the bass drum says The B-Radicles. They're wearing casual clothes, skinny jeans and long-sleeved T-shirts, not trying to match. But they're all good-looking, fit, young men.

The pungent odour of cannabis fills the space around me as a skinny man in a loose parka coat walks out from the toilets. The smell is carried so heavily in his clothes his coat must have been in a room where he spends hours smoking dope.

My health made Simon and me law-abiding teenagers; we did not have the choice to become involved with drugs. I was too ill, and he was too busy looking after me. But Dan came home with the smell of cannabis smoke in his clothes sometimes, especially in the last few months we were together.

The entrance door opens again. I look over.

It's Susie, looking over her shoulder at the woman behind her: a friend I recognise from her pictures.

Susie's shoulder-length dark brown hair is down tonight and there's a recently died silver streak falling to the side of her face.

In the day, she wears her hair up in a high ponytail. She also doesn't wear very much make-up, but tonight she's wearing smoky-grey eyeshadow that highlights the attention-grabbing contrast of her pale pastel-blue irises.

She walks over to the band, sliding her arms out of a leather jacket, revealing a flesh-hugging top to accompany her barely-there skirt.

'Hi,' Susie says in the direction of the guy with the guitar hanging from his neck. He looks up and gives her a smile that suggests they know each other well.

She walks up to him, wraps her arms around his neck and

presses her lips against his. It's a possessive hold. The kiss claims the man, telling other women in the pub he belongs to her.

He pats her bottom in the second between the end of the kiss and when her arms fall away.

'Have you got drinks?' she asks the band.

'Yeah,' the guitarist and the drummer reply. The guy sorting out the sound system looks over his shoulder and nods.

Susie's fuller-figured friend turns a pale red.

I would guess she has an interest in the third man in the band but hasn't been as successful as Susie in winning his attention. He straightens up, steps around the sound system and picks up a bass guitar from behind the drums while Susie turns and walks over to the bar.

Her blushing friend follows.

Jealousy whispers, and I don't think it is Louise's feeling. I don't like Susie. I don't like her because she has the children and I don't. The sensation causes my teeth to clench, and my muscles to tighten, bracing, as if this will become violent. But I don't move from my seat.

'Gin and Tonic and a white wine,' Susie says to the barman as the door opens again and a group of about eight people files in. Susie and her friend wave them over.

I sip from the pint glass of fragrant, hoppy-smelling ale trying to hide in plain sight in the corner. But I assume, if she notices me, it will not be too odd to see the woman who hangs around in the local park in a local pub.

The group of eight surrounds Susie and her friend.

The door opens again and another large group walks in, bringing a rush of cold air with them. They head to the bar.

I can't see Susie any more.

The door continues opening, with cold air sweeping into the

room, as a few notes from the band reach through the crowd, testing the sound.

'Hi, everyone. Be with you soon,' Susie's boyfriend says into the microphone.

A few of the people at the bar turn, drinks in hand, and face the band.

Susie frees herself from the crowd at the bar and occupies a chair at a table near the band, with a thin glass containing her G and T in her hand. Her girlfriend follows and sits next to her.

The lead guitarist's lips quirk on one side with a little recognition that tells her he knows she's there, then his concentration returns to tuning his guitar chords.

I watch every detail of Susie's expression and movement.

What can I do to get a healthy young woman out of Alex's house?

The door continually creaks open with a waft of cold air and then thumps shut as the pub fills up, until every table but mine is full. So, I'm not surprised when four men ask to share my table once it has become standing room only.

'Yes, go ahead.' It'll give me more cover.

I straighten up in the seat as they sit down.

'Do you know the band?' the man who sits next to me on the cushioned bench asks, as he puts his pint down on a cardboard beer mat. He smiles and leans back.

The ginger-haired young man next to him wraps his arm around the shoulders of the man on his other side.

The men are older than the band's average following who are spread around the rest of the pub.

'No. Are they good?'

'Brilliant. They played here before. You'll like them.'

'What sort of music do they play?'

The conversation between me and him develops into a conversation between me and the rest of the group, circulating around music tastes. Favourite songs. Favourite artists.

A drumstick hits the symbols, silencing our conversation.

A drumstick hits the snare drum once, then again, and again. Then the drummer launches into a full stream of sound.

The bass guitarist joins in, and the sound becomes a rhythm, then the lead guitar comes in and after three bars the vocals start.

It is Susie's boyfriend up front, singing the lyrics.

She stands up and moves in front of her table, dancing to the music. Everyone around the front four tables gets up as the music drowns out every other sound in the small pub.

The sound is deafeningly loud. It hits the walls all around me, bounces back and makes the table tremble with the weight of the vibrations thrusting out from the sound system.

The song is good, though.

My foot taps on the floor as the men around me sing along, in loud off-key abandon.

The men make me smile, they're enjoying themselves so much. Everyone in the bar is enjoying this.

A pungent waft of cannabis sweeps towards me. A skinny man walks past on his way to the toilets.

As I look back at Susie an idea rushes at me.

A moment ago, my thoughts were vague, but suddenly I know exactly what to do. It is as if Louise's spirit has sprinted through me to draw my attention away from the music and tell me the answer. I have it. It's so obvious. Easy, really.

I stand. 'I need the toilet, sorry,' I yell over the music to move the man next to me out of the way so I can slide out from the corner.

With my coat over one arm and my handbag hanging from the other, I turn to go into the toilets.

The skinny man who reeks of cannabis comes out of the door just as I am about to open it.

Our gazes clash. I try to smile but I must look silly and hesitant because my heart leaps into a nervous pace, jumping along with the people who are dancing in the area in front of the band.

There are two cubicles in the women's toilets and one sink outside them, with a long mirror hanging above. My breaths rush in and out as my heart races.

I breathe in deeply, forcing the feeling of panic to calm down.

I have never done anything like this but people do it every day. I hold the edge of the cold, white, porcelain sink, my handbag and coat sliding down to hang off my wrist, and stare at the woman in the mirror. 'You can do this. It's the easiest way. If you want to be with the children, you have to do this.'

If I'm caught I won't even be arrested these days – at the most it will be a warning. I just need courage.

I breathe in and out again slowly. Listening to the sounds inside me, trying to draw courage from Louise.

My heartbeat slows, preparing to pounce like a cat onto a mouse.

I look into my eyes in the mirror and see Louise's eyes.

I have seen spirits often, but to see her within me ... It's creepy. But I'm certain she won't harm me.

The nonsense they create in the film industry isn't real. Spirits can't physically do anything to harm the living.

Before I leave the cubicle, I unzip my handbag, take out my purse, find the forty pounds I have in cash and slide the notes into the back pocket of my jeans. When I come out of the toilets, nearly everyone in the bar area is either standing and watching or dancing and shouting along with the song. But I can see the skinny man through the moving bodies.

He's sitting at the end of the bar, near the front door, with his elbow leaning on the bar and his hand holding his pint glass.

His uninterested posture hints that he's a regular who doesn't appreciate the intrusion caused by a live band.

I walk across the pub in the direction of the skinny man, my one-third-drunk glass of ale deserted on the table with the men who joined me there.

How do I ask for drugs?

I stand at the bar next to the skinny man and lift a hand to obtain the barman's attention. He sees me straight away. 'Another pale ale, please. A half this time.'

The man nods at me and turns away to pick up a glass.

A false smile pulls my lips wide as I look at the skinny man. He's not young. He doesn't look very far off my age. 'Hello.'

'Hi.' It is a gruff, uninterested acknowledgement that I can barely hear over the music.

'You're not dancing; don't you like the band?'

'Not my thing.'

'Two thirty-five, love.' The barman puts the brim-full glass, with one shiny dribble of ale running down the side, onto a damp-looking bar towel in front of me.

'Thanks.' I reach for the cash in my back pocket and pull a ten pound note free. The barman takes the note, rings up my drink in the till and hands me the change. 'Thanks,' I say again as panic threatens to throttle me.

I glance over at the skinny man.

He's looking at his pint glass.

I take another breath, sucking in courage, as the barman walks to the far end of the bar. Then I turn to face the skinny man and breathe out the words in a brave rush. 'Do you know if anyone sells cannabis in here?'

Louise applauds – there's a rush of pride mingling with my terror.

The man looks at me. Hard. Questioning if he can trust me.

There's a moment of silence while I hang onto his gaze, determined not to shrink from it and show weakness.

He lifts his pint and takes a drink. 'Yes ...' he says, in a questioning tone as he puts the pint back down. No one is standing near us and the music means no one can hear us.

'Who?' I think he'll sell it.

He takes another drink from his pint, as if he's deliberately drawing this out because he knows I am a novice.

He smiles when he puts the pint down. I amuse him.

'I have some I can sell you. How much do you want?'

Jackpot. But how much cannabis is it normal to buy? How is it measured? If I say one packet, how much is that? I pull the cash out from the back pocket of my jeans, gripping the uncrushable slippery ten-pound notes and the change from my drink. Then hold the money out making sure my hand is lower than the height of the bar. 'How much will this buy?'

His eyebrows lift and his lips purse for a second as he makes the decision to do this. 'Meet me outside in ten minutes, but move away from me now.'

'Okay.' I pick up my drink and turn away, unsure where to walk. I can't go back to the same table with another drink.

I walk around the edge of the people dancing, between them and the people buying drinks at the bar. Trying to avoid the arms that are thrown out in careless excitement.

There's a space where I can lean against the wall.

Between sips from my half-pint glass my foot taps and I nod along with the rhythm, trying to blend in and enjoy the music, with my coat and bag hanging from my arm.

I keep glancing at the hands on the clock behind the bar. It's 9.17 now.

The skinny man is still sitting at the far end of the bar – and maybe I am staring at him too obviously.

I look at the band again and open my mouth like a fish; pretending to utter the words that everyone else is singing. Every muscle in my body is tense and my heart is clenched so tightly it feels a little like the heart spasms I used to have. The pressure is wringing the air out from my lungs and I can't squeeze it back in.

The music becomes just a sound with no rhythm, the people crushing.

The hands on the clock say 9.20.

I hold onto the half-pint glass as if it is a crutch that will keep me on my feet. Breathe, just breathe, for a few more minutes and then this will all be over.

9.22.

I try to slow my breaths, as I did when I was ill, counting slowly to three every time I breathe in and then to three when I breathe out.

9.23.

9.24.

I catch a movement in the corner of my vision, a sideways movement that is different from everyone jumping up and down. The skinny man is moving from the stool beside the bar. He picks up his dirty green parka coat.

I look at the clock and put my drink down on a table. 9.25.

Breathe. Breathe. Breathe.

My throat is so dry. I pick up the drink and take a sip, afraid I won't be able to talk when I get outside. Then I leave my drink on the table, turn and head for the door.

The sky is black beyond the yellow hue of the streetlights.

The music thuds through the walls and door of the pub behind me, invading the otherwise quiet street.

A whistle rings out.

The skinny man is standing on the far side of the street, in a shadow beyond a streetlight, at the head of a back alley.

As I walk over there, my arm braces, holding my bag and coat in front of me like a shield, while panic throbs through every muscle. I want to run. My heart is racing and running already. But those are not Louise's feelings – she's pushing me, making my legs move towards the danger. She has nothing to be afraid of, and everything to gain.

The smell of cannabis floods the cool air when I reach him.

'Hi.' The word slips through my lips because I have no idea what else to say as I delve into my back-pocket for the shiny ten pound notes and coins.

'Here.' His hand lifts and a small clear plastic bag, containing what looks like dried, crushed leaves is held out. Time hovers as I lift the cash and make the exchange.

He turns away without speaking, his gaze reaching over the road as he steps off the pavement and heads towards the pub door.

I must go back into the pub too.

I put the plastic bag in my back pocket.

One more thing to do and then I can go back to my room and leave everything to fall into place.

The loud music in the pub comes to a dramatic halt, and I

hear muffled words that the lead singer must be saying through the microphone. The music doesn't recommence.

Go back.

I keep hearing these short statements that seem to come from Louise.

My feet move, as if I'm sleepwalking. This is so unlike me. It is not me. But it has to be done.

The pub door is heavier than I remember as I push it open with a grip on the brass handle.

The noise inside the pub is now a tangled mass of conversation. People are crowded around the bar buying drinks, in a disorganised queue, four people deep.

I spot the silver streak in Susie's hair. She is right at the front at the far end of the bar, surrounded by half a dozen people waiting to order.

The tables near where the guitars are now left balanced against the drums are empty of people.

Susie's jacket is hanging over the back of a chair.

My heart is no longer racing from panic, it races with excitement, filling my arms and legs with adrenalin.

I weave through the chairs and stools moved out of the way so people can dance, my focus on Susie's jacket, Louise cheering me on from the sidelines.

When I reach Susie's chair, I sit and hide the movement of my hand, under the coat over my arm. I take the plastic bag from my back pocket and put it into the chest pocket of Susie's leather jacket, stand and turn away.

My heart beats so hard it tries to burst out of my chest as I navigate the slalom back to the front door and leave.

'Yes.' The word announcing my success mists in the air as the pub door thumps shut behind me.

I juggle my bag so I can pull my coat on as I walk, smiling and laughing. Smiling and laughing in a way that doesn't sound like me.

There is one more step for me to take and then this is done.

I keep walking while I unzip my bag and search out my phone. My thumb taps the numbers 999 on the screen. Call.

'Hello, what's your emergency?'

Chapter 21

11 weeks and 5 days after the fall.

A woman wearing tailored black trousers and smart patent black heels, which imply she's wearing a suit under her long blue Moleskin winter coat, is unlocking the door of the shop I'm waiting near. The gold lettering on the window says 'Shearing and Smith Recruitment Agency'.

I am occupying a different public bench today. In the street outside the agency. The coffee in my cup is cold because I have been here for an hour. I've hardly slept over the weekend because anticipation has been nibbling like a rabbit at my sanity.

Today is going to change my life.

It's the beginning I have been waiting for.

Louise's voice is loud in my head; it's not words but a jumble of sound. The sound has the blurred connections of a whisper, but the tone is loud.

My phone is in my hand. For the last half an hour I have just been watching time pass. Looking from my watch to my phone and back.

The woman locks the door behind her.

I can see her through the window, taking off her coat and

hanging it up. Then she disappears through a door at the back of the office.

My heart pulses with strong firm strokes – the pace mirrors the second hand on my watch. Waiting for the moment of success.

The electronic numbers on my phone slide over to 9.00.

The woman comes back into the room, puts a branded mug on her desk and moves to unlock the office door.

I stand and walk towards the door, meeting her gaze through the glass. She pulls the door open for me.

'Good morning,' I begin.

'Good morning. Come in. How can I help you?'

'I've recently moved to Bath and I'm hoping you can find a suitable job for me. I can start work immediately.'

'Take a seat. I'll have a look at your CV and check if there's anything right for you. We do make sure that people are a good fit for our clients so even if there isn't something now there might be in the future.'

I sit in the chair she raised a hand towards, on the window side of a desk. She moves around to sit on the other side, facing the window as the shop door opens.

'Morning,' the woman says in a casual way that immediately identifies the newcomer as a co-worker. She looks back at me. I lift the black A4 display folder I've been carrying, open it up and lay it on the desk with my CV on display. There are also letters in there from the parents of children in the schools and nurseries I worked in before I became too ill.

She reads as I put my handbag down beside my chair and slide my arms out of my coat. I cross my fingers and lean slightly forward. 'I want to move from working in a school to being a nanny.'

She looks up. 'Why?'

'To do something different. I had a difficult childhood. I lost my parents when I was very young and I'd like to support other families, children, to grow and live beyond difficult things.'

She nods, as though she doesn't actually care.

The phones on the four desks in the office ring simultaneously. The woman glances to the side. The other woman is still somewhere at the back of the office. The woman looks at me as she reaches for the phone. 'Excuse me. Hello. Shearing and Smith Recruitment Agency. Denise speaking. How may I help? Oh. Yes. Oh. Well, I'm not sure what to say.'

My crossed fingers tighten. Is this the call? Alex must have sacked Susie.

Of course, she wasn't arrested – she wasn't dealing drugs – but the police picked her up when she left the pub on Saturday night and they took her away somewhere in the car.

An hour and a half later, from the bench in the dark park, I saw the police draw up outside Alex's house with Susie in the back seat.

The police had probably questioned her about how she'd acquired the cannabis, especially if she'd been denying any knowledge of it.

'Yes. Yes. When by? Yes. I'll see what I can do. I am sorry. Yes. I do apologise again.'

Alex can't manage without a nanny. He'll need to work. He'll need someone else.

He'll need me.

'Thank you. I'll call you back as soon as I can. Goodbye.' The woman puts the phone down, and then, with her freshly applied, early-morning scarlet-red lipstick, smiles at me. 'You might call this perfect timing – a position that sounds ideal for you has come up. Are you available for an interview this morning?'

'Yes.' *Yes*, the voice inside me screams with excitement and my heart leaps with victory. *Yes*. The final voice saying yes inside my head is a breathy sigh. *At last.*

The door at the back of the office opens and the woman in front of me, Denise, looks over.

'Catherine, will you take a copy of these for me?' She closes my display folder and lifts it up, holding it out for the other agency representative to come and collect. 'Thank you,' Denise says as the other woman takes the document folder and turns away.

She smiles at me again, before reaching to pick up a pen. She writes Alex's name and address down on a branded pad of paper, peels the sheet off and holds it out, looking at me. 'This is where the interview will be, at the client's residence.'

'Thank you.' I take the piece of paper.

She looks at her watch. 'Can you be there for ten-thirty?'

'Yes.'

The other woman comes back with my folder and holds it out to me. 'Everything copied.'

I take the folder and slide the sheet of paper with Alex's details into the slot containing my passport.

'I'll let the client know you are on the way and check your references. He'll be interviewing others but he's looking for someone to start work as soon as possible. This week, prefer-ably.'

'That wouldn't be a problem for me.'

'Wonderful. Well, good luck and I'll let you know as soon as we hear the outcome of the interview from the client.'

'Thank you,' I say as I stand, tucking the folder under my arm and picking up my coat and handbag.

I'll drink a coffee in a café and walk to Alex's. I don't want to sit outside the house today because I don't want him to recognise me as the woman from the park bench. I am wearing my hair down to help prevent the recognition.

I don't knock the fox-head brass doorknocker but press the button for the electric bell for a good few seconds before lifting my finger. I received a text an hour ago to confirm that Mr Lovett is expecting me.

The heavier footsteps of a man coming down the bare wooden stairs creep from within the house. Less than a minute later the door latch turns on the inside and the door opens.

I lift the strap of my handbag higher on my shoulder with my thumb.

The youngest child is braced on his hip. A dummy is moving in her mouth, implying she's sucking hard on the teat.

An urge to grasp her from his arms pulses through me.

I smile, trying to look only at his face and not stare at the child. I want her. Even if I didn't have Louise in my head wanting her too, I would want her.

His pale eyes look at me. They're hypnotic, because the not-quite-blue makes me stare, looking for more blue in the grey.

His unruly hair is sun-bleached in places, making the blond multi-layered.

I thought of so many words to say but none of them will come out of my mouth. I swallow, trying to lubricate the dryness in my throat. 'Hello.' I open my hand and stretch it out towards him. 'I'm Helen Matthews. The agency sent me.'

Alex accepts my hand, not with an aggressive, dominating firmness but with the assertive hold of a confident man. 'Hello. Thanks for coming at such short notice. I'm Alex and this is Hope.' His eyes glance in the direction of the little girl who is clinging to his shoulder, her hands fisting, scrunching up the material of his mid-blue T-shirt. 'Come in.'

Louise is using my heart to thud out an annoying rhythm that will not be ignored as I step across the threshold. She wants my body to be hers. She wants to control me.

I am not her, and I don't want to be her. But I do want her children.

I smile at the baby. She looks a little over a year old.

'We'll talk in the kitchen,' Alex says. 'Through there.' He looks towards an open door. The flooring in the hall and kitchen is the old wooden boards.

He's wearing the pale jeans with the coffee stain, and his feet are bare.

The little girl, dressed in a nappy and T-shirt, watches me as I walk around him, her head moving to look over his shoulder.

He shuts the door and follows.

The kitchen is large. The front end of it is a seating area, where a wide white leather sofa wraps around the corner on one side of the walls. The space in the middle of the long room is broken up by a black granite breakfast bar surrounded with four tall chairs and a highchair. Glossy black kitchen units fill the wall space at the far end.

'Do you want a cup of tea?' he asks.

'Yes, please.'

The baby's legs hang loosely on either side of his hip, in a way that says she sits on his hip often and is very comfortable there. Safe. He may be a womaniser, but he isn't an aggressive man who frightens his children.

The children are not in physical danger at least.

But their small vulnerable minds ...

'So, you're older than the average person looking for a nanny's job ...' he says with his back to me as he crosses the large room, walking towards the kettle. The girl stares at me over his shoulder.

I follow, but stop beside the breakfast bar at the front edge of the kitchen. 'Am I?' I don't want to be drawn into a conversation about age in case it progresses to Susie.

This is about me.

'It's probably a good thing.' The kettle clicks as he presses the switch.

He turns and walks towards me. 'Would you hold Hope while I make the tea?'

'Yes, of course.'

He untangles the girl from his hip. I put my bag and coat down on one of the breakfast-bar chairs then reach out to take her, but she is clinging to his T-shirt. 'N. N. N.' The sharp sounds of denial come from behind her dummy.

Louise wants me to pull the child out of his arms. It must be difficult to see her child distressed.

This is a test. He's testing to see if I can manage Hope. But she lost her mother only a few weeks ago – who can blame her for wanting her father? It's wrong of him to try and thrust her at a stranger. This sort of behaviour is what will harm her mind.

'I'll make the tea,' I say. 'Hope and I can get to know each other when she's a bit more comfortable with me.'

'Thank you. She's fussy,' he says as she settles back on his hip. 'But the children's mother died a few weeks ago, unexpectedly, and it's made her clingier than normal.'

I walk around him to the boiling kettle. 'How awful.' I look at him, trying to think how I would act if I had only just heard that news. 'I'm sorry. That must be difficult.' I force my face and eyes to express empathy and interest, with appropriate emotion.

He doesn't answer, but his chest lifts under the baby's grip on his T-shirt as he takes a deeper breath.

Don't pretend you're upset, Alex. I know about the other women.

'Daddy.' A small voice travels down the stairs with the sound of small feet. 'Daddy.'

Alex looks over as the owner of the small voice, the small girl, comes through the door.

'Da—' She looks at me and her high-pitched voice slides to silence. She hurries towards him. Her arms wrap about one of his thighs and she presses herself against him as she looks up to meet his gaze. 'Daddy, will you come back and colour with me?'

His hand drops and his fingers brush through her very light blonde hair. Her hair isn't untidy; her curls have been carefully combed by someone, recently.

She's wearing a loose striped blue and white adult's T-shirt the size of a dress on her, with stains on the front of it.

'Who is she?' She looks at me then looks at her father.

'This is Helen. I'm speaking with Helen about maybe looking after you. If you like each other then she can look after you and play with you.' He looks at me.

I remember I am making him a cup of tea. 'Where are your cups?'

'Above the kettle.'

I open the cupboard and lift out two mugs while silence descends, except that the youngest girl is sucking on her dummy.

Louise screams, jolting my body in shock. It's as if she was testing how much noise she can make.

The scream isn't in my head, though. It's in the air, in the corners of the room and it surrounds Alex. Is she trying to make him hear her?

I look over my shoulder. 'Do you want milk or sugar?' Alex

didn't notice me start; the little girl is still clinging to his leg and he's looking at her.

'Just milk.'

'Where's the fridge?' It's behind one of these glossy-black cupboard doors, but I'm not going to play hide and seek with it.

'There.' He points to one of the tall cupboard doors.

I search out the milk and the room returns to silence. But in the spirit plain, Louise's anger is a vicious riot of emotion and sound.

I glance at Alex. His eyes are on the youngest of his girls, but his fingers comb through the curls of the eldest. He looks comfortable with silence. Nothing in his expression says he can hear Louise. But that unusual aura swirls around him, jet black in places and steel grey at its edges.

I drop a teabag into each cup, pour the boiling water out from the kettle, over the teabags, chasing them around the mugs with the flow of water, and then add milk.

I find a teaspoon and lift the teabags out. 'Bin?' I look at him. 'There.'

I press the cupboard so the gliding opening mechanism works and drop the teabags into the bin. After that, I pick up the mugs to take them to the breakfast bar, where he's standing.

'Thank you. Shall we sit down?'

He takes the baby off his hip and forces her buckling, denying legs into the highchair. 'N. N. N,' she moans as he attempts again and again to make her fit her legs into the chair.

'Hope.' It's a low-pitched order that says, do not fight me.

She concedes, her legs sliding into the necessary holes. He buckles up the strap that will hold her in place, then he looks at his eldest daughter. 'Fetch your colouring and bring it down here.'

She nods and runs off.

He looks at me as I pull out a tall chair and sit.

'The agency emailed through your CV and references. You have a lot of experience.'

I nod, unsure how to answer.

Louise is distracting me. I don't think she cares if I succeed in this. I don't think she wants me to move in, I think she just wants to get the children out. I can't do that. I can't take them. I have nowhere to take them to.

'But what about with younger children?'

'The nursery I worked in at the beginning of my career cared for children from the age of three months.'

He stares at my face. The conversation running dry again. Then breathes in suddenly. 'If children are difficult, what do you do?'

'Speak in a quieter voice, apply understanding and kindness to find out why and if necessary restrict their activity and raise the tone of my voice, but not the volume.'

His hypnotising eyes spark with electricity that warns me not to try to read his mind. He doesn't want a nanny to know him well or to understand his motivations. This is business to him.

Yet the way he looks at me says he's trying to see something in me that my words haven't said.

I think he wants to see something that tells him he can trust me.

I know, though, that trust can only be established by the evidence of time, and, in my experience, trust is a rare commodity, because people will often betray you.

Louise sweeps back into my body. I feel her looking at him through my eyes. I feel as if she is trying to change my view, to make me see something beyond the man in front of me.

I know he is a businessman, a photographer, a womaniser and a father. She must know much more.

The back pocket of his jeans buzzes with the sound of a

vibrating phone. He reaches behind him and looks at the caller identification. Then looks at me. 'Excuse me, I need to answer this,' he says as he presses the phone to his ear.

'M. M. M.' Hope reaches out for the phone.

'Daddy.' The other girl rushes in through the door carrying a piece of paper with a drawing on it and a fist full of crayons.

'You colour, sweetheart. Daddy needs to talk on the phone. I'll be with you in a moment.' He walks a little away from the children and me. 'Yes. Yes. Okay.'

It must be a work call.

The gravity-like tug on the tide that drew me to this house weeks ago pulls me closer to the children.

'I told you the other day. No. No.' He walks towards the hall as he talks, as though he intends to go out of the room, but he stops at the open door and turns. His eyes are looking at me but his expression tells me his mind is absorbed by the conversation. 'I said, no.' His voice rises in tempo. 'No, David.'

'D. D. D.' Hope reaches out her hands towards her father. Then she takes the dummy out of her mouth, drops it on the floor and repeats the pleading gesture with a clearer sound. 'D. D. D.'

The little girl is looking at me, with large eyes that are a true blue.

Misty pastel shades of sadness flow around her. Hazy colours that can only just be glimpsed, like a barely-there rainbow trying to break through in front of a rainstorm.

'I don't trust them, David.'

'D. D. D.'

The partially completed drawing and crayons left on a coffee table, the girl comes over to pick up her sister's dummy. She carries it over to a small step beside the sink, climbs up, turns on the tap and washes it.

At least Alex has taught the children cleanliness.

'Look, I don't care what they say. I don't trust them. No.'

The girl holds up the washed dummy. Hope reaches out to take it.

The girl has often pacified Hope.

I want to wrap them both up in my arms and squeeze them tight – give them all the love inside me. All the love that has been waiting years to find a child to give it to.

Perhaps it isn't so ridiculous to believe they are my fate. Perhaps they are why I was born with a broken heart. Perhaps they are why fate gave me awful parents and paired me up with an unfaithful man. If Dan were faithful, if my parents kept me, I would not be here today. I would not have found them.

'My name's Helen.' I whisper so I don't disturb Alex's phone call.

'I'm Rosie.' She holds up her small hand.

Louise weeps.

'Shall we take Hope over to the sofa and colour together?'

She nods as her hand slips free, looking at her sister.

'Come on, then, Hope.' I undo the buckle and, with her sister's approval as a recommendation of me, Hope lifts her arms, asking to be taken.

Louise reaches out with me, and then Hope has become ours, settling on my hip, as she was settled on her father's, with a fist clasping the back of my pink shirt.

I ignore the energy Louise is surging into my legs, trying to make me grasp Rosie's hand and run, and we sit on the sofa.

Rosie kneels in front of the short coffee table and slides her drawing over, to begin colouring.

I move Hope from my hip to my lap. 'What are you drawing?'

'Mummy. She's in heaven with the angels.'

Pain clasps my throat as if Louise has wrapped her hand around it and is squeezing tight.

'Just tell them I said no!' Alex shouts from the corner, no longer facing into the room.

Pulses of Louise's energy rush through my body urging me to get out of the house with the girls. But if I do that they'll just be brought back, and I'll be in a jail and unable to see them.

Miss Matthews, tell me why you took the children.

Their mother's spirit told me to.

Lock her up.

'What colour crayon are you going to choose next?' I ask Rosie, to stop her listening to Alex shout.

She picks up a grey crayon.

'I don't care. They can sign a statement swearing whatever they like. They're my children. No one can dictate what I do with my children.'

It's interesting that a man who's a womaniser and not trustable lacks trust in others. 'Shall Hope and I draw something too?'

'The paper is there.' The girl points at a packet of blank sheets of printing paper on a shelf under the low table. She doesn't appear upset by Alex's shouting. Is it normal?

'Yes. Yes. I know. I know. I'll cross that bridge when I come to it. But they're not having them now. Look, I need to go. I'm busy. Yes. Thanks. You too.'

He sighs. I do not look up but give Hope a crayon to use. She leans forward to tap on the paper, as I balance her with a hand over her stomach. It's been a long time since I've had the chance to hold a child as young as this. The warmth inside me, the brooding warmth that I have known for so long, drowns out every sensation that Louise is trying to force into my body. I love children. I love holding children and playing with them.

And these children are special – related to me in a way. And they need my love. They are as good as my own.

Alex coughs as if trying to clear his throat of something.

I look up as he comes towards us.

His hand slides the phone into his back pocket.

Hope drops the crayon and reaches for him. 'D. D.' He bends to take her off my lap.

'I'm sorry,' he says. 'This isn't a great time. You can leave. I don't have anything else to ask.'

I feel as if he's throwing me out of my own house. It throws me back to the day that Dan shut the door on me. The dismissal – rejection – cuts into the soft flesh of my heart. I want to stay.

Dan stood at the door, holding onto it, as if shutting me out physically and emotionally. Discarded, betrayed and banished.

'Thank you for coming,' Alex says, his voice hesitating, because I haven't moved. 'Please. Sorry.' His free hand lifts and slides through the muddled curls, then falls.

The please is a plea that tells me he's longing to be alone with the children. He wants to be shut away after his telephone row, not on public showing.

What is he like behind closed doors?

Whoever the real Alex is, Louise is angry with him. She's outside me, shouting from every corner of the room again. Screaming at him and me. She doesn't want him to have the children and she wants revenge.

I'm letting her down. This is not going according to her plan. Or mine.

This isn't how this is meant to end. He's supposed to ask me to stay, so he can go to work.

'Okay.' I stand, uncertain what to say. 'Will you call the agency to let them know the outcome?'

'Yes,' his voice says but his tone implies, no – after that phone call he doesn't care about anything but getting me out of the house.

Louise's spirit slips into the shadow around Alex as I walk over to the breakfast bar to collect my coat and handbag. I can hear her speaking to him, in that jumbled sound that is a whisper but not a whisper.

He moves aside, moving out of my way. His expression hasn't changed; he can't hear Louise.

As I walk towards the door to reach the hall, I glance at Rosie. 'Bye, Rosie. It was nice to meet you.' I lift a hand and wave.

She lifts a hand and makes one waving movement.

When I reach the doorway, I turn, look at Alex and hold out a hand. 'Thanks for considering me. It was nice to meet your children. They're lovely. It would be a pleasure to look after them.' It would be heaven to look after them.

He shakes my hand with that firm, confident hold. 'Thank you for coming.' There's something about that practised handshake, the handshake of a businessman. It is mastered. It presents like a shop window. But if I opened the door of that shop, walked past what was on sale and down into the cellar, what would be there? I feel as if there will be horrors hidden in his basement.

I don't think Alex is strong emotionally, and I know in his home life he's not as organised as his business presents him to be. He can't even manage to brush his hair, or wash the stains out of his clothes.

I walk into the hall.

He follows as I turn the latch and open the front door.

I glance back. 'Thank you, again. Goodbye,' I say as sunlight breaks through the gap of the opening door.

As I step out, his free hand grips the door and then the

doorknocker rattles with the sound I have become used to as the door bangs shut, heavily, behind me.

I am shut out of their lives and now I can't even sit in the park because Alex or Rosie might recognise me.

The green leaves of the trees in the park become a blur, misted by tears. I walk away with nowhere to go, my hands pressed to my ears, as Louise screams.

The strength of her emotions scares me, while the black hole inside is trying to rip me apart with its need for love.

My mind is being pulled to pieces on a medieval rack in a torture chamber, the wooden wheels creaking as they turn, stretching my emotions in opposite directions as far as they will go.

I need those children.

Louise wants some sort of revenge.

The phone on the desk beside the laptop bursts into life, vibrating as the ringtone chimes. My hand trembles almost as much as the phone when I pick it up.

Chloe.

Not the agency.

It's been hours.

I was so sure of my plan.

'Hello.' My voice lacks enthusiasm and energy.

'Hello. How are you?'

'Fine.' We have been speaking to each other at least once a day since I moved.

'You don't sound fine.'

'I ...' The truth presses on my tongue, longing to be spoken. I went for a job interview this morning and didn't get the job. I really wanted to work there. I swallow the words back. I can't say them. She thinks I have a job already. 'I'm tired.'

'It must be strange, working after so long. Are you sure it's not too much?'

'Yes.' I lift the pitch of my voice a bit higher, to make it sound brighter. 'I'm sure.'

'Are the children difficult?'

'No. No. They're lovely. The father is difficult.' And his wife's spirit is screaming inside me.

'But you said he lost his wife recently? You have to give him some allowance for that.'

'I know. But it's just ... difficult.' I can't think of another word. Sad. Heartbreaking. There's a drowning level of sadness inside me. A rain cloud dripping rain on my head, which streams down my face and drips from my chin. 'I don't know what to say to him.' How to persuade him that I should be the one to care for the children.

Louise is no longer working with me; her screams are aimed at me. She lost her children. She wants them back.

But spirits can't physically do anything. She needs me. She can't be a mother again. But I can become a mother.

When I realised that I could communicate with dead people I was eight. I watched the film *Ghost* with Patrick Swayze and Whoopie Goldberg, and thought, That's me. I hear things – people. I've never been afraid of the skill. It's like having an imaginary friend, and it makes me special – better than other people.

'If it's emotionally draining, it'll be harder to work there. You need to go out and do things other than work.'

All my mind and body want me to do is crawl into bed.

'You said you saw that band in the pub on Saturday. Do more things like that.'

'Mmm.'

'Okay, you aren't in a mood to talk and I have my date to get to. When I visit you at the weekend I'll drag you out for the evening. We'll find you something to do in Bath.'

'Enjoy your date with the man with amazing brown eyes and a mole near his lower lip.'

She laughs. 'I love that that's what you remember, not his name.'

'I remember, it's Ben. It's just your description stuck. If it works out I'll look forward to meeting Ben and his mole.'

Her laugh becomes a giggle. 'Talk tomorrow.'

'Yes. Talk tomorrow. Bye.'

I put the phone down, my breath coming out in a rush of air.

What to do? What to do? The words circulate through my head.

'It's six o'clock,' the electronic clock on my laptop announces.

I should take my tablets.

The packets and bottle are in a stack on the desk beside me and I have a bottle of water too. I close the laptop, leaving Robert Dowling's Facebook page open, reach for the first packet and pop the first pill out of the foil packet, then reach for the brown bottle, unscrew the lid and tip out the little white tablets, before reaching for the next box of foil capsulated drugs.

If I weren't taking my medicine maybe I would be worried that this is becoming an obsession, but I am taking it, so I know there's nothing irrational about this. It's just about love for me – and revenge for Louise.

Chapter 22

12 weeks and 3 days after the fall.

'Here you are.' The man who sat next to me last Saturday puts the gin and tonic he's bought for me, and the white wine he's bought for Chloe, on the beer mats on the round table.

'Thanks,' I say.

He pulls out a stool to sit down and join us at the table.

I assumed he was gay last week because the friends sitting next to him were a couple, but he's been chatting to us, or rather me, ever since we arrived, in a way that says he's doing more than being friendly. Now he's left his friends at the bar to join us.

'So, do you like Bath?'

I've told him half my life story already, and I'm enjoying the evening talking to him. It's the first time for weeks that my own thoughts and emotions have completely drowned out Louise's.

'She hasn't got a social life yet,' Chloe says, before I can answer.

He sends me a smile. 'I can show you the nightlife if you want me to?'

He has a nice look about him. His hairstyle tapers in length to fit closely over his ears and at the back of his neck. The cut and a clean shave shows off a strong jawline. He uses a gym, I can tell; the material of his long-sleeved T-shirt outlines well-defined, but not overly worked, biceps and pecs. 'Tomorrow night?' he says, throwing in the offer of a date with extreme subtlety.

A slight smile is dragged from me, because he's nice to look at as well as talk to. I might accept. There's no harm in that. I have nothing else to do. But – 'I'm visiting my brother tomorrow.'

His eyebrows lift. 'Monday, then.'

He's keen – the words Chloe will say the minute he's out of earshot slip through my mind.

'I'm working Monday evening.' It's not a lie. The agency didn't offer me the position with Alex, but they have offered me temporary work elsewhere.

I'm still determined to work for Alex, though. It will happen. It must. I've watched the house from the corner beside the busy road. His parents are living there and looking after the children. Alex's father walks the boy to school while Rosie stays with her grandmother.

'Then whenever you're free, if we swap numbers, you can text me.'

Oh, he's smooth, and his interest is flattering.

I catch Chloe's gaze; she's smiling. Her eyes open wider, urging me to accept the offer.

'Here.' He's taken the phone out of his front pocket and holds it out. 'Put your number in my contacts and I'll text you so you have mine.'

This is a big step. As big for me as Neil Armstrong taking the first step for mankind on the moon. I've only been romantically involved with one man. I do not find trust easy, and that man destroyed it even more. But I'm healthy now, and I've become trapped in a small rented room. I want to experience life and I want friends to do that with.

Becoming friends doesn't mean I'm giving anything of myself away. I can make it whatever I want it to be.

I put down the cold glass full of gin and tonic and take his phone.

I want the children, but Louise has been taking over my life. For weeks now – for the first time in my life when I have been healthy and not afraid of dying – I have been focused on death anyway because of Louise.

I will do this for me.

I am grateful to Louise for her heart but I am still me.

I open a new contact, type Helen Matthews and my mobile number. His and Chloe's eyes are on me.

I hand the phone back.

'Thanks.' He looks at it and touches the screen, then types something in with his thumb. My phone chimes in my handbag.

'Thanks,' I answer.

'So, let me know when you're free. Any night. If I have plans I can change them. I'll leave you two to talk now.' He smiles as he rises from the stool he straddled; the movement is easy and controlled, which can only be credited to the fact that his muscles are in good condition. He probably runs on the treadmills in the gym, or up and down the hills around Bath.

'He's keen,' Chloe whispers. 'You didn't say you'd met someone last Saturday.'

A smile breaks my lips apart. 'I didn't know I had. We spoke, that was all.'

'Well, whatever you said he liked it. His mate told me that he insisted they come back to the pub tonight so he could see if you were here, because you slipped through his fingers last week.'

'I wouldn't say that.' I glance at his friends. The gay couple are looking at me. He's talking to them about me. I look back at Chloe. 'He's nice, though.'

'He's more than nice. He's better than Ben with the mole.'

'You said you liked Ben.'

'I like Ben, but I adore your fella. If you don't want him I might try. Did you ask him his name?'

'Oh, God. No.' A laugh rushes out of me. 'I don't know how to do this.' I pull my handbag across the table, unzip it, take out my phone and look at the text. 'Andy. Andy Arnold.' I smile at Chloe. I'm still smiling when I look back down, a sudden mood-changing decision lancing through my mind. I type into my phone, using both thumbs. 'What about Tuesday? 7.30. Tell me where to meet you.' Send.

I look up at Chloe as a train whistle goes off at the bar. His text signal.

Chloe is grinning. She wants me to be happy, to make up for my lost years. She always thinks happiness comes from a man, though, as I thought with Dan.

But I know happiness will only come with children – Louise's children. I will not give up.

My phone vibrates and chimes in my hand. 'Perfect. I'll meet you outside the entrance of the Pump Room at 7.30. '

'Okay '

'Are you two going out?' Chloe asks as the train whistle goes off again.

'Yes.'

Chapter 23

18 weeks and 3 days after the fall.

The stadium's steep, graduated seating is slowly filling up. We have been seated for about fifteen minutes, plastic pint glasses in hand, the speaker system playing music. It's like no other bonfire night celebration that I've been to – sitting on a cold, plastic, fold-down seat in the tiered stadium of the Bath rugby club, looking at a floodlit empty pitch and empty stands on every other side. It's only this side of the stadium that is populated because the fireworks will be set off on the far side of the opposite stand.

I'm used to everything being dark on bonfire night, and the smells of hot dogs, roasting chestnuts and fizzing sparklers filling the air. Here the smells are pizza, the yeasty bitter in Andy's clear-plastic pint cup and the sweeter smelling lager in mine. Nothing seems right.

But to Andy and his friends this is normal.

'This is how the city of Bath celebrates Guy Fawkes,' was Andy's proud answer when I queried the idea of sitting in a stadium and not oohing and ahhing into the night sky in a dark park.

It's even odder because I haven't attended a celebration on

bonfire night for years, so I'm returning to memories that are precious.

'Are you all right? You're very quiet.' Andy looks at me with one of his slight smiles that suggest he has put all his trust in me. He lets his feelings show all the time and his expressions and words all say he cares if I'm happy.

Andy isn't like me, he trusts easily, and his attitude is rubbing off on me. I'm tentatively starting to trust him, too. He's such an open book I can see everything he feels and thinks in his expression, and his aura is beautiful; it's a halo of glowing gold and mauve.

But my relationship with Andy is not solving things. There's a constant sense in me that the world is skewed at an odd angle and I need to make it level. I'm not in the right place. Or doing the right things. Louise confuses everything. She doesn't want me to feel content, she wants me to hunger for the children.

I do hunger for them.

'Here, Grandad,' a young boy's voice calls out.

My heart staggers mid-beat. I know the voice. The boy is walking up the steps and pointing with a black and white striped glove-covered hand, at a row of mostly empty seats four rows down from us.

I've never seen the boy as close as this.

Louise's spirit rushes forward in my thoughts, urging me to stand and reach out – call out.

The boy is more like his father than the girls. He has Alex's face shape. He walks along the seating followed by his grandfather, who is carrying Hope. Hope is snug inside a winter onesie.

Alex is further down the steps holding Rosie's hand as they climb. Her head is down, looking at the steps, and all I see is the lime-green woolly bobble on the top of her hat.

As Alex and Rosie reach the seats, Rosie looks up; her gloves and scarf are a bright lime colour too, and the scarf has a row of bobbles on the end that hang down over her pink coat.

Rosie's hand slips free from her father's as she walks into the row of seats.

'I'll take Hope.' Alex holds out his hands to his father.

My hands itch to reach out and take her.

In my head, I'm climbing through the rows of people to reach her.

Andy's palm rests on my thigh. The warmth from his body seeps through the denim of my jeans and reaches my skin.

I glance at him.

'People watching?' he asks. He's joked before about my habit to drift off into thoughts and stare at people.

I can only answer with a nod. My heart has cracked, like the shell of a soft-boiled egg.

I'm in the wrong place. I should be four rows down with the children.

Being here with Andy is not resolving anything. Either what I want or what Louise wants.

But if I weren't here, I wouldn't have seen the children tonight.

Perhaps Louise has instigated this somehow? I've been trying to push her further back in my mind, because I can't do what she wants me to. Maybe she thinks this will make it possible.

Louise wants me to rush down there, take Hope and run.

I've become better at controlling my connection with Louise. I'm not led by her wants.

The bobble on the top of Rosie's hat sways as she shuffles on a seat between her grandparents.

Alex is sitting in the seat on the end of the row, with Hope braced on his lap. It looks as if she's asleep.

I can't watch them in the day, but in the evenings sometimes I walk down and sit in the park, in the dark, looking at the illuminated windows of the house. It's very rare that I see the children.

Andy's hand strokes up and down my thigh, lightly, slowly. He wants children. He's told me that, under the influence of a few beers. But even if there's a chance to have my own children I can't forget Louise's. I love them as if they're my own flesh and blood.

'Good evening. Welcome.' The sound system breaks into life. 'Thank you for joining us tonight. The display will start in fifteen minutes so please purchase your drinks and snacks and find your seats.'

The boy looks at his grandfather, who leans down to listen to the boy speak.

When the man straightens, he looks across Rosie's head and says something to the grandmother, who speaks to Alex.

Andy laughs at something in his friends' conversation.

There's a boisterous atmosphere all over the stand, with groups of students from the university as well as gatherings of families and friends.

Alex hands a limp, heavy-looking Hope to his mother. A fist of emotions, love, longing, clasps around my throat and my heart – my own emotions urging me to go to her. To be the one that holds her.

Alex stands as the boy does, turning side-on. The boy squeezes past his grandfather, navigating his way back along the row of seats.

When the boy reaches Alex, he lays a hand on his son's shoulder. Alex's lips are set in the firm unsmiling expression I have often seen in the weeks I've watched him in the morning.

That expression implies he never has an urge to smile.

The blond stubble on his jaw glistens in the floodlights as he turns to the steps. He's not shaved for days, again.

'Excuse us,' I hear Alex say to a couple who are coming up the steps as he and the boy descend.

I put the plastic pint cup on the floor under my seat and lean to speak to Andy. 'I'm popping to the toilet.' I don't wait for his acknowledgement. This is the chance I've been waiting on for weeks.

Alex and his son disappear down the exit steps.

I squeeze past half a dozen people to get out of the row, trying not to stand on the women's handbags, or anyone's feet, and hurry down the steps.

The space under the stand is crowded with people still.

Alex and his son are on the other side of the melee, walking along the far wall towards the toilets.

'Excuse me.' To get through the river of people walking the opposite way I push and shove, using elbows and hands. 'Excuse me. Excuse me.'

I can't follow Alex and the boy into the men's toilets, though, and if I go to the loo, I might lose them. I need another reason to be down here.

The queue at the bar beside the steps is only two people long. I join that, and wait, looking over my shoulder at the people walking towards the stairs, searching for Alex's blond head. Or a glimpse of the boy with a black and white scarf.

'What can I get you?'

'Oh.' I look at the server, then at the board of items and prices behind him. I can't buy another drink; I left mine with Andy. 'Salt and vinegar crisps, please.'

'Is that all?'

'Yes.'

He turns to pick them up from a basket beside him as I pull out the change from my back pocket to pay.

The till rings and springs open. I give him the cash and pick up the crisps.

The corridor has gone from being virtually full to nearly empty; everyone is queuing to get up the steps into the stand. Alex and his son are at the back of the queue, waiting patiently for the bottleneck to clear.

My throat dries, draining all the words of greeting I was considering in my rush down here, like water soaking quickly into dry, thirsty ground.

I swallow as I walk in their direction, trying to lubricate my mouth and throat. The cover-up bag of crisps hangs from my fingers at my side.

The boy's standing in front of his father. Alex's hands are on his shoulders.

The pace of my heartbeat persistently throbs in my ears. Louise is fighting to win my attention.

My child. Louise's words scream through my head. *My son.* Speak. 'Hello.'

Chapter 24

19.26.

A lex's head turns.

I'm standing less than a metre away.

The boy looks up.

I look down at him and smile.

He doesn't smile back.

I look at Alex and wait for what feels like minutes but is probably scarcely a second.

There's no recognition in Alex's expression.

'Helen Matthews,' I remind him. 'I came for an interview.'

'Oh. Yes. Now I remember. I'm sorry. A lot's happened since.'

The boy moves forward following the herd moving up into the stands. Alex takes a step forward.

I move too. 'Did you find a nanny?'

In a moment, the bottleneck will clear and they will be gone.

'No.' He's no longer looking at me, he's looking at the people in front of him. 'My parents look after the children.'

'Oh.' I try to sound interested. We shuffle a few more steps towards the stairs. 'I'm doing various temporary jobs, so if you need anyone for an odd day, or evening, you can give the agency a call. Or if you still have my CV, my mobile number is on that.'

A slight grunt of acknowledgement is my answer. I don't push any more. Pushing will push him away, not bring the children closer.

The bottleneck is clearing; people are climbing the steps quicker. 'It was nice to meet you again,' I say in the moment before he and his son move forward and begin climbing.

'Yes.' I can just about hear the reply that expresses no interest.

'Who was that, Dad?' The boy's question is clear as they reach the corner of the first set of steps and turn to begin climbing the steps for the seating.

Louise's spirit is rushing between us, urging me to move faster.

My heart wants me to be involved with these broken-hearted children. They need me.

She wants me to run up and push Alex down the stairs.

As I climb the steep steps for the seating, Alex steers his boy to their row.

The family have moved along so the two spare seats are at the end. The boy sits at the end and looks at me when I walk past.

I smile.

He looks at the pitch, his short legs swinging because his feet do not touch the floor.

Another slender hairline crack creeps through the middle of my heart.

'I bought some crisps to share,' I say to Andy as I reach my seat and hold out the bag.

'Cheers.' He takes the bag and pulls down the plastic seat for me.

'Thanks.' I sit and pick up my drink, my gaze reaching four rows forward.

Andy tears the crisps open as the floodlights go out.

'Are you ready for the best firework display in the south west?' a voice crackles through the sound system.

'Yes,' a cheer rises around the stands.

'Let's count down together,' the sound system voice encourages, then begins, 'Ten. Nine.'

The crowd in the stand participates in the countdown with an excited burst of energy.

On five, Andy leans to put his empty cup down, and on three he wraps an arm around my shoulders.

I lean into the embrace as the first huge boom goes off and a flash of light sparks through the dark sky.

Everyone looks up, following the light until it bangs again and bursts into a pattern of green and pink.

'Ah.' The expression of awe rises as I hear a child's cry, and look down.

Hope has woken.

Alex takes her and presses her head against his shoulder, covering her ear. She continues making grizzly child sounds as the fireworks bang and boom, flashing bright colours across the sky.

Alex presses a dummy into her mouth, then covers her ear again, to muffle the loud sounds.

A string in my heart pulls, but the fireworks drown out the calls from Louise for me to pull the child from him.

I watch the children in the coloured lights that are sprinkled across the sky.

I love their reactions.

Rosie and the boy end up on their feet, staring at the sky.

As soon as the display ends, Alex and his family get up and move out of the seats, among the first to leave.

We hang around, letting the rush of people go ahead.

Afterwards, Andy and I walk to the pub with hands clasped and fingers threaded. We are close. I have let myself become close to him because I was lonely, and he's done nothing to make me distrust him yet.

When I'm sitting in the pub with Andy and his friends my phone vibrates and chimes. I unzip my pocket and pull out my phone. Simon, the screen tells me. Andy glances at me. I signal with a pointing finger that I'll take the call outside and get up.

'Hello,' I answer as I walk across the busy pub.

'Hello. Did you and Andy have a good evening?'

Andy and Simon had hit it off when they had met last weekend.

'Yes, thanks. The fireworks were good. But watching them from a stadium is strange. What about you? Did the twins love it?'

'They did. I think this is the first year they'll really remember. They're already asleep, they were so excited.'

'I'm glad.'

'I'm glad you had a good night with Andy too.' He wants Andy and me to become something serious, because that'll ease his guilt over his cheating friend. I teased him about that in a private conversation in the kitchen at the weekend. 'And not because I feel guilty about Dan, because I want you to be happy.'

I laugh as I pull on the brass handle of the heavy pub door to get outside.

'Andy's nice. He's a good bloke.'

The night was chilly earlier but now it's really cold. 'I know,' I answer, my breath turning to mist in the air as my free arm folds over my chest and my fingers tuck under my arm to keep warm.

'Okay, I get the message, don't push you.'

A shiver runs through me. I want to tell him that I saw the children. I want to tell him everything. But I can't. He'll think it's strange. 'It's cold tonight. My teeth are going to start chattering in a minute.'

'Where are you?'

'Outside the pub, we're still out.'

'Sorry, then, I didn't mean to drag you out. I'll let you go.'

'Simon,' Mim shouts in the background.

'That's okay,' I answer before he can close the call and respond to Mim. 'I like to hear your voice. I miss you being close.'

'I miss you too. Even if you are hard work and crazy.'

That makes me smile. Calling me crazy is only half a joke, but it breaks the ice and frees tension in me every time he says it. I am crazy sometimes, and when he says that, it makes it all right to be crazy sometimes. But even so, I do not tell him about the children.

'I'm going back inside,' I say. 'I love you.'

'I love you too.'

'Simon!'

Mim needn't have chased. He wasn't on the phone long. I push the pub door open and the heat from the bar rushes out.

'Hey. Do you want another drink?' Andy's at the bar, buying a round. I walk over and slide my cold hand into the back pocket of his jeans.

I, me, Helen, I'm happy. I am. I've found this nice man, and I like him. A lot.

My children. My children.

But I can't forget them.

Chapter 25

18 weeks and 4 days after the fall.

I slide one foot, then the other, onto the edge of the metal park bench. My hands hold my calves, wrapping myself up in a self-comforting huddle. It is so cold, but it feels cleansing.

My breath floats away in a mist.

Alex is a framed picture in the window of the first-floor living room.

There's a low-level-light behind him, a table lamp perhaps, defining his silhouette as he holds Hope's head against his shoulder and walks around.

I couldn't sleep. Louise is in my head. The children are in my head. I had to come here. To be close to the children while they sleep.

Almost as soon as I arrived a light turned on, illuminating the window of an attic room on the third floor. Then that light went out and other lights switched on and off, travelling about the house, down to the ground and then up to the second floor.

Hope had woken Alex.

The timing was so precise to the moment that I sat down here, that I feel as if she woke because she knows I'm close. I think she sensed her mother.

I haven't moved from the park bench to walk and warm up, afraid that if I move they will move from the window.

Hope looks as if she's asleep now; limp in Alex's arms as she was in the stadium when they arrived last night.

Louise's spirit has taken me up to that room. I can feel Hope against my chest, held in my arms, warm and heavy as I walk back and forth, and her sweet childhood smell fills my nostrils.

Louise is getting to know me better. She's learning how to manipulate my thoughts and energy in a different way.

I love the children, and she knows that.

They feel like mine, and Louise is telling me that she wants them to be with me. I think because, then, she will have what she wants too – revenge on Alex.

'But how do I get through the door now?' The words hover in a mist in front of me.

A tepid tear rolls from the lower eyelashes of my right eye, cooling as it runs down my cheek. Another hairline fracture in my heart bursts open. 'How can I reach you?' The words reform the mist. 'What do I do?'

My hands slide from my calves to my ankles, holding on as I watch Alex move away from the window.

The light goes out.

He must be climbing the stairs in the dark so as not to wake Hope now she's settled.

My children. Louise's words form a mist in my thoughts.

I stay on the bench as Louise's heart beats a slow pained rhythm of loss in my chest; the rhythm of a break-up-film theme song with a melody that continues to move me to tears.

I am a child. Sitting in the darkness. In the corner of a room. Hiding. While someone shouts in the distance. It is a memory. My memory. From a foster home long ago.

A police siren reaches across the city, through streets, over and around the houses. The sound moving towards me.

The siren merges with my memory. Spinning blue lights flash through the thin curtains of my bedroom.

Loneliness is a swamp. Quicksand.

This evening wants to suck me into my black hole.

I stare at the second-floor windows of the house, where I think the children sleep.

My children. Mine.

Chapter 26

21 weeks and 4 days after the fall.

Kevin's small hand pulls heavily on mine as he lifts his feet up to make Andy and I swing him again, over the top of a pile of crisp leaves, as our boots rustle through them.

'That's enough, Kevin. You need to be gentle with Auntie Helen,' Simon shouts behind us.

'It's okay,' I call back over my shoulder. Liam swings forward with his feet tucked up, in the grip of his mother's and father's hands.

I look at Kevin. 'It's okay, you can swing.'

Kevin's legs lift immediately.

Andy smiles at me as we take Kevin's weight and swing him forward, to land a little in front of us. A sharp breeze carries freshly falling golden leaves from the branches of the plane trees that reach over our heads.

'I could get used to spending Sunday afternoons like this.' Andy's lips slide into a smile, implying he's thinking of the potential outcome of a bit of afternoon delight.

The quietly spoken comment pulses a dart of longing out from my brooding womb. I love that he often speaks about having children even though our relationship is young.

But growing fast.

I send him an answering smile. I'm falling hard for Andy. Trust is burrowing its way into my heart like a caterpillar eating its way into a soft, ripe apple. I don't mind that things are moving quickly between us. I think I've been lying to myself about how hard I'll find it to trust again. I trusted Dan quickly too. I think in reality I just desperately want to be loved by someone.

There's a stutter in the rhythm of my heart. It protests whenever I think about settling down with Andy.

But this is my life, and my chance to do whatever I want to.

I hear Louise all the time, but I screen the noise out as much as I can. Thinking about other things. Listening to other things. She may understand me better, but I am also getting better at understanding her.

Kevin lifts his feet, hanging by his hold on our hands so we'll swing him forward again.

I glance up at the house on the outer boundary of the path. The path runs along the edge of the Avon. The river is far below us on the left and the roof of the Georgian end-terrace house is high above us on the right.

The river path has brought us to the end of the row of terrace houses where Alex and the children live.

Kevin hangs his weight from our hands again. We swing him forward. His boyish shout of pleasure rings back from the side of the end-terrace.

'Don't make yourself sick,' Simon calls.

The boys' stomachs are full, from a small plate from the carvery in the pub and a large three-scoop bowl of chocolate ice cream with chocolate sauce, chopped nuts and marshmallows.

In a house only a stone's-throw distance from where we are

walking, there are three children who must feel empty no matter how much they eat. The hunger inside them is mother-shaped.

Images and feelings tumble me back through time until I'm a small girl, desperately longing for a mother.

When I was a child, sometimes I dreamed about drifting on a piece of wood in dark, deep, swaying water. Like Rose at the end of the film *Titanic*, in the middle of a vast, cold ocean, and on the horizon was one small light. The dream always ended with the light becoming Simon's hand reaching for me from a rowing boat.

I glance back at Simon, letting go of Kevin's hand. 'Simon.'

Simon's hand releases Liam's, and he comes, jogging forward the few paces to join me.

'Are you okay?'

'Yes.'

I turn to Kevin and say, 'Daddy and Andy will swing you for a little while, and you can take turns with Liam.'

Simon takes Kevin's hand in my place as Andy's eyes look at me with concern.

I slot a hand into Simon's free hand that's hanging loose on the other side.

Simon glances over at me as he swings Kevin forward, and squeezes my fingers gently in the ageless way he has of telling me that he will keep me safe.

'Liam. Your turn.'

As I call Liam forward, I catch sight of Mim's expression. Her eyebrows have lifted and her lips have pursed. She's annoyed with me.

Chapter 27

22 weeks and 1 day after the fall.

Chloe and I are laughing over funny stories from her failed attempts at meeting a man through online dating sites. She put Ben with the mole aside for a better option only for that man to be a player. She's been on about seven dates since then and had no luck.

A vibration rumbles in my handbag that's hanging from the arm of the café chair, accompanied by the chime of my phone's ringtone.

I pull the handbag onto my lap, unzip it and dig my phone out from the bottom. The screen displays a mobile number I don't recognise. 'Hello ...' My pitch is tentative as I encourage the caller to declare themselves.

'Hi. This is Alex, Alex Lovett.'

My heart skips, star-jumping on a trampoline. With my emotions, not Louise's. 'Oh. Hello. How can I help?' I press the phone hard to my ear so Chloe will not hear the conversation.

'I know this is out of the blue, but I'm ringing because you offered to do some child-minding, and I really need to take you up on the offer, if you're available?'

'Sure. I'm happy to help. When?'

'Now. Are you free?' The urgency in his voice sends up a bright orange flare of panic.

I look at Chloe, but I can't let her prevent me from taking this opportunity. 'Yes.'

'I have to go to the school to fetch Josh, my son. My parents are away on holiday, Hope's sick and Josh had a meltdown today. I probably only need you for an hour. How quickly can you get here?'

He's desperate, otherwise he wouldn't have called me. 'It'll take me half an hour to get there.' I stand, turning to pick up my bag, coat and scarf from the back of the chair.

'Thank you. I'll see you soon?'

'Yes. Goodbye.' My thumb moves to end the call as I take the phone away from my ear.

I meet Chloe's gaze as I drop my phone into the open handbag. 'I'm really sorry. My boss needs me.'

'But it's your day off.'

'I know, but one of the children is ill and he has to go to the school.' I'm juggling my bag between my arms and pulling on my coat as we talk.

'So, you're leaving me in this café.'

'Sorry, but I have to rush. I'll call you later.'

'Am I meant to go back to London, then?'

'It's up to you. He said he only needs me for an hour or so.' I throw the straps of my handbag onto my shoulder and pin them there with a thumb tucked under the straps. 'Message me if you hang-around and I'll let you know when I'm free. Sorry.'

I'm not sorry. Inside I am happy-dancing with excitement. My feelings overwhelming any opinions Louise might be trying to thrust on me. I'm not going there to steal the children. I'm going to see them.

Chloe stands, we hug and kiss each other's cheeks and then I'm walking away, going to the children.

When I cross the road to reach their street, I don't use the crossing but dodge through the cars. Then I run along the pavement to the front door, my handbag bouncing against my side as my thumb keeps the straps firmly pinned on my shoulder.

I press a fingertip on the electronic doorbell as I try to slow my heavy breaths so that it won't sound as if I've been running.

The door opens almost immediately. Alex must have been downstairs, in the kitchen.

He pulls the door wide to let me through.

He's balancing Hope on his hip again, only today she's wearing a cotton Babygro with little teddy bears printed on the material.

Louise's keening cry pushes through my thoughts, refusing to be silenced as she sees Hope and tries to make me reach out, surging her desperate energy through my arms and into my hands.

'Thank you for coming. Sorry I need to go right away. Rosie is primed. Hope hasn't been sick for about four hours and her temperature is down. I gave her Calpol an hour ago.' He shuts the door behind me and lifts Hope off his hip to hand her over.

She looks at her dad and her face screws up as if there is going to be a scream but it becomes a hard suck on the dummy in her mouth. I wrap an arm around her and hold her leg, bringing her to my side.

She reaches back for Alex. 'N. N. N. D. D.' The demanding sounds come from around her dummy as her hands stretch out. Straining for him.

'Daddy has to go, sweetheart. Come on, we'll find plenty to

do.' I turn her away from him. But glance back over my shoulder. 'It's okay. Don't worry. We'll be all right. Just go. The quicker you go, the quicker she'll settle and the quicker you'll be back.'

A look of uncertainty passes over his expression – he needs to go but he wants to stay.

'Go,' I repeat.

'The nappies are in their bedroom on the second floor, and there are snacks in the fridge.' He pauses as if he's trying to remember something he's forgotten.

'Rosie will help me if there is anything I can't find.'

He looks at me again, and for the first time I think he properly looks at me – notices me. 'Thank you, and whatever Rosie wants, let her have it. It won't harm this once.'

I nod. 'Go. We'll manage.'

His lips lift ever so slightly at the edges. 'Thank you.' His gaze reaches past me, into the kitchen. 'I'll be back soon, Rosie.' He doesn't have a choice, but even so I see the moment of decision to trust me in his eyes in the instant before he turns to take his coat off a hook that's on the wall behind him. 'Thank you,' he says again as his fingers curl around the door handle. 'I'll be back soon.'

When the door bangs shut behind him, and the brass doorknocker rattles on the outside, I walk into the kitchen.

Hope stretches her legs and fidgets constantly to communicate her desire to escape me.

Rosie is kneeling on the floor, leaning over the low coffee table, colouring. 'Hello, Rosie. It's nice to meet you again.'

Rosie looks up with eyes that express acceptance and nothing else. 'Hello.'

I give Hope her wish and put her down on the L-shaped sofa, on the end that is farthest away from Rosie and her colouring.

I put my handbag down too. Then return to the hall to take off
my scarf and coat and hang them up.

When I come back Hope has unzipped my handbag and is
sitting beside it with my keys and lipstick in her lap and my
phone in her hand.

'Sweetheart.' I reclaim my keys and lipstick, put them back
in the bag, zip it up and hang it up. 'You can keep my phone
for now,' I say when I come back.

'She'll drop it,' Rosie warns without looking over. 'If she wants
toys, they're in our bedroom.'

'What's your favourite game?' I ask Rosie. 'Shall we play
together?' An atmosphere has been left in the room, a sense of
something missing. Or is it Louise trying to tell me that she's
missing from this house.

'What do you like doing, Rosie?' Tears are gathering in my
eyes, which is silly. But if I've had hairline fractures through my
heart, like those in the glaze of an old china vase, for weeks, the
hearts of these children must be shattered into a million tiny
pieces. The cracks might be glued but they will always show.

Rosie doesn't answer and I don't push her. She can make
friends with me when she wants to. There will be plenty of
chances. I'll make sure there are. I am inside now, and I have
the children. I will not let them go again.

My children.

'What are we going to do, Hope? If Rosie is colouring.' Hope
sucks on her dummy staring at the things she's moving on my
phone. 'Do you want to go down on the floor?'

'She likes to be held,' Rosie answers, without taking her attention away from her colouring.

'Then I'll hold you, Hope. Do you want anything, Rosie?' I
pick Hope up and sit her on my hip.

Rosie shakes her head, still focusing on her drawing. But I know her answer, she wants her daddy – or her grandparents – or her mummy.

My children.

'Well, if you change your mind, tell me.'

She doesn't answer.

'So, Hope, how are we going to fill our time?' I want to turn the TV on. The sound would make the silence in the room stop screaming at me. Louise is everywhere, yelling at me to take the children. 'Shall I see if I can find a game on my phone?'

'She's not old enough to play games,' Rosie answers. A three-year-old calling me a fool with her tone of voice.

'What about music – does she like music?'

'Some.'

'Nursery rhymes?'

Rosie looks up. 'Mummy used to sing nursery rhymes.' Her child's voice, which would normally be full of the lifting and lowering cadence of excitable emotions, like Liam's and Kevin's, is flat. The pitch says, bluntly, that her mummy has gone, and she took the singing with her.

I expect to hear Louise crying, but, no, she's still screaming.

'Shall I see if I can find some on my phone to keep Hope happy until Daddy comes back?'

Rosie nods then looks down at her drawing.

At the age of three she's speaking for her sister's happiness when she's not happy. I remember how hard Simon fought for me when we were younger, to stay together, in homes and hospitals.

I sit down beside Rosie and move Hope over to sit between us.

'Hope, look.' I hold the top of the phone as she holds the bottom. She stares, sucking hard on her dummy while I open the music app and look up nursery rhymes. I find some rhymes to stream and smile, laughing internally, as I fight her thumb away to touch play.

'M. M,' Hope complains through the dummy she is sucking because I continue not letting her touch the screen so I can bring my photographs up. At least if she is flicking through photographs it will not harm anything, and the music will play at the same time.

'She's saying me,' Rosie explains.

'Old MacDonald ...' sings into the room as Hope's little fingers flick through my photographs quickly as if she thinks the music is coming from them.

'She can walk now,' Rosie tells me without looking up from her drawing. There's a box drawn in grey in her picture, with a car on top of it, that she's coloured in red.

'You are so clever, Hope.' A sharp pain pulls like a needle and thread through my heart. Louise would have liked to see Hope walking.

Rosie looks at me. 'Josh was naughty.'

'What did he do?'

'He bit someone.'

Wow. I did not expect that.

'Daddy said Josh is in trouble.'

'I am sure it will be okay when he says sorry. He probably did not mean to do it.'

Rosie nods. She's worried about her brother.

Simon slips into my head again. 'Is that Daddy?' I point at the stick man she's drawn.

She nods.

Nothing feels right in this room. I constantly hear Louise wailing with pain and loss.

I lean closer to Hope, to lean closer to Rosie, implying I am sharing a secret, to make Rosie feel confided in. 'Do you want to put a film on and eat snacks? What film do you like most? My favourite is *Beauty and the Beast*.'

'I like that too.'

'Have you got it?'

She nods, then stands and walks over to a cupboard underneath the breakfast bar.

The house is meticulously tidy; there's no clutter or dust anywhere in the room.

Someone else must be involved in cleaning this house, because Alex doesn't even look after himself. As usual, today, his hair was untidy, he may have shaved recently but not today, and the jumper he was wearing had not been near an iron.

Rosie pulls out a DVD case, opens it and presses the button to open the DVD player then puts the disc in. She takes the TV controls out of the cupboard, and looks up at the TV on the wall as she turns it on and fast-forwards the film to the start. She puts everything away as the introduction music plays, shuts the cupboard and comes back to the sofa.

She sits beside me, on the opposite side of me from Hope, who's still flicking through pictures. 'The wheels on the bus go ...'

'I don't like the bit with the wolves,' Rosie says.

'Shall I put my hand over your eyes when the wolves come on? Or shall I cover your ears?'

She looks at me. 'Cover my ears.'

'Does Daddy have any microwave popcorn in the cupboard?'

She shakes her head. 'We have a bag of Wotsits.'

'Shall we have some, then?'

She nods.

I stand, walk over to the kitchen and open cupboard after cupboard.

The sound of a giggle makes me look back. Rosie is laughing. 'They're in that one.' She points at a top cupboard.

I smile, in a conspiratorial way. 'Thank you.'

There's plenty of food in the cupboards. Alex may not be looking after himself, but he is looking after the children.

With a large packet of Wotsits tucked under one arm, I open the fridge, looking for drinks. There are some small cartons of apple juice with straws. I pick up two and head back to the sofa.

'Girls' time,' I say to Rosie and hand her a carton of apple juice.

'Thank you.'

I put the Wotsits on the table then pierce the other carton with the straw, for Hope, and sit down.

Rosie leans forward, picks up the Wotsits bag, pulls it open and balances the open packet on her lap.

I take the dummy out of Hope's mouth. Her eyes look from the phone to me. I hold the straw of the apple juice out for her. She takes a long drink. 'Is that nice? You must have been thirsty.'

Rosie's fingers rustle in the Wotsits packet.

Alex may not thank me if her fingers leave orange stains all over the white sofa cushions, but I want the girls to be happy while I'm here, and leather can be wiped clean.

Louise breathes through me, as though she's longing to speak. My body is full of her thoughts and emotions.

I want to hug the girls. But physically I am someone they barely know.

No matter what Louise is urging me to do, for today, I'll take pleasure in every minute I spend here, and not risk making them unhappy in my company.

At the sound of a key in the lock, I rest my bottom on my heels in my kneeling position, slip the brush of the pale pink nail varnish back into the bottle and look over my shoulder.

Alex walks in, bringing in the cold air and his son. 'Hello,' I say brightly.

I'm in the middle of painting Rosie's fingernails – with Louise breathing impatiently down the back of my neck, creating a tickling, heckle-rising sensation along my backbone. There are two unpainted fingernails on Rosie's left hand.

When I took a Wotsit from the packet, Rosie told me she liked the colour of my nails. I told her that I had the nail varnish in my handbag, and it became something to do.

'Daddy.' Rosie rushes to slide off the sofa, her hands pressing down on the white cushions – hands that are covered in orange Wotsits flavouring and nails that shine with wet pale pink varnish.

Hope takes the dummy out of her mouth, leaves it on the sofa and pushes herself to the edge, rolling to her side and sliding down until her toes touch the floor. Then she proves she can walk, and not only walk, because she runs across the room to welcome Alex and her brother.

A lump fills my throat. A lump of tears that want to break free. They're my tears.

Louise's anger has increased with a continual momentum in the hour I've been here – a snowball of anger rolling downhill, turning faster and faster and getting bigger and bigger.

I'm a spirit barometer. The pressure in the air changes when they're near. I feel them like gravity, like the heavy humid air of a summer storm.

The atmosphere has become heavier. Louise's spirit is frustrated.

I think she's frustrated with herself as well as me because she wants to speak and do, and she can't, and she wants me to take the children, and I can't.

What I do know now, though, is that as much as Alex can't hear Louise, nor can the girls. They've shown no sign of feeling the tension circulating around them and there's been no changes in their auras.

I get up from the floor.

'Okay?' Alex asks his son, raising his eyebrows. The question, and the expression, punctuate a conversation that they must have shared on the walk home.

Josh breathes in deeply. It is a grown-up expression of controlling emotion. But he's a child and Rosie said he bit another boy. Maybe Alex has been trying to teach Josh to control his emotions. Temper, yes. But distress – they should let it out in tears, or shouts, or smash things in a controlled environment. That's my view. Do not shut pain away and trap how you feel.

My hands slide into the back pockets of my jeans.

Josh's aura is reds and greys, dark reds, and greys like his father's.

'Daddy.' Rosie's arms wrap around one of Alex's legs.

'Hello, darling. Oh, your nails look pretty.'

'D-de.' Hope runs up for her cuddle and claims his other leg, with my phone still firmly gripped in her right hand.

Alex bends and picks them both up, so he has a girl on either hip.

The empty look on Josh's face, as he stands a little behind his father, yells – what about me?

Louise's spirit is close to Josh. She can see his locked-up anger too. I sense her trying to manipulate that. But Josh has no natural spirit barometer either. Nothing in his expression says that he has any awareness of her, or the emotions she is trying to transfer onto him.

I want to move forward and hold Josh, but I can't. Josh would not welcome it. But Alex can't hold three children at once and they're all desperate for his attention.

'What have you girls been doing?' Alex looks at me for the answer.

'Watching a film. I'll get out of your way now,' I say.

I want to rush out of the house, to escape suddenly, because Louise's behaviour here and the whirlpool of dark, consuming pain that hovers around Alex is disturbing.

I thought Louise brought me here to fulfil a mother's role, but every time she gets close to the children, she expresses anger or rage, not love. I want to take Louise out of the house, away from the children. It is not right for her to try to upset Josh even more.

'Have the girls been okay?' Alex asks.

'Yes. But I might need to wrestle Hope to get my phone back.' A smile that is more of a nervous expression moves my lips.

He glances at Hope's hand. The phone is still playing nursery rhymes.

'Hope, sweetheart, you have to give that back.'

She frowns and holds it to her chest.

I bend down and pull a cheesy Wotsit out from the half-empty packet on the coffee table, then walk over to Alex, holding the tempting Wotsit out. 'I'll trade, Hope.'

She reaches out, leaning away from Alex and making him balance her more carefully, but I pull the treat away and shake my head. 'No. You give me the phone, you get the Wotsit.' I hold out my free hand, palm up, to receive the phone. 'Phone. Please.'

A sound of amusement escapes Alex's throat and his gaze

catches on my mine, in a way that says I have won his confidence. 'She doesn't eat those; she's never been given one.'

I smile. 'Sorry. She's going to get one now if she gives me the phone.' The phone lands on my palm, with a light slap. I offer the Wotsit.

Hope sucks on the Wotsit as I walk past them to fetch my bag and coat.

I put my phone in my handbag, then take that and all my outdoor things off the peg.

Alex squats to put the girls down.

As I put my scarf and coat on, I turn around and watch Alex put the girls down. They return to the sofa and Alex walks over to fill the kettle.

Josh looks for something in the fridge.

'Thanks for the girl time,' I say, looking at Rosie and Hope as I hang my bag on my shoulder.

The fridge door shuts. I look at Josh. He has a carton of apple juice in his hand.

I want to walk over, run a hand over Josh's hair and kiss the crown of his head, as I might with Liam and Kevin. He looks so lost and desolate. 'Nice to meet you again, Josh.'

I lift a hand, waving at him.

'I hope that Hope feels better soon. She's had some apple juice and she's been fine.'

He nods, resting a hip against the work surface. 'And a Wotsit. Thank you again. I mean it. I had no one else to call. How much do I owe you?' He moves suddenly, as if he's only just thought about payment.

I don't want money. 'You can pay me in kind if you like. I wouldn't mind some tasteful photographs to give to my boyfriend as a Christmas present.'

His mouth opens. He doesn't know what to say.

A surge of emotions sweeps through me, as Louise expresses her temper, as if she has thrust her energy through my body, in the way that I imagine it would feel if a ghost ran through me. My stomach twists over. Nausea stirring. An echo, as the cells in my body realign.

'I ... I'm busy at work.' His arms fold over his chest.

'Sorry. That was forward of me.' I turn to open the door.

'No.'

I look back.

He smiles. 'I mean, no, it's all right. I'll let you know when. It won't take long to do a couple of nice shots.'

'Thanks.'

'No. Thank you.'

'You're welcome. Whenever I can help feel free to call me. I'm only working temporary jobs, no fixed hours. I'll wait to hear from you?'

'Yes.' The kettle boils beside him, steam spewing out of the spout.

He turns away and so do I, with no further goodbye.

The metal door handle is cold, and the heavy front door swings wide. I hurry out and try to close the door gently so the doorknocker doesn't rattle.

As soon as I start walking along the pavement, I take my phone out from my bag and ring Chloe. 'Are you still in Bath?'

'No. I got on a train home.'

Chapter 28

20.45.

My phone vibrates and chimes in my clutch bag just as I lift my hand to open the door to go out and meet Andy.

I stop still and fumble with the buckle as my heart stutters as though someone has jumped out at me. My heart has been jumping over everything and anything since I saw the children. The rhythm of its beat races against the number of rings on my phone.

The screen says 'Alex'. 'Hello, Mr Lovett ...' I answer in an uncertain voice, caught out by Louise's life colliding with mine when I'd not expected it to – for the second time in a day.

My heartbeat becomes an anxious rhythm pulsing in the back of my throat.

Louise is hovering at my shoulder, trying to prevent me from speaking.

'Hi. Call me Alex, please. Sorry if you're busy. I just thought I'd clear my debt now the children are in bed and arrange your sitting for those pictures.'

I lean back against the double-glazed front door, my heart smashing against my ribs.

'My parents are back on Saturday. They have the children in

the day when I'm working. They can have them for an extra hour. So, I can do early or late.'

'What's late?'

'As late as a job runs. I can't give you a time until the day.'

'All right, early, then. What time is that?'

'Seven-thirty.'

'Will the children even be up?'

'Believe me, they will be up. I don't get much sleep.'

This is a bad idea. I see that woman at his front door. I have to spend time alone with a womaniser. A bitter taste swells my tongue up against my tonsils.

I see Dan. I see him and the woman he's with in the pictures on his Instagram Stories.

I watched his stories when we first split, fixated on scratching the itch of jealousy, but then I realised that he could see who'd watched them and I stopped. I didn't want to give him the satisfaction of knowing that I still cared. It's hard to turn love entirely into hate, a bit like the alchemy needed to create gold from base metals – although it felt as if Dan had been very good at turning what was gold into something as valueless as tin.

'Shall we say Monday, if that's all right with you? At my studio. I have your email – I can send you the address and details.'

'Okay. Monday. Thanks.'

'No. Thank you for today.' A second of silence follows, which implies he's moving the phone away from his ear and is about to touch the screen to end the call.

'How's Hope?' I say it loudly, hoping I'll bring the phone back to his ear. That's why I want to spend time with a womaniser. That's the only reason. An important reason. Because I want to be with his children.

My children.

'A lot better, thank you,' he answers.

'And Josh? Rosie said he bit someone.'

'He's not a bad child.' A defensive response to protect his son surges into his voice. A response that makes me forget about his disloyalty to Louise, and nudges an element of respect and trust into my mind.

'Another boy was taunting him about his mum and Josh became angry. I've told him he has to hold himself together.'

But maybe you should give him the permission to fall apart, then after that he might be able to put himself back together better.

'He's been excluded from school for a week.'

'But if he was being taunted—'

'There's no excuse for hurting someone.'

Yes. Alex. Physically and emotionally. There's no excuse. You are right. There's so much I want to say, and Louise wants me to say things too, but I can't speak without giving myself away. He would know that I know more about his family than he thinks I do.

'So,' he says, to end the conversation. 'I'll see you on Monday. But I'll have limited time. I have a big contract afterwards.'

'I shan't be late.'

'Good. Goodbye.'

'Goodbye.'

A deep breath pulls into my lungs. I am no longer watching Louise's life; instead I have stepped into it. Into that vacancy. But not far enough.

'Are you okay?' Pippa, my landlady, calls into the hall from the kitchen.

'Yes,' I shout back.

Another breath pulls to the bottom of my lungs and I breathe it out slowly, trying to slow the pace of my heart.

'I thought you were going out?' Pippa pushes the kitchen door open wider and walks into the hall, wiping her hands on a tea towel and bringing the smell of frying onions with her.

'I am.' I move away from the door. 'Just having a moment.'

'A problem?'

'No. Something good. Just a surprise.'

She nods, then turns away.

I turn and open the door. If my heart had only ever been my heart perhaps it would be happy to go to Andy and want nothing else, because there is the chance of a family with him. But this heart had already fallen in love with three children and it wants them back.

Chapter 29

22 weeks and 3 days after the fall.

The woollen beanie hat that I bought on the way here makes my forehead itch. I throw my blue scarf around my neck for a second time and pull the front of it up over my chin to the tip of my nose as I enter the park.

My hands slide into the long pockets of Andy's best winter work coat that falls to my shins, hanging loosely on my smaller figure, and making my body shape indeterminable.

My purse is in the pocket. I haven't even brought my handbag in case that identifies me.

But I couldn't resist the desire to come back.

I want to see the children.

I was tossing and turning in Andy's bed for most of the night because my heart has been aching for them. It's a physical pain to be apart from them now I've been in the house, talked and played with them.

I would say that I can imagine Louise's pain, but I can't. Because her pain doesn't seem to be coming from love. I have realised that now. I think it is coming from her need for revenge.

She and I have fallen out.

Like friends who've argued over a major difference of opinion.

I will not do what she wants me to, which is impossible anyway, because I can't kidnap the children. I wouldn't even want to. They obviously love Alex and it would hurt them to take them away from him and I don't want to hurt the children. I want to make them happier.

But she seems to be in a sulk now. Her emotions are still within me and in the air around me, making me and the air heavier. But she's silent.

Her silence is ominous.

My hand holds the phone in one deep coat pocket.

It is freezing today. A hoar frost glistens in the naked branches of the plane trees and dusts the grass with white icing.

If the iron bench was cold in the autumn, today it is like sitting on a freezer shelf. The icy bars of iron radiate cold even through the thick material of Andy's coat. The heels of my boots tap on the floor and my hands press deeper into the pockets as my breath dampens the scarf covering my mouth.

The children might have already gone out for the day. They might be Christmas shopping somewhere. But whether they are in the house or not, I know I need to be here.

I wanted to come earlier but Andy would have thought it strange if I left his house in a rush. He cooked breakfast, and it would have been rude to leave without eating it. In the end, we ate lunch together too.

I'm shivering within ten minutes, my chin burrowing into the scarf and the raised collar of Andy's coat.

I rub my hands together, the wool of one glove chafing on the other. Then I clap my hands. I'll need to buy a coffee soon. It's too cold to sit here without something to keep me warm.

I last another five minutes before the cold becomes too much and I stand up to move around.

The familiar sound of number twenty-two's doorknocker rattling draws my gaze across the street.

Josh steps out; Rosie's behind him. Then Hope, walking, an orange band around her wrist attached to a lead-rein. The other end of the lead-rein is around Alex's wrist.

Alex leaves the house, turns back and locks the door.

He must be on his own with the children still.

My hands slide into my pockets as I walk towards the park exit and they walk along the street.

Hope is slow. Her small mitten-covered hand runs along the railings that guard the basement level of the houses, bouncing from rail to rail as she trails, a couple of steps behind Alex.

'Come on, Hope,' Josh complains from about twenty of his steps ahead of the rest of his family.

Louise's spirit moves away from me – flying over the empty moat-like dip at the edge of the park. Moving over there, with them, where I want to be.

Alex says something to Hope that I can't hear. I hear her grizzling about it, though. Then he bends, picks her up and settles her on his hip.

'D-Dee,' Hope complains. Her voice runs another stitch through my heart, securing me to them. I feel every millimetre of the thread pulling through me, pulling me towards them.

They do not see me as they walk on; their eyes are focused on the end of the street. I slow down. Alex's car is left behind in the street.

They disappear around the corner. I follow and reach the park entrance as they walk across the pedestrian crossing over the first busy road, in the direction of the town centre.

I cross Alex's street, taking a long route around the merging streets to avoid getting too close to them.

Hope fidgets on Alex's hip while Rosie holds her brother's hand.

My heart pumps hard. It is a risk to follow them, but the chances of Alex thinking he's being followed and looking back are small.

They walk towards, and then past, the cinema, then across the pedestrian area that even in this cold is crowded with a high density of young people, probably university students, drinking and eating, talking and laughing.

The activity and excitable December atmosphere continues as I follow them around the corner onto Westgate Street and then along to Saw Close. There are lots of parents and children in the area in front of the Theatre Royal. Josh glances back at his father, looking for some confirmation, or just checking that Alex is there, and then he turns and walks into the open door of the theatre.

Josh, Rosie, Hope and Alex disappear inside.

To the left of the door is a poster display that promotes the pantomime they must be going to watch. Jack and the Beanstalk.

Tepid tears trickle onto my cheek. I wipe them off and turn away. Pantomime ... It is something I have always thought I will do with my children.

Once, when Simon and I were in a foster home, we went to a pantomime with the family. I stared at the families in the seats around us as much as the stage, watching them laugh, shout, sing and clap along to the music.

I should have suggested taking Liam and Kevin with Andy. I will.

I walk away, unsure where Louise is. I can't feel her. But she is still fed up with me, and I don't think she likes it that I've fallen in love with her children.

She wants our connection to be all about her.

I care less and less about her, and her screaming. I care about the children.

Chapter 30

22 weeks and 5 days after the fall.

The rhythm of my heart joins the pace of my feet as I hurry up the stairs to Alex's studio. A man who works in one of the other offices has let me in.

My thumb tucks under the shoulder straps of my bag as I reach the top of the stairs.

'Hello,' I call as I tap a knuckle on the glass door. The sound is muffled because I'm wearing my gloves.

'Come in,' the call comes back.

I pull my gloves off, then turn the cold, round, brass handle.

'Hello,' he says as I walk in. 'You're early.' He hasn't looked at me. He's on the other side of the large room, looking through a camera lens, at something on the far wall.

'I didn't want to be late.'

'There's nothing wrong with being punctual.' The camera lowers and he looks at me.

The dark, cloudy mist around him is just like a brewing storm. Storm Alex is drawing in. A severe cold front.

An inexplicable anger rises in me. Louise's anger. She's been shouting constantly since the morning after I saw them go to the pantomime.

Ever since I came through the door downstairs it's felt like having a wildcat inside me. Scratching, hissing and clawing.

My connections with spirits have never been this close before; I've never been hounded by them. I've never become tired of hearing them or angry with them. But her continual obsessive racket is hard to live with. Especially when I can't do the thing she wants me to, so I can't silence her.

An invisible rush of aggression thrusts out towards him – her spirit flying at him. But as a spirit, there's nothing she can do.

'How do you want to pose? Sitting? Standing?' The camera is balancing in his right hand and a strap dangles over his wrist. Our gazes catch and hold. Pale blue-grey eyes wait for my answer.

An image dives into my head, of that woman, in her night-before little black dress and heels, walking away from his front door.

Womaniser, womaniser, plays through my head, sung in the voice of Britney Spears.

His eyes are so dramatic, and his gaze is so rarely bestowed, that his eyes almost literally deliver the electrical shock of a stun gun when he does look. It is the warning his eyes hold too – back off.

But he is really looking at me – attention and interest in his expression.

I breathe in deeply, restoring my courage. 'What do you think? I want a few to choose from, but I just want one really nice picture to give him. A picture that will make him smile every time he looks at it.' I drop my coat on top of my bag and walk across the room.

What would he tell me about Louise if I asked? I do not ask. I will not ask. I don't want the gate to be slammed in my face.

'Let's take some standing shots first.' He hangs the camera's strap around his neck and points across at the white wall at the end of the long room. 'Stand there.' The room is a loft space, with a high ceiling and windows at two levels. Lighting equipment stands around the room, and there are curtains along the back wall. He must draw the curtains across to change backdrops.

The black high-heeled shoes I chose this morning clack on the wooden floor.

'If you look to your right we'll get the morning sun on one side of your face.' He looks through the camera. 'This will look good in black and white too.'

I am wearing a white blouse and have tucked it into a pair of fitted, calf-length black trousers, with a side zip on my hip so my stomach looks flatter.

'Turn your body to the right too.' He's clicking the shot button already. 'Don't move your feet. Turn back round slightly. Pose as though you've turned to look at your fella.'

He stops clicking and the camera lowers.

I turn to face him fully.

He breaks into motion, the storm sweeping a high wave in from the sea towards the beach. 'If I were you—' he lets the camera hang, heavily, on the strap and his hands lift as he nears me '—I would undo another button on your blouse.' He doesn't wait for me to agree; his fingers undo the button, his fingernails brushing the skin of my chest.

A cold shiver runs through my whole body. A feeling like goosebumps rising over my skin as he opens the collar wider so it frames my neck.

'Let me show you the shots – you'll see what I mean.' His voice is matter-of-fact. Making his touch a business thing. He felt my shiver.

The other woman is in my head. I think Louise is putting

the other woman in my mind. She's seeing me as the other woman now. I think she would rather get away from this, from me, but we have an inextricable link, our bodies are tangled together and somehow it's meant our spirits are too. I don't think it's her choice to be with me any more. She *has* to be with me.

'Look.' He holds the camera out, showing me a picture on the screen. 'What do you think?'

He's right. I look ... buttoned-up in the image.

As the camera lowers and he turns away I rearrange the open collar myself, trying to remove the feeling of his touch on my skin.

'I would turn the collar up at the back.' I didn't realise he was looking at me again.

The camera lifts and then it clicks repeatedly. 'Turn your head and shoulders towards this window. Lift your chin a little. Look into the lens. You're looking at him, not me, remember. Make your expression say what you want to say to him.'

He stops clicking after a few minutes and stares at the camera screen, glancing through the shots.

I've had professional photographs taken at school. That was very different from this. Alex's skill oozes from his confident stance.

'Are they awful?' I ask after seconds of silence.

'The shots are okay, but I think they could be better. You don't look relaxed.'

I am nervous. Of saying or doing the wrong things. Of Louise watching. Of him. I can't read Alex, his personality is so closed. I can't even say for certain whether he loved Louise. He looks after his children well. He's gentle with them, kind. But he also has one-night-stands with strangers.

Womaniser. Womaniser ...

'Why not wipe all your make-up off and let him have a picture of who you really are?'

Who I ... 'Pardon?'

'If I was your boyfriend, then the picture of you I would want in my wallet is the woman that just got out of my bed. Have you ever seen the portrait Queen Victoria gave Prince Albert of her face without any adornment? There's something very sensual and precious about the side of someone that no one else usually sees. If that blouse is long, you could take off your trousers and sit in the leather chair over there; I am sure he'd appreciate the image ...' His voice is deep; it resonates across the loft space.

My fingers stroke through my hair – in a self-comforting movement.

I also can't tell if he likes me. I was afraid of him coming on to me, and he's saying things and doing things that are turning my stomach over with nerves, but showing no sign that he's affected by the privacy in the room. There are no hints in his voice or body language that tell me if he's taken to me. I don't mean physically, I mean I want him to like me. To trust me. So that he'll choose me over anyone else to care for the children.

'My blouse is long.'

'I'll turn my back, while you take your trousers off and get into position. Sit sideways in the chair and hang your legs over one arm while you lean on the other.'

When he turns, I see a stain on the shoulder of his shirt. 'Did you say you have an important shoot after this?'

'Yes.'

'Well, you might want to change your shirt before that. I think Hope left some of her breakfast on your shoulder.'

His head turns as he tries to look, pulling at the shoulder of his shirt. He breathes out heavily, finally expressing some personal emotion. That sigh was an expression of tolerance, of having to endure. 'Excuse me,' he says as he puts the camera down on a table. 'I'll change my shirt. I keep spares in here in case I work late.'

When I walk over to the leather chair, barefoot, in just my underwear and a blouse, he's sliding his arms into a grey shirt.

His body's firmly crafted, muscular definitions under his skin with no insulating fat. He may not be shaving or ironing his clothes, but he's exercising a lot.

Louise breathes down my neck as I position myself in the leather chair, in that silent threat of hatred and jealousy.

But why would she be jealous of me, when she hates him?

'Ready,' I say when I have the blouse positioned at the top of my thighs.

He's tucking the grey shirt into his dark grey jeans as he walks back over to pick up the camera.

But I found it hard to turn love completely around to hate with Dan. Maybe she loves and hates him.

'Good,' he says as he walks towards me with the camera in one hand.

He leans down. My stomach turns over and the moisture in my throat evaporates as his free hand moves to my thigh. His nails brush the top of my thigh in the same way they brushed my chest as he straightens the hem of the blouse.

I feel as if I will throw up as the goosebumpy feeling races up between my legs.

I cross my legs as he walks away, changing my position and straightening the hem of the blouse myself.

When he looks back at me, he nods, and lifts the camera back to his eye.

I can't help feeling as if he deliberately tried to unsettle me. But why would he do that?

Because he was checking that a future nanny would not be someone who tried to come on to him?

'Relax your shoulders. Look into the camera. Remember you are looking at him, not me. I presume you're hoping he'll be returning that look for the rest of his life?'

He walks around the chair, taking shots from different angles. His storm and Louise's energy accompanying him.

When he stops clicking, the camera is held at waist height as he scans through the pictures. 'These are going to be good.' He looks at me. 'Do you trust me to pick out the best ones and just send you those?'

'Yes.'

'I've got five minutes but then I need to go,' he says. His tone telling me to get dressed.

An image of the walk-of-shame woman is back in my head as I pull on my trousers. His manner when he spoke to her at the door.

'Thank you,' I say. 'I appreciate this. It's worth much more than an hour of child-minding.'

He doesn't answer. His dirty pink shirt is on the floor a few feet away.

An idea illuminates in my mind. I have another plan. Another chance to get inside the house.

I walk over, pick up the shirt then push it into my bag as I look at the clock on the wall near the door. His five minutes are up.

I slide my feet into my shoes, pull on my coat and pick up my bag. 'Goodbye, Alex.'

'Yes.' He slings the straps of a couple of equipment bags over his shoulder, and his keys rattle in his hand as he walks towards me.

'Thank you, again.'

'You're welcome. I'll email the images to you.'

When he opens and holds the door, Louise returns to my body, pressing her pain and anger into me.

As soon as I have closed the front door, I take the pink shirt out of my bag. The personal smell rising from the shirt, as I lift it out, makes me feel that I should see memories. Of course, I don't. I can't. Why would I have memories of being close enough to Alex to smell his skin or clothes? But Louise is in my senses. She can smell Alex, and she's connected to that smell.

She may hate him, but there's an echo of love there too.

I put my bag down on the kitchen table and take off my gloves, scarf and coat.

Then I pick up the shirt again, lift it to my nose and draw in the smell. It's not an action that came from my mind. Which is a little scary. I feel as if Louise controlled my movement.

But she can't have done ...

I bend down, open the washing machine, put the shirt in with an all-in-one liquid pod, shut the door and press the buttons to get the machine going.

Chapter 31

22 weeks and 6 days after the fall.

The pink shirt is washed, ironed, folded and wrapped in a white plastic carrier bag that was under the kitchen sink. But the shirt doesn't matter. What matters is whether I see the children.

I'm hoping that returning a clean shirt will lower the drawbridge and let me enter the house again.

I press a finger on the bell for a moment then take a step back.

I've judged the time carefully. I waited until his parents left, and then another twenty minutes. The light in the kitchen turned off ten minutes ago and the light in the living room turned on.

The sound of his footsteps announces that he's coming downstairs.

The door opens.

His frown asks why I am here.

'Hello.' I keep my voice cheerful. I don't want to seem strange or pushy. 'I picked your shirt up yesterday and washed it to say thank you.' I hold out my neatly folded gift in the white plastic bag. 'I wanted to do something to help ...' The words hover in a moist mist between us, as cold air races into the house and warm air rushes out.

He looks at the gift, the Trojan horse, that I am hiding behind. 'You didn't have to.'

'I know. But I can't even imagine how hard life must be for you, having lost your wife. So, I thought you might appreciate it.'

He takes the shirt. 'I ... Thank you.' He looks at my eyes. Capturing me with that Taser-like look.

I think he sees something odd in me.

He really does find it hard to trust.

There's an expression of decision, a movement in his lips forming creases at the corners of his eyes as he steps back. 'Would you like to come in for a minute?'

'Yes. Thank you.'

My heart skips over the threshold.

But Louise's energy is a screaming wildcat once more. She's pressing me to hurry upstairs, gather the children and run.

He closes the door on the cold night, with me inside, in the warm.

Where are they? 'Are the children awake?'

'Yes. They're upstairs in the living room. Would you like a cup of coffee?'

'Yes. Please. That would be nice.'

'Hang up your coat and go and see the girls. Rosie has been talking about you since the other day. She still has some of the varnish left on her nails and she wants me to buy more.'

As he walks into the kitchen a heavy sadness travels with him, but Louise has remained with me; screaming and trying to push me into movement.

I hear the children as I take off my coat and hang it up: small feet running across the floorboards in a first-floor room above and shouting as part of a game.

I climb the steps, my trainers making a heavy noise on each stair as I move further into their home.

The stairs turn at the top, onto a wide landing that leads to a set of stairs that go up again. There is one open door. A high-pitched babyish squeal of excitement pierces the air just before I reach it.

Hope is running about the living room, balancing mostly on her toes, her dummy in her hand not her mouth as her brother aims a plastic bow and arrow at her. She's squealing with happiness though; she giggles with absolute abandon when the arrow strikes her back, and then falls with a soft, quiet, impact onto an Egyptian rug that covers most of the floor. Then she falls backwards, dropping like a stone onto her nappy-cushioned bottom.

The air in the room smells sweet, clean, of soap and shampoo. The children have had baths and are in their nightclothes.

'Hello. Your dad sent me up.'

'Helen.' Rosie uncurls from a hunched position, dropping a crayon as she stands, deserting a picture that looks like the one she was drawing the other day.

'Daddy said you still have some nail varnish on,' I say as Rosie comes to me.

'Hope wants her nails painted too.'

'Coffee.' Alex is at the door, with a mug in either hand.

'D-Dee.' Hope crawls towards him.

Josh has put his bow and arrow down on a chair that is farthest away from me.

A bristling wariness surrounds him. He doesn't like strangers in his house.

Alex puts the mugs down on a pale oak coffee table, beside Rosie's crayons, and leans to pick up Hope.

In my mind's eye my hands reach out to take her from him. I sit on the sofa, so if Rosie returns to her colouring, she will sit next to me.

I pick up the mug of coffee, smiling at Alex and Hope.

Rosie climbs onto the sofa beside me. 'We are going to buy our Christmas tree with Grandma and Grandad tomorrow.'

'Are you?'

'I'm going to hang the stars that Mum likes on it,' Josh tells me from the other side of the room as his father shifts Hope into a position that allows him to sit at the far end of the sofa.

'We're making paper chains,' Rosie adds. Her brother's tone was flat but her voice expresses excitement that Christmas is coming.

'Mu. Mu.' The dummy is back in Hope's mouth. She reaches towards my hand, sliding off Alex's lap to come to me. She's looking at my rings. I hold out my hand so she can touch them.

'I have something to ask you,' Alex says as he picks up the other mug and shifts back into the corner of the sofa, turning a little in my direction. Louise the wildcat is clawing at him, because she's had no effect on me. 'My parents are going away soon – they spend part of their winters in Florida.'

Rosie slides off the sofa, to kneel on the floor, and picks up the crayon.

Alex's pupils have flared in the electric light. It makes his irises bluer. 'I'll need someone to look after the children.'

My children. Mine.

The offer is coming; it is a tension that I can see in the muscles in his jaw. Why would Louise not want this for me?

'Have you got a job yet?' He sips his coffee.

'Not a permanent job. No.' I, we, Louise and I, will be close to the children all the time.

'I need someone to start the first Monday after Christmas. Would you be able to do that?'

'Yes. I can fit around you.' I sip my coffee, trying not to leap, or faint from the pace of my heartbeat.

'Sometimes I have to work late; would that be an issue?'

'No.'

'And early starts? Generally, it'll be a seven-thirty or eight start.'

'Okay.' He's not asking me to move in, just to spend days with the children. That will be enough.

'I try not to work over the weekends, so you can have those off.'

I nod. Holding tightly onto words that want to scream my happiness.

'That's agreed, then.' He takes a long drink from the mug then puts it down. 'I better get the children to bed. Hope.' He grips her hips and pulls her away from the game she's playing with my rings.

'And I should go.' I haven't finished my coffee, but I didn't really want it. I put the mug down and stand.

'Rosie. Say goodnight to Helen. You'll see her after Christmas.'

I want to stay and be the one to tuck the children into bed, pull their duvets up to their chins and kiss their soft cheeks.

The crayon falls out of Rosie's fingers and she gets up, smiling at me. 'Goodnight.'

'Goodnight. Sleep tight and don't let the bed bugs bite,' I answer.

I reach out and run my fingers through her fine, pale hair. The curls release the sweet perfume of shampoo.

'Josh,' Alex calls.

He's playing with a car on the other side of the room. He doesn't answer, but he does obey the command in Alex's voice and puts the car into a toy-box by the wall.

'Ready?' Alex asks as Josh comes over to join his sisters.

Alex looks at me. Goodbye, his expression says, get your things and get out. You've served your purpose.

But at least now I have a purpose that will bring me back.

I smile at him, then look at the children. 'I'll see you all after Christmas.'

Josh ignores me.

Rosie lifts a hand and waves.

'After Father Christmas has been,' I add. 'Goodnight.' This I say to Josh particularly. Then I walk out of the room with a heavy ball-and-chain feeling dragging on my ankles.

Alex follows me out of the room, with Hope on his hip and Rosie trailing behind. 'Thank you,' I say to him. 'Shall I let myself out?'

'If that's all right?'

'Yes.'

He and Rosie walk with me to the top of the stairs.

As I step down onto the first stair she grips her daddy's leg, pressing into Alex. His hand drops down onto her head.

Josh is as far back as the living-room door, merely waiting for me to leave.

'Have a good Christmas,' I say as I walk down the stairs, watched by them.

Pain, grief and misery is so deeply embedded in this house it is in the mortar in between the bricks in the walls.

I take my coat off the hook, pull it on, awkwardly, under the gaze of my watchers, and pick up my bag.

'Goodnight, Helen.' I look up. 'Thanks for washing the shirt. I'll send you the pictures tomorrow and I'll call you after Christmas and let you know what time I need you to start.'

'Thanks. Goodnight.' I lift a hand then turn to the door.

Louise claws at me to turn back. She's trying everything she can to make my body move as she wants it to.

Do not leave them! My children! No! No! Don't go!

Louise's screams are not a distinct voice. The words are sharp sounds. But she's learned how to thrust her energy into sounds that are so like words I can understand. She isn't capable of simply talking to me though – telling me why she's enraged.

I turn the latch, pull the heavy door open and leave.

After Christmas, I'll be back five days in every week.

The fox-head knocker rattles its goodbye.

I skip my way into the city centre, smiling, and dodge through the tourists staring at the strings of white Christmas lights.

A jugful of energy has been poured into me.

When I sit in the pub with Andy I'm so talkative and fidgety Andy jokes about what I must have taken. I can't stop smiling. 'Happy pills,' I answer with a smile. Children-shaped happy pills.

His forehead creases with lots of frown lines. I stroke them flat with my thumb, laughing. 'Prescription happy pills,' I reassure him.

His lips twist in a lopsided smile. 'You are nuts tonight.'

'Thank you, I'll take that as a compliment.' He knows I have bipolar. He also knows it is under control with the medication. He isn't frightened of it.

The sunlight edges around the curtains in Andy's bedroom, and it looks bright. I lean up on an elbow and look at the clock on his side of the bed. 7:22. Andy's alarm will go off in eighteen minutes. I push the covers aside gently so I don't wake him, climb out of bed and walk quietly over to my jeans, to get my phone out from the back pocket. I pull last night's knickers on, pick my long-sleeved T-shirt up off the floor, slip it on and walk out of the room into the open living room.

I sit in the chair there and open my phone to look at Facebook – to look at the pictures on Robert Dowling's page. I want to look at the children's faces.

I'll be with them soon.

My children.

Louise hasn't settled since our visit.

There's a notification on my phone, saying I have an email from Alexander Lovett; received at 3.03 in the morning.

My heartbeat rises to a thud that resounds all the way to my fingertips as I open the email.

It is my pictures. He must have gone through the pictures for at least half an hour in the middle of the night.

I open the images. He's made me look extraordinary, sexy, but in the simplest, most unadorned way. My thumb slides across the screen as I scan through the twelve images he's chosen. As he said, the pictures of me in the chair look as though I have just got up in the morning.

'Thank you. They're lovely,' I reply. 'Have a good Christmas.' I'm not sure if that's the right thing to say to a man who's been widowed this year, but I send the email anyway.

I look through the pictures again. They are simply beautiful.

Chapter 32

Christmas Day.

Simon reaches across the table, balancing a couple of slices of turkey between the carving knife and fork.

I hold Andy's plate out to receive the slices, then pass the plate to Andy.

'Thanks,' Andy says.

Andy spent last night here, with me, squeezed into the narrow spare bed, where I had lain for months unsure if I would live or die.

Now I have a wonderful life.

Louise's spirit is not with me today. I imagine she's with her children. But I have her heart, and Andy, and I'm going to be with the children soon. I am so excited I've been struggling to sleep at night, worse than Kevin and Liam being too excited because of Father Christmas coming.

'Pull my cracker, Auntie Helen,' Kevin calls across the table.

'Pull mine, Auntie Helen.' Liam pushes his arm over his brother's, reaching further.

I cross my arms and take hold of the crackers. 'Ready. Tug,' I call. The crackers bang and I end up with the largest part of both, but the boys snatch them back and begin investigating the toys and jokes.

'Pull.'

I look at Andy. He's holding out his cracker.

My cheeks ache, I have smiled so much this morning; watching the boys unwrap their presents, sitting on the floor between Andy's parted legs with his warm hands on my shoulders.

'I'll pull it,' Liam shouts across the table.

'No. I want your Auntie Helen to open this cracker.'

The boys like Andy. He makes them laugh with silly jokes, plays the rough games they love and he'll kick a ball around in the garden with them for hours.

I take hold of the end of the cracker.

'Ready?' he says.

'Yes. Go.' I pull.

His thumb and finger grip his end of the cracker harder but he doesn't pull, just holds it steady so I can.

The cracker bangs, releasing a wisp of smoke and the smell of gunpowder and something chinks on china then plops into the pale turkey gravy in the white gravy boat.

The gift from the cracker, something metal, sinks to the bottom of the gravy. A puzzle. A keyring.

'Shit. Sorry.' Andy swears and sends an apology to Mim. The chair scrapes back as he stands and leans over, dipping his fingers into the gravy to retrieve the something. 'Sorry, everyone.'

Simon breaks into laughter. The carving knife and fork held carelessly in the air.

'What are you doing?' I say to Andy.

'Sorry.' Andy picks the gravy boat up with his other hand, as his fingers carry on wading around.

'Andy ...'

The boys are laughing too, and Mim is smiling as though she's about to laugh.

'No one will want that gravy now. Leave it in there,' I say. 'We can use what's left in the saucepan.'

'Or we can use that and it will be like a traditional Christmas pudding with a sixpence buried somewhere in it,' Simon suggests, and then laughs again.

'I can't catch it. It keeps sliding out of my fingers,' Andy says, to Simon, not me. 'I am going to have to tip this out.' He carries the gravy boat over to the sink. 'This isn't going as I wanted it to.'

I look over my shoulder.

Andy is frowning at the sink, his fingers searching through the gravy he's tipped out.

I am laughing internally. Whatever it is that's metal makes another sound.

'Got it.' He turns the tap on and rinses it.

I turn back to the table to help myself from the bowls loaded with different vegetables, sausages wrapped in bacon and flaky, crispy roasted potatoes. Simon has also gone back to carving turkey. 'Can you bring the saucepan?' I ask Andy without looking back.

'Helen.' The serious tone makes me turn. Andy is down on one knee, beside my chair, holding something out to me. A ring.

A ring!

'Will you marry me?'

'Oh, my God.' My hand is against my chest, and my heart skips. Shock. Shock. But. 'Oh, my God.' This time I say it in a whisper. He's looking at me. Waiting for an answer.

'I didn't expect—'

'I know. I wanted it to be a surprise. So, will you? Will you marry me? I know we haven't been together for long, but I think we've been together long enough to know this is going to work and I don't want to wait. I've waited long enough to meet you and I want us to make a family.'

The kitchen light is on, because it's grey, miserable weather outside, and the electric light catches on the diamond at the centre of the ring as his hand trembles.

'Yes.' Yes. I lean forward, wrap my arms around his neck and kiss him.

His hands embrace the back of my head, one fisted so he doesn't drop the ring, as he responds to my kiss. 'Yes,' I say against his lips. Grasping at this new life and holding on. 'I love you.'

'I love you too.'

I let him go and he gets up off his knee. Then takes hold of my left hand and holds my ring finger with one hand while the other hand slides the ring on.

I lift my hand to watch the diamond sparkle in the light. Then I look at him. 'Thank you.'

'Congratulations. But can we eat now, before everything is cold?'

I spin around, looking at Simon. There was a smile in Simon's words and there's a grin on his face. 'You knew.'

'He asked my permission yesterday.'

In the new year, in my new life, I'm going to be a mother and a wife. I'll have five days a week with the children and every night and weekend with my husband and I'll love them all and be loved by them.

My black hole will be filled to the brink. I don't even feel it there any more. I don't feel empty. I am full. Whole.

THE SPLIT

Chapter 33

The first Monday of my new life.

The pedestrian-only streets feel empty this morning. The tourists left with the Christmas market and everyone in the streets is walking to work. I don't feel as if I am walking to work – it feels as if I'm walking home. Louise may hate Alex, but she still has positive emotions that connect her to the house and they reach beyond the children.

I've left Andy in our home, eating a bowl of cornflakes.

I moved my belongings from the rented room over to Andy's flat on Boxing Day and gave Pippa the last week's rent.

I split in two on Christmas Day, divided down the middle: half Helen and half Helen-Louise. From now on I'll be leading a double life.

Helen wanted to stay in bed this morning, snuggled into Andy. Louise wanted me to get away from him.

She's uncomfortable when I'm in his bed. He's another reason for her to be angry, because Andy's a distraction. Her focus is her family, and I'm not doing what she wants me to do but she still needs me to have any chance of connecting with them. They can't hear her.

Every step I take closer to the house, the ache inside me increases.

My hands are pressed into the deep pockets of the long winter coat I bought in the sales and my boots splash through puddles formed by a night of rain. It is a twenty-five-minute walk from Andy's to Alex's.

The smell of freshly ground coffee in the cold air lures me into buying a takeaway cup. I am too used to buying a coffee to take to the seat in the park.

When I cross the road to reach Alex's street, habit wants me to turn left into the park.

I walk straight on along the wide pavement beside the railings that protect the spaces at basement level.

Hope's mitten-covered hand ran along these railings before Christmas.

My heart hammers against my ribs with excitement. The feeling takes me to when Dan told me to move out. Then, my heart hardly moved when it beat, its strength was so feeble. I had no hope of having children.

Today I face the door – a foot away from it, not metres away in the park – and press the doorbell.

Alex opens the door.

I hear the children in the kitchen. 'Good morning.' His tone is all business, but the drawbridge is down and I walk in.

'Good morning.' I turn and shut the door. I have a right to be in the house today; I have a position and the authority to be here.

He turns his back and returns to the kitchen. Louise rushes after him, a surging aggression pulsing into the air with the high pitch of her screams.

'You have made a good impression on the children already,' he says as he walks. 'Rosie decided to stay with you rather than walk Josh to school, so, Josh has decided he wants you and the girls to walk him to school.' He looks across his shoulder. 'It's now your job to get him school.'

'Okay.' I put the hot takeaway cup on a stair, drop my bag on the floor under the coat hooks, take off my coat and pick up my coffee cup.

'There's a key on the side here,' he says. 'The children are finishing their breakfast. Josh needs to be at school by 8.30. Obviously, he can show you the way, but the address and phone number are next to the key. If I am not back, he'll need to be picked up at 3.30.'

'Okay.' I say again as I walk into the open-plan kitchen.

He picks up his keys from the breakfast bar.

Hope is in the highchair, Rosie and Josh are on the high seats beside her, eating cereal from bowls.

'You have my number?'

'Yes.'

He walks past me, towards the hall. 'Hope will get grumpy after one o'clock – she needs a nap. Rosie hates napping but she still gets tired; she's better doing something quiet in the afternoon.'

'All right.' I turn as my gaze follows him into the hall.

He takes a leather jacket off a hook and pulls it on. 'Sorry I have to hurry today. Call me if there are any problems.'

'I will, but I'm sure we'll be fine.'

'Good. I'll see you later. I have no idea when I'll finish but I'll call if it looks as if it is going to be late.'

'Okay. No need to worry about us.'

He walks past me again, into the kitchen, towards the breakfast bar and presses a kiss on Hope's head. She looks up and gives him a sticky-looking smile. 'Dadee.'

A hand strokes over Rosie's head. When she looks up, with a

mouth full of cornflakes, he kisses her forehead. 'Be a good girl for Helen.'

A smile forms on her milky lips. He brushes his hand over her curls again, and looks at Josh.

'Bye, mate. Have a good day at school.'

'Bye, Dad.'

'Bye. Bye.' Hope waves a porridge-coated plastic spoon, flicking globules across the kitchen and narrowly avoiding hitting the leg of the pale jeans with the old coffee stain.

'Be good,' he looks back and says when he reaches the front door.

'Bye, Daddy.' Rosie waves vigorously.

'Goodbye,' I say.

'Goodbye,' he answers just before closing the door, taking his dark storm out of the house with him.

The doorknocker rattles from the outside. But I am inside. *My children. Mine.*

No, Louise. Mine. I smile to myself, over the mental taunt, as I walk towards the sink. 'You seem to be managing your breakfast without any help, Hope.'

I put my coffee down and rip a piece of paper towel off the kitchen roll, so I can wipe up the porridge that was thrown around the room.

'She's not a baby,' Josh tells me; his voice calls me a fool for thinking his sister might be incapable of feeding herself.

He's stepped up to help care for his sisters, and Alex said he counselled Josh to fight his emotions after Josh bit the other child. Both of those things will have trapped his grief inside.

'I know she's not.' I squat down to wipe some porridge off the floor while Josh watches from his perch on the chair by the breakfast bar, his spoon left in the bowl.

'Ah.' The squeal launches out from my throat as I fall back. My fisted hand breaks my fall, and I hit my hip on the wooden floorboards.

I lost my balance. But something pushed me.

'Helen!' Rosie yells.

'Are you okay?' Josh has slid off his seat and is next to me.

'Yes. Yes.' I smile, to reassure them all. 'No harm done.' I turn onto my knees and finish wiping up. 'Is there anything else I need to know?' I ask Josh. If he feels responsible the best thing to do for him is give him responsibility. The worst thing for him would be to feel he had no control.

With the dirty paper towel crushed in my hand, I stand up. My legs are wobbly. That frightened me. There was no reason why I should have fallen over.

There's no trust in Josh's eyes. He wants his mother here, that's all. He wants his life to go back to what it was. I can't give him that, any more than I can give Louise what she wants no matter how violently she tries to make me.

I walk over to the bin, pop the lid up with the pedal and throw the paper towel away. 'How long does it take to walk to your school?' I ask as if I don't know.

'We need to go at ten past eight.'

I look at him again. 'Do you have everything ready?'

'Yes.' It's strange to hear that hollowed-out, hard, curt tone that Alex uses in a child's pitch.

Did I sound like that as a child? No wonder I terrified foster parents and scared off potential adopters. And no wonder Simon protected me so energetically.

Louise wants me to wrap Josh in my arms and squeeze him tight, as though he's a small boy, but he would hate Helen to do that.

I, Helen, want to see him laugh. I want to make them all smile and be happy. The dark mist has left with Alex but the house is still haunted by memories and grief.

I take a sip of my coffee. 'Would any of you like anything else? A drink? Juice?'

'Juice,' Hope repeats.

'Her beaker's in that cupboard.' Josh points up. 'I'm going to clean my teeth.'

'Me too.' Rosie climbs down from the tall chair.

'You haven't finished,' Josh answers.

'I've had enough.'

When we are left alone, Hope's eyes track my movement as I find a beaker, open the fridge and fill it with a little apple juice. 'Here you are.'

Her fingers close about the handle then she twists around, pointing at the door with her free hand. 'Go. Go.'

'When you've drunk your juice, then you can get down.'

The strength of the pressure around me is intensifying by the second.

I am pouted at and she puts down the beaker. Then she asks to get down again.

Ignoring any potential impact on our future relationship, I slide out the front of her highchair, release the buckle and lift her out. Her legs stretch and wriggle, expressing her desire to walk – to get away from me.

Louise wants me to pin her tight to me and not let her go. But I do let her go and she runs after her brother and sister.

A headache thumps through to the left side of my skull. My fingertips press against my temple, a build-up of pressure. 'Shut up, Louise.' The words are a whisper.

'Where are you?' I call as I climb the stairs.

'Here,' Rosie's muffled voice replies. Their voices come from the second floor, above the living room.

'We're getting ready,' Josh shouts – We don't need you.

I walk into the living room to wait for the children to come down. There are two wide, long, Georgian sash windows at either end. The windows at the front cast sunlight rectangles on the floor.

The Christmas tree is still in one corner, with a scatter of needles on the bare floor where I imagine a few days ago the presents would have been crowded. The paper chains I saw Alex hanging, from my cold perch on the park bench outside, have fallen over the Christmas holiday and are draped across a set of shelves that covers one wall on the other side of the room.

There are numerous family pictures on the shelves, in wood or enamel frames. They're beautifully posed images. Life captured in a moment.

Alex has taken most of them.

I look at image after image of the children. Ranging from the moment Josh was born, until now. The children grow through Alex's camera lens. There are some pictures that include him, but none with Louise.

Have her pictures been taken away?

The pictures must be upstairs. That would make sense. If the children and Alex wanted Louise's pictures with them.

Curiosity leads me out of the living room and up the wooden stairs. 'Hello,' I call up. 'Are you ready?' Each step takes me further into Louise's life.

A stairway to heaven or a stairway to hell.

Heaven for me. I run up the last few steps.

The first door along the landing is open. But bangs and squeals come from a room farther along.

The first room is large, decorated in white with pink flowers.

On one side, there's a cot, and on the other there's a single bed; the duvet is in a tussled muddle.

The blue and white T-shirt I have seen Rosie wearing as a nightdress has been thrown on top of the duvet, discarded hurriedly.

Louise breathes down my neck, sending that shiver down my spine.

Everything she's doing to me gives me shivers today. Her presence is threatening. I feel as though she would be violent if she could be – and I do not know how, but I still feel as if she was the one who pushed me over downstairs.

There's a tall chest of drawers and a short wardrobe against the wall, a nappy-changing unit, toy-boxes at the end of the beds and plush toys and dolls spread about the room. But no pictures of Louise.

I straighten the duvet, fold the T-shirt and put it on top of the pillow then leave the room, following the sound of childish amusement.

They're in a room a couple of metres along the landing, on the other side of the bathroom. The door's open. The girls are bouncing on a bed crushing an image of Spiderman.

'Are you nearly ready?' I say, from the open door. I don't want to walk into Josh's space uninvited.

'I am,' Josh answers. He's on the other side of the room, sitting at a desk, playing with a handheld electronic game. He's very tolerant for a six-or-seven-year-old older brother.

'Come on, Hope, Rosie.' I beckon, encouraging them off the bed, without stepping into his room. 'You need to put your shoes on.'

There are no photographs of Louise in this room, unless they're behind the door.

My curiosity stretches to Alex's room.

There's only one other door on this floor but there isn't enough space for it to be anything other than a cupboard. 'Where's your dad's room?' I ask Josh as he puts his toy down.

'Upstairs.'

'Where?' The stairs don't go up another floor, but I know there are rooms in the attic, I've seen the windows.

He points towards the closed door. 'The old servants' stairs go up to the attic and down to the basement flat. Dad's rented the basement out now Susie's gone.'

A jab of desire calls me upstairs. I want to know everything about this family.

Do not get obsessed ... The words are spoken in Simon's voice.

No. Anyone would think it's strange that there aren't any pictures of the children's dead mother – and Alex is a photographer.

Josh helps me find everyone's coats, then he buckles up Hope's shoes as I tie the laces for Rosie's. His last job is to wheel the pushchair out from the under-stairs cupboard. He leaves me to settle Hope in the pushchair and opens the door.

When I've seen him with Alex he always runs ahead, but he doesn't today. 'Rosie has to hold the pushchair. So she isn't lost.'

'Thank you for letting me know.'

He walks either just in front of us or beside us – the girls' protector.

I want to tell him not to worry, to run ahead. I won't let anything happen to his sisters.

At the school gate, he kisses Hope on the top of the head and Rosie on her forehead, in the same way that Alex did.

He waves a second goodbye to them as he walks around the corner into the school playground, then disappears.

We wait by the gate for a little while, to make sure he hasn't forgotten something, but he doesn't come back.

Now I have a full day with the girls.

It's cold, but not too cold to play on the swings and the seesaw in the park.

With Josh not here to watch me, I hug Hope tight, braced in my arms, as we sit on one end of the seesaw while Rosie sits at the other.

We warm up afterwards with a cup of milky hot chocolate and satsuma segments. Then we go up to the girls' bedroom and sit all their dolls and cuddly toys in a round to play nursery school. There's one teddy bear that will not behave and sit up straight. He tumbles backwards, sideways or forwards again and again as we practise letters and colours. I sit beside the errant teddy, wondering if Louise has found a way to move things.

Is she practising moving things?

After lunch, I lift Hope into the cot so she can sleep and Rosie and I return to the living room. We put _Peppa Pig_ on the TV and I paint her nails pink. Then we sit together and she presses against me, so I wrap an arm around her.

I have cuddled both girls today.

My girls.

Rosie's breathing slows and quietens. Her body is heavier. I switch off the television so the sound will not wake her, carefully slide away and rest her head on a cushion.

For a while I stand watching her, with a sense that Louise is beside me, watching me.

Then I walk upstairs and watch Hope's stomach rise and fall, the jerking movements of the dummy as she sucks it in her sleep and the occasional flutter of her eyelashes as she dreams.

I have children.

Mine.

Words can't do justice to the warm and alternately melting and tight sensations in my stomach. I have children. I have a family Monday to Friday every week now.

This is what I have always wanted.

My girls.

A hard thrust of emotion sweeps into me, pushing me to pick Hope up and shake her. The thought jerks bile into my throat. I could be sick.

I swallow and turn away, my arms folding over my chest in denial, until I reach the stairs. Louise may have given me my life back but spending time with her family is teaching me to dislike her. Why would she want to hurt her child?

Rosie is still sleeping in the living room. I go down to the kitchen to make a cup of tea.

My thoughts are reeling at such a pace it's hard to hold onto any one thought. I am hanging onto a roundabout, my thoughts flying out of my head as I spin; I'm excited about being with the children but struggling to work out what is going on with Louise.

I carry the mug of tea up to the living room and sit and watch Rosie breathing slowly.

The room is quiet. There's no painful screaming. No dark mist of pain. But Louise is here watching Rosie too.

I stand and move around to look through the front window; my fingers touch a pane of glass. I can see the park bench.

I sat outside for months, and now I am inside. I have what I want. But I won't take the children and give Louise what she wants.

But if she's learning how to move things, what will she do to get what she wants?

'Why, Louise?' The whispered words form condensation on the glass. She doesn't answer me.

I look at the photographs on the shelves again. Years and years of the children growing. What was Louise like as a mother? How did she spend her days with Hope and Rosie?

'Why did you fall?' If it was suicide, why is she so determined to take the children when she'd chosen to leave them? Is it just about revenge because Alex slept with other women?

I was too busy thinking about staying alive with Dan, to think about killing myself. But I understand the blackness of depression. I've been inside that deep pit. Bipolar sometimes drags me down there still.

Why aren't there any photographs of her in this house? I can't think of a good reason.

The phone vibrates in my back pocket. The alarm has gone off to remind me it is time to collect Josh from school. I need to wake the girls. Hope first, so I can change her nappy.

Rosie is full of chatter. She tells Josh everything we've done. Hope joins in with contributions of a string of three or four almost words that do not present a sentence any of us can understand.

As I navigate the crossing over the main road with the pushchair, I catch Josh looking at me. The look acknowledges that I have been nice to his sisters.

I've earned a teaspoon's worth of his trust.

When we reach the front door, Josh offers to take the key, opens the door and holds it so I can bring the pushchair in.

'Thank you.' You're a good boy.

I've worked with young boys in challenging schools in London. Boys who are aggressive and ungovernable. Josh may have lost his temper with another boy, but he's not normally naughty or violent.

My son.

A sigh escapes. I'm tired of hearing her. But I can't shut her up.

I close the door as Josh undoes the buckle and helps Hope out of the pushchair.

When Hope's released, she wraps her brother up in a bear hug.

'Do you have any homework to do?' I ask Josh.

Hope climbs the stairs with feet, knees and hands.

'He's not allowed to play until he's done his homework,' Rosie answers for him.

'Reading,' Josh answers.

'Would you like to read to me?' I ask.

He nods.

'Rosie, will you be happy drawing for a little while? So Josh can read.'

She nods too, with the same head movement as her brother. These children are desperate for love. Alex's love can't stretch around three of them constantly. They need a mother.

Mine.

If Louise could scratch me from beyond the grave I think she'd be clawing at my face. She doesn't want me to replace her. She didn't bring me here for that.

The living room is quiet. Rosie is kneeling in front of the coffee table with a piece of paper in front of her and she's busy finding a colour. Josh is sitting on the sofa with a book open on his lap. Hope is beside him, leaning over to look at his book, her dummy in her mouth again.

But the silence isn't quiet. The silence is crying.

'What are you reading?' I ask as I put three cups of orange squash on the coffee table.

Josh looks at me, with an electric charge, looking into my eyes in the same way that Alex does. 'Roald Dahl, *The Twits*. Mum liked Roald Dahl. *The Twits* made her laugh.'

I wish she were laughing now.

I sit next to him, an urge to hug him sweeping through me. 'You can read it to Hope and me.' I put my arm along the back of the sofa behind him so I can turn a little and see the words in the book.

He reads well; he's an intelligent boy. There's no need to correct or help him.

My thoughts drift, travelling through time, reeling again. I can see that woman, standing at the open front door in the early morning, with smudged eye make-up, unbrushed hair and the clothes she must have worn the night before, talking to Alex.

Why did he do that?

I labelled him a bad parent. I thought that Louise wanted me to rescue her children from their father. But the closer I have come to the children, the more I see a good father, who loves them, and who they love.

'Ah,' Josh shouts, disturbing my daydream, as the book tumbles out of his hand onto the floor.

'Helen.' Rosie climbs onto the sofa, claiming my attention, waving her picture. 'It's Mummy.'

A spasm of nausea twists through my stomach.

'Look,' Rosie presses me.

Josh climbs off the sofa to get his book.

The drawing is ... Of ... Air thrusts out of my lungs, as if I have been hit by a wrecking ball. There's the grey box, with the red car on top, but now there are two stick people on the top edge of the grey box. One figure has their arms outstretched; another figure is falling back.

A third, shorter stick figure is standing beside the car.

Oh, my God. The children were there. That's what this picture says. What other reason would a three-year-old have to draw something like this?

Is Louise speaking through her daughter?

My mouth opens like a fish's. Poor Rosie. She's looking at her drawing, as if she's studying it for accuracy. 'That's Mummy.' She points at the lopsided person on the edge of the grey box. 'That's Daddy pushing.'

A small amount of bitter-tasting bile lurches from my tummy into my mouth. I swallow it back.

Pushing.

Oh, my God.

He did it. Alex did it.

That's why she wants me to run off with the children.

But how can Rosie have witnessed her father murdering her mother and speak so calmly about it? And if he pushed Louise, and the children saw it, why isn't he in a prison?

'She draws that all the time,' Josh says with a dismissive voice. 'It's all she draws.'

Why isn't he upset? Why isn't he blaming his father and telling the police?

'Pushing?' The word creeps out on my breath.

Josh stares at me, watching my reaction. 'Dad told her it was an accident. It was an accident that Mummy fell. He didn't push her. He tried to catch her.' He looks away immediately after dismissing Rosie's words, sits back down and begins to read again.

Pushing.

Why are there no pictures of Louise in the house? 'Do you have a photograph of Mummy?' I ask Rosie.

It can't have been an accident she fell. I know the wall was too high. It was murder or suicide and either way the children watched their mother die. They must feel anger, not just grief.

I have been angry with my parents my whole life because they chose to leave me.

If Josh is telling the truth then it was suicide and they watched their mother choose death.

'Yes,' Rosie says excitedly, very willing to talk about her mother, in a way that says she often talks about her mother. It implies that Alex talks about Louise too.

Rosie slides off the sofa and runs out of the room. I hear her socks slide on the floorboards on the landing.

'Careful,' I call out.

Josh is still reading.

A door opens and then Rosie's feet sound on the stairs that lead to the attic. The picture is in Alex's room.

After a minute or two, Rosie's footsteps come down and then she's at the door.

Josh stops reading to look at her.

'Here.' She holds out a crumpled, print photograph as she comes back to me.

I take it and look at the image the picture has preserved.

Louise is holding a small baby and Alex's arm is around her.

'That's Josh.' Rosie points at the baby.

Louise looks the same as she does in the picture on her Facebook page and obituary, a lot younger than she was when she died.

'Does Daddy have any pictures that he took of Mummy?' I ask.

'No,' Josh answers. It sounds like a rehearsed answer. A learned answer. I imagine the children asking, why aren't there more pictures of Mummy? And the answer, because there aren't.

'Put it back and keep it safe.' I hand the photograph back. 'I think your mummy is very pretty,' I add.

'I've read enough,' Josh declares as Rosie leaves the room. He puts his book down on the coffee table. Hope reaches for it. He picks the book up and returns it to his book-bag. 'I'm going to play in my room.' He doesn't ask but tells me as he puts the book-bag on a shelf, out of Hope's reach.

'Is that the agreement you have with your dad?'

'Yes.' His voice says I have no right to challenge him – you are not my parent.

My son.

'All right. But please put a film or something on for Rosie before you go?'

He nods, then goes to the door and shouts to ask his sister what she wants to watch.

She shouts her choice of *Paddington*.

He sets it up as I entertain Hope with my phone.

When Rosie walks back in he presses play.

My phone vibrates in Hope's hand and the screen displays the first line of a text message.

'Is that your phone ringing?' Josh asks, staring at me with the intense Alex-like look.

'It's a message,' I answer. 'Thank you,' I say to Hope as I pull the phone out of her hand. I stroke a hand over Hope's hair as the children watch me as if they're desperate to know who the message is from.

'Hi. I'll be back around six. Also, I forgot to say, do not answer the phone. If anyone calls let it ring. Alex.'

'Ok,' I text back and give the phone back to Hope.

'Susie looked at her phone all the time,' Josh says.

'Well, I'm not Susie. The message was from your dad. He said he'll be home around six o'clock.'

Josh doesn't answer. He deserts us to shut himself away in his room.

'Hope likes your phone,' Rosie says as she cuddles up next to me.

I wrap an arm around her.

She slides down as we watch the film, until her head is in my lap.

My fingers comb through her curls. My heart dripping love and happiness, while I feel regret and sadness in her aura.

Louise is watching in silence for a change. But I don't think it means she's happy.

I don't know what to make of Louise now.

I think it was suicide, not murder.

But why? Didn't she love her family? Didn't she love her children, if not Alex? But if she loved them, how could she have chosen to leave them, knowing that she would hurt them?

Leaving children behind is something that's unforgivable.

I don't want to be on Louise's side any more.

Chapter 34

18.10.

The noise of the doorknocker rattling comes from the floor below and the front door bumps shut.

Louise instantly recommences her high-pitched, aggressive screaming.

'Daddy.' Rosie slides off the sofa and runs towards the landing. Hope rolls onto her tummy to slide off the sofa and follow. I stand.

My heart is hammering.

Pushing – the word is spoken in Rosie's voice. That word will not leave my head.

When I reach the top of the stairs and look down, Alex has picked Rosie up in a bear hug and Hope is busily bumping down the stairs on her bottom to receive her cuddle.

'Hello.'

He looks at me, the dark mist swirling around him.

Did Louise kill herself? Why? How did she end up on top of the wall? Did you push her?

'Hello,' he says.

'Dad.' Josh squeezes past me and runs downstairs, passing Hope, who is navigating the last few steps.

Alex puts Rosie down and rubs a hand over the top of Josh's head as he wraps his arms around Alex's waist and holds on for a moment, claiming the attention I know he longs for.

'Dadee.'

Josh lets go of his father, letting Hope have her moment of attention. He's a rare child, I haven't met many children who love their family to the point they put themselves last at the age of six or seven. This is a family that know their places, though. They work together like defending soldiers in an ant army. There's a captain and a lieutenant, and the girls fighting on behind them.

To the death …

The smell of freshly cooked, warm Chinese food rises up to me as Hope is picked up and receives her hug and a kiss on the cheek. There's a full white bag on the floor at Alex's feet.

'Chinese.' Josh has smelled it too.

'Yay. Chinese.' Rosie claps her hands as Josh carries the bag into the kitchen.

Hope, who asks to be put down, follows.

Alex looks at me as I walk downstairs. 'You're welcome to stay for dinner, if you'd like to. There's plenty.'

Yes. I want to, because I want to break through Alex's shop window and ask him questions. But …

'No.' I have Helen's life to go back to. Andy will be home from work soon. 'Thank you, but my fiancé will have cooked something.' I've forgotten about Helen's life nearly all day.

Alex's gaze drops to my left hand, which is hanging at my side. His gaze lifts again. 'How was your day?'

The rattle of china plates and an increasing smell of Chinese food comes from the kitchen. 'Can I eat mine with chopsticks?' Josh calls.

'Yes,' Alex answers, his gaze shifting to the kitchen. 'Help your sisters to what they want.'

I stop about three steps from the bottom of the stairs, because Alex is in the way. 'The day went well. They were well behaved. I can't fault them at all. You have lovely children.'

My children. My children.

The pressure that wants me to snatch the children is back. I lean around Alex, my arms heavy as I reach for my coat, as if I am battling against gravity to control the movement.

He steps aside. 'Are you sure you wouldn't like a drink before you go? Coffee? Beer? Wine?'

'No. But thanks for offering.' I lift my coat and descend the last two steps. I'm imaging the scene in the car park. Louise falling from the high wall – him reaching out. The children watching. None of that shows in his manner.

There are so many questions I want to ask him. So many questions I can't ask him. 'What time will you need me here tomorrow?' I say as I slip my coat on and reach for my scarf.

'Same time as today. Is that all right?' He looks at Josh. 'If you want Helen to walk you to school?'

Josh nods.

He is not happy to walk with me, it's because he thinks his sisters are safer with him, even if it is only for little more of the day.

Alex's hands slide into the pockets of his jeans.

I look down at the movement, imagining his hands reaching and failing to catch her – or pushing her.

I look up, remembering that he's watching me. 'Yes.' A nervous smile, trying to hide my thoughts, pulls at my lips. I pick up my handbag. 'I'll leave you to eat your dinner.'

'Thanks.' One hand rises as if he'll touch my arm or shake my hand but then it falls.

I turn to the door, turn the latch and pull the door open. 'Goodbye.'

The hand rises again, to hold the top of the open door. The cold air of the already dark evening dashes in.

I cast him another nervous smile. 'Shut the door, you're letting the cold in.'

He nods. Then the door closes and the doorknocker rattles. Shutting me out of Louise's life – away from the children.

Headlights glare at me as I navigate the pathways alongside busy roads.

The pedestrian streets in the town are cluttered with rubbish bags awaiting collection and noisy seagulls swoop in, gathering in gangs to rip the black plastic open.

My heart is pounding from the effort of walking up the hill to Andy's flat. The heart focused solely on me; keeping me alive.

It's my heart now, but I can feel Louise watching like a seagull, waiting to swoop down and rip me open.

I can see Andy through the living-room window. The light is on and he's left the curtains open. He's sitting at the desk, with his laptop open. A smile rises from deep inside, expanding from the love I feel for him.

I unzip my bag and find the key.

The inscribed leather keyring Andy bought me hangs down as I put the key in the lock. I know the inscription by heart already. *I want to be your favourite hello, and your hardest goodbye.*

I open the door, then walk into Helen's life. My life. 'Hello,' I call through to the living room.

Chapter 35

The second Saturday of my new life.

Andy's thumbs rest on my hips and his fingertips reach towards the cheeks of my bottom over the fabric of my black pencil skirt. The gentle pressure of his embrace guides my movements as we dance. My upper arms are on his shoulders and my forearms are crossed behind his neck, hands hanging loosely.

We are dancing on the dark dance floor, lit only by the spinning multicoloured lights projected from the DJ's stand; rocking, moving slowly and talking to the pace of the R & B song. He's not pressing close, but standing a few inches back, leaving a space between us, a space that says we can be everything we need to be without being physically all over one another.

I don't think I've been this happy before.

I have everything. Andy – the chance of long-lasting love and a safe, happy home. Children – young children who feel like mine.

The wedding date is set. Ten weeks away. It is going to be a small wedding because I have no family beyond Simon, and only Chloe. My other friends are part of my past – part of Dan's life, not mine. All that is behind me now. I don't even know that poor sick Helen who survived such cruel, disloyal love.

I trust Andy. With everything I have I trust him. We are together all the time when I'm not at work, and his verbal reassurances, telling me what he feels for me, are constant. And I am not ill – he has no reason not to love me.

Andy brought a brochure home for a wedding venue in the garden of a historical house. A small folly, that can fit only a couple of dozen people inside. I love it, and I love that he thought of my need to keep the wedding small but still make it special. It's going to be intimate. Perfect.

For the reception, we've booked a room in an historic coaching inn where we can eat dinner, then we've invited Andy's friends and work colleagues to an evening celebration in Bath the next night.

I love this man. I'm glad Dan ended things because that gave me Andy, and Andy is better for me.

My arms slide further around his neck as he whispers in my ear. 'Do you want another drink?'

'Yes, please.'

'Another gin and tonic?'

I nod and my arms slide away from his neck as his hands brush over my bottom before he lets me go.

I smile over my shoulder as we separate; my balance is a little bit wobbly as the previous gin and tonics descend into my legs. I sit down at a table to wait for Andy to return.

My heart is full enough to burst. I am wholly Helen, so Helen, I don't even care about Louise. I have a functioning heart and a wonderful life, and the music in the club entirely drowns her out.

She should have given up by now, but she still screams at me every day.

Feeling the need to move because I feel odd sitting alone, I get up and walk about the darker edge of the dance floor to ambush Andy on his way back from the bar, hiding out of reach of the circulating lights. The bar is a stretch of blue light on the far side of the nightclub. I move in that direction, a smile generated purely by happiness on my lips as I weave through groups of people, trying not to knock the drinks held in their hands.

There's a heaviness in the air, a darkness that is nothing to do with the low levels of light. My gaze is pulled to a man. He's standing at the end of the bar, alone. Perhaps I notice him because he's the only person standing alone. It looks as if he's hiding in plain sight. He's like a ghost, but he's not a ghost, just a person people watching with an open bottle of beer in one hand.

I know that silhouette.

Alex.

Why is he here?

'Who's with the children?' I ask as I walk up to him, as though he ought to be chained to them every hour of every day.

He steps forward a pace, into the blue light thrown from the bar. 'Hi.'

'Where are the children?' I ask again, as panic rises.

'A neighbour is sitting with them.'

'Your neighbour?' I've never heard of the involvement of this neighbour. 'Are you on your own?'

'Yes.'

His face, the expression ... The shop window has cracks. He doesn't like me speaking to him here.

The hand that's not holding the beer bottle slides into the back pocket of his black cotton jeans. He's wearing his black leather jacket – in a hot nightclub.

'You can join Andy and me if you like?'

'Andy?'

'My fiancé.'

'Thanks, but no, thanks.' He's withdrawing – closing up the shop's shutters, hiding his emotions, as a moment ago he hid in the corner.

Alex. Louise breathes her emotions into me. She's hurting. There's that rare feeling of love merging with the hatred.

His gaze reaches over my shoulder, his body language stiff and awkward.

I turn to look where his gaze has reached to.

The rush of energy that comes from Louise knocks me a step back as I lose my balance.

Alex holds my arm to steady me and stop me falling, his grip pulling my gaze back to him.

He was looking at a group of women, and the woman I saw on his doorstep is among them. I recognise her profile.

My gaze clashes with Alex's with a sharp electric spark.

Is he looking for sex?

'Excuse me. I'll see you on Monday.' He puts his bottle of beer down on the nearest table, then walks around me.

I turn, my gaze following him.

He doesn't go over to the woman, but leaves the club.

My children. The words are a scream that I want to get away from.

My eyes turn to the bar, looking desperately for Andy. He's reached the front of the crowd now and is being served. I walk around people to reach where he's standing and squeeze between them. I touch his T-shirt at his side and feel the reassurance of his proximity. He looks over his shoulder and smiles.

Chapter 36

The third Monday of my new life.

My finger presses the doorbell, pushing hard as anger throbs from my heart all the way to my fingertip. I haven't slept since Saturday. I can't sleep. Louise hasn't let me. There has been a battle in my head between her and me ever since Alex walked out of the nightclub.

She's angry over his disloyalty.

Betrayal.

What am I to think? She's dead. He's alive. She's been dead for months now. At what point is it okay for someone who has been bereaved to move on?

I don't know the answer. But I feel my pain over Dan, and I can feel Louise's pain. If it happened before she died, as I'm sure it did, it would have been terrible for her.

But for me ... I don't care what he did before because I'm only here to be with the children and if he's a good father that's all I care about. I'm not Louise. I have no love or hate relationship with him.

The door opens, the doorknocker rattling.

Alex's skin colour rises in redness as his gaze meets mine. He doesn't look into my eyes; his gaze glances at me then darts away as he turns to the kitchen, where the children are.

I walk in, shut the door behind me and hang up my coat.

Alex is talking to the children. Cereal pours into bowls.

I breathe deeply before I join them, feeling Louise walk with me. The weight of her presence indicates that she's ready for a fight. She would walk into the room with accusations flying.

There's deep-seated hatred in the dark aura around him too. Perhaps it's Louise's hatred of him.

He leans to stroke a hand over Hope's head and kiss her temple.

When he looks at me, his skin colour lifts to the light red of embarrassment again, then his eyes dart away. 'I need to go. Hopefully, I won't be back late.' He moves past me. His façade is crumbling this morning. Everything about his manner says he feels guilty.

If he cheated during his marriage, then he must have felt guiltier then. If he can't meet my gaze, then he must barely have been able to be in the same room as Louise. That must have been horrible for her. It would have made her feel isolated and lonely. A memory of those feelings whips at me, opening my old scars, drawing my sympathy in lines of blood on my skin.

But she had the children, and parents who loved her. Why hadn't she just left him?

I don't understand her, or him.

If their marriage was so terrible, why did they stay together? For the children?

Louise breathes down my neck.

I hate to think of children being deserted. Maybe they fought over who would have the children? Or how much time they would have each?

But why kill herself, then?

Was their argument an accident after all? Were they arguing, and she climbed up on the wall?

I wish I knew. I want to know. I just want to understand. I need to silence Louise, and I don't think her noise will ever stop unless I can understand and work out what to say to her – or what she wants me to say to Alex.

For now, though, I push it all out of my head. I can't solve it, and I, Helen, am here for the children.

My children.

Shut up.

'Goodbye.' Alex walks back into the kitchen, talking to the children.

He goes to Rosie first. She's on a chair at the breakfast bar. She turns her head to present him with a cheek to kiss. This is a morning ritual that I have watched and learned by heart over the last two weeks. He walks over to Josh, pats his shoulder and then kisses the top of his head. Josh is a little man; he doesn't welcome kisses. Then Alex kisses the top of Hope's head. 'Goodbye, sweetheart.' The words are a whisper.

Rosie smiles at him; he reaches his hand out to her as she reaches out to him. Their hands hold for a moment before his slides free. 'Goodbye, darling, have a good day. Be good at school, Josh.' The last words are called back as Alex walks away. He glances at me, without any semblance of a smile. 'Have a good day.'

'Thank you.'

I walk further into the kitchen as he walks out.

The front door opens, the knocker rattles and he and his dark aura have gone.

'Good morning,' I say brightly. Ignoring the screams that echo about the room. 'How are we all?'

'Tired,' Josh moans.

'What are we doing today?' Rosie asks.

I have won over the girls; we laugh when we play every day and there's no sense of sadness surrounding Rosie, although I know she misses Louise desperately. But Josh, the man in miniature, hasn't let me in at all.

Whatever Louise wants, I want to see Josh smile and hear him laugh.

'Let's make some salt dough today – we can make things, paint them and cook them so you and Hope can keep them. Does that sound fun?'

'Yes.' Rosie's voice leaps with excitement.

'Does anyone want anything else with their breakfast?' I ask as I walk over to click the switch to put the kettle on.

I open the cupboard above the kettle, and reach up to get a cup, looking at the children. 'I'm going to make a cup of tea. Do any of you wan—?'

'Ah!' Rosie squeals as the cup slips from my hand and drops onto the granite work surface, making a horrendous china clatter as it cracks in half.

Two separate pieces roll off the surface and drop with a thud onto the floor.

'No need to worry,' I say quickly, squatting down to pick the pieces up.

'Ow!' This time the shout is mine as I lose my balance and fall. My hand lands on a piece of broken china.

'Ow,' I say more quietly.

'You're bleeding,' Rosie declares with terror in her voice.

'I'll get a plaster,' says Josh, slipping off the chair.

'Thanks, Josh. It's not bad, Rosie, just a little cut.' I put my hand under the tap and run the cold water as I reach for a sheet of paper towel to wrap around it until it stops bleeding.

Rosie is asleep on the sofa. Alex has said she rarely sleeps, but she often sleeps for me because I wear her out doing fun things. Hope is asleep in the cot upstairs. This is the time of day when I revel in how lucky I am. It is when I want to dance around the room, and sing to let all my happiness out. The girls are completely mine in the days.

The room is quiet, so quiet that Rosie's childish breaths whisper through the air.

There's no emotional screaming from Louise. She's often quiet at this time of day. But I think this is when she plots – watching, thinking and planning.

She's getting cleverer. Moving things and me as she wants to.

I look at my phone, enjoying the noise of Rosie's breaths, and without even thinking about it open Facebook and look at Robert Dowling's wall. My thumb scrolls through the posts. I'm looking at the images but not reading.

There are no recent pictures of the children; they are all of Louise when she was a child, a teenager or a young adult. *I miss this girl. I will not forget. Twenty-five years ago, our lives were perfect.* The last post reads, *I will never forgive him.*

Him ...

Alex?

Do they think it was Alex?

No one else was there except Alex.

But do they know he was there? I forgot about the Dowlings asking for witnesses weeks ago.

A rush of energy wants me to fight. Punch. Kick. Run. Scream. Pushing. Pushing.

My hands shake as I sit down. For a moment, Louise was the loudest part of me.

'Accident,' I whisper at Louise. I don't believe that Alex pushed her. Why would he have done that? He has this house and a successful business – he would not need a payout from life insurance. If their marriage was bad, he would have just left and insisted on his share of the time with the children.

There was no reason for him to push her.

But if she thinks that she was pushed ... Is that why she wants to take the children? Because he pushed her into depression, perhaps. The whole thing is tumbling back to the fact that Louise wants revenge.

What can I do to get her out of my head and out of this house, then? Because I am not going to reap revenge on her behalf. That would be the worst thing for the children.

For the next hour, I walk around the room, scrolling through Robert Dowling's Facebook posts trying to understand through the lens of Louise's eyes.

There is a tone that speaks from between the lines.

I hear it now.

They do not like Alex. Alex has always been almost non-existent in Robert Dowling's posts. The children could have no father on the scene from the way 99.9 per cent of the posts are phrased, prior to Louise's death, not just after that.

Questions begin bubbling inside me like boiling water.

They definitely had problems in their marriage, and those problems played a part in her death for whatever reason.

Rosie rolls onto her back, making a sound that means she's waking up.

I look at the time on my phone.

It is time to collect Josh anyway.

When the doorknocker rattles, questions have been bubbling in my head for hours.

The smell of pepperoni, mozzarella and freshly cooked pizza dough wafts upstairs.

The children rush downstairs ahead of me.

When I reach the top of the stairs, Alex is carrying flat cardboard boxes with the Domino's logo towards the kitchen. At least three nights a week he walks in with takeaway food.

'Pizza,' Josh shouts, jumping off the bottom step.

'Pizza,' Rosie echoes, following Josh.

'Pia,' Hope copies, bumping downstairs on her bottom.

Words pop in my head. Questions want to spit out of my mouth as the pot of curiosity keeps boiling.

'Get the plates and drinks,' Alex says to the children as they, one by one, wrap their arms about his hips and legs, building up like a rugby scrum.

'Hey, hey.' He holds the boxes full of pizza higher, his concentration consumed by the children. He might have been seeking a woman to have sex with on Saturday but his main focus in life is the children.

My children.

I have never seen him as a man who could commit murder. Never. I have watched him a lot. The only man I have seen is a good father who loves his children. I don't think I even care that he's a womaniser now. He's single. He's not made any promises to anyone that he's breaking. And most importantly the children love him. A parent's love is a precious thing.

'Go on, then, if you want tea, get the plates.'

When the children peel away, he looks at me. 'Hello. Good day?' His shop window is back in place. Confident, unruffled Alex. There's no hint of embarrassment.

'Yes. The girls have made you some baked salt-dough sculptures.'

'Thanks, I think.' There's a twitch of his lips in the corners, the biggest smile I ever get out of Alex.

Louise is screaming. It is directed at him. She spends most of the time in this house battling with me to say and do things to Alex; she rarely tries to get me to say and do things for the children. Her spirit is still here because of her love-hate relationship with Alex, and not because she wants the children.

She did not bring me here to help them, but because she could not leave things with Alex as they were.

I was shattered by Dan and stalked his social media because it was hard to let go. Receiving Louise's heart was my point of closure.

But she's stalking Alex from the other side of the grave. She needs some sort of closure. How can I give a ghost closure?

Alex is opening the pizza boxes, releasing the hot cheesy, meaty and baked dough smells.

He glances at me. 'Do you want to join us?' There's nothing abnormal about the invite. Alex invites me every time he brings takeaway food home.

I could stay – Andy's out tonight at a boys-only thing, and I have a million questions. 'Would it be rude to accept?' I walk farther into the kitchen.

'Of course not. I invited you.'

'My fiancé is out tonight.'

'Stay, then.'

Josh puts plates on the breakfast bar in front of their seats as Alex lifts the slices of pizza onto the plates.

He seems such a normal man, but the darkness surrounding him tells a tale of horror. He watched Louise die. If he didn't push her, he failed to save her. How would that feel?

There is guilt in his aura.

'Which do you prefer, cheese and tomato or pepperoni?' His lips lift at both corners to make the clearest impression of a smile that I have seen.

'Both. If no one else will go without.'

'We can accommodate that.' He lifts a slice of cheese and tomato pizza onto my plate.

'Thank you.'

'Sit down, then.'

It's strange; I thought that I had stepped into this family as deep as I wanted to go. But this is different – more intimate – as I sit up on the breakfast-bar chair beside Rosie.

Louise's emotions tell me she used to sit here.

'And pepperoni,' Alex puts the second slice on my plate, then moves the second empty box to the cooker. He brings a knife and fork back and cuts Hope's and Rosie's pizza into smaller pieces, as Josh and I lift our whole, wobbly, fragile thin-crust pizza slices and take a bite.

The questions inside my head try to break free, but I don't want to ask them while the children are listening.

Alex asks Josh and Rosie about their day.

My children. My children. My children.

Louise doesn't want me at their dinner table. It's that jealousy again, the evidence that she still loves him to some degree.

It's also evidence that he didn't push her. Why would she still love him even a little if he killed her?

The phone in my back pocket vibrates. I ignore it until we have finished eating. I take a look when Josh gets down to help Alex tidy up.

'You ok? How was your day?' Andy's checking that I'm home.

'Fine. Still at work. I stayed with the family for dinner.'

'Ok. See you later.'

'If I'm in bed kiss me when you come in.'

'Xxx Will do.'

'Xx' I add a few heart emojis and touch 'send'.

I look up to see Alex looking at me, and remember Josh talking about Susie always looking at her phone. I slide the phone into my back pocket, and smile.

Rosie climbs down from her chair and Alex leans to release the straps on Hope's highchair.

'Would you like a cup of tea before you go? Or something stronger? Wine? Beer? I'm going to have a beer,' he says as he lifts Hope and puts her down on the floor so she can follow Josh and Rosie out of the room. 'It would be good to discuss how the girls are settling with you.'

'A beer sounds great.'

He turns to the fridge and returns with two brown bottles, holding one out across the breakfast bar.

'Thank you.' I take the bottle and take a sip to clear the froth from the top.

He puts his down on the black work surface and opens the dishwasher.

'How did your wife die?' The words spit out from my boiling pot of curiosity.

He straightens up, his movement stiff, controlled, and breathes in deep. He looks at me, throwing an electric charge, then he looks away and picks up a dirty plate. 'She fell from a car park.'

'Fell.' I lift my voice and rock back, acting shocked.

He loads a plate into the dishwasher. Not looking at me.

'How?'

There's another significant intake of air, and he straightens, his gaze clashing with mine. 'I'd rather not talk about it, Helen.' He turns away and picks up another dirty plate from the stack Josh put on the side.

'Sorry. I'm just thinking of the children, if I can help them cope better. I didn't have a mother or father – my brother and I were in care. I know what grief feels like.'

'I'm sorry.' He's still busy loading the dishwasher.

'It's just … It's strange there are no pictures of her. The children must want to see her?'

'She didn't like herself in pictures. I can't give them what I don't have. There aren't any.'

Except there is one picture. That he keeps in his room.

'Do you think the children are coping? Rosie draws that picture of you both all the time …'

He closes the dishwasher; the china rattles as it shuts. He picks up his beer and his gaze penetrates me with the strength of his scrutiny as he leans a hip against the kitchen work surface. 'I presume, as you have seen that picture, you know they were there? I probably should have warned you of that.'

'It must have been awful.'

'That's an understatement.'

I want to smash the shop windows and push through the door. I want to see what's inside. He's a puzzle and I like puzzles, and maybe, if I work him out, I can work out what would be a possible conclusion for Louise.

I sip my beer, holding onto his gaze. 'Did you have a good marriage?'

The beer bottle pulls away from his lips, in a sudden, sharp movement. 'I don't think that has anything to do with you looking after the children.'

'Sorry.'

'I know the children are struggling. But I'm doing what I can.' His beer bottle moves around, expressing his words. Then he takes long draws from the bottle.

'Did you argue that day?' I can't help myself. 'Is that why Rosie—?'

'It's none of your business, really, but, yes, we argued. We argued a lot.'

How did she fall? Why?

He puts his bottle down on the side. It's empty already. 'I better go up and start getting the children ready for bed.'

'My fiancé isn't going to be home until late so I can stay and help get the girls ready for bed, if you and Josh want some time together?'

'Are you sure?'

'Of course.' The best gift I can give Josh is his father.

'I'll pay you.'

I'm not here for your money.

'Come on.' Alex moves away from the side in the kitchen. I slide off the chair. Our paths meet near the end of the breakfast bar. His lips lift; it's almost a smile.

I smile, as inside I laugh.

Louise rushes through me, sweeping her anger and bitterness through my heart. The emotions overwhelming for a moment.

I cough, choking as I fight to catch my breath.

Alex's palm rests on my shoulder. 'Are you all right?'

'I'll just get a glass of water, then I'll follow you up.'

'Okay.' His hand slides from my shoulder, and I hear his heavier footsteps jog up the stairs.

'Girls,' he calls. 'Rosie. Hope. Bath time. Helen has said she'll help you have a bath tonight. Is that okay?'

The sound of their feet on the floor above is the answer.

When I reach the landing, Rosie, Hope and Alex are waiting for me.

Rosie looks at me, her eyes saying she might like me, but I can't replace her father.

Susie must have bathed them at least sometimes, though.

'I'll go on up to the bathroom and start running the bath,' I say to Alex.

He nods.

I smile at Rosie as I walk past.

'Come on, then, double piggyback.' Alex squats.

As I climb the stairs I watch Rosie wrap her arms around his neck and climb onto his back, clinging like a little monkey. While Hope lifts her arms in front of him. 'M too. M too. M too. M.' He holds her under the arms and picks her up as he straightens. Rosie's arms brace his neck as Hope settles in tight against his chest, her arms wrapped the other way around his neck.

The balancing act does not look safe, and both girls are giggling as he starts up the stairs with one forearm in front of him under Hope's bottom, and the other twisted behind him under Rosie's bottom. 'Here we go.'

I hurry to the top to get out of the way.

The door to the bathroom is shut, but, beyond it, the door into Josh's room stands open. The screech of car wheels reaches into the hallway.

I walk farther on, close to the bannister, to look at Josh. He's sitting on the bed, his fingers and thumbs working a control for a PlayStation.

'Hurry up, Daddy, I'm slipping.'

I turn and open the bathroom door as Alex reaches the landing and turns towards the girls' bedroom.

Squeals of glee and giggles pursue me into the bathroom. I imagine he dropped the girls onto Rosie's bed.

I turn on the hot and cold taps. The stream of water falls into the deep cast-iron roll-top bath with a reverberating splatter, catching the light and sending patterns across the white and black tiles surrounding the bathroom.

I check the water temperature with my fingertips and adjust the cold tap a little as I listen to Alex talking in the girls' room. Contrasting aggressive sounds come from Josh's game.

When I go into the bedroom to get the girls, Hope is lying on the changing table as Alex removes her soiled nappy.

She's playing with a plastic duck, looking at that, not him. He lifts her legs and wipes her bottom off, then throws the nappy and wipes into a pedal bin beside the table. 'There, you are good to go for your bath.'

As he lifts Hope down his gaze travels to Rosie, but it catches on me. For an instant.

I smile.

His lips twitch with an acknowledging movement before his gaze falls to Rosie.

This is ten times more intimate than my position at the dinner table. I'm walking deeper and deeper into Louise's life. Wading into a sea that swells with waves of various heights depending on Louise's mood. I feel as though one day, if I'm not careful, this is going to drown me.

'Come on, then.' I raise a hand, encouraging the girls to come with me.

Rosie is stripping off, throwing her knickers onto the disorderly pile on the floor.

'Take your Flounder into the bath with you and show Helen where your bubble bath is,' Alex says. 'Then you can play.'

When we get into the bathroom Rosie walks across to show me the shelf where the bottle of bubble bath is. 'It's there.'

'Thank you,' Alex says from the door. I look back as I realise he's talking to me.

I smile, again, the smile reaching out like a touch on a shoulder. He's the gatekeeper, and he's a good father, no matter what else.

Now I can be just like their mother.

My children. Mine.

'Shall we mix up the bubbles?' I say as I reach for the bright orange bottle. 'I'll pour a little of this magic liquid under the running water.'

'It's not magic,' Rosie says in answer to my conspiratorial tone, but she is smiling broadly.

'Are you sure ...?' Piles of bubbles grow below the running tap.

Alex's deep voice opens a conversation in Josh's room.

'Bubbells,' Hope says as I hold her under the arms and lift her in.

'Yes, sweetie, bubbles.'

I lift Rosie in.

My children.

Hope slips as she tries to sit and falls back. I catch her, my hand bracing her head in the moment before it would have hit the side of the bath.

'Let's mix up the magic potion,' I say as I help Hope sit.

Inside me, panic is flaring.

Would Louise have done that? Pushed her own daughter?

The conversation next door has become bursts of exclamations and comments about the game they're playing.

Surely, she would never want to hurt the children?

I kneel beside the bath and play with Hope and her duck and Rosie and her plastic fish.

Louise is in every corner of the bathroom, screaming. Wanting to be heard. Hating that I'm here.

I'm not listening. In my head, I have covered my ears. I have no empathy for a woman who would hurt her child.

My children.

Chapter 37

The fifth Sunday of my new life.

M y phone trembles and rings on the bedside table.
I lift my head from Andy's naked chest and reach for
it, imagining that I'll see Chloe's name on the screen. She's
coming to Bath tonight with her new boyfriend, who we haven't
yet met. She's on about number thirty-third time lucky. 'Hi.' I
rub the sleep from my eyes.

'Hello, Helen.' At the sound of Alex's voice, I automatically
sit up, the duvet falling below my breasts.

'Hello, sorry, I thought you were someone else.'

'Sorry to disturb you on a Sunday.'

Andy's fingertips stroke down my back, and he mouths, Who
is it?

My boss, I mouth back. 'How can I help?'

'I need someone to look after the children tonight. I am doing
an overnight shoot. My parents were coming for the weekend
but Mum slipped on the ice outside the back door and she's
broken her ankle. I asked my neighbour, but she's busy.' His
urgency and stress press through the phone. 'I can't pull out of
this. The magazine's spent thousands setting it up. It'll ruin my
business if I let them down over child-minding problems.'

'I'm sorry to hear about your mum.' I'm wasting time. Thinking. I'm busy tonight, but spending a night in the house will give me more time with Josh and I don't spend enough time with him. Louise's life is pulling me away from my own. But I can spend a day with Chloe any time.

'If you can't do it, I suppose I could try and get through to the agency. But, of course, they're not open today ...'

I breathe in, holding the duvet up to my breasts, covering the aggressive-looking operation scar. 'Yes. Okay. What time?'

'Nine this evening. The sofa in the kitchen area has a fold-out bed; I'll put some bedding out for you. All you'll need is an overnight bag.'

'All right, I'll be there for nine. See you later.'

'Thank you. You are a lifesaver. Goodbye.'

Bitch. Bitch. Bitch. The density of the air in the bedroom increases – an incoming thunderstorm.

I sense sharp strokes tearing at my skin. Louise trying to rip me open from the inside and the outside.

She was my lifesaver.

But she destroyed her children's lives when she chose to climb up onto that wall. And she did not save my life by choice, but rather sought to destroy her own, as well as the lives of her family.

My feelings of empathy for her have completely died.

I put the phone back on the side.

'Later?' Andy queries as he turns to get out of bed. 'What did you agree to?'

'He needs someone to look after the children overnight, tonight. I'm going to go around there at nine and sleep over.'

He's picked his jeans up from a chair; the belt buckle, which is still threaded through the waistband, jangles as he pulls his jeans on. 'We're going out tonight.'

'I can rearrange it.'

He secures the button of his jeans and pulls up the zip. 'Rearrange it?' His eyebrows lift with a sarcastic expression as he does up his belt then leans to pick up a long-sleeved T-shirt. 'It's a bit unfair to Chloe. This is a big deal for her, and her fella. How many times did you say to me how important Chloe is to you, and if I did not get on with her we wouldn't work?' His arms slide into the sleeves and then he pulls the T-shirt over his head.

'I know. But she understands how important the children are.' I push the duvet away and get up to go into the bathroom and wash.

'I would have thought that you would be more interested in planning your wedding with your bridesmaid. Most women would be.'

'He has a job he can't cancel. The children know me. I would rather I'm there than a stranger. If they can't have their father, I'm the next best thing.'

Andy moves forward suddenly, blocks my path and holds my elbow. 'That family is just your job. Sometimes, the way you talk about them, it's as if you think they are your children; your phone is full of pictures of them.' He pauses, breathing in. 'You know I'm open to having a baby.'

Emotions that are so deep they might drown me sweep over my head. 'I know.' My arms and legs are flailing. He's offering me everything that I've ever wanted. But it's knocked me off my feet, because now I have another family to think about. I already have children.

'We can start trying before the wedding,' he adds.

The pressure in my chest wants to blow my heart to pieces – with joy. I see colours, streamers and confetti, dancing around me. I can have both. I can have my own child and Louise's. 'Can we start trying now?'

He nods, his hand sliding up from my elbow to embrace my upper arm, and we kiss, sealing the bargain.

As he pulls away his hand slips to pat my bottom. 'Ring Chloe, tell her to come earlier if she can. You can spend the afternoon with her and we can have dinner with them.'

'Thank you for understanding.'

'I'm just hoping this obsession with someone else's children will end when we have our own. I want us to come first in your heart.'

My palms press against his cheeks and I kiss his lips. I want my family and Louise's.

Bitch.

'I'll make you a cup of tea, while you have a shower,' he says when he pulls away.

'Thank you.'

When I walk into the living area later, there's a full mug of steaming tea on the table, with a plate of buttered toast beside it, and the medicine bottle and packets are there on the side too.

He puts my breakfast out for me most mornings like this.

I was never meant to marry Dan; Andy and I were, at some point in the creation of the universe, made for each other. And, oddly, not only am I alive now because of Louise, but I would never have come to Bath and found him if not for Louise. I owe her for more than just a heart.

But that knowledge doesn't stop my impatience with her screaming and selfish anger.

I hear nothing but jealousy.

Chapter 38

Alex takes his coat off the hook as I stand on the second stair, hands braced in the back pockets of my jeans, my outdoor things already hung up and my overnight bag left beneath the coat hooks.

'It's really cold outside tonight. The weather on the news said it'll snow. Where's the shoot?'

'In the gardens of an old house about two-hours' drive away. And it's already started snowing there. The magazine is thrilled by the idea of the models in evening dresses with moonlight reflecting off bright white, snow-covered lawns. The models aren't going to be as pleased. I hope they have hot coffee and blankets.'

I am unsure how to answer, so I smile.

'Thank you again for this,' he says. 'You can't imagine how grateful I am. I'll see you in the morning. I should be back by nine.' He turns to open the door.

There's a stray hair on the shoulder of his leather jacket. I feel like stepping forward and brushing it off, then kissing his cheek in parting, as I might with Andy. I rigidly withhold the silly urge, pressing my hands deeper into my pockets. 'Goodbye.'

That urge must have come from Louise, an echo of her past, before things went wrong.

'Goodnight,' he says before closing the door, deliberately less vigorously than normal so the knocker doesn't rattle as much.

I breathe in. His aftershave is hovering in the air. For once he shaved, and his hair was wet from the shower.

It feels like another step deeper, to be here at night. Like the other day when I stayed late. I'm not just caring for the children, I have breached their family life. I'm living the way I always wanted to live. Loving and being loved – I do think the girls love me.

There are no lights on down here, but light is falling down the stairs from the first-floor landing. The children are in bed, and the house is completely quiet.

The silence means Louise's racket is deafening, and she hates the idea of me staying the night. She hates any interaction I have with Alex, and she hates it that the girls want me here.

I sigh out a breath, turn and walk upstairs, my socks slipping on the wooden treads.

'What can I do?' I whisper at Louise. 'You've gone. You need to go. You need to move on and find peace.' My feet brush quietly across the landing and over the soft rug in the living room. I drop down onto the sofa.

I reach out and pour some of the red wine from the bottle Alex has left open for me into the glass on the coffee table: The table Rosie leans on to draw her daily picture of her mother's death.

Louise's energy in this space is telling me that I should be as angry as she is. She doesn't understand why I'm not angry with Alex.

'Because he's a good father.'

Her screaming intensifies, taking on a sinister tone.

She invades my thoughts most of the time. Making me fight to hear what I'm saying to myself over whatever she is trying to say.

I wish she would go. I want my mind back to myself.

I lean back in the chair, cross my legs, sip the wine and talk to her, because if I can't enjoy my own thoughts I may as well try to converse with her and persuade her to go. 'Maybe Alex did cheat on you. Maybe he was a bad husband. But he's a good father. You should let your anger go. I know it must have been awful at the time. But it doesn't matter now. You chose to leave. This is what it is now.'

Her noise grows in tempo. She's angrier with me. The sound vibrates through my body.

I turn the TV up as loud as I dare without risking waking the children on the floor above.

Alex went into the children's rooms, to kiss them goodbye, while I waited down here. He confirmed that they were asleep. I'll go up and look again in a little while.

I sip the wine, repeatedly, until I have drunk two glasses' worth. I screw the cap on the bottle to stop me being tempted to drink more. I'm here to look after the children. I don't want to be drunk if they wake up.

Plus, the wine is drawing my mind to the noise that Louise is making, rather than helping to drown her out.

'I don't even know what you think I can do?'

There's no answer. She hasn't learned how to control her energy enough to hold a conversation with me. Or she doesn't want to hold a conversation with me.

'I think he had an affair. I think he had an affair, you argued and, somehow, you fell.'

I still don't understand how it could have been an accident, but I can't adjust my mind to the fact that she chose to leave the children either, and I don't believe that Alex would have picked her up and thrown her over the wall.

'Was it an accident, or did you deliberately fall? But if you killed yourself, why are you angry? And how could you do that to your children? They were watching! You're making me angry.' I thrust the words out across the room. 'I'm not angry with Alex – he can live his life however he wants to if he doesn't hurt the children. But I'm angry with you. His infidelity is his problem. You've left him to live with the guilt. But you left the children too.'

The atmosphere in the living room is thick with Louise's temper storm.

I press the off button on the television controls, and stand.

I'll go to bed. Louise can't growl and shout at me when I'm asleep.

I lean forward to leave the controls on the coffee table and get up, but halt in mid-movement because there's someone with me. Beside the sofa. The TV control drops out of my hand as my heart jumps and I turn to my left to look. I haven't—

Of course, there's no one there.

Anxiety pulses in my blood, pushing the rhythm of my heartbeat all the way to my fingertips. The figure was as human as me for a moment.

I walk out of the room to look along the landing and upstairs. There's no one there and no sound that suggests a person has run away. A spirit. Louise.

The shadowy figure was as tall as me.

Has she learned to present herself in some sort of form?

'Louise. You need to let your children go,' I say as I turn the hall light on and the living-room light off. I refuse to let her know she's scared me.

I walk downstairs, to get my overnight bag, the blood pulsing wildly through the arteries of my body and air pulling quickly and unsteadily into my lungs.

Alex told me to use his bathroom on the attic floor rather than risk waking the children, but I stop on the second floor, put my bag down and look into the girls' room.

They have a night-light, spreading a moonlight-like soft glow around the room. The air smells of their bubble bath and shampoo. They're tucked under the covers, their breaths quiet and relaxed. I don't go nearer, to avoid disturbing them.

Josh's bedroom is dark but in the light on the landing I can see his silhouette under tousled bedcovers. His breathing is noisy, as if he's dreaming.

I pick up the bag, walk on towards the door at the end of the landing and turn the cold brass door handle.

A low groan comes from Josh's bedroom.

'Help!' The shout rings into the hall, with a piercing sound of panic.

The bag falls from my hand as I turn back.

'Josh. Josh.' He's breathing quickly.

When I look in his room, he's sitting in the bed, curled over, his hands holding his head.

'Was it a bad dream?' I walk in without asking permission.

His hands fall, his head lifts and he looks at me, shrouded in shadows, his eyes black. A young man looks at me through the eyes of a small boy.

'Would you like to talk about it?'

'No.' His head shakes.

'Talking can help.' This man-child is sitting here in blue and red Spiderman pyjamas that tell the truth about his age. I walk closer, smiling slightly. My heart yelling, Please like me, Josh.

My children.

Then love them, or leave them!

'Do you want a drink?'

'No. Thank you.'

His words might be wrapped in bristly thorns but he's not told me to leave him alone, so I dare the last few paces to reach his bed. 'Is it okay if I sit down?'

'Yes.'

And now I know the bad dream has shaken him, because he doesn't want to be alone. He's just a boy.

The mattress dips beneath me as I sit. 'Do you have many bad dreams?' I assume the dream was about Louise.

'Yes.'

'What do you normally do when you have a bad dream?'

'Sometimes I go upstairs and sleep with Dad.'

'It must be difficult ...' I say, leaving the end of the sentence open in the hope he'll fill in what is difficult.

He doesn't.

After a moment of awkward silence, I stand. There's no benefit in pushing him into talking. 'I was just going to bed, so if you have another dream and you need me, I'll be downstairs.'

'Dad said you're sleeping on the kitchen sofa.'

'Yes.'

Josh slides down under the duvet. I lean further down instinctively, lifting the rumpled duvet over his shoulders and straightening it. Longing to kiss his forehead. 'Shall I leave the hall light on for you in case you want to come downstairs?'

He shakes his head.

'Goodnight, then. I hope you sleep better this time.'

As I leave the room there's a shadowy figure at my shoulder. I look over but, again, there's no one there.

Louise is learning all the time in her spirit world.

A sigh escapes as I walk to the door for the stairs up to Alex's room. Josh deserves a chance to move past his mother's death.

I turn the cold door handle and pull the door open.

The light switch is on the wall in the small square of landing. The narrow stairs go up and down. Josh said that this staircase goes all the way down to the basement flat, but the door must be locked down there.

There's a weight on my shoulders as I climb the stairs – a pressure that's trying to prevent me from climbing any farther. I hold the handrail. Afraid that she'll try to push me. She wants to get rid of me.

Louise has brought me to this house and now she doesn't want me here.

'I don't understand you,' I whisper.

Before I came into this house Louise's presence was full of sadness and called for help – now it's an ominous threat. I feel as though I was lured here to perform a despicable act. She feels evil.

What if she pushed Alex when they were on top of the car park? Then, would Alex have pushed her back? But even a hard push would not have toppled her over that wall. He can't have just pushed her in the way Rosie keeps drawing. He would have had to lift her. But then Rosie never draws the wall. Three-year-olds do not capture that sort of detail.

Josh knows what happened that day, and he has probably just dreamed about it. Poor child. I won't ask him. He wouldn't want to talk to me.

'You should be comforting your son and making life easier

for him, not raging at me.' Talking to Louise reduces the fear.

My words resonate in the narrow steep staircase.

If I were Louise, all that I would want is for my children to be happy. Even if I hated their father.

At the top of the stairs there's a door on the left. It creaks when I open it. This house is full of creaky doors and floorboards. I know the house is old, but it's as though it's trying to frighten me too.

The long master bedroom is dressed in moonlight that reaches in through two dormer windows and the room is decorated, like much of the rest of the house, in black and white, with wide black and white stripes painted on the walls. The lack of colour gives the space an eery leer.

A queen-size double bed stands on the opposite side of the room to the windows. The headboard is black, the duvet white.

Even the top of the bedside chest is black granite and the wooden cupboard underneath white.

The door creaks behind me. I look back, thinking someone is there again. No one is. I walk back and shut the door, leaving the stair-light on. Now the light in the room is a line around the door behind me and moonlight.

I carry my bag to the far side of the room, where I can see the open door into the en suite.

It's cold in here, but the window has been left open by a couple of centimetres.

Water splashes into the sink as I release the zip of my bag. I clean my teeth, watching myself in the mirror. But then my eyes are drawn away from my image to an image beside me. A face. A transparent woman's face.

When I turn to look, fooled into believing Louise is there, again, the toothpaste drips from my mouth onto the black floor-tiles.

A clattering, then shattering sounds, has me turning the other way. The other mirror has fallen off the shelf into the sink.

Seven years' bad luck.

But I did not touch it. I have not been near it.

Louise is walking all around the house tonight, playing poltergeist.

I lean over the sink and spit out the toothpaste, rinse my mouth with cold water from the tap, then wipe the toothpaste off the floor with toilet paper. I pick the mirror up out of the other sink and put it on the granite top.

There are elongated, triangular shards of broken mirror in the sink. I lift them out one by one. A quick burst of pain lances into my finger as one of the fragments pierces my skin. A round bulb of scarlet blood grows on my fingertip and then the blood is staining the white sink, and smearing the pieces of mirror.

Is Louise's DNA mingled in with mine in that blood?

I grasp the loo roll, pull off a few more sheets and wrap them tightly around my finger. Then I finish moving the shards of the mirror onto the side and turn the tap on to rinse away the blood.

When I walk back into the bedroom, it is colder. But the central heating must have switched off.

My heart drums as I look at the bed where Louise once lay night after night, when she had my heart. I can't help myself. I put the bag on the bed. The scent of lavender rises as I walk over to the bedside chest. If the picture of Louise is kept in here, I imagine it will be in a drawer in a bedside chest.

As I sit on the bed I remember that the one-night-stand woman has been in this bed too, and, as I saw him at the club watching her, perhaps it means she's been here more than once.

I lean and turn the bedside lamp on, then open the top drawer. There's nothing in there except for an orange patterned and scented paper drawer-liner. There is nothing in any of the drawers.

Was this Louise's side of the bed?

I walk around to the other side of the bed, sit down and open the top drawer of the bedside chest.

It's there. The picture. He keeps it beside him at night, within reach.

She looks happy. They look happy. But it was taken a long time ago.

Alex is still looking back to this; what does that tell me?

I turn the picture over. There's nothing on the back to say when or where it was taken.

I put it back in the drawer. The other items in the drawer I think are keepsakes. I pick up a necklace. There's a hinge on the silver pendant. It's a small locket. I open it. Inside there's a tiny picture of two very young blond children with Alex. I know then I am touching something that has rested against Louise's skin, probably for years.

Bitch!

My body jolts in a jump when she screams the accusation. I close the locket and put it away.

Mine!

There's a small pebble in the shape of a heart lying next to the picture. My thumb rubs over the smooth surface as I pick that up and I lift it to my nose; it smells of the sea. It was picked up on a beach.

There's an old-style pound coin in the drawer too. It could just be a discarded thing in anyone's drawer but my eyes focus on the date it was minted: 1990. It represents some sort of memory. If only a heart carried memory, then I would know everything.

The drawer also contains a small troll toy with orange hair, an old Comic Relief red nose and a sentiments wallet card.

I put the pebble back and pick up the plastic wallet card.

My husband ...

My best friend
My pillar to lean on
My place to run to
My reason to smile
My inspiration
I love you

A bang somewhere downstairs makes me throw the credit-card-sized sentiment back into the drawer and push the drawer shut. My heart and breathing are rushing again as I turn off the lamp. My nerves are humming.

There's a double duvet and a pillow on the sofa in the kitchen. Alex said the base of the sofa would pull out, but it is a wide sofa and I'll be fine stretched out on it without fiddling around to make it up.

A car passes the house in the street outside; the light thrown by the car's headlights spins around the kitchen walls as it stops at the end of the street and turns.

I put my bag down. I can't hear Louise now. There are only the noises from the people getting out of the car outside.

I spread the double duvet out on the sofa, folding it in half so it will be a mattress and a cover. Then lie down and pull the pillow under my head.

There's no more noise in the room, none from Louise and none from the street.

My buzzing brain listens to the silence, exploring it, trying to find sound. Until I do hear a sound. Music. A very quiet, slow song, coming from below, from the basement flat.

I listen, and try to keep my mind focused on positive things, on the children. I think about them one by one, and recall every special moment with Rosie and Hope, as new ideas of things to do gather in my mind.

Chapter 39

The fifth Monday of my new life.

'Daddy! Daddy!'

Rosie's shouts drag me from other thoughts and out from under the duvet into a kitchen that's illuminated by the early daylight. 'Rosie,' I shout as I stand. Her feet are running along the landing above. 'Rosie, down here.'

'Rosie!' Josh's yell comes from the second floor.

Hope is crying.

'Daddy!' Rosie calls again, still looking for him on the floor above.

She's at the top of the stairs when I walk into the hall.

'Rosie. Daddy's at work.' Josh's voice lowers in pitch with each word as his feet thunder down the stairs from the second to the first floor. But Rosie has already remembered.

Her eyes and expression tell me I'm not who she wants, but she knows why I'm here.

'Good morning.' I climb the stairs. 'Were you frightened?'

'I thought Daddy had gone.'

'It's okay.' Josh reaches her before me. His arms surround her. The little Spiderman superhero and the small girl in the oversized T-shirt. They're a picture of the lost children from Peter Pan.

I'm sure Simon and I presented the same picture as children.

The shadows and movements in the house last night fill my consciousness as Louise's energy presses on top of me like a ton weight. With the presence of a black, stalking panther, hiding in the shadows, waiting for the moment to leap.

She doesn't want me to go to them. She wants me to leave them as they are, with just each other for comfort.

Louise, stop hurting them. Help them move on and move on yourself.

I stop halfway up the stairs. Not because Louise is trying to make me, but because Rosie wants her brother in this moment, not me. She is shutting me out of their family.

I glance at the finger wrapped up in bloodstained toilet paper. If I have Louise's DNA I have theirs. I am physically connected to them – a family member.

My children!

A shadow wraps around them. Or rather it's not a shadow, but I can see it, because their auras fade slightly, smothered by Louise. It's not an embrace, it's a barricade to keep me away.

I climb two more steps, afraid that Louise doesn't mean well, that she might harm the children in some way. 'Rosie ...'

Rosie releases herself from her brother's hug. 'I went to get Daddy because Hope is crying, but he wasn't there. I forgot he went away.'

I forgot to take the baby monitor from his room. He told me it was in there. 'Hope, darling,' I call upstairs in a light voice as Josh moves out of my way.

My hand rests on the bannister and slides over the wood as I walk along the landing and then climb to the next floor. 'Hope.'

'She'll want her bottle,' Josh calls. 'I'll make it.'

I look over the bannister. 'Thank you.' His gaze meets mine.

After last night, we have an understanding. He smiles before turning away.

'Hope. I'm coming.'

Her wails become louder, not quieter.

I run up the steps.

'Hello,' I say as I walk into the room, greeted by a tear-streaked face that's a picture of misery. 'What's the matter, sweetheart?' But I know the matter – the room smells of the matter; she needs a nappy change.

Josh and Rosie join me in the room while I change Hope. Josh puts the warmed bottle near me, and then finds her a clean Babygro.

As I dress Hope she looks past my hip, watching Josh and Rosie, with a smile dancing on her lips. Josh plays around making faces at her.

'I'll take her down to get breakfast,' Josh says, reaching to take Hope as soon as she's dressed. She rolls to her side and reaches for him to lift her off the changing mat. He talks to her as he hands her the milk to hold herself. She starts drinking as he carries her away – the little superhero.

These are wonderful children. Let them heal here, with their father. Leave them in peace, Louise.

'Josh,' I say when I join them in the kitchen. He stops and looks up. 'Will you be all right if I wash and change quickly?' He nods at me and turns away.

After a sleepless night, I need a shower to revitalise. I'm tired and have a whole day to get through with the girls.

The narrow stairs that lead to Alex's room in the attic have a different feeling in the day. There's a mottled tunnel-light in the ceiling that stops the space from feeling so oppressive.

In the en suite, I lock the door and strip as I stare at the pieces of broken mirror on the side. It is a reminder that feels like a threat.

I don't know how she moved that mirror.

I shower quickly using Alex's soap. He's left a folded white towel out on the side for me. There's a bloodstain from the cut on my finger marring the perfect white.

When I reach the kitchen, the children are sitting around the breakfast bar in their pyjamas, Hope strapped into her highchair, eating cereal. The room smells of toast.

All I want to do is care for these children and help them come to terms with the loss of their mother. My mind is buzzing like a bee moving from flower to flower, trying to think of ways to help them.

You must leave them alone, Louise. You are not helping.

She descends in a weight of emotion, screaming and clawing.

When the doorknocker rattles, announcing Alex's return, the children are in the middle of rushing to get dressed, to take Josh to school.

We are late. They usually dress before breakfast, but I broke their routine and like a pile of cards the morning plan has collapsed.

'Dad!' Josh shouts first and runs off. He's the only one who's completely dressed, but he's dressed himself.

'Daddy.' Rosie's foot pulls free from the pair of tights I am trying to get her into and she follows her brother.

'Dadee. Dadee.' Hope runs away, still dressed in her Babygro. My plan is to put her in the pushchair dressed like that and wrapped up in her winter onesie.

'Help Hope on the stairs,' I call after them. She has two flights to bump down.

I gather up the remains of the clothing that I am trying to dress Rosie in and take it with me. I offer to pick Hope up on the way past but she refuses help, concentrating on achieving the task alone.

'What a lovely greeting,' Alex welcomes them.

'I smell donuts,' Josh shouts as he leaps from the bottom step.

'Fresh, warm donuts,' Alex confirms. The brown paper bag in his left hand rustles as he lifts it, looking at his watch. 'There's just time to eat one before I take you to school.' He looks at me. 'You can stay to share the donuts or head straight off. I'll look after the girls today.'

'Are you sure? You haven't had any sleep.'

'We'll be all right. We can lie on the sofa and binge watch Disney movies.'

So, I am cast out of the family again, an employee put in her place. The memories and emotions of foster parents taking us in and passing us on sweep back into me.

'It didn't snow here, then ...' he says as he gives Josh the bag of donuts and picks Hope up.

I haven't looked outside.

'We had about three inches. Enough to create a good effect in the pictures.'

I nod.

The donut bag is put in the middle of the breakfast bar, and the children climb onto the seats to help themselves.

Alex walks to a cupboard to fetch plates.

Louise stands at my shoulder laughing because Alex is sending me away.

But I have Andy at home. My mind was absorbed in Louise's life last night, but I have my other life to return to.

Alex puts the plates down in front of the children then walks across the room, around me. 'Would you like tea?' he asks as he passes.

I turn, my gaze following him. 'No. Thank you. I'll leave you to it.'

Chapter 40

The fifth Tuesday of my new life.

The alarm clock beside the bed is ringing. I reach out to press the button to stop it.

I have slept as heavily as a stone.

Andy isn't in the bed but the shower's running.

I throw back the duvet and get up. 'Andy.'

'Yeah?' he answers through the bathroom door.

'Do you want a cup of tea?'

'Please.'

I need something to get my brain going this morning; it still feels dense and heavy. As I walk into the kitchen my gaze turns to my tablets. My energy, thoughts and emotions are swinging all over the place lately. But I have been taking my medicine.

I suppose, it's because of Louise. Because her spirit is draining and attacking at the same time. Pulling my mind in a dozen directions.

A ringtone reaches through the apartment. It takes a couple of seconds for my still-tired brain to realise that it's my ringtone.

I can't remember where I left my phone. It's not in the kitchen – that's the only thing I do know. The noise is louder but still muffled in the living room. It's coming from somewhere near the door. It must be in my coat that's hanging there. It rings and rings as I search through the pockets, checking the same pocket twice. It will ring off in a minute.

'Ah.' I find the phone in the second that the ringtone dies.

Recent calls. Alex.

My heartbeat leaps into the quick pace of a shoe-tapping Irish dance. I touch the number to call back. It rings twice.

'Hello.'

'Hello, Alex, you called?'

'Yes. I wanted to let you know you don't need to come today. We're having a snow day.'

'A snow day?'

'You haven't opened the curtains yet, have you?'

'No.'

'There's about eight inches in the park here. It's the first time the children have seen snow this deep. I'm meant to be in Bristol but trains aren't running yet, so I've cancelled my booking, and Josh's school has shut for the day. We are hunting out the sledge and taking it up to the Royal Victoria Park.'

My head nods as if he can see that. But it's not with agreement. For the second day he's showing me that I'm not included in the family, that at any moment he can shut me out of the children's lives.

A sigh escapes.

'Of course, I'll pay you,' he says, insulting me.

'You don't have to.'

'Is Helen coming?' Rosie's shout rings in the background.

'Ellen,' Hope's high-pitched echo squeals.

'The other option is, you could come and play too if you want to be part of a snowball fight, boys against girls?'

Yes. 'Yes, please.'

'If you want to make some first footprints in the snow with us, you'll have to be quick – we are nearly ready to go out.'

'Okay.' A smile pulls my lips. 'I'm coming.' Just try to stop me from playing with the children in the snow.

He ends the call as Andy walks into the room, with one towel hanging around his waist and another in his hand, rubbing his hair.

'Who was that?'

'Alex. It's snowed. Have you looked? He's staying at home but he said I can go over anyway and help entertain the children in the snow.'

'When he's there?' His eyebrows lift and fall.

'He has three children, including one toddler. It'll be easier with someone to help.'

His eyebrows lift and fall again, and the hand drying his hair drops. He walks past me, his bare feet making no sound on the carpet as he goes over to look out of the window. 'Yes, it has snowed. I better ring and check the office is opening.' He looks back at me. 'Maybe we should have our own snow day?'

My palm presses against his damp chest, to stop him from coming closer and cuddling me. 'I want to play with the children. I've never played with children in snow like this.'

His eyebrows descend into a v as his brow creases with a frown. 'We'll have children to play in the snow with in the future.'

'I know. But that isn't today. Let me go and play in the snow. You know how many years I was trapped indoors.'

His next expression is a sigh of acceptance. 'Okay, but when you've finished playing with the children give me a ring, and I'll take you on for a snowball fight.'

My hand slips off his skin, my heart leaping as I embrace him. His wet chest dampens my pyjama top.

Chapter 41

The sixth Saturday of my new life.

Thousands of white snowdrop flower-heads form a carpet over the lawn in the London park that Andy and I are walking through. The sky is blue above us and the park is beautiful. 'Wait a moment.' My hand slips out of Andy's. I can't help it. I want to look. I squat down and capture a single white flower between my finger and thumb.

The structure of the dainty flowers has always fascinated me, and I'm pulled into a moment of mindfulness that makes me appreciate the world I'm living in, the life I've got.

I look at Andy. 'It's pretty.'

He leans down, smiling. 'Yes. Very pretty.'

I've been enjoying life a lot recently, smiling a lot.

We walk along holding hands – the closer we come to the wedding, the happier I'm becoming. Excitement is making my cheeks ache from smiling so much, and my heart plays a constant happy rhythm.

I've started thinking of Louise's noise like a form of tinnitus. Just a constant noise I must learn to ignore. I must let her go – even if she can't let go.

Everything else just keeps getting better. I'm closer to Josh since the snow day and I've stayed for dinner once more and played a game with them all afterwards.

As I straighten up Andy leans down lower and picks a single snowdrop. He straightens and slides the flower into the hair behind my ear, with a smile, then presses a kiss on my lips.

We are a couple from a movie most of the time now. Perfect. Too perfect perhaps.

Andy's hand embraces mine and he pulls me into walking. 'Your brother is going to wonder where we've got to.'

I only smile in answer while my other hand slides my handbag higher on my shoulder.

I have pictures of pageboy outfits in my bag, for the boys to agree which one they will be willing to wear. I also have pictures of the dress I want Chloe to wear, and some fabric samples to agree colours. It's exciting.

I'm getting married!

We are getting married.

I swing Andy's hand, as I would if I were holding Rosie's. He looks across and laughs.

When we reach Simon and Mim's house, he knocks on the door and Simon answers.

'Hell—o.'

I wrap my arms around him before he can get the greeting out.

His arms envelop me in return and hold tight, squeezing.

'I missed you,' I say against his shoulder.

'Auntie Helen.' The shout comes from behind Simon.

I bend to hug the boys, but not so far down now; for five-year-olds they're tall and they get taller every time I visit.

'We have a trampoline in the garden. Will you come and play?'

'A trampoline?' I look at Simon; I hadn't heard about that.

'Mim's idea. I gave in. Hello, Andy.' Simon looks past me.

I'm dragged into the house by the boys clinging onto either hand.

'Helen.' Chloe comes out from the kitchen. I didn't expect her to come for lunch. This is going to be a wonderful birthday.

'Hello, you.' I free myself from being the boys' hostage and embrace her as firmly as I embraced Simon.

'Auntie Helen. Auntie Helen.'

'Don't pester your aunt. She will look at the trampoline when she's ready,' Simon silences the boys.

'Mim and I found a shop near here that stocks that dress you like. We think you should go and try it on, and others too. We should spend the whole afternoon wedding-dress shopping.'

'Oh.' That's a great idea. 'I agree, Mim,' I shout towards the kitchen.

'Good,' she calls back as the kitchen door opens. Sweet and savoury baking smells fill the air. She's dressed in an apron. 'The boys have been baking bread for lunch. The rolls are in the shape of dinosaurs but fresh bread tastes nice no matter its shape. We'll eat and then go out.'

I smile and hold the hand that she has lifted out to me.

'How are you?' she asks.

'Well. Very well.'

'And how is Helen really?' Mim's voice travels from the kitchen.

My senses have been on hyperdrive today – hearing every layer of sound, seeing every colour in its brightest form and catching smells on the air from the restaurants and cafés we have walked past.

'This is my favourite. I think it suited you the best,' Chloe says, picking up another wedding-dress catalogue, turning to the page we have dog-eared and adding it to the pile on my lap.

'It's also the most expensive,' I say.

'Fine,' Andy answers Mim, in the kitchen. 'But she works too late sometimes. She's too involved with the family. She makes it personal, because the father's on his own. She feels sorry for him.'

Chloe doesn't appear to be aware of anything beyond the glossy magazine she pulls off the pile and thumbs through quickly to find another dog-eared page. 'What about this one? You looked amazing in it.'

The smell of peeled, chopped carrots carries in the air as well as the sound of someone, I think Andy, cutting them. He offered to help cook dinner, so he won't risk seeing the final decision on the wedding dress.

'You know Helen can become obsessed,' Mim says.

'Obsessed?'

'Her bipolar. She has an unhealthy obsession with people sometimes. Including Simon.'

There's no answer from Andy.

Chloe is flicking through pages. I want to reach out and grab her hand to stop her; the sound, the movement and the sweep of air as the pages turn are annoying. I want to concentrate.

'Has Helen told you?'

'That depends on what you're asking about.'

The muscles in my body tighten, bracing to stand up and storm into the kitchen – an aggrieved defendant. But then how will I know what they will say if I go in there? I want to know what she says and how Andy will answer.

'What about this one?' Chloe puts another magazine, with an open page, on my lap. 'It has to be on the shortlist.'

'I presume you know she was sectioned when she was fourteen?'

'Yes.'

'Do you know why?'

'She had a manic episode.' There's an eating sound, crunching. I think it's Andy eating a piece of carrot. He doesn't sound upset.

'That's what you should do, make a shortlist and write down the pros versus price. That will help us decide.'

'You write the list.' A crocodile snaps in my voice.

'She was stalking her social worker. She thought the woman knew where her mother was and wasn't telling her. She used to avoid school so she could spend all day following the woman. In the end, she was ringing her constantly and knocking on her door in the evenings, insisting that she tell her where she was.'

I imagine Andy's eyebrows lifting, in the responsive expression that I know well. But there's no verbal answer – just another crunching-carrot sound.

'This one. Definitely.' Chloe looks at me for agreement on the shortlist she's typing into the notes on her phone.

I nod.

'The police picked her up and then she was referred for psychiatric help.'

'And that was when she was diagnosed?' Andy confirms, in a stiff tone of voice.

'Yes. But it has happened again since. A couple of times.'

'This one?' Chloe asks.

'Yes.'

'And …?' Andy asks, the stiffness in his tone lifting to ask, so what are you telling me?

'There was a female teacher at her school. Helen was sixteen. She really liked this woman, and the woman liked Helen. She felt sorry for her, I think. She used to invite Helen to her house for dinner and Helen would play with her daughters. Then she started offering Helen babysitting so Helen could earn some money.

'In the end, Helen used to go there all the time. Uninvited. The woman contacted Simon and asked him to stop Helen going there. It was when we had just married.

'But it wasn't Simon that stopped it. Helen had another heart attack and ended up in hospital. During that time, the teacher left the school and moved to a new house.'

I am washed away, swept on a tide, out into a deep swaying sea where my arms and legs thrash against the waves trying to keep me afloat. That's my story. Mim has no right ... But if I go in there now to tell her to stop, Andy will know I've been listening.

'After she came out of hospital Helen called Simon every night for hours. She was still in care then. Simon and I talked about her living with us. But she'd been in the same foster home for a while and it seemed better to give her stability. We'd planned for her to live with us when she left care, but I just wanted Simon to myself for a few months. She didn't let that happen.'

Andy's only answer is a long release of breath. I can't tell what the sigh means.

'So, these are the ones I think deserve to be in a shortlist of six.' Chloe has laid the magazines out on the floor with the pages open.

I glance at the pictures, not really seeing them, my concentration on the conversation in the kitchen.

The smell of hot cooking oil carries into the room, and I hear the oil spit.

'Okay. Thank you for telling me. Now, I know she can become obsessed. But she's all right at the moment and she's taking her tablets.'

'Good. It's just she was being very clingy with Simon before she left here last year. It's usually a sign that something isn't right. I thought you should know.'

'Thank you for making me aware. But that was a three-quarters of a year ago, she was recovering from a break-up and major surgery. I think she had good cause to rely on her brother. Helen's okay and she's happy.'

'Good.' I picture Mim smiling, to soften the blow of her words and the way he pushed them back at her.

A swarm of bees is in my blood. Charging around. 'I need a drink,' I say to Chloe as I stand. 'I'll be back in a minute.'

Andy is standing in front of the chopping board, knife in hand, with a pile of diced carrots in front of him. He reaches for the celery that's on the side near him as Mim tips the chicken breast from a bowl into the hot fat. The fat pops and spits.

I walk over, embrace Andy from behind and kiss his neck as he starts chopping again. His head turns and I move to the side so we can exchange a proper kiss. 'I love you,' I say.

He smiles. 'I love you too. Have you chosen your dress?'

'Not yet.' I go to the cupboard. 'But we are narrowing it down.' I take out a glass and move to the sink to fill it with water. I drink it in the kitchen – to stop Mim continuing the conversation about me.

Chapter 42

The sixth Sunday of my new life.

Andy's arm is hanging around my shoulders. I lean into his chest, appreciating the cuddle, even though it's not very comfortable to sit like this in train seats that are designed for strangers to be able to avoid any chance of contact.

'You know one thing we haven't decided yet ...'

He pauses, as though waiting for me to speak. I don't know the answer. 'Pass.'

'Where we are going on honeymoon.'

My palm presses on his stomach so I can straighten up in the seat and turn to look at him. 'Honeymoon?'

'You say that as though you hadn't thought we'd have one.'

'I ...' Hadn't.

'Tell me you've at least told your boss you will be taking time off after the wedding. I have two weeks planned.'

'I ... didn't think.' I smile.

He looks annoyed. His colour has risen in redness and a frown is playing with lines on his forehead. 'Helen.' My name is a complaint.

'I didn't think,' I repeat. The things Mim said flood through my mind.

'Well, think now. And tell your boss on Monday. Don't ask.' The words are as sharp-edged as the knife he cut the carrots with. 'Where would you like to go?' he asks in a softer voice. 'Where have you always dreamed of going? I have enough money saved to go somewhere exotic.'

'I have money too.'

His arm lifts and I settle back in against his side. But anxiety is now spitting at me like the hot oil that Mim fried the chicken in. I don't want to be apart from the children for two weeks.

My children.

Who will care for them in the day?

If Alex brings someone in to work temporarily for the two weeks, how will the children cope with another new person in their life, another fake mother?

They will want me. And I'll miss them.

Mine. Bitch.

Chapter 43

The seventh Monday of my new life.

I breathe in deeply and press the button to ring the bell. The woollen fingertip of my glove slips off the button. The bell stops abruptly. I press and the bell rings again.

My hand is trembling.

I lift my finger away and wait.

Alex usually answers quicker than this. But it's earlier. He has a job on the far side of London. He texted and asked me to be here for six-thirty.

The door opens. Slowly. The doorknocker doesn't rattle.

I didn't hear him come downstairs, but his feet are bare and his shirt is untucked.

'The children are still in bed,' he says in a low voice, as if he's trying to prevent them waking. 'We had a restless night. They've all been up, and I overslept. They're in my bed.' He steps backwards, so I can come in. Then shuts the door, carefully, behind me. 'You can make yourself a cup of tea. I need to finish getting dressed.'

'I need to speak to you about something.'

'Is it urgent?'

'Yes.'

'Come upstairs and talk to me, then.' His hand grips the newel post and he starts climbing.

I follow. 'I'm getting married in five weeks. I need to take some time off for my honeymoon, over Easter.'

He glances back at me but keeps climbing. 'I'm not going to deny you a honeymoon. Take whatever time you want but just let me know the dates.'

'I need a fortnight.'

'Okay.' He walks along the landing on the first floor. The house is silent apart from the noise we make. I can't hear Louise.

'Who will look after the children?'

'Who knows ...?' he answers in an impatient tone. 'My parents ... I'll work something out.' He's focused on hurrying upstairs.

The pace of my heart and breaths increases as I run up the stairs after him. 'I'm worried about them. I don't want to leave them for two weeks.'

'We can cope without you, Helen.' His tone lifts from impatient to annoyed as he reaches the top of the second flight of stairs and opens the door to get to his room.

I follow him up the narrow staircase. The door into his room is open.

The children are spooning. They're in a little toppled stack on one side of the bed. The biggest to the smallest. Hope is sucking her dummy in her sleep; it trembles in her mouth when she stops. Rosie's arm is around Hope's waist and Josh's around them both. The other side of the duvet is pushed back and I can see the creases and the indent in the pillow that says Alex was there.

He's tucking his shirt in as he walks across the room.

I wait near the door.

He's cleaning his teeth in the bathroom.

When he comes back in, he smiles at me. 'I might take a fortnight off and look after the children myself,' he says in a hushed voice. 'It's my birthday. We could go on holiday.' He walks to his side of the bed, and bends down to open the drawer beneath the one that had the keepsakes from Louise in it. 'We haven't been away for a long time. It would be good for us.' He takes out a pair of socks.

'Where would you go?'

He balances on one foot then the other as he pulls the socks on, displaying a core strength that implies at some point in his day he crams in an addiction to exercise.

'I have no idea.' His fingers comb through the curls in his hair when he straightens, and he looks past me, at a long mirror on the far wall.

His hand touches his jaw. He hasn't shaved.

There's a jumper on the floor near the bed. He picks it up and pulls it on as he passes me. 'You can stay up here with the children if you want to. The alarm clock is set for them. I'll see you later.'

'Yes.'

As he passes through the bedroom door I see something. A shadowy figure entering the room. The shadow passes in front of the mirror too.

The sound of Alex's footsteps reaches the bottom of the stairs.

I turn and look at the children.

An ache increases inside me, longing swelling like fluid around a broken bone.

I started bleeding last night, my first period since I've been trying to become pregnant.

I lie down on the bed, careful not to shake the mattress and disturb the children, facing Hope, looking at a row of blond heads as my head rests in the indent Alex has left.

My children.

Oh, go away, Louise. Please.

Chapter 44

Shrove Tuesday: the eighth Tuesday of my new life.

The doorknocker rattles. The sound of the door shutting is heavier than normal.

The children push themselves off the sofa and run as Alex's feet pound up the stairs.

'Daddy.'

He didn't stop in the hall, and he beats the children to the landing.

They gather in a small pile-up by the door, then part to let Alex through. He holds a stack of magazines in a hand raised above their heads.

'Disney World. Florida.' Alex drops the magazines on the coffee table. They're holiday brochures. 'You can look through these and decide which hotel we should stay in.'

'Cool.' Josh grabs a glossy brochure. Rosie takes one too, and Hope.

As I stand they sit back down on the sofa in a row, with brochures open on their laps, making a very sweet picture.

'Disney World.' My hands slide into the pockets of my jeans. Andy and I have booked to go to Italy. Sorrento. I wish I could go to Disney World with the children.

'I think we deserve it after the year we've had.'

A sympathetic smile touches my lips. My hands lift out of my jeans. 'Do you want me to get you a cup of tea before I leave?'

'No.' He looks at Josh, whose head has come up.

Josh gives his dad a broad smile. The broadest smile that I have ever seen from him.

'Josh and I make the pancakes and we need to get started on the mix.'

'The batter's made. It's resting in the fridge. Rosie and I made some this afternoon.'

'No!' Josh screams, and the brochure is launched at me.

I lift an arm. The brochure hits my elbow.

'Josh.' Alex moves in an instant, takes hold of Josh's slender arm, pulls him off the sofa and makes him stand upright, facing me. 'Apologise now.'

I rub my elbow.

Josh looks at Alex, not me. 'But she made the pancake mix.' The word 'she' is spat at Alex as if I am the evilest person in the world. 'We do it.'

'Helen didn't know that. I should have told her this morning. Blame me.' Alex breathes out restrained anger with a shaky exhale. Then his gaze comes to me. Anger rages in his electric eyes and storms in the mist around him. The anger is directed at me.

'I'm sorry, Josh,' I say.

Alex shakes Josh's arm a little, in a nudge for him to respond. 'I'm sorry I threw the magazine. But you shouldn't have made the pancakes.' He pulls his arm free and runs out of the room.

'Helen hasn't cooked them! We still have to cook them!' Alex shouts after him.

'I don't care! She spoiled it!' The return shout comes from the second set of stairs as Josh stamps up them.

'I'm sorry,' I say to Alex. 'I'll get out of your way.'

He sighs and his fingertips rub his temple as if I've put the weight of the world back on his shoulders. 'You didn't know. It's my fault. I should've said something this morning. You were trying to help.'

No answer comes to my lips except for an apologetic smile.

But is it his fault, or my fault, or Louise's? The idea came to me while the girls were playing in their room this morning. Louise was with us, and her presence was vindictive. The toys would not do what they wanted. They kept falling over and rolling away. I chose to get the girls out of the room and away from her meanness. But perhaps she put the idea into my head as another way of being mean.

'I need to go and talk to him.'

'That's all right. I can let myself out. What time tomorrow?'

'I can walk Josh to school, so, eight. I'll leave the girls with you.'

'All right. See you then.'

I leave the room before him.

He climbs upstairs as I walk downstairs.

'Come on, Josh. Don't spoil the evening.' As I take my coat off the hook Alex's deep, exhausted, grief-stricken and heartbroken tone drifts downstairs. 'Rosie will want to cook with you.'

Laughter floods the air around me and bombards my mind in peals that will not allow any other thoughts.

I hate Louise. She's like a bitter taste in my mouth. A bitter sound in my brain.

I pick up my bag, open the door and leave.

The knocker rattles as I pull the door shut. My hand is trembling. How did she manage to control my mind, though? It's frightening to see and feel her learn to manipulate things, to manipulate me.

What will she do next?

Chapter 45

The eighth Friday of my new life.

I am unstrapping Hope from the pushchair when the landline phone on the wall in the kitchen rings.

Josh hangs his coat and scarf and runs to answer it as I unzip Hope's winter onesie.

'Nanny.' Josh's telephone greeting brims with excitement.

Rosie drops her coat on the floor and rushes to speak on the phone.

'Yes. Yes. No. Dad isn't home yet. Yes. A nanny.'

'M too. M too,' Hope pleads, fighting with me as I try to get her arms out of the sleeves of her onesie.

'In a moment,' I say to Hope, as behind me Rosie is reaching out a hand begging Josh for a turn on the phone.

I think it's Pat Dowling on the phone. If Josh had to tell them he is with a nanny, it must be Louise's parents, because Alex's parents know about me.

'We're going to Disney World! Yes. I am. We are.' Josh continually turns his back on Rosie as she makes grasps for the phone receiver.

'Is Grandad there?' Josh asks. Then after a moment he says, 'Hello, Grandad. Yes. Yes.'

As soon as Hope is free from her coat she joins the impatient Rosie and excited Josh in the kitchen, her hand reaching out in the same way as Rosie's.

I put the pushchair away while the yes and no conversation progresses in the kitchen. But Rosie and Hope are making complaining noises.

'Let me talk,' Rosie declares as I walk in. She's pulling on Josh's arm, trying to take the phone.

'Josh,' I say quietly. He and I are still not on good terms – after pancake-gate. He ignores me when he can and barely says a word when he can't. I am grunted, nodded or shrugged at.

Louise has taken him away from me, when I had only just won him over to my side.

On this occasion, he chooses a shrug. 'Rosie wants to talk to you.' He holds the phone out. 'I want to talk to him again after you.'

Rosie eagerly takes the phone with a happy smile. 'Grandad. Yes. Yes. I love you too. We're going to colour now. Yes. Josh reads after school. Yes. Yes.'

Josh is waiting, itching to get the phone back.

'M too. M too.' Hope has climbed onto the sofa, and is standing on a cushion, holding out a hand to express her desire more strongly.

I walk over to the fridge to sort out some drinks and snacks as the phone call continues.

'It's Grandad,' Rosie says to Hope as she holds the phone to Hope's ear. 'Grandad,' she says again when Hope listens but doesn't speak.

'Ganda. Yes.' Hope nods, and nods, and nods. It makes a smile touch my lips as I imagine Robert Dowling on the other end of the phone.

They talk for an hour, as I rest my crossed forearms on the work surface and watch, taking pleasure in their happiness.

Louise's negative energy hovers everywhere. But I can't tell what she makes of this. Does she try to communicate with her parents too? Can she influence them?

A shiver runs down my spine. She's breathing down my neck. Threatening again. Trying to put some distance between me and this phone call.

At some point the phone call must come to an end. 'Josh,' I say quietly. 'You need to do your homework. You should let your grandparents go.'

A glance over his shoulder sends me the evil eye. A look he learned from his mother or father?

'Josh,' I say again.

A grunt. He holds the phone receiver out towards Rosie. 'You say goodbye, then I'll say goodbye.'

Her eyes focus on her brother as she takes the receiver. 'Josh says I have to say goodbye. Yes. Yes.' She kisses the phone. 'I miss you too. Goodbye, Nanny.' She kisses the phone again. 'I love you too.' She holds the phone out to Josh.

'Hello,' he says into the receiver. 'I have to go. Yes. Yes. Goodbye, Nanny. I miss you too. I love you. Yes. Can I say goodbye to Grandad? Goodbye. I love you. Will you ring again? Yes. I miss you.'

Hope is reaching for the phone.

'Hope wants to say goodbye.' He holds the phone to her ear. She laughs, and nods. Then waves. 'Bye. Bye.'

Rosie laughs at her as Josh puts the phone back to his ear. 'Bye, Grandad. Yes. I love you too.'

As the phone call ends, the positive energy they've thrown about the room drops like a stone into a pond. Sadness runs out about the house in ripples. 'Come on, snack time. Then homework, Josh.'

A glare.

Louise laughs.

When Alex opens the front door, Josh is sitting at the far end of the sofa in the living room, reading aloud. He hasn't had time to play on his PlayStation because of the call from his grandparents.

Josh discards the book on the sofa as the door shuts downstairs, and leaves the room.

The girls follow.

So do I.

I can smell pepperoni and pineapple as soon as I walk out onto the landing. I lean over the bannister. Alex has two takeaway pizza boxes in his hand. They eat junk food night after night. Takeaway after takeaway. 'Hello.'

He looks up. 'Good evening. Do you want to stay?' He lifts the pizza boxes a little.

'No. My fiancé will be cooking.' I walk along the landing losing eye contact with him as he looks down and sets a hand on Josh's head. 'Josh hasn't finished his reading yet,' I say. 'But missing it for one night won't do any harm and it's because he was talking to his grandparents.'

Josh is looking up at his father with eyes full of adoration. 'They said we can go over there one weekend. To sleep over. Like we used to.'

'No.' Alex's whole demeanour changes. A Jekyll and Hyde shift. The shop window shattering. The refusal is growled.

'Dad?'

'No. Why were you talking to them?' The pizza boxes are almost thrown onto the stairs.

Alex usually shows himself in 2D to me, but this is full-on three dimensions. The hidden Alex.

'Nanny rang us.' Josh's voice is high and defensive.

Alex leans down, gripping Josh's head, not hard but holding him in place in a way that says you will listen to me. 'I told you not to answer the phone. You are not to talk to them.'

Josh's face screws up in a hard frown and his eyes glitter. He pulls free and punches his father in the stomach with one hand, then the other. 'I hate you.' He runs off, upstairs, past me, and keeps running, with Alex watching.

Josh's heavy footfalls run along the landing, up the next flight of stairs and then the sound of his bedroom door slamming reverberates through the house. A message from the house, not just Josh.

From Louise?

Get out!

I think she wants Alex to blame me.

I walk down the last few steps. 'You shouldn't have spoken to him like that.' I can imagine this Alex pushing someone in a temper.

Alex picks up the pizza boxes and turns away. 'Is it your job to tell me what I can and can't say to my son?'

The girls are keeping their distance. How often does he fly into a temper like this?

I don't like his temper. It's not just broken his shop window, it's shattered the family feeling that I love.

I follow him into the kitchen. 'If you tell him he's not allowed to speak to the parents of his deceased mother ... Yes, it's my job.'

'Leave it, Helen.' He puts the boxes on the side. 'You don't understand.' He moves forward to hold Hope under the arms and lift her into the chair.

'What is there to understand?' We are arguing like a couple. I'm another step deeper – up to my neck in Louise's life. But it's cruel of him to stop them from seeing Louise's parents.

'Daddee?' Hope says. The cautious note in her voice asks why Josh isn't here, as she slots her legs into the highchair.

My arms cross, holding onto a temper that wants to let loose at him as hard as he let loose at Josh.

Rosie is quiet as she climbs onto a chair. 'Can I have a piece of pizza?' she asks tentatively.

'Yes, darling. Help yourself.' He slides the boxes in her direction and then carries on buckling Hope into her highchair.

I step forward and help Rosie open the boxes. It restores some of her confidence. 'We told Nanny and Grandad that we are going to Disney World,' she dares to say now Alex has stopped growling.

'Did you? Thank you.' He looks at me, not Rosie. 'I told you not to answer the phone.'

That was weeks ago. I had forgotten. But … My hands lift, expressing my words. 'I didn't, I was taking Hope out of the pushchair. But what did you expect me to do? Would you have really wanted me to take the phone off them? It made them happy.'

'I said I love you,' Rosie adds.

Alex turns to fetch plates out of the cupboard.

'I miss them,' Rosie offers, her voice lowering in pitch again, as though she's frightened to say it.

Alex doesn't respond, but puts the plate down, moves a slice of pizza onto the top plate and cuts it up for Hope. I think he's not answering because if he lets any words out of his mouth they will not be nice.

I should go, but I don't want to leave when he's angry and the children are unhappy.

My thoughts are upstairs, where Josh is either crying or stewing with anger in his bedroom. I think he'll have taken control of his tears long before he reached his bedroom. The young man.

A sigh escapes, and I lay a hand on Rosie's shoulder. 'Your wife's family have a right to be in the children's lives.'

I am stared at with ice-grey-blue eyes that tell me to be quiet. In 2D his eyes can deliver electric shocks; in 3D his eyes can be menacingly violent. 'I'm the one that makes that decision. Please go, Helen.'

Another impatient sigh escapes. I want to be able to shout at him. To make him let Robert and Pat in. This is why Robert hasn't posted recent pictures of the children: Alex isn't giving them any contact.

'You can't take their grandparents away. They lost their mother ...' I thrust the words at him like throwing knives before I walk out of the room. I expect a sharp retort to follow me – none does.

I lift my coat off the hook, pull it on, wrap my scarf around my neck and slide my hands into my gloves. I breathe in. Then look into the kitchen. 'What time on Monday?'

He's sitting at the breakfast bar with his share of the pizza on a plate. He's not going to go upstairs and speak to Josh.

Alex's gaze meets mine. For a moment I think he'll say, don't come back.

'Eight.'

'Okay. See you then. Goodbye, Rosie, Hope.' I want to walk into the room and kiss the tops of their heads, in the way that Alex does when he leaves. Instead, I wave.

'Bye.' Hope twists around to wave.

Rosie looks at me with misery in her eyes.

I want to pick her up and take her with me. I love you.

My children.

'My children,' I breathe out on a whisper as I open the front door.

Chapter 46

The ninth Monday of my new life.

When Alex opens the front door, he and Josh are ready to leave.

'Good morning. The girls have eaten,' he says. 'I'm taking Josh to school.'

Josh doesn't look at me. There's a tension between him and his father that says their argument on Friday has rumbled on over the weekend.

Alex reaches past me to open the door. I move out of the way. I haven't even taken my coat off.

Josh trails after his father with heavy feet.

'Goodbye.' I say it to Josh, not Alex.

Josh glances at me, telling me I am the problem.

Alex pulls the door shut from the outside.

I take my coat off and look at Rosie, who is standing at the open door into the kitchen holding Hope's hand. Alex and Josh forgot to say goodbye to them.

The shop window hasn't been fixed; 3D Alex must have been raging about the house all weekend.

'We can't go to Disney World,' Rosie says. 'Daddy said Nanny and Grandad won't let us go.'

'Why?'

'We aren't allowed to leave Britain.'

'Oh.' A frown pulls at my brow. Why? 'Would you like to go to the park and play?' Instinct draws me to distract them.

They can't leave the UK? What does that mean? She's confused me.

Rosie lets Hope's hand fall and without a verbal agreement climbs a couple of steps so she can reach her coat, agreeing to the idea of the park. 'Nanny and Grandad want to take us away.' The announcement is delivered with a sad note of acceptance. 'They don't want us to stay with Daddy. Daddy said they told the lawyers not to let us go.'

Oh, my God. She does know why.

Why would lawyers be involved?

She puts her coat on as she stands on the stairs, a tear sliding down one cheek leaving a snail trail of moisture. The tear falls from her chin as another breaks free from the other eye.

I step forward. 'Oh, sweetheart. I'm so sorry.' My arms wrap around her and I hold her. I press a kiss on top of her soft curls. She smells of the children's soap and toothpaste.

I have no words to say to make this better; all I can offer is physical comfort. I love you, darling.

My children.

Bitch.

You are the bitch.

'Come on.' I let Rosie go. 'Let's cheer ourselves up on the swings.'

Hope is beside me, arms up, asking for her share of the cuddle. I bend down, pick her up and balance her on my hip. 'We won't worry about the pushchair, it's only over the road; you can walk, Hope.' I reach for the little coat that Alex has recently bought for Hope and help her put it on while she balances on my hip.

'Okay. Ready? Let's go.' I take the spare key off the hook near the door.

I don't like Robert and Pat any more. If they ring again I'm going to grab the phone out of the children's hands. The children should be going to Disney World.

'Daddy said we'll go to Cornwall instead. There's a beach and a fairground there.' Rosie's small hand clings to mine as we cross the road to reach the park entrance.

Good for Alex for coming up with an immediate alternative. 'Cornwall is nice.'

When we walk through the park entrance, I put Hope down.

They run across the park ahead of me, to reach the swings. I lift them both into swings and push them in turns. There's no laughter. They are as sad as they were the first day I watched them come to the park with Susie.

Louise brought me into these children's lives to take them from Alex, but I will not. So, she's found another way.

The children are happy with Alex and me.

Leave them alone! I shout, at Louise, as I push Rosie's swing higher.

When we leave the park, I take the girls to a café to treat them to hot chocolate topped with whipped cream and marsh-mallows. I help Hope drink hers so she doesn't spill it. Images in my mind remind me of the days I watched the girls with Alex or Susie.

I will not let them be taken away.

My children.

Not any more.

If Louise were flesh and bone I'd slap her.

I know what it's like to lose my parents. To have no family. Louise had everything, and I'm sure she chose to throw it away. I won't let her selfishness destroy the lives of these children any more.

She has an enemy now and her heart and her life are mine.

I buy the children a pack of small, mixed filled rolls from the chiller cabinet in the local supermarket. Then we take our lunch to the cinema and find a children's film to watch.

The film finishes at two-thirty so we have time to collect Josh.

The girls haven't smiled all day, and when Josh walks out through the school gates he throws them a meagre, 'Hello,' and walks several paces ahead of us, his thumbs tucked into the straps of his rucksack that contains a crushed book-bag.

Josh turns and looks back when he reaches the front door of the house, his hand out, palm upwards, waiting for me to hand him the key.

'There you are.' I place the key into his palm, speaking to break the silence.

He doesn't respond, just turns, slots the key into the lock and pushes the door open. He holds the door as normal but Hope is walking so there's no pushchair to wheel in.

'I'll do my homework in my room,' Josh says as he hangs up his coat.

I don't want that to be a new way of doing things – but for this evening: 'Okay.'

The landline phone rings as I'm unzipping Hope's coat and Rosie is hanging hers up. I look at Josh, who is in the kitchen taking drinks out of the refrigerator. He glares at the phone. As though it's evil.

He must now have a love versus hate relationship with his grandparents.

The phone continues to ring.

Josh and Rosie ignore it as Hope looks from one to the other.

Rosie's gaze catches mine, her eyes sparkling, full of sorrow.

Louise has found a way to make her screaming heard by everyone.

'Come here.' I open my arms wide, encouraging Hope and Rosie to come to me, wrap them up in a hug and kiss Rosie's then Hope's cheek as the phone carries on ringing.

They may no longer have their mother or her parents but they have their father, me, Alex's parents, and each other. They have so much more than Simon and I ever had as children.

When the phone stops ringing, Rosie pulls away from me and walks into the kitchen. Hope follows her.

Josh holds out two cartons of apple juice.

'We went to the cinema,' Rosie declares, 'and we had hot chocolates.'

Josh looks from Rosie to Hope, who gives her big brother a questioning smile that implies she's struggling to understand and navigate this new period of sadness. Josh looks at me, with eyes that are asking questions I can't read. But even if I could, how would I answer?

He can trust me, though. If he wants to talk I will listen. I smile to tell him that and I want to touch his head, comb my fingers into his curls and show him the affection of a mother that he desperately needs.

He looks away.

I turn to pick up the letters that have been pushed through the letter box by the postman after we left this morning. There are four. Two in white, stamped, official-looking envelopes marked as private and confidential and two in glossy coloured and motif-decorated envelopes that look like junk mail. I take the envelopes into the kitchen and put them down on the work surface for Alex to find when he comes in.

I lift Hope into her highchair so she can have her drink.

Josh walks off with his drink and a packet of crisps. 'Are you allowed to take those to your room?'

He looks over his shoulder, with an expression that tells me I have no right to challenge him. 'Yes.' He turns and carries on his way.

A sigh of frustration escapes, as my heart experiences the pain I know his must feel too.

'What shall we do now?' I say to Rosie and Hope.

'Can I draw?'

'Yes, you can draw.'

'Moosick.' Hope claps her hands. Music means she wants to look through the photographs on my phone as the nursery rhymes play.

As I fetch my phone, Rosie gets her crayons and puts them out on the coffee table in the kitchen's sitting area.

I think she's chosen to stay in the kitchen because it's farther away from her brother and the anger, arguments and broken spirits that rip this house to pieces every time one tiny shred of happiness appears.

'Leave the children alone, Louise.' I let the words out on a whisper. I'm desperate for her to listen. But I know she won't. She doesn't care about them. She only cares about herself.

I lift Hope out from the highchair and hand her my phone – it's playing 'The Grand Old Duke of York' – and glance at Rosie. She's kneeling on the floor, grey crayon in hand as she draws the car park again.

Until Friday I persuaded her to draw flowers instead. But I

do understand the car-park drawing. It is Rosie's way of saying, I want my mummy.

She wants her mummy to hold her today, and so she draws the last moment that she saw her.

This is what you did to her, Louise. This is the pain you've created in your wake. A riptide of pain.

I sit down on the sofa beside Rosie and rest a comforting hand on her back as she draws.

After we've been sitting for about ten minutes, the phone rings again.

Rosie doesn't look up but carries on drawing, resolutely ignoring the sound.

The phone rings twice more before Alex opens the door.

'Hello.' His tone is deep and heavy and the mist of negative emotion and energy around him is darker than ever. His spirit has died by another few breaths, withering, tired, and struggling to fight on. 'How have the children been?'

Sad. 'Quiet. But okay.'

'Daddy.' Rosie hops up from the floor, to go to him.

Hope discards my phone on the sofa and moves too.

Alex has a shopping bag in his hand. More takeaway. He squats down and the bottom of the bag hits the floor. I see him look at the drawing and notice what the picture is and I see his spirit shrivel further, losing life like a wilting flower. A punctured tyre. A deflated balloon. I am seeing depths in him that have been fought and concealed before. 'Did you have a nice day today, darling?' he asks Rosie as her arms wrap around his neck, and his arm slots around her waist. Hope clasps her arms around him from the other side.

He stands up, with a girl balanced on either arm and the bag left on the floor. Their arms remain about his neck. The pose reminds me of the first time I saw Rosie and Alex, in the picture on Robert Dowling's Facebook page.

'We went to the cinema,' Rosie announces proudly.

'I 'ad chocklet.' Hope pronounces the most complex sentence I have heard her say.

'Did you, now?' He kisses one girl's cheek, then the other girl's, as I stand.

My hands slide into the pockets of my jeans.

He's wearing those silly pale jeans with the stain on them. That had always been a sign that sometimes his shop windows were broken.

'I treated them. Rosie told me ...' I leave the rest of the sentence unsaid; Rosie doesn't need to be reminded of why.

His lips part in an odd expression. He's heard the unspoken element. His expression suggests acceptance of a hated fact.

'I'm sorry I let them answer the phone,' I say quietly. Rosie isn't listening to me; she's pressing her head into Alex's neck.

'At least now the children understand that I'm not just being cruel.' He walks over and sits both girls on the breakfast bar. The granite top must be cold under their bottoms. 'Stay there,' he says to them as they let him move free from their hold. I walk closer to make sure Hope doesn't decide to try and climb down and fall.

He's moved to pick up the shopping bag and returns to unload it beside Rosie.

Tonight, dinner is prepacked elements of a Chinese meal, in cartons to go in the oven. He turns and twists the knob to set the oven running.

'Would you like to stay?'

The offer is not really spoken to me. Heartless in sound. Perhaps his shop isn't open, perhaps it is just shutting down.

Closing-down sale items thrown out into the street, free for anyone willing to take them away.

'Yes.' I have to. I can't leave them like this. 'I will. Thank you.'

I walk back to the sofa to pick up my phone, stop 'Puff the Magic Dragon' mid-song and message Andy to tell him I need to work a little later.

Alex stabs the plastic covering the cartons of food with a fork. I want to tell him that I'm sorry that the Dowlings are pressuring him.

The phone vibrates in my hand. I look down at the text. 'Okay, let me know if you want me to come down and walk home with you.'

'I will do,' I text, then slide my phone into my back pocket and look at Alex. 'Can I help?'

'No. Thanks. It'll be forty minutes. I'll get the children ready for bed while this is cooking. Where's Josh? In his room?'

'Yes. He's been up there since he came home. Shall I bath the girls so you can spend some time with him?'

He looks at me. It's not an electricity-charged defence but a look that lets me see straight through to his miserable soul. Yes, his innards are tumbling out into the street. He's falling apart. 'That would be kind, and probably what he needs tonight. Thank you. I'll pay you for an extra couple of hours, of course.'

Why does there always have to be a moment that tells me I am not a real part of the family? I feel a real, necessary part until he talks about money.

His gaze falls to the small pile of letters that I left on the side beside where Hope is sitting.

I move out of the way as his hand lies on Hope's thigh. He smiles at her as he picks up the letters with his other hand. 'Are you happy, sweetheart? Are you smiling?'

She is.

He opens one of the white letters.

'Would you like a drink?' I ask.

'Yes. A beer, not tea. Take one out for yourself if you want one,' he adds, looking over his shoulder before looking back down at the letter.

'Shit,' he says a minute later as I pop the metal caps off the beer bottles.

He doesn't usually swear.

'Is everything all right?'

'No.' He answers without explanation as he puts the letter down on the side, to pick up the next white one. His thumb tears the second letter open, quickly, as if he suspects who the letter is from or what it might say and is desperate to have his suspicion denied. The letter is unfurled from its folds quickly and his eyes scan over the lines as I carry the open bottles over.

There's a cough, a cough that suggests something is stuck in his throat and he's choking. A fisted hand presses against his mouth.

I'm side on to him; I can't see his expression but I see his fingers pressing into and creasing the paper. The paper trembles.

'Alex?'

His fist drops and hits the breakfast bar as he looks up.

I move slightly, moving around to try to see his face better.

His eyes are red-veined and glossy when he looks back down at the letter.

He puts the letter on top of the other, folds them in half and throws them over the top of the electric hob to the far side of the kitchen.

He looks at Rosie and slides his hands under her arms. 'Come on, let's go upstairs and see if we can cheer your brother up.'

He lifts Rosie down to the floor, then turns back to pick up Hope. 'I'll start the bath running,' he says to me. 'I'll shout when it's ready for the girls to get in.'

I assume that's a polite request for me to wait downstairs for a little while.

His beer is left on the work surface.

Once they've left the room, I follow, quietly, stopping at the door and watching.

Alex has Hope's hand in one of his and Rosie's hand in his other. The girls climb the stairs slowly, a step ahead of him.

I lean against the doorframe, sipping from the beer bottle, my heart aching with love. They're my family. My children.

Mine! Mine! Bitch! Get out!

My eyes are drawn to something at the top of the stairs. A shadow. A human figure that disappears when I look properly.

'Leave them alone, Louise.'

I turn away and walk back into the kitchen. The life I have with Andy put on pause for the sake of the children.

The folded letters are at the far end of the kitchen.

The cast-iron bath fills slowly. Alex will be upstairs for ages.

I put the beer bottle down beside the one I left for Alex, go over to the letters, pick them up and unfold them.

'Oh, my God.' The top letter tells him the date of an inquest that will look at the cause of Louise's death. Because her death was unexpected and unnatural, the coroner has summoned a jury to hear the evidence and conclude on a cause.

I move that letter to the back and read the next. It is a court date for him to attend a custody hearing. Robert and Pat are trying to obtain partial custody of the children.

That isn't good for the children. They're being vindictive and cruel to their grandchildren. I agree they should be able to see them, but to take them away for part of every week ...

They may have been good parents to Louise, but they are terrible grandparents. As bad as Louise seems to have been as a mother.

I put the letters back in the right order, fold them again, and put them back as they were.

Tears run onto my cheeks as I walk to the sofa. I do not wipe them away but let them run. I may have found these children because of Louise, but I hate her.

I pick up my phone, with a desire to message Robert via Facebook and tell him what I think of him. My thumb itches to do it. Anger urges and screams for me to do it.

Instead I open a game app and let my thumb blast bullets at bubbles.

'Helen.' The call comes from upstairs for me to run up and bath the girls.

I play with the girls, wash their hair and then lift them out and dry them off.

In their bedroom, Rosie slides on the woman's T-shirt she uses as a nightdress. It has stains on it and it doesn't smell of sweet, small child. It smells and looks as if it hasn't been washed for ages.

A breath releases on a sigh as I turn to the chest of drawers and take out a clean Babygro for Hope. This family needs me. I will not let anyone take them away, not even for one day a week.

The boys are playing a game on the PlayStation next door, avoiding discussing complicated emotions.

A high-pitched attention-grasping buzz draws my and the girls' attention. It is the sound of a phone alarm.

'Dinner's ready,' Alex shouts.

A moment later he's standing at the bedroom door to lead the pyjama-clad procession downstairs.

The shadowy figure of Louise is merged into his dark aura. A shadow of a shadow.

I am part of the family at the breakfast bar; Rosie and Josh speak to me as much as they do Alex, as Hope smears her dinner across her face, bib and highchair.

Alex's method of feeding a toddler is to let her get on with it and not react to anything that misses her mouth.

He has a very relaxed parenting style, but, in this context, I like it.

Despite the disappointment over their holiday and the grief that lies at the core of this family, when they eat dinner they're like any other family.

I am just another facet of that – their mother figure.

'Would you like me to put the girls to bed before I leave so you two can have a little more time together?' I offer, looking at Alex then Josh, as Alex gathers the dirty plates.

Alex looks at Josh. 'What do you think? We could get the dishwasher going and then you can read a book to me for a little while?'

Josh nods.

Alex looks at me. 'Thank you. Yes.'

'Find us a book to read,' I say to Rosie, to send her off ahead as I release Hope from the highchair. There's a small set of shelves in the corner of the girls' room that contains a pile of thin story books.

'Can you put the beer bottles in the recycling?' Alex asks Josh.

Tired and ready for bed, Hope willingly wraps her arms

around my neck and lets me carry her upstairs as Rosie runs ahead of us.

For the sake of comfort, I sit in Rosie's bed to read the story, with her on one side and Hope on the other. They're tucked under my arms, Rosie resting her head against one of my breasts and Hope against my other.

Hope sucks her dummy, and Rosie begins sucking her thumb halfway through the rhyming rhythm of the story.

I juggle the book in my hands, trying to turn pages without disturbing the girls as they become heavier the more they relax. Hope falls asleep before I finish the story. Rosie's breaths slow as she sucks her thumb gently.

A shadow spreads across the room, coming from the door. Alex is there. Our gazes catch but only for an instant before I look back down at the book. He's blocking the light from the hall. I turned the light off in their room to help the girls settle.

He doesn't move until I have read the last page.

As I close the book, he walks in.

I lift my arm so he can pick Hope up and carry her to her cot. He kisses her head before putting her down as I carefully move Rosie's head to the pillow.

I can't help myself, I bend and kiss her cheek softly before I move away.

He walks past to reach Rosie and kisses her brow as I put the book back on the shelf. Lastly, he turns on the night-light and lifts a hand, telling me to walk out of the room ahead of him.

He pulls the door up until it is almost closed.

'How's Josh?' I whisper as we walk along the landing to the stairs that will take us down to the first floor.

'He fell asleep reading. He was awake for most of the last two nights, though, so he's tired. Hopefully tonight they will all stay asleep.'

I nod. I have as many questions bubbling and burning behind my lips as I had the last time I was alone with him. How can I ask them? 'Alex,' I say as we start walking downstairs. 'How have they stopped you from taking the children to Disney World?'

'Do you want another beer?' he answers with a question that denies my question, closing the shop.

'Yes, please.' There's no point in pushing for answers. I know Alex well enough to know he will not speak unless he wants to.

But if I stay perhaps he'll choose to speak – patience is a virtue. My illness has taught me patience in multitudes.

He glances back. 'To be honest, I appreciate you staying. I need someone to vent to.' He speaks in a low voice so his words will not carry.

The sudden decision to trust me catches me out. Trust received from Alex is a rare gift. I accept it as a gift. I know the value of trust.

'I don't want to worry my parents and I don't like taking problems to work.' He looks ahead again as he descends the last few steps.

This moment of vulnerability has opened him up; the door is only open with a slight crack, like the first day I came here, when Susie put the chain on the door, but he's letting me look in.

'My wife's parents applied for an emergency court order from the Court of Protection on Friday evening.'

He steps off the bottom stair and turns towards the kitchen. His body language closed but his words opening up.

'They were so concerned that I was running off with the

children their solicitor contacted an out-of-hours emergency number.'

'Why would they think you would run off with the children?'

He walks across the kitchen to the fridge.

I stop by the end of the breakfast bar.

'Because they think I am evil incarnate.'

Are you? The doubt flashes through my head.

No. He's not.

'They think I murdered my wife.'

Someone so kind to his children could not murder. I don't believe it.

He takes two beers out of the fridge.

I wait for the phone to ring – for Louise to scream for his hearing. It doesn't. The Dowlings know he'll never pick up.

The fridge swings shut. He takes the caps off the beer bottles and holds a bottle out for me as he walks over.

'Why?' I ask, when I take the bottle.

He leans forward, his elbows resting on the breakfast bar.

His hands surround the beer. 'Louise.' His gaze lifts from the bottle to me. The window shutters open, folding back and letting the light and me in, displaying a vulnerability and confusion of emotion that's as intense as his usual look of defence. 'We argued a lot. She turned to them a lot. They blamed me; as most parents would. They were wrong. It wasn't my fault. I never held it against them. But now ...' he looks into my eyes in the way he did in the early days, trying to see something in me '... they think things were so bad I killed her.'

'Did you?' The words spring from my lips. He's given me the chance to ask and even though I don't think so, I want to hear what he'll say with the shutters open.

He reels back. 'God, no, Helen.'

'Josh said it was an accident. Rosie said you pushed her.'

He straightens up, standing back, and drinks from the beer bottle, in a way that deflects my words, buying time. Trying to shut down from 3D to 2D.

But his body is leaking 3D. His skin has paled. He's not embarrassed. He's shocked.

The beer bottle lowers. 'When did they say that?'

'The first day I looked after them.'

'I'm surprised you did not run for the hills. It was ...' He swallows, his Adam's apple sliding down then up. 'A horrible accident.' His eyes glisten, reflecting the kitchen down-lighters.

I watch every tiny movement he makes. Trying to understand. 'I'm sorry,' I say.

'So am I,' he answers before taking another drink. 'But anyway, the long and the short of it is that Louise's parents don't believe it was an accident, and I can't prove it was.' He takes another long drink from his beer. His tone of voice is closing on me too. He's getting a grip on his emotions, packing them all up again.

I drink. I want him to continue but he doesn't. 'What will happen next?' I ask before taking another sip from my bottle.

He shrugs, in a movement I have seen lift Josh's shoulders many times. 'Who knows? It's up to the coroner's jury now.' He takes another long drink. His bottle is already almost empty. He leans his head back, drains the bottle, puts it on the side and turns around to walk to the fridge. 'I'm not bothered about myself. I really have no strength left to care. But the children. They deserve better. They deserve to be left alone now.'

He takes another beer out of the fridge and holds the bottle up, looking towards me, to ask if I would like another. I shake my head. I still have more than half a bottle and I should go home after this drink. Back to my other life, my normal life.

He pops the cap off the bottle and stares at the work surface. He shuts his eyes, and the muscles in his cheeks clench as his jaw stiffens. He takes a deep breath in, and the bottle and his hand tremble as he lifts it to his lips. The windows are breaking again. He drinks. 'The problem is ...' he turns to face me, looking at my eyes '... they don't want to know the truth. The truth is sometimes more painful than a lie.' He drinks again.

I drink, not looking away from his gaze, feeling as though I'm trying to pass a test. It's like a children's game where you stare and try not to blink.

'Sorry.' He looks away. 'It's unfair of me to burden you with this. It's not your problem.'

It is my problem. If they take the children I'll lose them too. 'That's all right. I'm a good listener, and I would rather know anything that impacts on the children.'

The beer bottle lowers in a rush. 'They don't know about the hearing.'

'But they told me that their grandparents want to take them away from you.'

'I had to give them a reason not to answer the phone, and explain why we can't go to Disney World.'

'I would have done the same thing.' I drink the last of my beer, and put the empty bottle down on the breakfast bar. 'I should go home.'

He nods. I think he thinks I am trying to avoid any further conversation. I doubt he would have talked to the barely out of her teens Susie about this. This is a new thing for him, and it is not something he does naturally. But I need to get back to Andy.

I walk forward, lay a hand against his arm and hold him gently. 'I'm sorry, Alex. If you need me to do anything; look after the children in the evenings or the weekends ... I'm happy to and I'll do my best to keep them smiling.'

'Thank you.' His hand lifts and covers mine on his arm.

The touch lasts for less than a second before my hand falls and I step back.

His hand lifts and his palm runs over his face, as a sigh escapes. 'I can't believe she's still destroying our lives from beyond the grave.' The words are not said to me, they're a distress call sent out into the universe.

But I know Louise has heard them.

'What time do you need me here in the morning?'

'Do you know what? Don't worry. Don't come tomorrow. I'm going to take a day off. Come on Wednesday, at eight. I'll pay you, for tomorrow, of course.'

Money. Not family. I hate him offering me money like that. 'Thank you. I'll see you on Wednesday. Goodnight.' I step back and turn to go.

'Goodnight.' His voice floods with a tired acceptance of the facts.

I take my coat and scarf off the hook quickly, pick up my handbag and open the door.

My heart is thumping like a punching fist against my ribs as I pull my coat on and walk along the street, hurrying to get home to Andy – to Helen.

I pull my scarf out of the sleeve it is caught in, wrap it around my neck and wipe the tears from my cheeks. If he loses the children, then I lose the children.

I don't know how my heart would cope. I don't think I could bear the pain of losing them. I love them too much to lose them. It would be worse than losing my parents. Worse than losing Dan.

I fish for my phone in my bag and spend the walk home talking to Andy on the phone, telling him about the custody battle and the investigation into Alex's wife's death. His voice shifts from horrified to sympathetic, even though it annoys him if he thinks I am caring too much about the children.

When I walk through the door at home he's there to hold me. We hold each other. Just hold each other. For a long time. Because I know how precious life is and he thinks I'm a precious thing.

I'm happy hiding in Helen's life, because Louise's life is where sadness and madness lie.

Chapter 47

The tenth Thursday of my new life.

Andy's fingers are woven in between mine as we walk into the magnolia-painted consulting room to see my surgeon. Since the operation, I've mainly been supported by the extended medical team, seeing the doctors in outpatient appointments to check my progress. But today my appointment is with Mr Harris, the man who saved my life last year when he put Louise's heart in me.

'Helen.' He stands up and holds out a hand. I let go of Andy's to shake his. His hand is cold and probably recently smeared with sanitiser gel dispensed from the container on the wall near his desk. 'Take a seat. How are you? You look well,' he says as he sits down.

'I'm getting married in a fortnight,' I say as Andy and I occupy the seats on the opposite side of his desk and exchange a glance.

'Then congratulations are in order.' He looks at me and Andy. 'And you feel well? No problems?'

'None.'

'Infections?'

'Only minor things, but they heal without antibiotics.'

He looks at my notes. 'Your blood pressure is excellent, and your electrocardiograms have been good.' His gaze lifts to me. 'As you seem to be accepting the heart very well, what do you think about reducing the immunity blocking drugs? We can try and see if we can get you off those. It would be better for you in the long term if we can. I'll reduce the dose first and see how you go.'

I glance at Andy, as though he can decide for me. Then I look at Mr Harris and nod.

It occurs to me ... that ... stopping the immunity drugs that stop my body from battling Louise's heart will make her heart completely mine.

I smile.

I'll plant a flag in her heart; it'll catch in the flow of my blood and wave the colours of Helen.

'Yes. I would like to try.'

He writes on a page in my notes. Then pulls over a pink form and writes on that. 'It will take a few weeks for the impact of the drug to reduce,' he says as he writes. Then he looks at me, sliding the form towards me. 'I'll send a letter to your GP and let her know you need to continue with blood tests to monitor your white cell levels. And if you feel ill at all, please call the ward.'

I nod.

He pulls over a yellow form and fills that out, then picks up both forms and holds them out for me to take. 'Hand those in to Reception. You know the drill.' He smiles.

A smile parts my lips as Mr Harris stands and holds his hand out to Andy. 'Good luck for the wedding, nice to have met you. Take care of this woman. She deserves to be very happy.'

Andy smiles. 'Thanks. I know.'

I glance at Andy as we walk out, grinning with excitement.

He's never seen me unwell. It is one of the things I love about us, that to him I have only ever been healthy.

Chapter 48

The tenth Friday of my new life.

The doorknocker rattles as I close the door. The children are in their usual places in the kitchen.

I wave. 'Good morning.'

The girls wave back, their mouths full of breakfast cereal.

'Good morning.' Alex's voice has a deep early morning, running-over-gravel key. He's standing at the sink rinsing out a cup.

'I have a doll who has hair that I can brush, and I can make up her face,' Rosie says.

'Have you?' I add a very impressed note to my voice as I walk into the room. 'Happy birthday.' I hand her the card I have taken out of my handbag.

She grins as she accepts it. I unload more birthday things from my handbag, laying them out in a row: lots of edible paper flowers and a small plastic fairy. 'We'll use these to decorate your cake while Daddy's at work.'

'How did it go yesterday?' Alex asks as he opens the dishwasher.

I told him I had a dress fitting in London, which was partially true – I did go there after the hospital appointment. 'Good,' I answer.

I receive a brief, shallow smile as he puts the cup into the drawer of the dishwasher.

'I'll pick Josh up from school, then you can focus on putting out the party food.'

I nod, smiling again. He doesn't know the half of my plans. I have room decorations for Rosie and Hope to make in my bag, games planned and I am taking Rosie out to buy the things for party bags and pass the parcel.

'Are you excited?' As Alex picks up plates that are littered with toast crumbs, I stroke a hand through Rosie's curls and then kiss her head.

Alex carries on, with no reaction to my kiss.

I have been cuddling and kissing the girls, in a motherly way, ever since the last time I stayed to bath them. He's never appeared to think it's odd.

Rosie's nod and smile express every bit of her excitement.

She's four. She will start school for half-days in the autumn school term. I will miss her in the day. But she's happy because she will be in the same place as Josh.

Alex smiles at her as he runs a hand over Hope's hair and picks up her empty bowl.

The negativity in this house is being pushed away for today. Even Alex's mist of pain is paler, a thinner smog of misery.

As soon as Alex leaves with Josh, I help Rosie and Hope put their coats on and we head off for a morning of party shopping.

The rest of the day is spent baking and making, while Louise screams through the ringing phone on five different occasions. I put the radio on to drown her out.

When Alex hurries Josh through the door just before four, his mouth opens with a look of surprise and then – he smiles fully for the first time that I've seen.

My God, when those shutters open ... I've always thought him good-looking but with a genuine view of him ...

He looks at Rosie. 'You've been busy.' Streamers and helium balloons decorate the kitchen ceiling and the breakfast bar is full to the brim with sandwiches cut into small triangles for small fingers, tray-bake cakes cut into equally small triangles, crisps in a few varieties and a good old-fashioned cheese and pineapple hedgehog.

The birthday cake is on the far side of the room, with four candles pointing upward from a flower garden. The fairy has been placed in the middle of the square of candles.

Alex takes his coat off. Josh is already hanging his. 'Go and get changed out of your uniform quickly, before Grandad and Grandma get here,' Alex tells Josh.

Alex walks into the kitchen, looking at Rosie. 'Did you help to make all of this?'

Josh's feet pound up the stairs.

'Yes.' Rosie smiles.

Alex bends to pick her up. She wraps her legs about his waist as he carries her over to look at the birthday cake.

Hope trails behind like a little duckling. 'Me.'

'This is pretty,' Alex says.

Rosie nods.

'Did you lick the spoon?'

'Yes.'

'That was a treat.' He looks down at Hope. 'Did you help too?'

'Yes,' Hope agrees. Although I don't think she knows what she is agreeing to.

Alex looks at me. 'Thank you. This room and the food look wonderful.'

Apparently, since Christmas, Alex has been taking Rosie to

ballet classes and swimming classes on Saturdays. We are expecting fifteen children who are under five from those classes and his parents are coming to join me as helpers.

I am looking forward to this party. I have dreamed of holding parties for my child. I never had a party as a child and I've done everything for Rosie that I longed for when I was small.

Alex's parents arrive ten minutes before the guests are due. I'm introduced, 'This is Helen,' in a voice that says I've been spoken of. They're introduced as James and Mary. We shake hands, then we make polite conversation, until the doorbell rings announcing the arrival of the first child.

I take the role of doorwoman. 'Hello. Hello. Come in.' I take coats and send the children upstairs with brightly coloured presents held tightly in their hands.

Upstairs they're welcomed by Alex's mum, who directs them into the living room full of more streamers and balloons.

I follow the last child to arrive upstairs.

Rosie is sitting on the floor in the middle of a circle of children, ripping open presents, while music plays in the background; it drowns out the complaints from Louise that I hear.

She should be happy today, but she's angry even today. Angry because I am here celebrating with Rosie. Angry because Alex is still here to host the party.

All she wants to do is take Rosie and the others away from him.

Happy birthday from your mum, Rosie. You lost your mother, now she's taking your father.

Bitch!

Right back at you, bitch. If I can do anything to stop you, I will.

Hope's on the sofa with Josh, who is trying to keep her eyes on him and one of her multicoloured and multi-textured toys so that she doesn't climb down and break up the party.

Alex is kneeling beside Rosie, moving aside the presents once they've been observed and commented on.

His parents are kneeling at the back of the gathering of small people, his father, James, acting as DJ, and his mother, Mary, general helper.

Once the last present has been ripped open and the painting set moved aside by Alex, Rosie's gaze lifts to me.

I smile when her gaze finds me. She's asking – what now?

No one else knows. I'm the games-master.

'Who wants to play musical bumps?'

Squeals of excitement are the answer.

I am used to large numbers of young children, as a teaching and nursery assistant. I love orchestrating games like this.

As James plays and stops the music, I look for who is the last to sit until we whittle the children down to one winner. Then we play a very noisy, giggly game of Simon Says.

This house can't have known this amount of laughter for a year, at least. Rosie told me that none of them have had a party before. This is a special day for all of us.

'Sit down, everyone, time to pass the parcel.'

The children's high-pitched enjoyment means that when the doorbell rings the sound barely makes it up through the house to the living room. But I hear it when James stops the music and the first layer of the parcel is torn into.

I stand.

Alex's mum stands. She's heard the doorbell too. She looks at Alex. Her eyes asking, who?

It could be anyone. A parent needing to pick up a child early. A sales person.

She leaves the room, and I sit down. But I catch movement, a blurred shape, Louise following. Her shouting is louder. She wants to be heard over the children and music. Her energy is everywhere – it's heavy and threatening. A thunderstorm is coming.

James starts the music again.

When the music stops, a loud conversation rises from downstairs on a wash of cold air. A disagreement taking place at the open door.

Alex glances at his father and gets up from his knees. He leaves the room and shuts the door behind him. Closing off the heated conversation.

The children scrabble to rescue the chocolate frog that slips out from the ripped open-layer into the scrunched pile of wrapping paper in the middle of their circle.

Once the frog has been retrieved and is safely melting inside its wrapper in a hot little hand, James starts the music again.

The conversation on the ground floor is louder, drawing my attention.

'Not today,' I hear Alex say in a definite voice. 'Not ever, if this carries on.'

My children! Mine! Mine! Get out!

'I have a right to be here!' Another male voice shouts – a voice I know in a gentler tone.

I stand. The children are managing this game on their own, and James has the music under control.

I walk to the door, open it, slip out of the room and shut the door behind me.

'You can't stop me!' a woman yells.

'Then call the police,' Alex replies.

I cross the landing and lean over the bannister to look.

Robert and Pat are outside the door and Mary is holding the door as Alex stands in front of them, guarding the house.

I am within metres of Louise's parents, her children and her husband.

Robert moves and Alex moves, Alex's hand reaching to the doorframe barring Robert's entry. 'I said no. You can stop me taking them on holiday, but you can't tell me who I invite to Rosie's party, and you are not invited.' The words are snarled. The only time I've seen him angry in this way was the day the children answered the Dowlings' phone call.

Robert steps closer. 'We have come to see our grandchildren.'

'Can I do anything?' I call down, drawing all eyes up to me, shattering the argument with a crack through the middle.

'Call the police, please,' Alex answers.

My heart stretches on a medieval torture rack as I take my phone from the pocket of my trousers.

If the children hear Robert or Pat, they will rush downstairs. They would hug and kiss their grandparents, no matter what Alex has told them. Loving-grandparents are good for children. But these people want to take the children away from us.

The argument continues below as I touch 999.

'I'm calling,' I shout.

Pat and Robert look at me.

For a moment, I wonder if they will recognise me. But why should they? When they saw me watching from the car park opposite their house, it was months ago.

'I suggest you do as Alex says and go,' I say.

Silence hangs over the hall.

I feel Louise's figure lean over the bannister beside me, as if she's calling down to her parents.

I move the phone to my ear.

'Ah.' The phone slips from my hand, falls and clatters onto the stairs below, as I straighten and grasp the bannister. I think I hear the phone's screen shatter.

Robert Dowling looks away, steps back and rests a hand on Pat's shoulder. 'We'll go. It's not right for the children to hear us arguing. They've had enough of that in their lives.' The words stab at Alex. 'Will you give Rosie her present and her card?' He holds out a white plastic bag.

Alex's outbreath is audible as far away as the landing. 'Yes.' He wants to say no. But he accepts the bag.

Alex shuts the door before Robert and Pat turn away.

Mary turns to Alex, her body shaking.

The Dowlings' present falls from Alex fingers onto the floor, then mother and son embrace. The next pull of breath into Alex's lungs becomes a sob.

The defencelessness and exposure in the embrace embarrasses me on one part, because I know that Alex would not want me to see him this vulnerable. The other part is pierced with jealousy. I wish I had a mother to hold me like that.

I turn away, go into the living room and close the door. My phone left, broken, on the stairs below.

The children have reached the red tissue paper layer. They have two more layers of the parcel before it is the prize.

James looks at me, his eyes asking me what was going on downstairs as he stops the music.

A disagreement begins over who is holding the parcel, which requires me to referee. But it's quickly solved when they discover it is only a lollipop between the wrappers.

I keep the game running, and lead the cheer when the last layer of wrapping is ripped open and a kit to make felt pirate finger-puppets is revealed.

As the cheer dies, Alex joins us. He glances at me, his expression hardened, denying any emotion, before his eyes turn to the ring of children. 'Is anyone ready for tea? Shall we move to the kitchen?' He presents a stiff smile, for the children's sake.

I look at James. He's spotted his son's fake smile.

Rosie gets up and runs to take hold of Alex's hand to lead the procession downstairs.

When the children have left the room, James asks, 'Who was at the door?'

I hesitate. Unsure if I should say. Alex did not say it. I shouldn't know them by name. But James doesn't know that. 'Mr and Mrs Dowling.'

'Robert and Pat. The cheek of it,' James mutters as he gets up. He leaves me in the room to clear up the wrapping paper and goes downstairs.

I take Rosie's presents up to her bedroom before I walk down to join the party in the kitchen.

My phone isn't where it was on the stairs.

The adults are circulating with plates of food, and the children are clustered on the sofa, and any other piece of furniture the right height to become seating, like swallows perched along electric wires.

I smile at Mary as I take a plate from her. Her hand is trembling, and her smile is nervous.

She fetches a bottle of lemonade to fill the paper cups on the coffee table.

My phone is on the work surface. The screen is decorated by more than a dozen cracks; it will need to be repaired at the weekend.

Alex takes charge of lighting the four proudly placed candles on the birthday cake.

James turns off the lights in the kitchen and Mary opens the singing. 'Happy birthday to you. Happy birthday to you ...'

The Dowlings have gone. But there's still something wrong. Something askew. The whole house feels angry. The air I breathe in is heavy and hot, as though the thunderstorm hasn't hit yet.

When the song ends, Rosie purses her lips and blows hard, extinguishing the candles one at a time.

'I'm just going to pop upstairs and use the powder room,' Mary says, quietly, to James, and leaves the room.

I reach for a knife and step forward to cut the cake. The sharp knife sinks through the soft butter icing. A sharp scream echoes in the hall and hard bumps and thumps trail down the stairs.

The children look as James moves. 'Oh, good Lord. Mary!'

Alex passes me. 'Mum.'

I put the knife down and follow them into the hall.

'Ring 999, Alex,' James says quietly. 'I think your mother has broken her ankle again.'

As Alex moves I see Mary, curled up in pain and distress at the bottom of the stairs. James is kneeling beside her, her hand clasped in his.

'Hello. Yes. Alex Lovett ...' Alex states the address as I turn back.

'What happened?' one of the children asks me. Some of the children have gathered at the door.

I can't help in the hall but I can save the children from distress. 'Come along, sit back down. Who wants birthday cake?' Hands rise about the room.

'... My mother. She's fifty-eight. It looks as though her ankle is broken ...' Alex says behind me.

As I cut the cake, Rosie tells everyone how she made it. Rosie, Hope and Josh were at the back of the room, too far away to see what was going on in the hall. I think they haven't realised that Mary is hurt.

I don't want them to know. But there will be an ambulance outside soon, and medics in fluorescent jackets, and I won't be able to hide the situation.

When the children are eating cake, I touch Josh's shoulder. His body jolts in a spasm that protests the unwanted contact. I lean to whisper, 'Do you mind keeping control for a moment?'

He looks at me, his eyes saying he is unsure of agreeing, but he nods his agreement anyway.

I open the door into the hall, step through and close the door behind me. Alex looks at me.

'I think we should ring the parents,' I say, 'and ask them to pick the children up early. Do you have their numbers?'

Alex shakes his head. 'No.'

Then the children are going to see an ambulance arrive. 'All right. I'll keep them in the kitchen.' I look at the watch on my wrist as I turn and open the door. I have forty-five minutes to fill.

Bitch! Ha, ha, ha.

Louise's cruel laughter sends a shiver down my spine.

A movement at the top of the first flight of stairs draws my attention – her human-shaped blur of movement.

Did she push Mary downstairs?

She tried to push me over the bannister when I dropped the phone. There was a surge of energy.

I should warn the children to be careful on the stairs. To hold onto the bannister or the spindles, all the time.

The ambulance arrives without the flash of blue lights or the play of urgent sirens. I think because Alex has warned them that the house is full of three- and four-year-olds.

I keep the children's concentration on a game of cartoon character charades as quiet tones of conversation seep through the closed door.

Bumps and scrapes follow the conversation. I imagine a trolley brought in for them to lift Mary onto and take her out of the house.

My heart thumps. The aftermath of the moment of fight or flight. All the time, while I keep the children involved in the game, Louise is laughing. It's a manic sound. It's a horror-film laugh from the ghoul in the attic. Or the basement.

I whisper, 'Bob the Builder,' in the next child's ear.

When the doorknocker rattles with the sound of closure, one of the children is enacting Belle from *Beauty and the Beast*, miming how she would ring bells.

The ambulance staff and James are outside the window, wheeling poor Mary to the ambulance.

The door from the hall into the kitchen opens. 'So how's this party going?' Alex says in a quick breathless tone.

'Well,' I answer. 'Very well.'

'Belle,' Rosie shouts.

Alex looks at her.

'Charades,' I say. 'Rosie, let Daddy have your turn? You've done it twice.'

Her face splits into a smile, expressing her excitement over the idea. Alex may not feel like this, but if he does this one silly thing it will fix a memory in Rosie's head that will last forever and blow away his absence after teatime.

He looks at me. I beckon with a hand for him to lean in. His eyes ask why. 'I need to whisper the cartoon character's name to you.'

He leans and turns his ear towards me.

'Rapunzel,' I whisper.

My view is of Alex, combing and tossing back pretend hair, while the children giggle, as beyond him the trolley carrying Mary is raised into the ambulance.

I can't believe that Louise has done this. I didn't think spirits could harm people. But now … What else can she do?

The thought terrifies me, but there's no one I can talk to about this fear.

'Rapunzel!' one of the girls shouts.

Chapter 49

The eleventh Wednesday of my new life.

I'm getting married on Saturday. I should be happy. Instead I'm sitting on the toilet in Alex's house utterly miserable. I'm bleeding. My period is a few days late, and I had begun to believe.

I grieve for what might have been for a few minutes, then address the situation and wash my hands.

A pathetic, pale-faced, red-eyed woman looks back at me from the mirror, and behind her a grey shadow.

Bitch. Go away.

I want to be a natural mother too. I want. I want. I want. The words are childish.

No. I need. I need. The words pulse through my mind.

I breathe out the frustration of failure.

Louise laughs.

The girls are waiting for me downstairs.

I unlock the toilet door, breathe deeply and step out, back into the life I have inherited from Louise's shadowy figure.

The girls are working on collages with glue sticks, piles of cut-up material, ribbons, lace and threads that we bought in the market. There are more things stuck on Hope than the paper. 'Oh, Hope, you've made a muddle.'

Rosie looks at her sister and giggles. Then sticks a button on Hope's nose.

Hope brushes the button off.

I sit down, pull Hope onto my lap, kiss her temple and breathe in her sweet child smell, letting her ease the longing in my heart as I peel material and decorations off her.

My child. Mine, I say, before Louise can shout it. I'm not in the mood for Louise's grumbling.

'Come along.' I put Hope on her feet. 'Let's wipe your hands and get ready to fetch Josh.'

We are collecting him later tonight because he's been selected for the school's football team. He's taking part in more things like that: nature club on a Monday, football on Wednesday and art club on Thursday. I've taken it as a sign that he's beginning to accept his life without his mother.

The children are happy, despite Louise screaming through the phone's ringtone at four o'clock nearly every day.

I run the water, tear off some paper towel, dampen it and wipe the smudges of glue off Hope's face and hands.

My gaze catches on the white official-looking envelopes waiting on the breakfast bar for Alex's return. The envelopes were on the doormat when we returned from the market. Poisonous threats from Louise, waiting to disturb the peace again.

Alex hasn't told me any more about the inquest or the custody hearing, but one of those white envelopes is A4 in size and almost bursting its paper seams with information.

Chapter 50

1745.

My period is heavy, my stomach is cramping and I'm light-headed. I didn't sleep much last night because I couldn't stop thinking about the wedding.

I look at myself in the mirror, then smile, for myself. To myself. Not looking beyond my face. I don't want to know if Louise is in the room with me.

The doorknocker rattles, announcing Alex's return.

I dry my hands, unlock the door and walk out of the toilet. This is my last day here before the wedding. Tomorrow, I'm looking for shoes with Chloe, in London. Friday, we are picking up the dresses and then coming back to Bath for our two-woman hen night.

When I walk down the last flight of stairs Alex already has Hope and Rosie in his arms and Josh hurtles past me, sounding as heavy as a baby elephant.

'Be careful, Josh.'

I don't want to leave the children for two weeks. I'll miss them and worry about them.

Josh leaps off the third step, throwing himself at Alex, arms out so he can wrap them around Alex's neck and hang on, his legs dangling. He looks like a cloak that has been hung around Alex's neck. But Josh is heavier than a cloak.

'Josh,' Alex complains. 'Let go.'

There are still not enough arms on one parent. They need another parent.

I walk forward.

If it were one of the girls I would take her from Alex and hold her but Josh will not want that; we don't do physical contact beyond shaking hands on deals. Deals like those I made when he was off school during half-term: if you don't tell your father you can have your pudding while I make lunch.

Alex bends sideways so Josh's feet touch the floor. He lets go, with a pout on his lips, sulking because he's always the one that's excluded.

Alex lets the girls down too, untangling himself from Hope's arms.

I think Alex will pick Josh up, but his head turns, looking into the kitchen; he's caught sight of the envelopes.

He leaves the children.

'Go upstairs, all of you,' I say. 'Daddy is busy for a moment. I'll make hot chocolate and you can sit on the sofa and cuddle Daddy while you drink them.'

Josh looks through the kitchen door. He doesn't like me stepping in between him and Alex. He wants to tell me that he won't go. He wants to walk into the kitchen and wrap his arms about Alex's waist and never let go.

Alex is reading the top page of a small stack of A4 paper.

Josh can see his father's attention is focused.

'Daddy and I will be up in a moment,' I say quietly.

Josh looks at me then turns and starts climbing the stairs. The girls take his cue and follow.

I turn to the kitchen. I want to speak to Alex.

His eyes scan across the printed lines of information.

I walk past him, finding a saucepan with a pouring lip and cups in the cupboards and taking milk from the fridge. Then I measure five cups of milk into the saucepan.

The hob ring clicks as I turn it on.

The papers flop down on the breakfast bar, hitting it with a slapping sound – dropped in disgust.

He rips open the second white envelope. It is a one-page letter folded into three. He unfolds it and reads.

'What do they say?' The pitch of my voice expresses my fear: that we'll lose the children.

He throws the letter onto the breakfast bar. It skims across the black granite and drops over the edge at the far side, fluttering to the floor.

'What do you want? The bad news or the really bad news?'

'Start with the really bad.'

'This—' he picks up the stack of papers '—is the information for the inquest into the cause of my wife's death.' The papers flop back down onto the breakfast bar. 'It contains evidence ...' He swallows, his Adam's apple shifting as he fights emotion. Then his hand lifts and runs down across his face before lifting again and combing through his unruly hair.

And, go on ... I want to push him, to make him continue.

'They've found a witness ...' he looks into my eyes '... who says he saw me push my wife over the wall at the top of a car park, although no one else except my wife, me and the children were there.' We stare at each other. 'Go on, then ...' he says. 'Ask the question everyone is going to.'

My lips form the words. 'Did you?' I have asked him before, though, and he said no. But people lie.

'No. Of course I fucking didn't.' He turns away and his hands grip the edge of the work surface as if he's grasping the edge of a cliff, as his head drops down, hanging in a hopeless expression.

The 3D Alex is running about in his shop, arms flailing.

It is wrong of me to like it when I can see him with all his faults on display. But I do like it when I see the raw honesty beneath his façade. It shows how close I have become to the children's gatekeeper. I turn away to see if the milk is boiling in case he sees me smile.

I glance over my shoulder as I stir the milk. He hasn't moved. The stiffness in his body that presents his effortless confidence is wiped away, and Louise's vindictive evil slides into his dark aura, turning it a gleaming jet black. She thinks she's won.

I open the cupboard to take out the chocolate powder, and a drawer to obtain a spoon. Then spoon chocolate into the cups. Giving him time to pull himself together.

I know he didn't do it. No matter what a witness says. I know too much about Louise's selfishness and I have seen too much of the man who loves his children. If you give that much of yourself to your children you can't be a bad person.

I pour the milk into a cup, and stir it into the chocolate, the metal spoon clinking against the cup. I repeat the action four times. Then put the pan and the spoon in the sink and turn to Alex.

He hasn't moved. I walk forward and rest a palm on his back. 'I believe you. Tell me the not so bad news.'

My hand slides away as he straightens.

'The custody hearing has been postponed until after the inquest.'

'When is the inquest?'

'Nine weeks away.'

Chapter 51

The twelfth Saturday of my new life.

My arm is threaded through Chloe's like the link of a single firm stitch that holds us up as we wobble up the steps of the hotel in razor-sharp four-inch stiletto heels. We have killed tonight and the whole day has been wonderful. From drinking champagne in the dress shop while they brought out our packaged dresses for us to being back on the train, to spending the afternoon in a spa here and hitting the town.

Our mission for the night, beyond drinking as many different cocktails as possible and dancing, has been avoiding Andy and his friends. But I have his phone on tracker so I know which bars and clubs he's been in.

The electric doors of the hotel slide open in front of us.

As soon as we are inside, I unwrap my arm from Chloe's and slip off my shoes. My brutally treated, sore, aching feet weep with pleasure from the comfort of the pale, cool, glossy polished stone tiles.

'Good evening,' the young man on Reception says as he smiles a corporate welcome.

Chloe glances at her watch, mid taking off her right shoe. 'Good morning, actually.' She laughs.

I'm laughing and I can't remember why as we walk into the hotel bar, barefoot, the beautiful and cruelly shaped high-heeled shoes dangling from our hands.

We are staying here tonight, and tomorrow morning Simon is picking us up in the car and taking us to the country hotel where I'll spend my wedding night.

I could leap and clap, and spin around dancing, arms spread wide with excitement. The bar is almost empty and I'm barefoot so I could do it.

A voice captures my attention. The low tone creeps along the room from the end of the bar. The man there is talking quietly but the place is empty so his voice is carrying and his attempts to prevent that sound shifty.

'I'm going to have one last margarita. What about you?' Chloe asks.

'Yes. Go on,' I say, while my mind whirs, spinning over who is at the far end of the bar.

Alex.

I can't see his face. So, he can't see me. But his voice and hair have given him away.

I glance over my shoulder, as if I can see through buildings and see his house. The children must be there. They're going to Cornwall tomorrow. But tonight, he's out with a woman.

It is weeks since I saw him in the club. I discarded the memory because I have no interest in knowing anything about Alex beyond him being the children's father.

But the hotel is minutes away from the house. Does he have a room here? Does he come here for sex now?

Does he come here to avoid me seeing him in a club?

His body moves in a way that says he's going to look around, as if he's sensed me watching.

I tuck myself in, hiding behind Chloe.

My heart is bump, bump, bumping. 'That's the father of the children I look after,' I whisper at Chloe.

'Where?' She looks over her shoulder.

'Don't look, you'll give me away. He's at the end of the bar.'

'Can I help you, ladies?' the barman offers.

'Two margaritas,' Chloe says, then looks along the bar.

'Stop it.' I smack her arm.

Ha. Ha. Ha. Ha.

Louise has broken into her manic laugh. I don't want to hear her tonight. She has nothing to do with tonight or tomorrow.

Chloe laughs and her eyebrows lift. 'He's handsome.'

'He's single. But he has one-night stands,' I say.

The woman he's with laughs. The sound is familiar. It touches a memory. I know her too.

I lean around Chloe to look. The room sways, with the unsteadiness of an over-indulgence of alcohol.

The woman's hair is black; an absolute black that is unnatural and says it is regularly coloured with cheap dye from a box, not the carefully crafted tinting of a hairdresser.

I know her. I just can't remember.

Alex leans in, talking, and she leans in to listen.

Click.

Chloe clicks her fingers in front of my face. 'Hello. I am here.'

'Sorry. I want to know who he's with. He's going to Cornwall tomorrow. I didn't think he'd be out.'

'So, because he has children he's not allowed a night life?'

I roll my eyes. A surge of nausea reels through my body. I should probably not drink the margarita. I need to avoid a hangover. 'I need the loo. Can you ask the barman if I can have a glass of water too?'

'Are you all right?'

'Yes.' When I feel high with life I can drink anyone under the table, alcohol doesn't touch the sides as far as making me drunk, but it still makes me feel sick and hungover.

I turn my back on the room, shoes still in hand, and walk out to the lobby to use the toilets. I think Alex's eyes follow me, but I don't look back to see if I'm right.

I slide the lock home in a toilet cubicle. No one else is in the plush marble-everywhere toilets.

With my clutch bag tucked tight under my arm, I lean over the toilet and put the forefinger and middle finger of my right hand into my mouth, trying to master the nausea. If I am sick now, I'll be able to sip some of the margarita and water and hopefully not have a headache in the morning. My throat spasms with a single, painful retch, but I'm not sick. I push my fingers a little further into my throat, and then it comes, a recycled cocktail of cocktails.

I vomit four times, until my stomach's empty, then pull off some sheets of the posh-hotel toilet paper, wipe my mouth and fingers, and flush the toilet.

At the sinks, I wash my hands, throw water on my face and lean down to rinse my mouth out under the tap.

I use the dryer and then open my clutch bag to repair my make-up.

The version of me in the mirror is blurry. I dab on some fresh foundation, to tidy up my night-out face. My hair has lost half of its curl that Chloe spent an hour creating earlier and my lipstick has been left on all the glasses and straws I have drunk from tonight. I slip the disc of foundation back into my bag and take out a lip gloss.

I hope I don't have black shadows under my eyes tomorrow.

Later today.

My hands fist and I jump up and down for a few seconds, allowing myself a moment of childish excitement.

'I'm getting married today! Ahhhh!'

When I stop jumping I smile at the me in the mirror, take the tin of mints out of my bag and pop one in my mouth before I leave.

Chloe is sitting in a booth a few feet from the bar, our drinks on the table in front of her.

There's no one at the end of the bar. The bar stools where Alex and the woman were sitting are left askew.

'They left ...' I look at Chloe, then look through the window. The glass is darkened but the electric light reaches through. The silhouette of a couple crosses the road, illuminated by the streetlights and the lights from the restaurants on the far side of the road.

'Come on.' I pick up my shoes and cram a swollen foot into one.

'Pardon?'

'Come on. I want to follow them.' I cram the other foot into a shoe.

'Why?'

'Because. Come on.' I push her shoes across. 'He only lives around the corner. Can you keep an eye on our drinks, please?' I call to the barman. 'We'll be back soon.'

He nods an acknowledgement as I get up.

I run out of the bar, as much as I can run in pinching, ridiculously high heels.

'You're mad,' Chloe says as she follows me out of the hotel and down the steps.

I'm clicking my way along the road, my heels making far too much noise for stealth.

But Alex and the woman are a good way ahead of us and cars are passing between us.

A shiver brushes over my skin. Now that I've cleared the alcohol out of my stomach I can feel the chill in the air.

Alex and the woman hurry across the road rather than wait for the crossing lights to change, but they don't walk into the street that leads to his house. They walk past it and on towards the road and the supermarket behind the house.

'Wait, will you?' Chloe's hand clasps my arm.

If he looks back all he'll see will be two drunk women on their way home. But perhaps he's already seen me in the hotel bar.

They're about fifteen metres ahead. His hands are in the front pockets of his trousers. Her hands are holding a clutch bag. There's no contact between them; nothing that suggests affection or even attraction.

He's laid out his shop window for her.

I can't say why that makes me feel happier, but it does. I've seen beyond it. My place in his family is deeper.

'I'm cold,' Chloe complains. 'Can we go back?'

'No. I want to see where they're going, and who she is.'

They turn and walk into the narrow, cobbled mews at the back of the Georgian houses.

I glance at Chloe, pressing my finger to my lips to tell her to be quiet as we walk on. But the metal caps on our heels scratch on the pavement and the sound echoes into the narrow, old alley.

When we reach the turn into the mews, I hold Chloe back and peer around the corner.

I can't see Alex but the woman is standing near the wall that separates the road from the mews. She wobbles a little on her heels.

The memory clicks into place; the last piece in a puzzle slotting in perfectly. I saw her outside his front door months ago. It's that woman. I saw him staring at her in the club too.

My feet carry me out from hiding. Chloe doesn't follow.

Where's Alex?

His car is parked at the back of the house, at the far end of the mews, as if it's been hidden. The passenger's door is open and I see him now, leaning into the car and getting something from the glove box. He pulls back and shuts the door. I duck back, hiding against the wall in a shadow between the streetlights.

When he walks back to the woman, he's holding out his hand to give her whatever he's taken out from the car.

She opens her bag as she walks forward. She doesn't take something from his hand, but gives him an item in return.

Alex turns to a back gate and lifts what she's given him. A key for the gate to the back of his house.

There's a small garden at the basement level of the house. I've never been down to it, because the basement is rented out.

But that woman has the key to the basement flat. 'Oh, my God.' I look at Chloe and whisper, 'He's such a liar.'

'Why?'

'He said his basement flat is rented out. He's taking that woman in there.'

'So? Maybe she rents it.'

'So ...' My answer is outrage.

'So, he's seeing a woman he doesn't want you to know about. Maybe she's married. But so what?'

'I've been working on top of their love nest!'

She bursts into drunken laughter, with a hand pressed to her stomach as if she has a stitch. Her legs crossing as if she's trying not to wet herself. 'Did you actually say that?'

But she doesn't understand. I feel ... Betrayed. That's it. I feel cheated on. A couple of days ago he stood at the breakfast bar, hanging onto the granite top, like the loneliest soul in the world – when, probably, downstairs, there was that woman he intended sneaking off to have sex with.

They even have their own staircase.

Chloe comes across, threads her arm around mine, and tries to pull me away, but falls against me instead. She reclaims her balance. 'Come on. Forget your boss who hides women in the basement, let's go back to the bar.'

She pulls me away, taking me back to the hotel.

But I'm thinking about the children. Are they in their rooms while a neighbour sits in his living room?

A shiver rattles through my spine. The rattle of a rattlesnake longing to spit venom.

I shouldn't care. But I do.

Chapter 52

12.08.

Awhoosh of steam rises from the hair curlers as Simon presses the button to fix the curl. He's taken over from Chloe because she was complaining about how sick she felt.

We left the hotel in Bath late, after I ran to Boots to buy paracetamol for Chloe.

I've not admitted, though, that I made us even later because while I was out I walked beyond the hotel in the opposite direction and looked across the road.

Alex was packing the car, sliding Hope's pushchair in on top of the suitcases – back where he belongs.

I don't know how to digest what I saw last night. He's been seeing that woman for months, that's what I think. She wasn't just a one-night stand. Maybe it began the first day I saw her, but it has continued from there.

Maybe I'm wrong, though, maybe he was seeing her before Louise died. I could have misunderstood the day I overheard them. I can't even remember what they said. Perhaps the one time was one more time.

My mind is pulling in every direction of thought. There's anger, a remnant of my own experience with Dan. I can recall in detail the moment Dan told me about the woman he'd been seeing. Every sound of his breath is in my mind, not just the words.

But there's also jealousy – because she lives in Alex's house. She's closer to Alex and the children physically.

There's an equal fear. What if she's emotionally close to them too?

I stare at Simon's reflection in the mirror, ignoring the words that fizz behind my lips.

He's concentrating hard on creating curls.

It is as if champagne bubbles are popping on my tongue. But I haven't taken a single sip from the full champagne glass beside me. The bubbles make me feel like talking, like telling Simon and Chloe everything. I want to know what other people think. I'm driving myself mad holding in all the lies I've told – caught in a web of secrets in one half of my life.

My gaze catches on the wedding dress hanging from the wardrobe door.

Chloe is spread along the sofa, draped in a hotel bathrobe. Her just-painted fingernails and toenails shining mauve and her hair and make-up perfect. But the expression on her face and the colour of her skin tell tales about last night.

I don't think she even remembers following Alex.

'Do you think you're going to be able to walk with me?' I ask Chloe.

She smiles through our reflections and gets up. She pulls the belt of the white towelling robe tighter around her middle as she walks over. 'Of course. I'm walking with you. Even if I end up vomiting on the shoes of your future husband, I'm walking with you.'

She leans down, embraces my shoulders from behind and kisses my cheek as Simon pulls the hot curlers away.

This is my life. This is Helen's life. This is the important life. I need Andy now, that's all; it's because he's not here that I have the jitters over Alex's sex-life.

I am with two of the people I love, but I want the third.

But what about the children?

I love the children too.

Every time I think of them I think of that woman in the house. With just a locked door between her and them.

A door that's locked when I am there. But is it open after I go?

There's nothing better than hiding your dirty laundry in the basement — dirty-little secret.

'There. Done. I think.' Simon looks at Chloe. 'But you'll have to style it. I may have curled her hair before but I can't pin it up.'

'You can ring downstairs and order more coffee, then,' Chloe answers.

So many years of the three of us have brought us to this moment. My illness meant I spent hours in rooms listening to Chloe and Simon banter and bicker.

Simon looks at me, through the mirror, as Chloe picks up the packet of hairpins. 'Can you manage without me? I'll order the coffee and check on Mim and the boys.'

'I can manage without you.'

One of his eyelids drops in a quick wink before he turns away.

'You're getting married.' Chloe states the obvious as she slides the first pin into my hair. 'It has just become real for me.'

A smile pulls my lips wide. 'Yes.' I swivel around on the chair and hug her about the middle. 'Yes. I am.'

Why am I thinking about anything else but that?

She embraces my shoulders, and we rock from side to side. Excited. Happy.

The folly where I will become a wife is a circular, temple-like, pale-stone building, on top of a hill that overlooks a scenic lake. I walk across the grass that was dampened by a rain shower about an hour ago, with my skirt hem held up in both hands, trying to tiptoe in satin shoes so my white heels do not sink into the mud. Simon is holding my dress, at the back.

Chloe and Mim follow; Mim herding the boys; Chloe also trying to save her silk dress from becoming water-stained.

We are almost there.

The building is steps away.

At least no one has seen us struggling. Because the doors are closed and everyone must be inside.

It's a chocolate-box building, in a chocolate-box setting, and Andy is waiting for me inside.

The event planner who showed us the venue steps out from behind a pillar. 'Hello,' she whispers, keeping my arrival secret. 'They're ready for you. When you're ready I'll open the doors.'

The smile that's been breaking my lips open all the way here, and making my cheeks ache, comes out again.

The sky above is a layer of miserable clouds that weep occasionally, but what I see is the brightest of blue-sky days.

I climb the steps, with Simon holding my left hand so I do not slip, up to the pillar-lined porch that embraces the whole of the eighteenth-century, mock-Roman Temple.

My right hand opens and the fabric falls, the heavy hem dropping to the ground.

Simon lets go of my left hand and instead raises his arm. His suit is the same colour as the boys', although the style is a little different, but their paisley-pattern, purple waistcoats are the same.

Simon looks at me and winks again, then his gaze travels over his shoulder to smile at Mim and the boys. 'Come on, boys. You are meant to be up front here.'

The boys run up the steps, around us.

They've managed to remain smart despite the challenge of the damp grass.

Chloe takes over the herding, as Mim comes up the steps last. She is going to walk in first. That will tell the violinist that I am here.

Chloe sets a hand on Liam's shoulder, encouraging him to stand still.

Mim looks at me. 'Good luck,' she says quietly.

'Thank you.'

She opens one of the double doors just enough for her to fit through and disappear.

Simon bends and straightens the knots of the boys' ties, as I fuss with the white rosebuds Chloe has pinned in my hair and she tries to stop her knicker-line showing through the figure-hugging satin.

The romantic pledge of the violin flows out.

'Ready?' Chloe asks the boys.

They look back, grinning at their father and me.

As the boys look away Simon says, 'Ready?' to me.

'Yes.' Yes. Absolutely, ready.

The wedding planner opens the double doors. Presenting us all. Ta da!

The warm air that escapes carries the heavy perfume from the flower garlands draped about the fireplace.

I am grinning as hard as the boys as they walk in first. Chloe, then Simon and I follow.

The small congregation has turned to look at us walking between the rows of chairs on either side.

The logs in the fireplace glow a vivid, warm orange in the grate, and the warmth catches up the scent of Chloe's and my own posies too; the smell of roses, lilies and green ferns mingles with the smell from the conifer branches in the decorations.

The boys and Chloe join Mim in the chairs at the front, on the left.

Officially, traditionally, on the left side would be the bride's family and friends. But everyone invited for my sake has arrived with me, so the small room has been filled by Andy's friends and family spreading out.

I walk to the front with Simon beside me. The violin our accompaniment.

Andy steps away from his chair and turns to look back, his eyes on me.

Everything is perfect. Exactly as I imagined it – as I wanted it.

He is remarkably tall in his suit, remarkably handsome and perfectly formed.

My lips tremble, the muscles suddenly too overwhelmed by emotion to smile.

My heart taps out the rhythm of a future – of a forever. With no fear of death. No need to leave my home.

'Hello,' I say as I near him.

'Hello.'

My hand slides off Simon's arm and I lift my arms to embrace Andy's neck, posy in hand. 'Later,' he laughs, catching hold of my forearms and lowering them.

His hands hold my hand. I look at the registrar as she talks through the official opening of the ceremony.

Andy speaks, and I watch his lips moving as he talks. 'It's so amazing when someone comes into your life and you expect nothing, but suddenly they're there. Right in front of me was everything I ever needed. I can conquer the world with one hand, Helen, if you are holding the other. But I know that a relationship means giving the best of yourself to someone who truly deserves it and that woman is you. I promise you my best, to be my best. Your best friend. Your best lover.'

Laughter ripples about the room.

'The best husband, and father – I hope. And the best foot-rubber. I love you, Helen.'

I love you too, I mouth.

'And now, Helen ... your vows,' the registrar prompts.

A long in-breath calms the fizzing words. I don't want to rush my vow. 'I can't promise that I'll be able to solve all the problems we'll face, or that I'll always get things right. Sometimes life will be hard and sometimes it will be as wonderful as today. But I promise you we'll spend every good and difficult day together. I'll be with you, as your wife, your friend and your lover.'

An ah sound sweeps like a soft brush about our audience.

'When I'm with you I'm able to be more of myself. I just want to smile and laugh with you for the rest of my life. I love you.'

I love you, his lips mouth in return.

'And now, it's time to exchange rings,' the registrar declares.

Andy claims my left hand, and in his right, is the ring. The warm gold, that John, his best man, has been nursing, slides onto my finger, as Alex recites the words the registrar tells him.

'Here.' John, who was at the table in the pub the night this began, presses a ring into my right hand.

'Hold out your left hand.'

Andy spreads out his fingers. I hold his left ring finger and push the ring as far as his knuckle.

The registrar announces that we are married.

'Hello, husband,' I say to Andy.

'Hello, wife.' Andy leans close. 'You can put your arms around me and kiss me now.'

I do; Andy the only thought in my mind.

COUNTING DOWN
THE DAYS

Chapter 53

The first Tuesday after Easter. 7 weeks until the inquest.

I press the bell and laugh. I've just said the word jubilant in my mind. I am jubilant. I feel jubilant. Euphoric. Ecstatic. There are so many great words for feeling good. Triumphant. Exultant. Gleeful—

The door opens when I am in mid-flow with happy words.

Alex barely looks at me and turns towards the kitchen, leaving the door for me to close.

Over the moon, I say to myself as I step in.

Victorious.

I hang up my coat.

Elated.

I push off one loosely laced trainer with the toes of my other foot on the heel, then do the same to take the other trainer off without bending down.

I'm not going to let Louise get me down. She was quiet while I was away on honeymoon. I didn't hear her at all until yesterday evening, when I got a text from Alex about the time he needed me here. She is just tinnitus. A sound that I refuse to let disturb me any more.

Euphoric is the best word.

Or gleeful.

I turn to the kitchen, where the children are eating breakfast.

I have been purely Helen for two weeks. No. Not just Helen. Helen and Andy. Mrs Arnold.

But Louise is more than noise here. She's a weight. Pressure. Like a toxin, she's a suffocating mist in the kitchen. Stealing through the air and stifling breath like petrol and diesel fumes in a tunnel. Pressing her hand over every nose and mouth so no one can live unless she lets them breathe.

Me. Me. Me. Me. My children. My children. My children. Mine. Mine. I mock her while I breathe out, breathing away the sound and sense of her. 'Good morning. What a lovely bright day. It looks like we'll be able to spend a good couple of hours in the park.'

Alex glances at me. He's loading the breakfast bowls into the dishwasher. His expression rigidly holding back emotion. I can't see if their holiday went well or not. But I don't see grief hidden behind his windows now. His expression doesn't stir empathy. I know the secret he's been keeping underneath the floorboards.

'So, is there a preference for which film we go to see this afternoon?'

'Are we going to the cinema too?' Rosie asks first, as Hope and Josh look at me.

'I thought it might be nice, as you're home today, Josh.' He has a teacher-training day.

He looks away, unimpressed by my blatant attempt to bribe him into liking me. No one would guess this family has just returned from a holiday.

'I'll leave some cash out for you to use,' Alex says as he shuts the dishwasher with a china and cutlery rattle.

Hope twists sideways and lifts her hands out towards me.

My heart melts as quickly as ice cream in a hot oven. It is the first time she's done that when Alex is here as an alternative. 'Hello, sweetheart.' I accept the embrace and look over her shoulder at Josh and Rosie. 'How was your holiday? Did you enjoy the beach?'

'Hope fell over and got wet,' Rosie told me.

'We went out on a boat,' Josh says at the same time. 'But Rosie was sick.'

'Ah,' I say to Rosie as I lift Hope into my arms.

Hope puts an arm around my neck, and then her fingers start to play with my ponytail. 'Ello. Ellen.'

'Hello, Hope. Did you like the seaside?'

'Yes.' She nods.

'She liked the roundabouts at the fair,' Rosie told me.

'And did you?'

'Yes. Josh liked the diggers best.'

At least it sounds as if they enjoyed themselves.

'Did you enjoy your honeymoon, most importantly?' My gaze is pulled to Alex, who is walking towards me.

'It was wonderful, thank you. The weather was brilliant and I loved every minute of it.' You liar, Alex.

He walks straight past me, without hesitating at all, and on into the hall. 'I need to go.'

Did he see me in the hotel that night or not? Does he know that I know? Is he trying to avoid me?

His skin hasn't coloured with embarrassment.

He pulls on his leather jacket. 'I've said Josh can go to his friend's for tea. It's only around the corner.'

I glance at Josh. Who ignores me. I look back at Alex. 'Okay.'

Alex walks back into the kitchen, pulling the wallet out from his back pocket. 'Here.' He opens it, takes out two twenty-pound notes and leaves them on the side. 'Have a good day,' he says to Josh. 'I'll pick you up after dinner.'

If Alex knows I saw him with that woman, he doesn't care.

He should care what I think, if he respects the part I play in this family.

Josh nods and lifts his arms, in a request to be able to hug his father. Something that is unusual to the morning routine. Alex holds him firmly and kisses the side of his head. Josh kisses Alex's cheek. 'I love you, son.'

'I love you, Dad.'

Alex walks around to say his goodbye to the girls, who are turning their cheeks to receive kisses, and then Alex has gone and the doorknocker rattles in his wake.

'Well, then, let the day begin. Get your coats on and we'll head over to the park.' I glance at the locked door at the far end of the room as Rosie and Josh get off their chairs.

In the park, my gaze drifts over to the house again and again as I push Hope's swing. While Rosie and Josh swing themselves and climb all over the high frames. I sat in this park, watching the house, often. But I never watched the basement, because the entrance is at the back.

Susie lived in there, though. But it has been weeks since Susie moved out and the flat was already let when I began looking after the children.

Has that woman been in the basement for that long?

Is it a serious relationship?

If it is serious why haven't Alex or the children spoken about her?

I treat the children to a McDonald's with part of Alex's forty pounds, and in a moment of silence when their mouths are full of nuggets and burgers I throw in the question, 'Do you ever see the person that lives in the basement? They use the back garden, don't they?'

Josh's smooth child's forehead creases into frown lines. He swallows his mouthful of burger and bun. 'No,' he answers. 'We own the garden. There's a path to the back door.'

'Oh.' I nod. 'How do you reach the garden, then? I've never been into the garden.'

'It's down the back stairs,' Rosie tells me. 'But it's never sunny in the garden. I like the park.'

'You'll have to show me later,' I say. Maybe I can look into the flat's windows from the garden.

Josh has his play-date to dash off to when we return from the cinema, so I try to cajole Rosie into taking me down the back stairs, but she doesn't like them.

'They're scary stairs.'

'Do you hear sounds?'

She nods.

The day I really want Rosie and Hope to sleep, neither of them does. Hope grumbles through the monitor, then cries with lots of tears. I think she has a tooth coming through, a particularly painful molar.

Her distress means that Rosie can't relax either.

Which means I can't go downstairs.

When Alex walks through the door, just after five forty-five, my mood has swung from euphoria to despair. Frustration tugs from every angle. Louise has screamed twice through the phone and constantly in my head. The knowledge of that woman downstairs is an itch, and the fact that he's lied is a poison.

Every time I think I understand him, I'm wrong.

The girls hurry out onto the landing to welcome him. Rosie holds Hope's hand as they make their way down.

Once he's taken off his coat and slipped off his shoes, they're lifted off their feet, one tucked under either arm. He kisses Hope's cheek, then Rosie's. 'How are my girls?'

Hope smiles and wraps her arms around his neck. Rosie kisses his cheek.

I walk down the last few steps. 'Hello.'

'Hello.' To me his voice is cold. But perhaps mine was.

He bends and puts the girls on their feet.

'Peppa Pig,' Hope pronounces perfectly.

'Ah. She comes before me now, does she?' Hope starts climbing upstairs on her feet, her small hand clasping each strut of the bannister, with Rosie following.

Alex is filling the kettle in the kitchen and I join him. I could begin with small talk but if I do it will be hard to progress to what I want to say. 'I know.'

Alex turns, kettle in hand. 'What?'

'I saw you.'

His eyes and his expression continue to look confused. So he didn't see me at the hotel.

'At the hotel, the Friday before you went on holiday. I was staying there. I was in the bar, and you were in the bar.'

A fleeting frown. A moment of confusion. His lips begin to form a word but stop. Then he knows what I know.

'I saw you walk back with her.'

He turns away from me and puts the kettle on its stand. 'Saw me or followed me?' Click; the kettle is put on to boil.

'Do the children know about her?'

Louise starts laughing. The sound echoes from the walls around me.

'I'm seeing a woman. But I think it's too soon to introduce the children to her. Do you want tea?'

'Yes, please. The children to her? Or her to the children?'

He glances over his shoulder as he drops teabags into the mugs. 'What's the difference?'

'It depends on what you're avoiding. Whether you're afraid of the children's opinion or hers.'

He turns back to the cups as steam rises from the kettle. 'The children's. Obviously. Their mother died. It's too soon after losing their mother.'

I step forward. 'How long has she been in the basement?'

'A while.' He picks up the kettle and pours the water into the mugs.

'Does she come up here?'

He puts the kettle down, heavily. Then turns, arms folding over his chest. 'What is this conversation? I don't think it's any of your business to know if she comes up here. I can understand you wanting to know if she's met the children, but you don't need to know anything else.'

I walk over to the fridge, wanting my brain to fizz with the words I wanted to throw at him before the wedding. But my thoughts dredge through thick mud. The right words are not there.

I open the fridge, take out the milk carton and hold it out for him to take, tilting the bottom of the carton in his direction.

'Thank you.' He turns back to the mugs.

'Why haven't you mentioned her?'

'Because, as I said, it is none of my children's nanny's business.'

Is there any greater way to be put in my place? It is an insult. An urge to slap him runs down my arm. My anger is playing into Louise's hands; I am less able to control my own actions when I'm caught up in emotion.

He turns to pass a mug of tea to me. His pupils are wide so his eyes look bluer.

'It might be my business,' I throw back sharply as I accept the mug. 'You told me a witness saw you murder your wife.' The words are a knife thrust, to get him back for insulting me.

A grimace tumbles through his expression as he looks away to pick up his tea. But he doesn't try to avoid the conversation. He turns around and rests his bottom against the work surface, settling in to argue with me. 'Really, you think I murdered my wife and moved my mistress in downstairs? Why would I do that?'

'I ...' The mug is hot, burning my hand. I put it down on the breakfast bar.

He looks into my eyes, his gaze becoming an electricity-charged wire fence that warns me away. 'I had a difficult marriage, yes. No, I didn't want to kill her. I am, for good reason, hesitant about going down that road again. I didn't have a mistress and I wasn't looking for one. But I just happened to have an empty flat, and she just happened to need somewhere to live.'

And you just happened to sleep with her weeks after your wife's death.

If he tells me that they met that way I'll know he's lying. I want to know if he'll lie. 'Is that how you met her, because she rented your flat?'

'No. I met her in a club before that.'

'When you were married?'

His skin colour rises to a scarlet red. 'No, afterwards. But if you're asking if I had sex with other women while my wife was alive, the answer is yes. But it doesn't mean that the witness is telling the truth.' His stare intensifies, pinning me down as tightly as an arm lock. 'I didn't kill her. She killed herself.'

He turns away and picks up the cake tin that contains the Easter chocolate. 'I'm going up to see the girls. Would you mind hanging around until I've fetched Josh from his friend's so I don't have to take them with me?'

'I don't mind. Shall I make dinner?' I follow him, trying not to splosh the tea over the lip of the mug as he races off.

Bitch! Liar! Liar! Louise's energy sweeps through me and rushes towards him.

'Shit.' His tea sploshes onto the stairs.

'Go on up, I'll get a cloth,' I say.

What does Louise get up to in this house when I am not here?

She should be spending all her energy annoying that woman downstairs, not storming around up here.

Chapter 54

19.12.

'Hello,' Andy calls from the kitchen within a second of me shutting the door.

'Hello.' The room is warm and I can smell basil and tomato. I've walked into my sanctuary.

'How was your day?' He walks out of the kitchen with a bottle of beer in one hand. A bottle that's coated in condensation in a way that suggests it has recently been taken out of the fridge. If I ran my finger over the bottle it would leave a line. 'Here.' He holds the bottle out to me.

I thought it was his drink.

'Thank you.' My heart clasps as I strip my coat off.

I exchange my coat for the cold bottle, and he hangs my coat up.

'You're welcome, Mrs Arnold.'

'I had a good day, and the children had a good holiday.' I rarely speak about Alex. I speak about the children. I toe off my shoes, and then, the beer bottle bumping his shoulder, wrap my arms around his neck and kiss his lips.

I am home. Safe.

I am me.

I don't want to think about Alex and his woman any more.

Chapter 55

6 weeks and 4 days until the inquest.

A woman walks along the road towards me. She's not wearing a coat, just a figure-hugging sweater with slim-line black trousers.

The morning is the warmest of the year so far.

She has a good figure. That's what drew my attention. She's a striking woman. But as we walk closer to each other and my gaze lifts from her body to her face, I see who she is. The first clue was in the way she holds her bag, the second is her matt-black hair. It's her. The woman from the basement.

Her gaze doesn't travel anywhere near me. She looks beyond me. Through me. Everything about her expression and body language says she hasn't seen me before.

She's walking to work in high heels, with a stride that's as confident as Alex at his most confident.

She walks past without looking at me.

If she doesn't know me it means she isn't interested in what happens in Alex's life beyond the basement, or that she's so confident in her hold on him, she doesn't need to be.

I glance over my shoulder.

I don't like her.

I don't know her, but I don't like her.

Bitch. I laugh aloud at the cruel reference in my head.

Does Louise shout bitch at her too? I hope so.

I must have walked past her dozens of times through the winter and not noticed her.

Does Alex know the time she walks to work? If so he'll know we are likely to pass in the street.

Anger is itching through my nerves when I press my finger on the doorbell. My mind wants to know everything, but I don't know what it is I need to ask.

Alex opens the door. 'Good morning. My first appointment has cancelled, so I'll walk Josh to school. You and the girls can stay here.'

'All right.' I slide off my coat. Does he think about that woman in the day? When he's doing the everyday things with the children? Do they text one another all the time?

I hang up my coat and turn to the kitchen. 'Good morning, Helen,' Rosie calls.

'Goo monning,' Hope repeats.

Alex turns to the stairs. 'Are you ready, Josh?' he shouts upwards.

I walk into the kitchen. 'Hello, darlings.' I rub the girls' heads, muddling up their pretty curls that were previously brushed into shape.

When that woman is downstairs, does she hear the children and Alex up here? I would find that comforting. When we talked the other day, Alex indicated that it was him who is holding back. What about her? Does she want this family? The children?

I lift Hope out of the highchair as Rosie gets down.

Because Hope still has a back tooth painfully pushing its way through her gum, I don't even try to put her down in her cot after lunch, but fetch a blanket from her room and let her lie on the sofa with her head on a pillow beside my lap.

I run my fingers through her golden curls as Rosie draws the picture I hate.

That picture feels part of a curse now. Part of Louise's haunting.

Does Louise go down to the basement? What does she do down there? Watch? Hate?

She must watch them in bed together.

Her breath sends a shiver creeping down my spine.

She thinks she's shown me why I should take the children away.

But even with a woman in the basement Alex is still a good father.

The dummy trembles in Hope's mouth, in the way it does when she is sucking in her sleep. I lift my hand away, so I will not disturb her.

'Rosie,' I whisper. 'Come and sit beside me.' CBeebies is playing on the television. Quietly. To drown out Louise's wailing.

Rosie drops her crayon. It rolls across the table and falls onto the rug on the far side. She climbs onto the sofa. I lift my arm so she can rest against me on the other side from Hope. Her thumb slides into her mouth. When that happens, I know she's tired, whether she sleeps or not.

'Are you missing Mummy?' I whisper.

She nods against my breast.

'I'm sorry, sweetheart.' I stroke her cheek with the backs of my fingers. Her skin is damp. She rarely cries; she's led by her brother's and her father's stoic denial of emotion.

Alex said he's holding back and not letting this woman into the children's lives. But he's been in the relationship for months. How long can it be before he lets her meet the children?

What happens if it becomes serious between them? Will he want a nanny when he has another woman here?

The house is filling up with threats, pulling at the children, trying to take them away from me.

My heart beats out a firm thumping rhythm that reverberates all the way to my fingertips. Anxiety turns in my mind and wraps around my heart, a slender spinning pillar of wind that whips around in a tornado of emotional destruction.

I can't lose these children.

The tornado picks up every thought in my head, growing in width and pace, setting everything into a spin.

For the rest of the afternoon I am fighting with fear, trying to act normal.

I will lose the children.

I don't know what I can do to keep them forever.

Anxiety's weed has long roots and they grow quickly.

I am going to lose the children. I know.

Chapter 56

18.10.

When I walk through the door at home, Andy isn't there. My hand trembles as I draw my phone out of my pocket to text him. The tornado in my body is wide enough to destroy the whole flat. I want to scream. Throw things. Rip. Scratch. Break. Everything. 'When will you be home?' Send.

Ping. I only had to wait a second. 'On my way now.'

'How far away are you?'

'Not far. Just coming up to the chip shop on the corner. Shall I buy tea?'

'No, I want you home.'

But. 'Yes.' I can't face starting anything for dinner.

The phone vibrates and then rings. His image appears, a picture I took on our wedding day.

'Hello,' I answer the call.

'What do you fancy?' he asks in a voice that tells me he's smiling.

'Chips will do.'

'Are you okay? You sound upset.'

'I had a difficult day with the children. Rosie cried for her mother.' And I am her mother.

'I'll be quick. See you in a bit.'

The phone call ends. But the phone remains in my hand, gripped tightly as though that is all I own.

My knees buckle, leaving me washed up like flotsam on the floor, and curling over, as small as I can be.

Tears drip onto the floor.

It might all be over soon.

If I lose the children ...

My children.

When Andy opens the door, I unfurl to get out of the way.

'What's wrong?' The white plastic bag containing the greasy-smelling paper parcels, drops on the floor.

'I am going to lose the children.'

'Has he sacked you?' Andy's strong arms wrap around me.

'No. No.' There are sniffs between my words as I sit up. 'I'm just ... I don't even know what's wrong with me.'

'Hormones. Probably,' he says. 'Come on. Go into the living room. I'll plate up the fish and chips and bring you a glass of wine.'

'I don't think wine will fix this.'

'We'll find out after you've tried it.'

The meal tastes like ash, and I can't swallow the wine because I'm sobbing.

I drop the fork on the chip paper. I can't eat.

'Lie down on the sofa,' Andy says, standing up to take my plate away.

I grab a tissue box and lie down, curling up like a baby in the womb. I want to be held that tight and loved that much.

Andy loves me. I am loved that much.

Louise is in my head, poisoning my thoughts, that's what this is. I've been in that toxic house and brought her home with me.

Go away! Leave me alone!

'Hello,' Andy says in the hall. 'I need your advice. No. It's Helen. She's upset, but there's no reason for it. Yes. Okay. I knew you'd have some good advice. Thanks, Simon. No. She'll be all right. Thank you.'

I look up when Andy comes into the room, but my head is heavy and it aches because of the overdose of emotion.

'What did Simon say?' I want him. Simon.

Andy smiles. 'He said if you are taking your medicine you'll be fine, but you probably need to sleep. And you didn't sleep that much when we were away. He suggested some warm milk with whisky and honey to help you nod off.'

I choke on a half-sob half-laugh. My brother loves me too.

After I have drunk Simon's remedy, I lie with my head on Andy's thigh as he strokes my hair.

I'm in the same position when I wake up only my head is on a cushion, not Andy's leg, the television is off and daylight is softening the colour of the curtains, making them a little transparent.

'Good morning. How do you feel?' Andy is standing near the sofa, with my phone in his hand.

'Rubbish,' I say. Tired. Heavy. Aching. Sad.

When I say the word sad in my head, sadness sweeps over me in a strong wave, washing up into every artery like a wave crashing over rock pools and reaching into every crevice.

He lifts my phone. 'I'm trying to work out your passcode so I can find your boss's number.'

'Why?' I sit up.

'Because I don't think you should go to work today.'

My feet slide off the sofa as I straighten up. 'The children will make me feel better.'

'You're exhausted. Are you sure you're up to looking after them? Take a day off.'

My head shakes in denial. 'I need to go.' When I stand up, every joint complains, I ache everywhere. But I force myself to move. I want to move. I want to see the children.

I stumble and Andy braces my arm. 'I don't think you should go.'

'I promise if I feel ill I'll ask Alex to come home from work and call you so you can walk me home.'

If I don't go, what if Alex turns to the woman downstairs for help?

He says he doesn't want her to meet the children, but there will be a first time some time.

A sigh trembles from Andy's throat.

I can't explain why the children are so important; Andy won't understand. He doesn't like it that I care so much about them.

'Okay,' he says, his gaze analysing my expression, doubt in his eyes. 'I'll make you breakfast and you can have a bath. But don't work late tonight.'

I nod. I just want to get there. Be there. With my children.

Every mouthful of porridge is hard to swallow. I take paracetamol along with my other tablets to try to stop the pain.

Perhaps it's because I'm no longer taking the immune blocking drugs? Perhaps that's why I feel overwhelmed? Because my heart is completely mine. Because it owns all the emotions I feel for the children.

Andy rings into work to say he'll be late, and walks to Alex's with me.

I don't see the woman walking into the town centre as we walk along the pavement.

Andy and I kiss on the corner at the head of the triangular

park, my arms around his neck and his around my waist. He kisses my cheek after he's kissed my lips. 'Have a good day and look after yourself. Get the children to do something calm.'

I nod and kiss his cheek. 'You have a good day too.'

'Text me when you're about to leave and I'll come and get you.'

'Thank you.'

We share another kiss before he goes. But as soon as he walks away the heavy doubt lies over me again. A thick layer of freezing snow. At odds with the warmer spring weather. This is coming to an end. I feel it. It's not just fear. Louise is warning me. Threatening me.

Because Alex will be arrested, her parents will win custody or that woman will move upstairs.

Every minute I spend with the girls through the day I feel as though I'm fighting for their lives.

When Josh comes home, we sit and read together and then, instead of letting him go up to his room to play electronic games, I encourage him to play with Rosie's butterfly-blowing elephant so that we can all play.

I need these children.

They are mine.

Chapter 57

5 weeks and 2 days until the inquest.

The music throbs through the nightclub like a pulse, vibrating around our dancing circle, which is made up of Andy's female friends and one of his gay friends.

I'm hot, sweaty and dizzy from too many gin and tonics.

Andy is on a sea-fishing trip. To celebrate one of the guys' birthday. I complained that it was sexist not to take the women, but I didn't fight for long because I didn't really want to be on a boat with drunk men and smelly mackerel.

I discovered today, when the rest of us went shopping instead, that no one else had wanted to go either and so that was the real reason it was a men-only day.

The trip was planned ages ago, but to Andy's credit he's been offering to withdraw from it all week because he didn't want to leave me alone this weekend. Especially as Chloe is away with her boyfriend.

He suggested I stay with Simon. But I don't want to leave Bath, and Andy will be back early in the morning. So, I promised to spend the day with everyone who wasn't going fishing.

I can't explain this, but although I've been accepted by his friends from day one, I've never felt comfortable, or normal, with them. I have stunted friendships with them. The conversations feel forced, they don't flow like a river as they do with Chloe, but ripple over stones in stops and starts. Perhaps my experience with the false friends that Dan and I shared has tainted my trust in their friendship. Perhaps it will take me longer to trust in new friendships.

The bass beat of the music develops the subtle change that will hook it into another song. 'I need the toilet,' I shout across the circle. People lift hands and smile, acknowledging my words. I turn away.

After using the toilet, I freshen up my lipstick, staring at my image in the mirror. My hand shakes, making the lipstick smear. I get a tissue out of my bag to wipe the edge of my lip then reapply.

Louise is there, a blurry image at my shoulder. She's there every time I look into a mirror now.

I don't feel well. This anxiety has been with me for days.

A breath sighs out on a rush. I am tired too. Ready to go home. To curl up again. Hide again.

But Andy isn't there to hold me.

The toilet door falls shut behind me. My gaze travels about the room.

A sway of dizziness, like vertigo, sends me off balance for a moment.

I have drunk too much.

I need a soft drink to sober up a little, before I walk home.

Andy told me to use a taxi, but it will take as long to wait for the taxi as it will to walk.

On the way to the bar my gaze is drawn to the man standing alone at the far end.

Alex.

He's here with that woman.

He's looking across the club, drinking from a beer bottle.

I look over my shoulder. I can't see her on the dance floor, but it's busy in here.

I weave my way through people to reach him.

'Alex. Alex,' I call and lift a hand, to get his attention.

He can't hear me over the music and hasn't seen me in the crowded club.

'Alex.' I am three metres away, but a group of women walks between us.

'Alex!' I shout around the last of the women. He looks in my direction. 'Hello.' I wave.

He recognises me and lifts his beer in a salute of acknowledgement.

I am held up by another group heading towards the bar. I think he'll move away but he stays where he is. 'What are you doing here?' I ask as I walk up to him.

He looks into my eyes, electric charge firing and his eyebrows lifting. 'Why? Are you going to tell me how to live my life again? And before you ask, my parents have the children for the night.'

I close my lips on everything I was about to say as his dark aura absorbs me in its midst. I am standing closer to him than I would in the house, so I can hear him, and he can hear me.

'Are you with your husband?'

'No. With friends.'

His aura is blacker than normal. Pitch black. Matt black. 'Are you here with the woman from the basement?'

'No.' His head shakes to confirm it.

Why was he here, then? 'Are you on your own?'

His eyebrows kick up, asking me what reason I have to ask. 'Yes.' He drinks from the bottle, tipping the base high.

'Have you nearly finished that? Do you want another drink? I was just going to buy one.'

The base of his bottle strikes the bar top heavily when he puts it down. 'I'll buy you one,' he says, reaching into his back pocket for his wallet. He sounds drunk. 'What do you want?'

'Gin and tonic.' I don't want to drink a soft drink when he's drinking alcohol.

After he pays for the drinks, we walk away from the bar. He grips a glass full of whisky and ice. I take hold of his arm and pull him towards a table that people are leaving.

The thin wool of his sweater slips out of my fingers as he pulls his arm free.

'Sit down.' My tone replicates an order to a child. He doesn't pick up on the negative tone of my voice, but his brain must be numbed by alcohol as much as mine is, if not more.

He sits on the end of the red leather seat that embraces a table in a crescent shape. I sit on the opposite end, laying my clutch bag down on the seat beside my hip.

The gin kicks at the back of my throat on the way down. It stirs up a flux of nausea. I swallow the feeling away with another sip. 'Why are you here on your own?'

'For fun,' he answers in an ironic voice, staring at his whisky, the glass held in both hands.

'You don't look as though you're enjoying yourself. Where's your girlfriend?'

'My girlfriend?'

'The woman in the basement.'

His shoulders lift and fall as a bleak look flows through his eyes. A hand lifts and rests on his forehead then runs down across his face.

Every time I think I know him, I discover I don't. The gesture expresses an emotional connection with the woman.

'We had an argument,' he says as his hand returns to the glass.

Did the children hear their argument? If they did, Rosie will be drawing her pushing picture on Monday.

'And?' I prod for more.

His elbows rest on the table and his shoulders hunch over. 'I have no idea what I'm doing. I'm lost and wandering around in circles.' The confidence slips out of him, the shop windows being flung open, and what's inside … surprises me.

My elbows rest on the table as I lean towards him. 'Literally or figuratively?' I joke.

'Both.' He leans back in the chair, smiling slightly. 'Sorry, am I keeping you from your friends?'

'No. They won't miss me. You can talk for as long as you need to.'

'I wish talking would help. Nothing helps.'

His voice expresses a naked honesty I haven't heard before. But he's never spoken to me when he's drunk before.

'Helps with what?'

'What do you think?' He drinks some whisky, the ice rattling against the glass.

'Are you worried about the inquest?'

'I'm worried about losing my children, pissed off with life throwing me the crap hands and fed up with the need to keep trying. She escaped. I can't get away. But, God, if I could just …'

He doesn't continue. I think he's speaking about suicide.

I reach out and brace his forearm that's resting on the table. I can't say everything will be all right because I don't know that it will be. The inquest hearing might mean he's accused of murder. Louise's parents might win custody of the children.

'Why did you argue with your girlfriend?'

His head shakes in a 'no' movement, but he answers, 'She wants more than I can give her. More of me. More of my life.

I'm not ready for that, and nor are the children. I can't just forget the past.'

I hear regret in his voice. Sadness and longing. Longing to rewrite the past?

I never heard regret from Dan. I've dreamed of receiving an apology, and him pleading for me to go back, only so that I would have the pleasure of saying no. To hear regret in Alex's voice is ... nice. I have a lot of respect for him as a father; I want to be able to respect him as a man.

Alcohol is like oil on a hinge, it lubricates and eases and makes it easier to open up.

'Does your girlfriend not understand that?'

'She's hardly a *girl*friend.'

'Woman, then; does this woman who lives downstairs not understand?'

His right hand strokes over his hair. Self-comforting. He shakes his head. 'I don't even know if I want her to.' The glass of whisky starts spinning as his fingers twist it around. 'If I let her understand I'm letting her in, and I'm not ready to let anyone in.'

You let her into the basement – my jealous thoughts snap.

But, he's thinking about Louise still. That's what he's telling me. That he isn't over her yet, and so he may have cheated, but he does regret it.

He looks up. Looking into me. Looking for something. His gaze open so I can see into him too.

His head shakes, as if whatever he keeps saying no to are words or emotions in his head.

'The problem with me is I don't do anything to let go, Helen. I have no escape. I haven't turned to drink or drugs, and I could have done. I have access to that stuff in my world. But I couldn't do that to the children. It means I have nothing to escape into. Nowhere to run to when I need to get away. Except one place. Something I will not become addicted to, but I can use when I want to ...' His eyes look beyond me, over my shoulder, for a moment.

I glance back. There's no one particular there. His mind has gone elsewhere. I think he won't continue. But then he looks back at me.

'I can escape when I'm with a woman.' The words are said with a bitter, hard disgust.

His voice, his eyes and the tight clench of his jaw say that he's not comfortable with acknowledging that.

Sex is the drug he goes to. He's been using that woman in the basement to escape other thoughts and now she's said no more. That's what they have argued over.

But that means he's looking for an alternative tonight.

'You used that woman just for sex.'

'It is better than using prostitutes, and sex is what we both wanted. She knew it was just about sex. I don't want to be close to someone. Louise is still ...' His words slip away on his breath.

Her energy is heavy around me. She's listening to this. Is she hearing it as an apology? He sounds as if he still loves her, no matter that he did the same thing with women when they were married.

The music pulses around us as I wait for him to continue.

His gaze falls to the whisky, his shoulders rounding further with the look of defeat.

'It is not a year yet,' I say.

The glass spins around in his fingers.

'It would be strange if you didn't still have feelings for her. You're grieving.'

He looks up. 'Am I grieving? It was like this before she died. I needed an escape route then.' The glass lifts and he drinks the whisky in large mouthfuls, the ice rattling in the glass as his Adam's apple slides down and back up. Then he wipes his mouth with the back of his left hand as his right hand sets the glass on the table.

'Not grieving. Guilty,' he says, spitting the last word out with a bitter sound. 'Guilty because I couldn't cope. Guilty because I couldn't fix things. Guilty because I needed to escape. And guilty because I still need to. Goodnight,' he says as he stands, moving out of the seat. 'I need to go.'

Is he going to go to that woman and accept her demands?

I stand, picking up my clutch bag, and follow.

I'm not going to let him leave without understanding that everything he does impacts on the children, and if he does something wrong, I could lose them. 'Alex!' He can't hear me through the throb of the music.

He doesn't look back before disappearing into the dense crowd at the edge of the dance floor.

When I reach the hall that leads downstairs to the exit, he's gone already. I run down the steps as fast as I can in heels. I'm not going to let him ruin this.

I pull the ticket out of my pocket to claim my coat from the cloakroom. There's no queue. I hang the coat over the arm my clutch bag is tucked under and push the exit door wide.

The street is alive with traffic and the streetlights are bright. A policeman and woman are standing on the far corner of the road.

My gaze turns one way then another. There are five different routes. Three roads. Two pedestrian routes. The pedestrian routes lead back to his house, but I'm not certain he's going that way.

Where has he gone? To another club? To another person?

The cold wind whips my hair at my cheeks

My fingers clasp the bag that's under my arm, and the cold makes me shiver, but I'm not going to waste time putting my coat on.

'Has something happened, miss?' The policewoman walks over.

'I am looking for ... my friend. He just walked out of the club. We had an argument.' Lies are easily told these days.

'Do you think it might be better to let him go? Does he need some time to cool off?'

'He's not violent. We shouted. Nothing else. I want to apologise.'

She smiles. 'Are you sure it's not better to wait until the morning when you're both sober?'

'Yes. I'm sure.' I can't be rude, but my voice is urgent.

'A man walked that way a couple of minutes ago, and he's the only person we've seen leave the club in the last fifteen minutes.' She points towards one of the pedestrian routes that will take him farther into the city centre. It could also be a route home.

'Thank you.' I run a few paces with my shoes on, then stop and slide them off and run along damp streets with my shoes, coat and bag gripped in my hands.

'Hey, love! Wey hey, where's the fire?' People, drinkers, call out to me as I run across the paved area outside a pub, where people are gathered, smoking.

'Steady up, darling.' A young man I nearly run into grips my arm. I pull it free, nearly losing my balance on a wobbling slab of paving. Then I run again.

I should have caught Alex up. I should be able to see him.

There's another junction in the pedestrian area, a crossroads. I can walk straight on, left or right. Straight on leads to the house, to the children, but it also leads to more pubs, wine bars, a casino and the hotel I saw him in the other night.

If she's in the basement it also leads to her.

I walk on, crossing over the uneven cobbles of the main street onto an arcade with an outer row of guarding pillars.

'Alex!' I see him. 'Alex!' He's walking quickly. His hands in his pockets and his head lowered a little.

'Alex!' My voice echoes back from the old Georgian stone.

He glances back, stops walking and turns around. To wait. A dark, stationary silhouette.

I stop and slide my shoes back on. The soles of my stockings are wet and uncomfortable as I start walking again, and the world is swaying.

The breaths that pull into my lungs are rushing along with my heartbeat. I try to breathe slower as I walk up to him.

'Why are you following me?' He speaks before turning to walk on.

'Because I want to help.' I fall into step beside him. I will follow, wherever he's leading, if it means we'll keep the children.

'Nothing helps, bar one thing, and that's only for a moment. Anyway, you live in the other direction.'

'Yes. But ...' We turn the corner, where the arcade opens onto the area that encircles the single-storey building containing the Cross Bath. There's a deep step in front of us, and no one is in the area around us. Although the noise of the nearby road and bars leaks into the space.

I catch hold of the sleeve of his leather jacket. 'Sit down and talk to me.' He doesn't pull his arm free, but looks at me. 'Sit and talk this out.'

'No, thanks. I'm drunk. You're drunk. The pavement is cold. And we both need to go home.'

I let go of his sleeve. 'Andy isn't back until the morning – I don't have to hurry back. And you should be seeking psychiatric help not sex with strangers.'

His eyebrows kick up, in disbelieving surprise over my words. I wouldn't have said the same words sober.

But there are more words that want to come. 'I'm sorry.' The words are fizzing, and then they spit. 'No. No. I'm not sorry. Tell me why there are no pictures of Louise in the house. Why did you sleep with women when you were married? If you feel so guilty now, why did you do it then? Is the lack of pictures due to guilt?'

Has he erased Louise's existence because he feels guilty?

Has he kept that one picture beside his bed because he regrets what he did?

I feel as though I am facing Dan; if I'd had the chance to ask him I would have wanted to know.

Why? Is that the answer Louise has been waiting for too? She's in the shadows all around us. Watching but silent.

If he tells me and apologises will it mean she leaves me alone?

I want to shake the words out of him. Wring them out of him. My hands grip my bag and coat tighter, so that I will not do either of those things.

A sigh runs through his lips and mists in the night air as his hand runs over his hair. 'I'm not talking about this in the street. But if you come back to the house, I'll tell you about my marriage. It's going to be regurgitated at the inquest anyway – you might be able to help the children if you know the truth.'

'I can come back to the house.'

We walk through an alley and into the main street, my stiletto heels scratching on the tarmac and paving slabs.

His hands are in his pockets. Mine hold my coat and bag.

We navigate the groups of drunk students in Kingsmead Square in silence, him leading and me following half a step behind. He doesn't even glance at me as we walk along the main road.

When he lifts a hand to press the pelican crossing button, he finally glances back, but in the same way he might check that one of the children is there and not lost.

We cross the road, and then we walk along the wide pavement towards the house. I glance at the dark park, and see myself sitting in there, months ago.

His hands slip out of his pockets. His pace quickens and he walks a few paces farther ahead as we near the house. The metal of the door key catches the light as one hand lifts.

I have walked through this door many times, but never with Alex.

Louise welcomes us. Her presence a concentrated weight in the air of the hall. A threat against me. I have no justifiable reason for being here alone with Alex beyond curiosity and self-preservation. Her intense relationship with Alex, which has meant she can't let go and move to the spirit world, has spun the hatred to the other side of that coin, love. Her jealousy is telling me to get out.

'Do you want another drink?' Alex throws the words over his shoulder as he takes his coat off and toes off his shoes.

'What sort of drink?' As I ask there's a sense of Louise's spirit pushing through me. Trying to push me back out of the door.

I hang up my coat and follow him into the kitchen, holding my clutch bag in front of me. It's strange to be in the house in evening clothes.

'I'm going to have whisky. But if you prefer you can have tea or coffee, or something else ...' The words drift as he slides the cuffs on the sleeves of his thin sweater up to his elbows and reaches to open a cupboard. The electric light catches the gold hairs on his arms. But his jawline is clean-shaven.

He shaved tonight, before going out. Before looking for sex.

'Have you got any gin?' If he's drinking more, I'll drink more, to keep him talking.

He looks over his shoulder at me while lifting a half-full whisky bottle from the cupboard that contains special crockery, entertaining platters and Christmas plates. The whisky must have been hidden at the back. 'No gin, sorry. Your choice is beer, whisky or something non-alcoholic.'

'Whisky, then. Please.'

He puts the bottle down and opens another cupboard, reaches for glasses, puts them on the side and then unscrews the cap of the bottle. 'We'll go upstairs. It is warmer up there.' The whisky flows into one glass then the other.

I'm standing, balancing on one stiletto heel, my legs crossed, gripping my clutch bag with my hands over my stomach. 'Is she downstairs?' It is uncomfortable being in the house with him on my own. But I want to be here, to find out everything I can. I might be able to help somehow. To help him keep the children – and push that woman away.

He looks at me as he stops pouring, his eyes and expression asking, who? Then he realises. 'No. She's gone away for the weekend.' To avoid him, the tone of his voice adds. 'Do you want some ice?'

'Yes. Please. What will happen when she comes back?'

He shrugs. 'Who knows? I'm not thinking about it. All I know tonight is that I need to do something to get out of here myself, and it's going to have to be through this.' He picks up a glass of whisky and lifts it high, in salutation. He takes a sip before turning back for the other glass and then filling them both with ice from the ice dispenser inside the fridge.

'Here.' He walks around the breakfast bar, holding a glass out in my direction.

'Thank you.' As I take the glass our fingertips brush awkwardly.

He goes back for the bottle, picking it up by the neck, then leads the way out of the room. I stop to slip off my stilettos before I climb the stairs behind him. The soles of my stockings feel gravelly from my run across the cobbles.

Louise moves in front of me when I reach the top of the stairs, trying to block my path as I follow Alex through to the living room. But she's just a shadow, she can't really stop me.

I look up, thinking about the children as if they are in their rooms above us, but he's said they're with his parents.

The house is an empty shell without them. Like a piece of discarded bird's egg that's dropped on the ground in the park.

'Do you miss the children when they're away?'

He's putting the bottle down on the coffee-table; he glances back as he straightens. 'You probably think I'll say no. That I'm glad to get some time to myself. But the truth is I do, because I have nothing without them.' His eyes say more. His eyes tell me a truth.

The sex, the drinking, for this weekend at least, is about escaping the knowledge that he might lose the children.

He drinks from the whisky in the glass. Then sits down at one end of a sofa.

I sit at the opposite end and lean forward to put my clutch bag down on the low table.

He swallows all the whisky in the glass, the ice rattling, and then puts the glass down beside the whisky bottle before reaching into his back pocket.

His phone is in his hand; his elbows rest on his knees as he leans forward, touching it with his thumb to unlock it and look for something.

I cross my legs, take a sip of bitter, sharp whisky and then rest the glass on my knee.

The whisky is going to go straight to my head.

'Come here. I'll show you a picture of my wife, then you'll understand.'

I lean forward and put the glass down, then slide across the leather sofa, moving next to him so I can see the screen on his phone.

'I met her when I was eleven. We were both eleven. She was in my class in our first year at secondary school.'

He isn't showing me the pictures.

'We started dating when we were fourteen. I know my parents have pictures of us on school trips and things. I think her mother does too. But Louise hated old pictures. She hated any pictures.'

He holds out the phone. I take it and look at the image displayed.

It's horrible. She's emaciated. She looks so ill.

'You want the children to have pictures. Would you want them to look back on memories like that?'

'No. What was wrong?' Louise is wearing a V-neck T-shirt in the picture and beneath it the bones of her clavicle push through a translucent layer of skin. Her arm is barely wider than the bones in it, and her cheeks are hollow, dark and sunken, denying her smile. Her eyes and her mouth huge, her hair thin and lank.

It is Louise. I can see her in the image. But she's so different.

My mouth is open in silent exclamation when I look back at Alex, asking why again.

'Anorexia,' he answers. 'Now you see why I can't put pictures up around the house. The children will forget how ill she looked. I hope they will just remember that she loved them.

'She was fine until we had Josh. She put weight on while she was pregnant. Within two months of giving birth she became obsessive about losing the weight. She wouldn't eat in front of me. She ate sometimes, I know, but when she did it was in secret because she hated herself for doing it and then she'd make herself sick. She tried to hide that from me but I lived with her, I knew.

'She blamed Josh for her weight gain and blamed me for wanting to have him. She was modelling at the time. She couldn't get back into it.

'It took me a year to persuade her she was sick and needed help. The private retreat I got her into helped. They watched her every day and monitored her eating and taught her to increase what she ate daily. When she came home she was getting better, and she became a mother to Josh, but she never worked after that. Her agency had dropped her when she was too thin. Instead we made a fresh start. Went to America. Built a new life. It was her idea.

'I built up my name out there. Working with some of the big fashion houses and magazines. While she came up with her own idea for a project. Another baby. Rosie was going to cement our future and make us an average family. No one is happy every day but we planned to be at least content. Content would be good, and happy often, she used to say.'

His mind has travelled back through time. The distant look in his eyes tells me he's there, listening to Louise say those words.

When he breaks free from the memories he picks up the whisky bottle and refills his glass. He drinks the whisky straight down, before moving the bottle in my direction and offering me a refill.

I drink all the bitter whisky in my glass, feeling it burn my throat, and hold the glass out. I want to be supportive. Maybe I'm stupidly expressing that through drinking whisky, but I want his trust and if I try to sober up while he keeps drinking he'll stop speaking.

He refills my glass, beginning to speak again as he does so. 'When

Rosie started to show, Louise's mind told her she was putting on weight and the fight she had with food began again. I made every meal for her and put out what I said she needed to eat to look after the child inside her. She forced down every mouthful.'

'I'm sorry.' I don't know what else to say.

I sip the whisky as he refills his glass again. My throat has been numbed by the last glass.

'Even before Rosie was born, Louise was pretending to eat, hiding food. Josh, at the age of two, told me where Mummy had hidden her lunch one day. Rosie was born four weeks early and they said it was probably due to a lack of nutrition. We were lucky Rosie didn't have brain damage. It was then that Louise spiralled into hell and we all went with her.'

I see her. I hear her. She lives in hell even now. 'What about Hope?'

'Hope ...' A harsh note of amusement that seems to laugh at himself slips out. 'Hope was Louise's idea again. She convinced herself, and me, that if she had a reason to get better she would, and what better reason than to have a child inside her? She proved to me she could eat and she would eat because she went back into the retreat and put enough weight on so her periods started again.

'She maintained the weight for about four months. I agreed then, to try for another child. She fell pregnant straight away. But as soon as the baby began to show she became ill. She couldn't stand to look at her body in the mirror with the bump.'

He looks me in the eyes. No electric charge, only that naked honesty glitters in the electric light from the lamp that's near him. 'It wasn't Hope's fault. She didn't ask to be created. But Louise hated her.'

Oh, my God. I feel that. I have felt it. The way she doesn't relate to the children as she should do. The way she focuses all her energy on Alex.

He drains another glass of whisky.

I have pushed open the shop door and now it's open it's as if he can't close it, and he's letting me all the way into the basement level of his emotions.

'We came home, to the UK. To be near our parents, so they could help with the children. We bought this place and I set up the studio. But the only way she would eat is if I cooked her food and stayed with her to make sure she didn't throw it up. It was like having a fourth child.'

He breathed out harshly. 'I couldn't work half the time. She was more like a child than Josh, and angry with me all the time because I made her eat. All she wanted to do was starve herself to death. She destroyed us and she didn't care.' The sheen of moisture in his eyes gleams. 'She didn't love me, us, she didn't love us.'

He fills his glass again, and reaches to top up my glass.

I cover the glass with my hand and shake my head. But I do take a sip as he sits back in the seat.

Sipping the whisky makes the bitterness stronger. My stomach trembles with nausea. I swallow all the whisky and put the glass down.

He mistakes the movement to mean I want more and refills my glass.

'So that's the story of me and Louise,' he says as he puts the bottle down and collapses back on the sofa, glass in hand.

It's not the whole story. He hasn't said how she fell from the top floor of a car park, when he and the children were there.

'The children have no idea what was wrong. Josh remembers how thin she was, and how she avoided food. He'll understand when he's older.' Alex's free hand strokes over his hair. 'But for now, all I want is for them to see her as an angel. I want them to have a mother they can look back and love.'

I lay a hand on his knee. 'But why do her parents think you're responsible for her death if they know she was ill?'

'Because they need someone other than her to blame for her anorexia.'

His free hand makes a second pass over his hair. 'And she rang them in tears the day she died. It's my fault she died, and they know. But that doesn't mean I should lose my children.'

His fault? 'Why was it your fault?'

'I pushed her into it.' He doesn't look at me when he says that, he looks across the room. But then he looks at me. 'The truth is ugly?' he says, and drains his glass.

His hand slides to the back of his neck and his palm holds there, his elbow stretching out wide as the empty glass rests on his knee. My hand is still on his other leg.

'God. I need to get away from this. I need to be out of my mind.' He looks at me. 'It's our wedding anniversary today. It's the first time she's not been here.'

I move my hand off his leg, drink my whisky and lean over to put the glass down out of his reach to discourage him from topping it up. My thoughts are becoming a fish swimming through reeds.

'I loved her.' He's still looking at me. 'Right until the end. Even now. I love her. But she was so fucking hard to love and help. She didn't want to be helped. And she died without knowing how much I loved her. But how do you show love to someone who has done that to themselves—' he thrusts a hand at the phone on the coffee table '—and pushes their children away for the sake of being thin?'

He leans forward, puts his glass down, and then both hands are behind his head, and he bends over, with elbows on his knees and head held down.

I think he's crying.

I touch his shoulder. For one moment, he rocks back then forward. 'If you knew the agony I've lived through for years? I hide it from the children, from my parents. From the people I work with. The friends who've drifted away because she never went out and I couldn't leave the children with her.'

His hands fall and lie on his thighs as he straightens, glancing at me. 'Sorry, I'm a sad drunk. I don't usually talk. I don't need to talk when I'm having sex. Sex is the only thing that gives me some help.' He looks into my eyes. 'But then that makes me feel guilty too, because I used it to escape her even when she was alive. She didn't want to be touched so she told me to sleep with other women. It was a relief and ...'

'Revenge,' I say. 'I understand what it means to be angry at life.' At someone and at fate. I know what anger can make you do – and what love can make you do. I have done some strange things.

'And how fucking cruel am I? What a bastard to want revenge on my sick wife. I sicken myself.' A sigh runs out from deep in his throat, a low-toned, heavy sound. 'I don't know. I suppose one day, this will be something I can label as the past, and there will be someone new in my life and ...' His words run dry. I'm not sure why. He's looking across the room, at nothing, to nowhere.

But he's right – one day there will be someone else. If he keeps sleeping with people, if not the woman in the basement, then someone else he meets will stay around. He will collide with fate at some point.

Then what about me? What about the children? If he finds someone else to be their mother where will I fit into their future?

Louise is laughing all around me. At me.

He's the gatekeeper. No matter where the children go, if I'm attached to Alex, I'll have access. If he wants me to stay, then there will always be a way for me to stay.

I need to feel safe. To quell this anxiety. I'm reaching for a rope. I need to know that I will not lose the children. I can't lose the children.

The living room spins in a single full circle as I lean forward, rest a hand on his thigh and stretch to whisper in his ear. 'If you want sex, Alex, I'm here.'

His head turns, and for a moment he looks into my eyes.

I'm so drunk, I can't hold his gaze.

His hand reaches to the back of my head and his lips press against mine, and in a moment his tongue is in my mouth. It's an awkward kiss, because he's drunk too.

I can't even say how we end up lying down. But he is on top, and no longer kissing my mouth but his hip is pressing against my hip and my skirt has been pulled up.

This is stupid. This is so stupid. My mind chants as I move to help him strip my knickers off. This is insane.

What are you doing, Helen?

Louise is pushing at me. Her energy is heavy on me and she's in my head, screaming and snarling and making my thoughts fuzzy.

One of Alex's hands unthreads his belt from the buckle.

He's on his side, balancing on one elbow next to me on the wide sofa, struggling to undo the waistband button of his jeans. When it's free, he releases the zip.

I can't remember how we ended up on the sofa. Lying on the sofa.

My skirt is pushed to my waist. My knees part as he moves over me. The ceiling spins, and spins.

I shuffle down on the sofa, because my back is uncomfortable.

His breath smells strongly of whisky, and his hands are near my shoulders where they press indents into the sofa cushions. 'Ah.' He pushes himself into me without any consideration for me.

'Ah. Ah. Alex.' Louise is shouting all around me.

My hands hold his shoulders. Holding on because I feel as if I am falling.

'Alex.' I feel a little sick. The movement is making me feel sick.

I bite my lip. I will not be sick.

His breath comes out in grunts of exertion.

There's no contact between us beyond the intimate connection, and he isn't looking at me, he is looking beyond me.

He pushes into me, striking against my body heavily, his belt buckle rattling.

As the movement goes on, my body begins to enjoy it, because he is doing everything my body needs to enjoy sex; it doesn't need kisses or touches, or love, to react by instinct.

I shut my eyes and let my body feel – and react. It is as though he's thrashing us both, as though his violent penetrations, which rock my whole body and shake my breasts, are determined to make us pay for doing this.

He wants the need out of him and he wants it out quickly and he wants to hurt himself when he does it.

Louise is laughing again.

Is this what it is always like for him? I feel sorry for him.

In my head, I feel Andy making love to me, kissing me, all

over my body, and then gently moving within me. Where is Andy? I need him, not this. I need to get home and be with him.

I want to grip Alex's arms as I feel the rush of an orgasm rising like a distant wave, growing bigger and threating to break over me. I want this to stop. To stop it feeling good. It shouldn't feel good.

I don't hold Alex's arms because he doesn't want to be touched.

My fingers claw into the sofa cushion near my hips, my teeth clenching, biting hard to stop me from shouting. My breathing is short sounds that slip out through my nose. If my mouth were open I'd be panting.

An orgasm sweeps through me. The wave washing into the harbour.

Tears roll from the corners of my closed eyes.

He doesn't stop. If anything, his movement increases in strength.

My fingernails press more firmly into the sofa cushions, clinging. My climax is not a moment of success for him. He doesn't care; this is his release. He's focused on the sensations inside him.

I see the shroud of dark mist around us. I feel it. It's as violently bitter as the whisky, angry and guilty, and grieving.

He's breathing hard. Pressing into me hard.

I tip my head back into the sofa and lift my hips, thrusting back against his thrusts to bring this to its end. I just want to go home. But I reach a second orgasm before his conclusion comes.

That orgasm inspires his end. He pushes into me one last time, then makes slight additional movements as he groans, with an ethereal sound.

His pelvis rests on mine, still and heavy.

I want to push him off me.

He withdraws and moves onto his side, next to me, his weight on his elbow.

I roll away, sitting up, getting up. We smell of sex. It's in the air, in the darkness around him.

Louise isn't jealous. She's still laughing.

My knickers are on the floor. I pick them up, step into them and pull them on, my hands trembling and my head spinning.

His belt buckle rattles as he does it up, and when he stands up his trousers have been done up again.

It is as though nothing has happened between us.

'I need to go home,' I say.

He nods, but says nothing.

I pick my clutch bag up off the coffee table.

He follows me out of the room, along the landing and downstairs.

I slide my feet into my heels as he stands on the third step of the stairs, watching me, with one hand on the bannister.

I take my coat off the hook, throw it over my arm and glance at him. 'Goodnight.'

'Goodnight. Thank you for listening, Helen.'

I open the door, let myself out and close it carefully behind me so the knocker doesn't rattle.

Oh, my God. Oh, my God. Oh, my God. I have done far more than listen. I have done too much.

After only five steps I lean over and I am sick into the grate for the rain water at the edge of the street.

Chapter 58

5 weeks and 1 day until the inquest.

A key turns in the lock. It wakes me. I've been dozing. I have not slept properly.

The door opens.

I roll over in the bed and look at the electric alarm clock. 5:09. A part of me wants to hide. To pretend I'm asleep.

I can't believe what I've done. It's been repeating in my head like a nightmare all night.

Another part of me desperately wants Andy.

'Hello,' I call out into the hall in a voice that's husky with hangover. I just need to touch him. To be back in Helen's life.

'Are you okay?' He appears in the bedroom doorway as I push up onto my elbows.

'Yes.'

'I had a text to say you disappeared from the club last night.'

I didn't even think about telling anyone I was leaving. 'I was drunk. I felt sick. I still feel drunk and sick.' I smile, feeling pathetic – and guilty.

Guilt is a physical sickness.

What did I do last night? Why? I was so drunk, I don't even remember.

'Would you like a cup of tea?'

'Yes, and some paracetamol. Then I want more sleep.'

'Your vote is for a lazy Sunday, then?'

'Yes, please.'

'A cup of tea is on its way,' he answers, 'and I'm going to get back into bed with you because I was drunk last night too.' A smile pulls at his lips.

I lie down as he walks away from the doorway and shut my eyes.

This is reality. I just want last night to go away. Louise pushed me into it. Pushed me into it through fear and then laughed as it happened.

He used me as a substitute for her while she watched. I was her vessel, that was all.

And his vessel; Alex wanted his childhood sweetheart underneath him, but he's not had that for years and so he used my body – in his mind he was with Louise.

'Andy. Andy.' I throw the covers back and rush out to the toilet to be sick.

Chapter 59

5 weeks until the inquest.

M y finger trembles as it presses the doorbell.
      I received a text from Alex yesterday saying, 'Sorry about last night. It shouldn't have happened.'

I didn't reply. I didn't know how to reply – and I was with Andy.

It feels like minutes before the door opens, but it's probably only seconds. The doorknocker rattles.

'Hello,' I say, as I see Alex.

'Hello.' His voice is low, gruff and dismissive and he turns away before the door has even opened wide enough to let me in.

He's in the kitchen with the children. They're eating pancakes. The smells of butter, batter and maple syrup fill the hall.

I take my coat off and at the same time slip my shoes off. I hang up my coat and leave my handbag with the shoes. 'Hello,' I say to the room, in a bright voice.

'Hello.' Rosie looks over, smiling. Hope lifts a sticky maple-syrup-coated hand and waves at me.

I look at Josh, who hasn't looked at me. 'How are you, Josh? Did you have a good weekend with Grandad and Grandma?'

He looks up. 'Yes.'

Alex brushes a hand over Josh's head, mixing up the short-cut curls. I think the caress is only given to avoid the need to interact with me. His skin is a vivid red.

Perhaps my skin is a darker colour too.

'What time will you be home today?' I ask Alex, creating an opening for conversation.

'Between five-thirty and six,' he answers, looking at the children, not me.

'Okay.'

His gaze turns to me for a second, then he looks away and taps Josh on the shoulder. 'Come on, get your things and put your shoes on. We need to go.'

I look at the clock on the wall. It's early for Josh to go, but Josh eats his last mouthful, climbs down from the stool and leaves the room. He loves the days when he has Alex to himself on the way to school.

'Let me clean you up, messy,' Alex says to Hope, moving in the opposite direction from Hope to pull off some paper towel. He dampens it under the tap, then comes over to wipe Hope's face and hands. She looks at him with adoring eyes as he does it, and his attention is all for her.

No matter what happened between us, I can't live without these children. I must forget Saturday night and carry on and if he wants to pretend it didn't happen, that helps.

After he's wiped Hope's hands, I unbuckle her from her highchair, my hands trembling, while he wipes Rosie's sticky face and hands.

Rosie smiles at him as Hope smiles at me. Rosie and Hope were second and third attempts at happiness for him and Louise. They've made me happy and I make them happy.

My stomach churns with a cocktail of guilt and embarrassment. I was so foolish. Too drunk.

Hope's becoming heavy, and quite capable on her legs; she doesn't need to be carried. But I want to hold her. I want her as my comfort blanket, and a shield.

Chapter 60

4 weeks and 4 days until the inquest.

When I open the door, returning from the school run to drop off Josh, an A4-sized brown paper envelope is lying on the coir doormat amongst other long narrow white envelopes and brightly coloured junk mail. I see at a glance the manila envelope is franked for first-class postage.

Rosie undoes Hope's wrist rein as I bend to pick up the post. The franking on the brown envelope doesn't have a company name but I know it's something unusual and personal. I put the post on a step of the stairs as I help the girls take off their damp coats and shoes.

Today is a very wet day. It's a day to spend indoors.

A craft day.

Rosie told me she wanted to make necklaces with the beads and buttons we saw in the market the other week. Hope would be too tempted to put them in her mouth, though, so instead I've bought coloured strips of paper for them to roll into bead shapes and thread onto ribbon.

'Go in the kitchen and get out the scissors and glue. We'll make the beads on the coffee table there.'

I'm avoiding the living room. I don't want to go in there. I don't want to have to look at the sofa.

I follow the children into the kitchen with what Rosie refers to as Helen's crafty-bag.

I bring the post in with me and put it on top of the breakfast bar, then turn to help the girls set up.

I roll beads with them, and help Hope with hers, my thoughts drifting ...

I can't stop recalling the moment that Alex and I ... The images run like stills through my head. Those still-shots were playing on a loop while I was with Andy. I want them to go away.

I've lied to Simon, Chloe and even Alex by omission over the last year. But knowing what I've done and not telling Andy is rotting what Andy and I have made, what we are making.

The memories are a flesh-eating infection spreading through my mind, chewing up my brain.

My lips want to betray me and shout the truth.

If I tell Andy the truth it might destroy us and I can't destroy us any more than I can lose the children.

It's Louise's fault. She scared me into it. Trapped me into doing it. Your fault.

She's watching now. Laughing with a vicious sound.

Bitch.

When Alex came in from work last night his aura was still pitch black and as thick as I imagine a 1950s London smog would be. As choking and poisonous as that too.

He spoke to the children and ignored me. His skin red and his eyes, which sometimes look so directly into mine, did not collide with mine once.

I am ashamed of myself, and shame is worse than embarrassment.

It was desperate, not only wrong.

Obsessed. Obsessed. That word keeps playing around in my thoughts too. Trying to connect itself with the things I have done in the past that were foolish. But I'm not ill. I'm taking my medicine, and I'm not obsessed with Alex in any way. It's just that I love the children. I'd do anything to keep them.

Is the woman downstairs? She could be underneath my feet. I feel her presence all the time when I'm in the house, not through a sixth sense but out of shame. I'm no better than her. I'm worse than her. She met Alex and they created some sort of relationship. I just …

Louise must know if the woman is downstairs.

Perhaps that's why Louise is laughing so much, because she's pushed me down even lower than his mistress.

A sigh drops out through my lips, a noticeable enough sigh that if Josh were here, he would know it was in response to a difficult or sad thought. But Rosie is too young to understand the silent language of human beins.

Hope looks at me with eyes that ask for help, because the paper isn't doing what she wants it to do.

I wrap my arms around her and lay my hands over hers to roll the paper.

'Can I use glitter?' Rosie asks.

She knows I have glitter in my crafty-bag. 'Yes. But make sure you do it over the paper so you can tip the leftover glitter back into the pot.'

I touch 'call' on my phone, another time, while Rosie watches me, clinging onto Hope's hand to make sure she doesn't decide to run off into the road.

The phone ring begins. It continues.

Pick up, Alex.

J. S. Lark

My heart is bumping against my ribs and I feel sick with fear. Come on.

Ring. Ring.

Ring. Ring.

'Hello, Alex Lovett isn't contactable at the momen—' I touch 'end' and smile at Rosie, who is biting her lip as I call again.

I have called four times— 'Hello, Alex's phone.' A woman answers.

My heartbeat stutters with relief. 'Hello, is Alex there? This is Helen, his nanny. It's urgent. It's about the children. I'm looking after them.' Or meant to be.

'He's in the middle of a shoot but I'll ask him if he wants to take the call.'

I hear voices in the room, in his studio, I assume.

'Hello.'

'Alex. Do you know about Josh going home with someone else? We're at the school. We waited and waited but he didn't come out. I took the girls in and asked the teacher where he is. She said he'd gone home with the mother of another boy.'

'Shit. Sorry. Yes. He's gone there for the night.' I imagine his fingers combing into untidy curls.

The breath rushes out of me in relief. I've been thinking all sorts. That Louise's parents had taken Josh. That I had lost Josh forever.

'I'm sorry I forgot to say this morning.' There's a note of frustration in his voice. But the frustration is directed at himself. His thoughts must have been jumbled up by Saturday night too. 'Now you're on the phone, though ... Can you work late tonight, feed the girls and get them into bed? I need to work late really, if I can.'

'Yes. Of course.'

'Thank you. Sorry again.'

'Don't worry about it. I'm just glad Josh is safe.'

'I need to go.'

'Can you say hello to Rosie, quickly? She's been worried too.'

'Okay. Hi, sweetheart,' I hear him say as the phone is moving.

'Daddy?' Rosie says, the pitch in her voice making his name a question. She nods a few times as I hold the phone to her ear then she says, 'Goodnight. Bye, Daddy.' She kisses the screen of my phone, then looks at me.

I assume he's hung up. When I look at the phone, he has.

Rosie looks at Hope, and I see her squeeze Hope's hand a bit tighter. 'Josh is at his friend's and Daddy is working late, so, Helen is staying with us for tea. Then we have to get ready for bed.'

'Let's cook tea together. We can treat ourselves to a stir-fry. We can buy the ingredients on the way home.'

Rosie enjoys helping me chop things, and Hope enjoys sitting in her highchair watching and chewing on raw sticks of carrot.

After dinner, I chase them up to their room to play, so I can run a bath, herding the girls upstairs like little Austrian mountain goats. Rosie hopping up steps and Hope hanging onto my hands so she can jump steps.

Daylight still illuminates their room. The evenings are drawing further and further out.

I go into the bathroom, put the plug in the plughole and turn on the taps.

When I turn to leave, I catch my reflection in the mirror above the sink. I see her, Louise, in my face – a superimposed image trying to reach out from inside me.

I'm scared. I know that she can trick me into doing bad things.

That sense of a breath runs a shiver down my spine as I return to the children.

Their room is untidy. Clothes and toys are spread across the carpet. I pick things up, building up a pile of clothes to be washed and throwing the toys they're not playing with across the room into the toy-box. Keeping myself active to fight the fear and anxiety.

When I'm finished, I go back into the bathroom and check the temperature of the water. The girls are tucking dolls and teddies into a toy cot and kissing them goodnight.

I leave them to finish the game, pick up the pile of washing and take it down the two flights of stairs to the kitchen.

Hope's giggles travel behind me. Rosie has started playing Mr Tickle and poor Hope is the one being tickled. Hope's giggles are adorable; they relieve some of the pain and confusion from the anxiety. Laughter lifts a mood like sunshine.

As I push the clothes into the washing machine, Alex's coffee-stained jeans come to mind. I would love to get my hands on those with an in-wash stain remover. Perhaps I should offer to start doing the washing.

I walk back upstairs smiling at the noises of the girls' game. 'Bath time,' I say as I walk into the bedroom.

They play with plastic fish and Hope's rubber duck amongst the bubbles in the bath as I wash their hair.

Rosie is the one to pull the plug out.

A swirling whirlpool draws the water and bubbles down the drain as Hope stands up and lifts her arms, so I can pick her up.

I lift her out and wrap her up in a thick warm towel. Hope waits, standing on the bathmat, a white fluffy parcel of sweetness, as I lift Rosie out, and wrap her up too.

'Into pyjamas and then we'll dry hair and find a book.' I kiss Hope on top of her damp curls.

Rosie lets her towel fall to the floor in a heap and Hope runs off, leaving her towel in my hands.

I get up, fold the towels and hang them up.

'My nighty's gone!' Rosie shouts. 'Where is it? Helen! Helen!'

'I put it in the washing machine,' I call back. 'Use another for tonight. It'll be dry by tomorrow, and it will smell lovely, like perfume.'

Rosie screams.

Oh, my God. I run into their room.

Rosie's hands are fisted and her face flushed, and she continues screaming. She turns to the toy-box and starts throwing toys at me as I walk across the room.

'Rosie.' I knock each toy aside. 'Rosie.' Some of the toys are plastic and they hurt.

When I reach her, her anger turns a sharp corner into distress, and she throws herself on the floor kicking and hitting the carpet.

'Rosie.' I drop to my knees, while poor Hope watches, bewildered. Rosie's never thrown a tantrum like this; her arms and legs flail as the carpet absorbs her screams.

The tone and pitch of my voice lower. 'Rosie. Stop it.'

She rolls to her knees suddenly and throws a hand at me, slapping my thigh. I catch her hand before she can hit out again.

'That was Mummy's. Daddy doesn't wash it. He said I can keep it.'

'Things have to be washed. It was dirty, darling.' The endearment slips off my tongue in response to the pain on her face.

Her eyes fill with tears that run onto her cheeks. 'It smells of Mummy.'

Oh, God. But it hadn't been washed for nearly a year, then. 'It needed washing, Rosie.'

'No. No.' She pulls her hand free and slaps me again.

'Rosie.' The tone in my voice tells her to stop as I reach out to hug her.

She pushes my arm away.

Hope chokes out a sob. I look at her and see slender streams of tears streaking her face.

'Would you like one of Daddy's T-shirts?' I ask Rosie. I need to find something to calm them down. To make Rosie feel better.

She nods, with a jolting shivery sniff as two more fat teardrops roll down her cheeks. 'I'm sorry, Rosie.' But you couldn't keep wearing that dirty thing. 'Do you want to come up to Daddy's room and help me find a T-shirt?'

Her thumb slips into her mouth as she nods. The girls must be getting cold.

'Let's all go and look for a T-shirt.' I pick Hope up and balance her on my hip. She's not even in a nappy yet. Then I offer my hand to Rosie. Her small hand holds mine.

'Do you have a favourite T-shirt of Daddy's?'

When we step into the narrow back staircase, I feel Hope shiver. It's dark and cold.

I turn the light on before we start climbing.

Louise is all around us.

I hold Rosie's hand tight. Feeling Louise's hand in this. Louise influenced me again. She knew what would happen when I picked the clothes up.

She's destroying this.

Rosie is still crying, only now the tears are running silently down her cheeks.

We are all in Rosie's bed, cuddled up together when the door-knocker rattles downstairs. A moment later it rattles again as the door bangs shut.

I expect Alex to shout upstairs, but he doesn't. Perhaps because he assumes the girls are asleep.

I should move Hope to her cot, but she's quiet now and dreaming. The dummy shivers as she sucks.

Rosie is on the other side of me, on the outer side of the single bed, her thumb trembling in her mouth.

If I unravel myself from them, Hope will be against the wall and Rosie will stop her from falling out of bed.

Alex still hasn't shouted upstairs or come up to the first-floor landing.

I carefully lift my arm and move Hope's head to the pillow. Then do the same with Rosie. They're both wearing one of Alex's T-shirts, Hope with a nappy underneath.

I cautiously shuffle my way down the bed and get up. Then move Rosie over a little, nearer Hope.

I lean across to kiss Hope's forehead, then kiss Rosie's hair before leaving the room.

When I reach the first-floor and walk along the landing, Alex is swearing in the kitchen, in a low husky voice.

My pace is slower as I descend the second set of stairs, because I think he's arguing with that woman. But I can't pretend I'm not here. He knows I am and I want to go home.

'Alex.' My questioning tone reaches tentatively from the stairs towards the kitchen.

'Hello.' The answer that comes back is a flat-toned acknowledgement. I descend the last few steps quicker, the soles of my socks brushing on the bare wood.

'The girls are—' I begin before I can see into the kitchen. But then I see him.

He's standing by the breakfast bar. The manila envelope is open, the contents in his hand. He looks at me, lifts the contents of his hand higher and then drops them down onto the black granite.

He looks up at the ceiling, and his hands lift to the back of his head, elbows out wide.

'What is it?' I take it he was swearing at the letter.

His hands fall and his eyebrows lift as he looks at me. 'You'll need to know.' He reaches out, picks up the letter and holds it out to me.

When I take the letter, he picks up an open bottle of beer that's on the breakfast bar near him and drinks as I read.

When I stop reading, he pushes the printed pictures that were underneath the letter towards me.

The pictures are of him and that woman having sex up against a wall at the back entrance to the house. I skim through them.

Why does he want me to look at these? But then I see why.

The next picture is of us. His hand is raised holding the key in the lock as the door opens.

The next picture shows me following him into the house.

The last picture is of me, leaving the house early in the morning, my hair and make-up a mess.

The letter says the pictures prove he's acting immorally and is unfit to look after his children. Robert and Pat have had a private detective watching him. Watching me too, then.

My gaze lifts to Alex as I put the pictures down.

'Sorry. You shouldn't have been dragged into this. Nothing should have happened the other night. You came back to talk. I was drunk and I'm sorry.'

I came back because I wanted to help the children – to keep my children. 'It was one night. And the children weren't here.' There's a note of pleading in the excuses bursting from my lips.

'How can they threaten you with that? People have sex. That has nothing to do with the children.'

'That doesn't matter. The issue is they're building a file of evidence to make me look bad. Sleeping with the children's nanny is another element.' His fingertips rub across his forehead.

He's ruined this.

He breathes out and his hand falls away from his forehead as he drinks another mouthful from his beer. He looks into my eyes, holding my gaze with that firm confidence of denial – electric sparks flying. 'You'd better go home.'

I look into solid panes of glass as a nod moves my head, because what else can I do? I can't undo what happened on Saturday.

I turn away, leaving him in the kitchen. Leaving the girls asleep in one bed upstairs.

I put my shoes and coat on, and pick up my bag. Then look back. 'Goodnight.'

He doesn't answer.

I open and shut the door, trying not to rattle the doorknocker and wake the girls.

As I walk home I realise I have no idea what time he needs me there in the morning and I haven't told him that the girls are in bed together, or that I have washed Louise's T-shirt.

Oh, God.

My heart and head hurt so much; I'm terrified of what might come next if all my lies come to light.

What else can Louise do?

I run the rest of the way home. To get back to Andy.

To get back to Helen.

Chapter 61

4 weeks and 3 days until the inquest.

'Your phone is ringing.' Andy's tone is a hard, cold judgement. The phone lands on top of the duvet. I reach out for it.

'It's your boss,' Andy says.

The ringtone stops trilling.

I sit up and reach for the phone. My head is a dead weight. I'm so tired.

I came home last night to Andy sitting on the sofa, drinking, and telling me my dinner was in the oven probably burnt.

I'd eaten with the girls but didn't tell him. All I wanted to do was curl up against him and cry. But he wasn't in a mood to be consoling; he was determined to be aggrieved.

'Do you want a cup of tea?' Andy asks.

I grasp onto it as a white-flag offering. 'Yes, please.' I smile. He doesn't smile back.

My knees pull up and I wrap an arm around them, over the covers, as I call Alex back.

'Hello,' he answers.

'Morning. Sorry I never asked last night – what time do you need me?'

There's a breath. A breath that reaches through the phone and tells me that this isn't good news.

'Actually, I'm ringing ...' another loud breath, that suggests his throat is dry '... to tell you not to come. My father's coming today. After those photographs, I can't have you in the house.'

His parents know about the pictures ... The children ... 'How?' I need to go to the house. I need to see the children.

'I—'

'Rosie is angry with you anyway; for washing Louise's T-shirt. To be honest we're all angry about it.'

'She doesn't want me to come today?'

'No.' The answer is blunt. Callous. But then there is another breath, and the tone of his voice changes to one that expresses long-suffering tolerance. 'Thank you for everything you've done for the children. I am sorry about the other night. I shouldn't have drunk so much.'

Josh shouts something in the background.

'I need to go. Goodbye.'

The connection dies before I can say goodbye. In my head – the door bangs shut, with the harsh rattle of the doorknocker. The door has been closed. Firmly. Forever ...

'Andy.' I get up. 'Andy!' I can't see him. I thought he would be in the kitchen but he's not. 'Andy!'

'What?' He comes out from the bathroom.

I throw myself into his arms dramatically, my heart crumbling into pieces. 'I've lost my job.' I've lost the children.

His arms wrap around me, holding me firmly. 'It's just a job. I can support you. We'll manage.'

No. It's not just a job. It's my life.

Chapter 62

4 weeks and 2 days until the inquest.

I spent twenty-four hours in bed. Crying. But today I got up so I could come to see the children. I can't sit in the park. They know me now. So, I stand at the corner of the street, takeaway coffee in hand, and hope they'll come outside at some point.

Andy's told me again and again that I don't need to find another job. I don't want to. I just want the children back.

But I want Andy too.

He keeps talking about his children, our children. I want them, but I can't just forget Hope, Rosie and Josh.

There's a tug-of-war in my head. Andy tries to pull me one way, forward. The children pull me back.

I'm not sure who I am without them. I am not Helen – even though they were originally Louise's.

I lean against the railing and ring Chloe.

'Hello.'

'Can you talk? I need to talk. I lost my job.' Lost my children. 'And I slept with the father.' I need to confess this to someone.

I could have heard Chloe's gasp even if the phone were about a foot away from my ear.

'What? Why?'

'It just happened. We were talking and drinking and it just happened.'

'Does Andy know?'

'No, I can't tell him. Don't tell him.'

Chapter 63

3 weeks until the inquest.

Arumbling noise wakes me. My phone is vibrating on the bedside chest of drawers. The electric clock says 8:42. Andy must have gone to work without waking me.

I reach for the phone.

It might be him.

The vibration runs into my arm.

It's Simon.

'Hello.' My voice is croaky and lacking energy. My whole body is heavy; I've slept for nearly thirteen hours.

'Chloe rang me last night. I called, but Andy said you'd gone to bed. She told me about your night out. How do you feel?'

My free hand lifts to my forehead. Chloe ... I knew she was worried about me, but I didn't want Simon to know. 'I feel awful.'

'Why, Helen?'

'I have no idea why.' Because I thought it would help me keep the children. Because I was drunk. 'Because I'm an idiot.'

'Are you taking your tablets?'

'It wasn't deliberate. It has nothing to do with bipolar.'

'Are you sure?'

'Yes. I wish I could blame it on that. I was just drunk.'

'What are you going to do?'

Stay in bed and sleep for the rest of my life, because I hurt so much. I miss the children. We'll never sit and make things together again, or cuddle up on the sofa on a cold afternoon. And Josh ... my man-child.

'Andy told me not to worry about getting another job. He can support us.'

'I mean, are you going to tell him?'

'I can't. It'll ruin everything.' Enough has been ruined already.

'If I was him, I'd want to know.'

'Well, you aren't him. Don't tell him.'

'I wouldn't do that. But I'm worried about you. This is going to be difficult with—'

'Please let me deal with it.' I just need to be able to think, to work it out. To work out how to get the children back. But my head is so heavy.

A sigh runs into the phone at his end. 'Okay. But I'm here if you need to talk.'

'I love you.'

'I love you too. Even when you do stupid things.' Immediately after the last syllable, he closes the call.

I send a text to Andy saying I love you, hiding my guilt behind kissing and heart emojis.

Images of Alex flow through my head. Would a message help? Just to keep in contact. No. I think I should be quiet for now. For a little while. Perhaps after the inquest, and the custody hearing, he might be more receptive.

The phone whistles. I look at the reply from Andy. '**Love you too. Look after yourself today. I'll bring something home for dinner.**'

I drag myself out of bed to make tea and toast so I can take my tablets.

While I wait I fetch my laptop, open it up and look up Robert Dowling's Facebook page.

The pictures of the children are all too old.

The children have changed so much since his last pictures were taken.

But when I look at them, I hear the children talking. I know the sound of their happiness, and their sadness.

I bet Rosie will be drawing her I-want-my-mother picture today.

I am her mother now. I am here.

Chapter 64

3 days until the inquest.

A sigh of anger and frustration slips through my lips as I flip the laptop lid down with a hard push.

Robert Dowling is a bastard.

I can hardly believe that I once thought him part of my ideal. That he was included in my visions of a perfect family.

I couldn't have been more wrong about him.

'Here.' Andy puts a cup of steaming tea down on the kitchen table beside my laptop. 'I still say you shouldn't go on Monday.'

He knows that I look at Facebook only to find out what's going on with Alex's family.

He knows I am still emotionally attached to the children.

He knows that sometimes I walk down to the house and stand on the opposite side of the busy road in the hope I might see them.

He knows I want to go to the inquest to find out what might happen next. If the children might lose their father as well as their mother.

Andy sits opposite me, rests his elbows on the table and his fingers steeple together. His chin presses onto the tips of his fingers. 'It's not going to be good for you.'

Simon, Chloe and now Andy have tried to persuade me that I need to speak to a doctor. They think I'm having an episode.

'It's normal to care about three children who have lost their mother.' I repeat the phrase I've said about a hundred times in the last few weeks.

I'm feeling depressed, but that's normal too. Anyone would feel low if they'd developed feelings for the children, and everyone would have developed feelings for three lonely, mourning children ... wouldn't they? 'I need to go. I might be able to say something.'

'You didn't even know her.'

'I know the family. I know what's true and untrue.'

His hands fall onto the table, then turn so his palms lay flat. He breathes out. 'When are you going to get a test? Shall I buy one on my way back from work? I know you don't seem to care but I want to know.'

I reach out to lay a hand over his. 'I care.' I'm over a month late. There's a chance that I'm pregnant. But I've been avoiding testing our theory because everything is going wrong and I don't want to know if we are wrong.

I want my own child, but I also want the children back, and at the moment my thoughts must be for them; they need me more than the possibility of a fertilised egg. I can't cope with thinking about anything else.

His hand turns under mine and his fingers surround my hand. 'I'm worried about you.'

'You don't need to be.' Simon has been scaring him. Or perhaps Mim with her whispers of obsession.

This is different.

This is very different.

'I want our child. I want it to be true. But wait a little longer. I don't want to see a negative symbol. I can't face that at the moment.' I can't face the fear that I'll have to carry for nine months that it might be Alex's baby and not Andy's. I don't want to think about that possibility and as soon as I know there's a child, then I won't be able to push the thought away.

He stands, keeping a hold of my hand as he comes around the table to kiss me.

His other hand embraces the back of my head as he leans down and presses his lips on mine.

I open my mouth and answer his kiss.

It is a long kiss.

His nose brushes against mine in a gesture of affection as he pulls away. 'I love you, Mrs Arnold.' The breath of his words strokes my check.

A smile pulls at my lips as love sweeps through my heart, like the brush of a soft broom sweeping my soul clean, brushing the guilt aside. 'I love you too.'

He lets my hand go. 'I need to get to work.'

I stand and follow him towards the door, my hands slipping into the pockets of my pyjama bottoms.

'Promise me you'll call if you need to.'

He wanted to take the week off work and go to the inquest with me, but someone else is off and he's not been able to take the time.

'I promise.'

When he's ready to leave, we kiss again, then he opens the door and goes.

I have no idea what to do today.

Alex took the children away with his parents the day before yesterday. I don't know where. They left in two cars, with suitcases, the pushchair and highchair for Hope and what looked like a bag of toys. It looked as if he'll be gone for a long time.

I walk into the living room, drop down on the sofa, tuck my feet up and press the button to turn the television on. I'll probably spend my day sitting here staring at a TV that I don't really hear – listless and miserable – and still be in pyjamas when Andy comes home as I was yesterday.

I wrap my arms around my legs and rest my chin on my knees. The people on a talk-show babble on.

I try to feel Louise around me, in me. She's nowhere here. She hasn't been with me since the day that Alex threw me out.

I've been used and disposed of.

But I still have her heart. She is keeping me alive whether she wants to or not.

Chapter 65

The inquest day 1.

I follow Chloe, walking in single file along the top row of the viewing-gallery seating in the courtroom.

I told her to go to the top of the tiered seating so we'll be able to see Alex wherever he sits. I want him to know that I'm here. To know that I still care about the children.

That I care enough to have come.

After all of this, I hope Rosie will forgive me and the children will want me back.

I catch hold of Chloe's arm as we reach the middle of the row. 'Sit here.'

I feel as if I'll be able to control everything from up here, like a conductor. But I know the truth is the judge and jury control this.

'Do you think they'll show images of the dead wife?' Chloe whispers, her face twisting into a grimace as she makes her shoulders shiver.

'I have no idea.'

I'm not sure why we are whispering – the only occupants of the court are people with notepads on their laps in the front row of the gallery. Journalists.

A door opens in the farthest corner of the courtroom. Three people clothed in black robes walk in; one woman is wearing a short white wig. They're the lawyers.

A man in a black suit and tie follows. He walks over to a computer. The clerk.

The courtroom becomes a theatre with a stage – a final performance. There are two rows of seating for the jury on the right, a stand for the witnesses on the left and a high long desk for the judge.

The door on the right by the gallery seating opens. Several people come in and file along the rows of seating in front of Chloe and me, filling up the wooden benches.

I look back at the door, with a sense of waiting.

I feel as though I'm going to see the children. But they will not come here.

Alex's parents are at the end of the train of people.

His father holds the door and looks back. He's not the last.

Alex is the last.

He is dressed in a dark blue suit and light blue shirt, a tie with a blue stripe and his hair has been cut significantly shorter, disposing of the unruly curls.

In my head, I see him dressing this morning and straightening his tie in front of the mirror with Louise watching.

My heart drops down to my heels, plummeting, like a heavy pebble thrown into water.

Louise fell and sent out waves – life-destroying waves. Waves that swamped her children.

The dark aura is consuming Alex's silhouette today.

I tap Chloe's leg. 'There's the father.'

She looks over.

He sits next to his father at the very end of the front row. The man sitting behind him leans forward, presses a hand on Alex's shoulder and speaks to him. Alex looks back and answers. They know each other.

He speaks to someone else a few seats along in the second row too.

The smiles and comments that pass along the rows say that they are a group of people who are here for his benefit.

My gaze stays with him. I think that he'll look at me, because I'm staring hard enough to reach through to anyone's sixth sense, but he doesn't. He looks forward.

A second later a young man in a black suit comes in; a lanyard holding a security card hangs about his neck. 'Please be upstanding,' he shouts across the room.

Everyone rises, in a wave that flows from front to back.

The judge walks into the room, his scarlet robe swaying in fluid movement as he climbs a step to reach his seat on the high stand.

The long, dated white wig makes him look stupid, not professional. We should have grown out of such things as a country by now.

My mind begins throwing mocking words. Angry words. Boiling-over, spitting words. I press my lips tightly closed.

When the judge sits, this is suddenly real. It's no longer the scene of a play, it's Alex's life and the children's future.

I'm sitting on a hard wooden bench in the midst of a tense crime drama. Mood music plays in my head and the dark aura that travels with Alex creeps across the gallery seating like a poisonous smog. Looming. Eerie. Frightening.

The judge raises a hand, telling people to sit with a downward movement. 'You may sit.' He looks at the clerk who introduced him. 'Bring the jury in, please.'

A single hard heartbeat strikes against the sole of my shoes.

The room is silent but for the voices of the jury as they swear to do their duty with an unbiased view.

I watch Alex, as if by looking at him I will learn something about the children.

How are they?

Where are they?

His palms rest on his thighs, lying on the blue fabric of his suit trousers.

I think he's itching to run from this but holding himself down.

The jury is told about Louise's illness, by the woman in a short wig and black cape. It is known that Louise had depression due to her eating disorder, however, it's not known if she had thoughts about suicide; she did not discuss suicide with anyone.

The barrister changes the pitch of her speech and begins speaking about Louise's 'unhappy and turbulent marriage'.

'It's possible that Mr Lovett became impatient with his wife in an argument, or perhaps deliberately chose to dispose of the burden of his sick wife ...'

The sound of Alex clearing his throat echoes about the room.

'... so he could focus on the pursuit of his increasingly successful career.'

This is going to be like a trial. The barrister must intend to prove Alex murdered Louise, and Alex has no voice here. He has no solicitor to defend him. He can only sit and listen while they slander him and decide if he might be guilty.

Professional witnesses come from the back door into the court-room, as if there's a conveyor belt on the other side. They tell the jury how ill Louise Lovett was before her death, and how her marriage had become a thing that caused her fear, not comfort. Their rows were noisy, if not violent. Things were broken.

At 12.22, Pat Dowling walks out from the door at the back.

I have not thought about why Pat and Robert are absent from the gallery. It's because she is a witness.

She relates the phone call that took place between her and Louise the day that her daughter died.

Another person in a black cape, but without a wig, picks up and unfolds a piece of paper. The neat, sharp creases that divide the paper into segments imply that it has been folded like that and kept in a folder of evidence for a long time.

'Do you recognise this drawing?' the bewigged barrister asks Pat.

Drawing?

'Yes,' Pat answers.

'Can you tell the jury what it is?'

A sigh leaves her mouth before the words do. But I know. 'A drawing that my granddaughter did just after her mother died. She told me that it is a picture of her father, Alexander Lovett, pushing her mother, my daughter, Louise, off the top of a car park.' When she stops speaking, she sniffs. The clerk appears with a pack of tissues. She dabs a tissue against her cheek, then wipes her nose as the clerk takes the picture from the barrister and carries it over to the jury.

Rosie's I-want-my-mother picture passes along the rows of decision-makers. Pushing. She told me that too. But they cannot rely on evidence produced by a three-year-old drawing out her pain.

I glance at Alex. I can see that the muscles in his jaw are tight with restrained anger. Or distress. He hates that picture. He hates it because he hates Rosie having that memory.

We know she draws that picture because the memory torments her and she doesn't understand it.

It is the last moment – the last memory – she has of Louise.

The judge looks at the jury.

Rosie's picture is passed back to the clerk.

The judge's gaze lifts to a place above my head; I turn and look. The clock.

'It's time for a recess. We will return in an hour.'

He stands.

The room stands in another flowing wave. Alex and his parents are the first to leave the gallery seating. Alex drops down off a step, as though he's jumped down. His hands sweep aside his suit jacket and slide into his trouser pockets.

He's so good at guarding what he thinks; his emotions are firmly shut up inside a hard case that says he doesn't care.

He does.

I have seen the expression of those feelings. I have been caught up in a net by his emotion.

Others file out from the gallery seating.

I want to talk to him, to ask him how the children are. Does Josh know what's happening? But by the time we walk out of the courtroom Alex is nowhere in sight.

There's a café in the court building. The legal team are there, buying sandwiches, in among a long queue of people who were sitting in the gallery.

Alex and his parents are not there.

Chloe and I join the queue.

Pat and Robert Dowling join the queue a few minutes later. They sit on a table on their own, while most of the spectators gather in a group around three other tables.

The afternoon's witnesses are people who were in the street when Louise fell. They heard a woman cry out. A few seconds before she fell, she was shouting.

I wait for the witness who has said he saw Alex push her. They must be saving his statement for a specific moment when they will produce the most damning information.

A doctor is called to take the stand. A forensic genius. He's asked about the evidence at the scene.

'The position of Louise Lovett's body strongly suggests that she did not jump, she fell backwards, not forwards. She landed on her back, facing the car park.'

This being an inquest, not a trial, there's no one to challenge his opinion.

The barrister folds her file and walks away as though the case is made as clear as day.

The moment of final condemnation is coming.

'Please call the next witness, Luke Martin,' the barrister says to the clerk as she puts her files down in front of one of the supporting solicitors. She is so confident about the next witness she doesn't need notes to refer to.

The clerk walks to the door.

The man who comes in has long hair that has been tamed in a ponytail. But it looks as if he hasn't cut his hair for months, or perhaps years. His facial hair is also long and uneven.

A memory, a sense, suspicion, tells me I've seen the man before.

His suit is oversized – three sizes too big for his thin frame.

A penny drops, with the metallic sound of a rolling coin in my head. I remember. It's the homeless man in the alley by the car park. The man who told me he had not seen Louise, he had not been there that day. So, he can have nothing to say to this courtroom, because he told me he didn't know anything.

'I know him,' I turn and say to Chloe.

'Please be quiet in the gallery,' the judge calls.

I catch Alex looking at me.

I open my mouth, wanting to speak, but he looks away.

What this man will say is not true. Alex has his faults. But this is not true.

'Please repeat to me what you have said in your witness statement,' the barrister asks.

He describes the scene as Rosie has drawn it. Two children outside the red car on top of the car park while Alex and Louise are fighting at the edge of it, by the wall.

Unlike Rosie's drawing, though, he describes the car park perfectly. The stairwell that I climbed, he says he saw Louise climb. When he is asked how high the wall is? He holds his hand up to his chest at exactly the right height.

'How was she pushed over the wall?'

I look at Alex; his skin is coloured crimson.

'She was on the wall. Sitting on the wall. They were shouting and then 'e pushed 'er back. Just like this.' I turn and look. He's lifted both hands, palm out.

'Do you know how she got onto the wall? Did Louise climb? Was she lifted?'

'I don't know. I was in the stairwell, then.'

Energy surges into my legs, and my throat. In my mind, I'm standing and shouting. That man is lying! He wasn't even there!

Pat and Robert found him, and somehow convinced him to lie. What with? Money?

Another witness talks through some CCTV footage. It shows Louise walk out of the stairwell. Seventeen minutes and twenty-two seconds later Alex's car is shown, circling through the car park, climbing to the top floor. It is obvious he knows she's there. That he's gone there to find her. He's driving too fast to be safe, which suggests he knows something is wrong.

The CCTV shows his car arriving on the top floor of the car

park; he gets out of the car, leaving the door open behind him, and runs out of shot. A moment later Josh appears from the open car door. He has climbed over from the other side of the car. Then Rosie appears. She must have climbed from the back seat. Hope's car seat, with her in it, is in the car too.

I wait for them to turn the camera. To see what happened in that horrible moment at the end.

'Unfortunately, we have no footage of the actual fall. The cameras' range does not reach to the corner of the car park.'

'Ah.' My sigh is audible.

Alex hasn't made a sound. Perhaps he knows all this already.

'With that we will finish for today,' the judge says as the last witness is led out of the room.

Everybody stands.

As soon as the judge and jury have gone, I climb on the seat to get around Chloe, and stay on the seating, walking along the wooden bench.

I need to find the barrister.

'Helen,' Chloe calls behind me.

I can't stop.

'Helen!'

The lawyers are not in the café or the halls. I dash around like a madwoman, with Chloe following. There's no one official anywhere, and when I press against the door that must lead to the rooms at the back of the courts it is locked. I turn and growl in frustration as Chloe runs up to join me. 'What are you doing?'

'Trying to find someone to tell them that I know the homeless man is a liar.' I walk around for the third time in a crazed pursuit for justice. I can stop this – stop the children losing their father.

The entrance area is full of people pulling on coats, readying themselves to go outside into a rainstorm.

The lawyers have to leave; they must be doing the same.

My coat is in the gallery, left, forgotten, and so when I push the door open and step outside the rain slams down on my head and shoulders.

Months ago, almost a year ago, I had stepped out into the rain. On the first day I stepped into Louise's life and knew I had found her parents.

The heavy drops thrown down from the sky soak my clothes and run down my face as I run towards a woman a few metres away, my shoes splashing through fast-forming puddles. 'Wait a moment! Excuse me! Excuse me! Wait!' My hand waves and beckons as I run. 'Wait, please!'

The lights flash on a black BMW as she nears it and I hear the locks shift free.

It's her. I'm sure of it – her hair, which is still dry under the cover of her umbrella, is auburn and the barrister had auburn hair underneath her wig. It's in the way that she walks too. With an assured stance. The umbrella dips forward as she moves towards the driver's door.

'Excuse me! Hello!'

The umbrella lifts again as she turns to look at the madwoman splashing through the puddles, with hair stuck to her cheeks. 'Hello.' I pant at her, out of breath and terrified of running out of time. 'That man, who said he saw Louise pushed off the car park. He lied. I need to make a statement. That evidence must be dismissed – the jury can't consider it.'

Her eyes judge me, evaluating me as someone of a lower class. But then my clothes are wet and dirty from the puddles.

'How do you know that?'

'I went to the car park months ago. I asked him if he'd witnessed anything the day Louise died and he told me he wasn't there.'

She stands still. Her eyes telling me that she's deciding what to do.

'Surely the inquest is about the truth? He hasn't told the truth.'

The rain runs off her umbrella and drips from my hair.

'You'll need to make a statement to the police and explain why you were there. Are you a friend of Louise's?'

'I ... I ...'

Who am I?

Chapter 66

21.53.

I am exhausted, my clothes are damp and my head is reeling. I've been through everything a dozen times. Asked to repeat my story until it has been turned backwards and upside down.

I'm so tired I can barely focus as I walk into the waiting room in the police station.

Andy rises from a plastic seat that is bolted to the floor. 'What's happened? What on earth is going on?' His arms envelop me. I lean into the embrace as across the room Simon and Chloe stand.

'Your clothes are damp.' Andy lets me go and starts stripping off his coat.

'What's happened?' Simon asks as Andy's coat rests on my shoulders.

'They asked me to bring your laptop with me,' Andy says.

I look at Andy. 'I know. They have my phone too.' They asked permission to take them. To confirm my statement. If I hadn't given them over by choice they would have applied for a warrant anyway.

'Why?' His forehead creases into a frown that I want to stroke away with my thumb.

'Can we go home, please? I don't want to tell you here.'

'Tell us what? What, Helen?' Simon asks.

Chloe's eyes ask more searching, silent questions.

I have told the police everything. From the moment I made my list of who my heart might have belonged to until the moment I recognised that man. They think I'm insane. They checked my records and they know I've been sectioned for stalking in the past. If I didn't have a husband or family to leave with they may not have let me go.

They also know about the night I slept with Alex. I didn't tell them that, but the pictures are already in the evidence. They knew.

Now they're checking my phone and my laptop to see how long I have known Alex for.

I am not only a new witness, but a new suspect.

They believe I have a motive. That I wanted her husband.

I have admitted that I want the children. I do. But I did not know about her or the children until after she was dead.

'We are staying in Swindon, for tonight,' Andy says, his arm and hand bracing my shoulders, holding his coat in place. 'We're booked in at the hotel over the road from the court.'

'You have to work.' I look at Andy.

'I have the time off. They're going to manage without me. Come on.'

We walk four astride to Simon's car.

Everyone is silent during the journey back to the town centre.

In the reception of the hotel, Andy looks at Simon. 'I know you want to ask her about this, but she needs to get in a warm bath and relax. I'm going to take her upstairs.'

I lean against Andy, tucked under his arm, but my gaze reaches to Simon. 'I'm sorry.' I look at Chloe. 'Sorry.'

Chloe reaches forward and rubs my arm lightly.

When Chloe's hand falls, Andy turns me towards the lifts.

My hand is caught.

I turn back to Simon. His smile offers comfort. 'Goodnight.'

I had nothing to do with Louise's death and the police will discover that. But Simon, Chloe and Andy will discover that I have lied to them.

In our small double room, I sit in a steaming hot bath, with a glass of red wine, and eat a burger that Andy has ordered from room service, from a plate balanced on the edge of the bath.

Andy is sitting on the toilet, watching me.

I've told him everything between sips of wine and mouthfuls of food – everything except that I had sex with Alex and that I planted drugs on his nanny. I haven't told the police about the drugs either.

His fingers rub his temple as though he has a headache. 'So you came to Bath because of that woman.'

'Yes.' The water is cold now. It sways around me as I reach for the wine glass again.

'And you wanted to get into his house to look after her children?'

'Yes.'

'Because you think it's her heart?'

'It is.'

'And she speaks to you?'

'Sometimes. But mostly I just feel her presence and emotions.'

A rough sigh rolls over gravel in his throat as his elbows rest on his knees and both his hands hold his head.

He's still dressed for work, in trousers, a shirt and tie. He was called by the police before he left his office, and they picked him up from there and took him to the flat to get my laptop.

'Helen,' he says, not looking at me but shaking his head with his face hidden behind his hands, 'that is not a sixth sense – you're unwell.'

No. 'I know you don't believe in spirits but they're real. Other people who don't have bipolar believe they're real.' I put the glass down and stand, turning to reach for the towel. The water sploshes over the side of the shallow bath and the splash catches his trousers.

He straightens and moves his leg over.

I wrap the towel around me before I step out of the bath. I meet his gaze. 'I am not ill.'

'Other people might believe in ghosts, Helen. But other people don't stalk the family of a dead woman, to the point they become her children's nanny.'

I walk out of the bathroom, trailing damp footprints. 'I just wanted to know them ...'

Andy's hand wraps around my arm and holds me still. 'Whatever your reasoning, it wasn't normal, or legal, Helen.'

The pace of my heart is firm and strong. I have done the right thing. I know I have. But it's as I always thought, that if I told someone they'd think I was having a bipolar episode.

'I'm not ill, Andy.'

His hold on my arm pulls me back to him and his cheek presses against my wet hair. 'God. What this means is that you met and married me while you've been ill.'

I would have pulled away but he doesn't let me move.

'If you'd been well would you still love me? Will you stop loving me when you are well again?'

'Don't be stupid. I'm well now.'

Chapter 67

The inquest day 2.

Andy's fingers are laced with mine, and his thumb is fidgeting with mine as we walk up the steps to the courtroom. Simon is beside him and Chloe beside me.

Andy and I have been arguing for about four hours about coming here today. He wanted me to go back to Bath. I refused.

I've been awake throughout the night, and my restlessness kept him awake, and because we were both awake, we talked. He wants me to see a doctor and promise never to see or communicate with Louise's family again.

I can't promise that.

I must be in the courtroom when the children's future is balancing on the scales of fate.

'Do you want a cup of coffee before we go in there?' Simon asks.

'No,' I answer, 'but you can if you'd like to.' When I say you, I mean any one of them.

'No, from me too,' Andy answers. He's going to stay by me through every minute of this. He's lost his trust in me. He said he's not sure who I am.

Simon and Chloe know nothing about my conversation with the police.

I have no idea what will be said about that in the courtroom today.

The police told me nothing last night about the conclusions they were drawing, only questioned and questioned me about why I was in the car park and why I ended up working for Alex after Louise died. I sat shivering in a silver blanket in the interview room, with both hands wrapped around a mug of tea.

Andy pushes the gallery door open and holds it for me to pass, then Simon holds it to let Chloe walk through.

We are the first people in the gallery.

'The back row,' I say to Andy so he can lead. His fingers remain woven between mine as he walks ahead, my hand tucked in behind his hip. When we reach the middle, where Chloe and I sat the day before, I pull on Andy's hand to stop him. 'Sit here.'

'Trust you to get yourself caught up in this,' Simon says as he sits on the other side of me.

'She's a trouble magnet,' Chloe jokes.

The heels of my shoes tap on the floor underneath the bench.

Simon's hand rests on my thigh, and he looks at me. His eyes asking if I am all right.

No. No. Because I'm losing the children. Whatever is said today, I'll lose them.

We sit alone in the gallery for about ten minutes before other people walk in.

There are more people than yesterday and nearly all of them sit close to Alex's parents. They are in Alex's camp – on his side. But Alex isn't there.

Andy's thumb taps on mine as the judge walks in.

'Please be upstanding,' the clerk calls.

Here I am again, on the set of a television drama. The jury walk in and find their seats.

My fingers are holding Andy's tighter than he's holding mine.

The judge begins by announcing that the evidence given by Luke Martin the previous day has been discredited. 'You are therefore required not to consider it when you retire to make your decision,' he says, looking at the jury.

I glance in triumph at Andy. Surely now everything will be all right.

'Please bring in Mr Lovett,' the barrister asks the clerk.

Alex?

Has he been prepared for this? Did he know it would happen?

He walks in from the door at the back of the court, and across to stand behind a pedestal with a microphone. He's wearing the same suit as yesterday, but today his shirt is white and his tie an amber-brown pattern, and he's not shaved this morning. The tailored suit makes him look taller than I remember.

Alex's chest lifts with a deep breath as he takes his position. His hands rest on the stand either side of the microphone.

Does he know that I have discredited Luke Martin's evidence?

'Tell us what happened the afternoon your wife died, Mr Lovett. Did you and your wife argue that day?'

'Yes.' He looks at the barrister, not the jury. 'We did argue. But we argued all the time. She made me angry. It was an expression of my exasperation. Frustration. We had a baby and Louise wouldn't eat to keep her body going so she could care for Hope.'

'Hope?' the barrister asks.

'Our youngest,' Alex answers. 'We had a very ... bad argument that day. Because we had three children who needed a mum to love them but she didn't care.' He pauses and draws in a long breath.

He may not look nervous, but the breath implies his breathing has been shallow for a long time.

'Louise focused on herself, on what she looked like and felt like. She was obsessed with herself. I didn't argue with her because I wanted her to care about me. I wanted her to care about her children and be well for them.'

He swallows, his Adam's apple moving up and down about three times.

'How did she fall from the car park?'

'It was suicide. She leaned back and just ... fell.'

'No note was found. No one else has said she spoke of suicide, not her parents, your parents, her friends or any of the psychologists who have supported her during her illness,' the barrister says.

'I destroyed the note. And what she did to her body said how much she wanted to destroy herself, surely?'

'Why would you dispose of the note?'

'Because in it she blamed her death on us. She said we didn't love her. *We*. Her words were, "you and the children". I didn't want her children to know that she thought they didn't love her. That note put the blame on them. It would have made them carry blame for the rest of their lives. I was not going to let them think her death was their responsibility.'

'When did you dispose of this note?'

'When we returned to my parents' house. After ...' He swallows several more times. 'I didn't want anyone else to see it.'

'Did that note tell you where to go? That Louise had gone to the car park?'

'Yes.'

'Would that not indicate that it was a cry for help?'

'I offered her help just before she left the house.' The barrister let the silence hang over the courtroom and did not ask more.

Alex swallowed, then ... 'We used to sit on that wall on top of the car park when we were younger.'

His lips move as if fighting a tickle under his nose and then his hand lifts and rubs under his nose. The catching tremble in his long in-breath is audible even in the gallery. 'When I got up there she was sitting on the wall. But it wasn't the person I'd fallen in love with sitting there—'

'How can you be so sure the note was not a cry for help? To draw you there to save her. To obtain help from the authorities, perhaps?'

'She was offered help daily. I had helped her for years. I offered again, before she fell. But anorexia owned her. She didn't want to be cured. She must've known I'd go to the car park, but I have no idea why she wanted me there. To watch her fall? I doubt she thought about what that experience might do to the children and I know she didn't care about me.'

'What happened in the minutes between when you left your car and Louise fell?'

'She shouted at me to go away. I tried to convince her to get off the wall.' The heel of his palm wipes under his eyes and then the back of his hand under his nose.

The clerk puts a box of tissues on the stand beside him.

He does not take one.

'I told her how much we loved her. I loved her. I hated the anorexia but I didn't hate her. I told her I would get her into a clinic again.'

'What did Mrs Lovett say in return?'

'She kept shaking her head. Then she told me that I was pushing her into doing this.'

'Doing this?'

'Falling, I suppose. She said she could not continue to feel as if she was letting me down.'

Pushing her into it. Those must have been the words that

Rosie had held onto. She would have been standing a few metres away listening.

'I told her that the children needed her. Then she said, they would be better off without m—' He swallows. It becomes a choking cough. No one says a word while Alex chokes on his tears. They catch the electric light in the room, sparkling on his unshaven jaw as they run down his face. He wipes them away with his hand, swallowing a lump of emotion in his throat. 'That was when she leaned back. I tried to reach her, but I couldn't catch her.'

I see two brown crayon stick figures, one with arms reaching out, the other leaning back.

There are coughs, deep breaths and sobs in the gallery. Louise's mother is in tears. Alex's mother is in tears.

'How was I meant to save a woman that was determined to kill herself?' Alex says, his voice gaining strength. 'And I'm not talking about the car park, I mean the anorexia. It was the anorexia that killed her.'

'Thank you, Mr Lovett.' The barrister turns away from Alex, to face the jury. 'You have been told about Louise Lovett's illness. But we have some pictures to show you that express just how ill Louise Lovett was. These pictures were taken a month before her death.' She looks back at Alex. 'Why did you take these?'

'To try and make her see herself. I mean really see what she was doing to herself and not see the person she imaged in her head.'

Six pictures are passed around the jury. I can imagine how emotive and graphic they are if they were taken by Alex.

Eyebrows lift and lips twist and people swallow back emotion as the pictures are passed along one row and then the other.

The barrister looks at Alex. 'Thank you, Mr Lovett. Did you ever hit your wife?'

'No. Never.' The answer is pronounced with shock.

'Not even a smack.'

The inquest is taking on the essence of his trial again. A trial in which he isn't allowed to defend himself.

'Never.' He swallows. 'But sometimes ... Sometimes, my hand would fist or stretch out in frustration. When I shouted I knew I frightened her, sometimes. But I wanted to frighten her. I wanted to frighten her into eating, not dying.'

'And that anger did not lash out on the top of the car park and push her? You are certain she fell of her own choice.'

His head expresses his answer with a firm shake. 'I did not push her.'

'You said you argued daily ...'

A breath pulls into his chest on the memory and the answer is given on his out breath. 'Yes.'

'How many times a day?'

'Sometimes all day, rarely less than twice.' I hear the weight of guilt in the statement. He believes that he pushed her over that wall emotionally. Guilt. He carries it around in that dark cloud.

'And was there anyone else there when she fell? We heard from a man yesterday saying that he'd seen you, but we have now been told he advised someone else he hadn't been there that day.'

'I didn't see anyone there other than myself and the children. But I wasn't looking around.'

'Thank you, Mr Lovett.' The barrister turns away, dismissing Alex.

'Thank you, Mr Lovett, you may step down.' The judge confirms, nodding at Alex.

Alex looks at Louise's parents before he moves, guilt and

misery glistening in the tears in his eyes. His hand rubs under his nose as he turns and descends from the stand.

I look at Andy. He lifts our joined hands, turning them so he can kiss the back of mine.

Does Andy understand now?

The judge looks at the barrister. 'I believe there is one more piece of evidence to be presented before I sum up.'

'Yes, my lord. A statement from Mr and Mrs Lovett's son. He was six years old at the time. He is now seven.'

The barrister takes a piece of paper from a lawyer in her team. 'Thank you,' she acknowledges before progressing. 'You have heard, although not in words but in a picture, from one of Alexander and Louise's children, now you will hear the account of another. The account of their eldest child.'

The door into the gallery opens. It's Alex. He sits in a space that has been kept for him by his father. People in the row behind lean forward and pat his shoulder but Alex doesn't turn to acknowledge them.

'Helen,' Simon whispers.

The implication in his expression and voice is that I am staring inappropriately.

I glance at Andy; he was looking at me looking at Alex too.

While my attention has been on Alex, the barrister has acquired a pair of black-framed glasses so that she can read, and she's facing the jury. '"The day my mummy died ..."' she begins.

I hear the words in Josh's voice. It is a story written in the voice of a seven-year-old.

'"... Mummy and Daddy argued. Daddy was angry. He gave us some ice cream in the kitchen and talked about going to the cinema. He told me to forget that Mummy was in a bad mood. She was always in a bad mood."'

The barrister looks up from the paper into the faces of the jury. 'The boy was in tears at this point, because he loves the mother he's lost.'

She looks down. '"She was never happy. I can't remember her smiling but Daddy says she did sometimes. Daddy left her in the living room and sat with me and Rosie in the kitchen.

'"I remember him getting up from the table when I had nearly finished my ice cream. He said, 'Your mum's quiet, I better check on her.' I thought that was funny because that was what he said about my baby sister sometimes, not my mum."'

It's strange listening to Josh's child's voice in the powerful pitch of a woman who is used to orating emotional stories.

'"Then Daddy came back and shouted at me to put my shoes on and put Rosie's on. He ran upstairs to get Hope. We got in the car and he strapped Hope and Rosie in, but his hands were shaking. I asked him why, but he wouldn't tell me. He said we had to go and there was no time to talk.

'"When he got in the car, I asked where we were going. He said to get Mummy."'

The barrister pauses, looking up at the jury for a moment. Not saying, but implying, why would Alex have gone to fetch Louise and then pushed her?

I look at Alex. Has he read this? Does he know what Josh has said?

'"He drove fast. The car threw me to the side when he turned the corners. He drove past a red light. I thought the police would stop us but they didn't and then he drove into a car park with roofs and we went up and around and up and around lots of times.

'"When we drove onto the roof of the car park I saw Mummy and I pointed and told him she was there. Mummy was sitting on the wall.

'"Daddy stopped the car and got out. I asked him to let me out but he didn't hear me. I climbed out and heard Mummy say that Daddy was pushing her, but he told her that we all loved her.

'"I wanted to talk to her too. I wanted to tell her I loved her."'

A choking sound becomes a cough. The noise comes from Alex. He has a tissue in his hand and tears are streaking the cheek that I can see.

'"Daddy told her to get down off the wall,"' the barrister continues, '"but she didn't. Then she fell. Daddy reached out for her, but she fell."'

I can see her, there, that day. Louise. On the wall. Leaning back. What did she think in the moment before she reached the ground? Did she regret it? Was she afraid? There was nothing she could have done to stop her fall.

I think of her heart as mine now. Wholly mine. But ... this heart was inside her body in that moment during that fall.

I do not feel Louise. She hasn't been in the courtroom.

Or perhaps she has been but she's not come close to me.

The barrister walks across and drops the statement on the desk where the legal team are sitting and removes her glasses. 'And there you have it. The picture of the event as spoken by her seven-year-old son.'

A muscle tightens in Alex's jaw, implying his teeth are gritting, holding onto the full extent of his emotion.

'That is all the evidence gathered by the coroner.' The barrister returns to her seat and looks at the judge as she sits down.

This is it. The end.

'Thank you, Miss Marshall.' The judge looks at the jury.

The judge spends half an hour talking over the evidence that has been presented, then breathes deeply and his grey eyebrows lift to the edge of his wig. 'And so, it is time for you to think through this evidence and decide, did Mrs Louise Lovett die through misadventure? By that I mean through accidental death occurring from a deliberate action taken by Louise Lovett that resulted in her death? Through suicide – did Louise Lovett voluntarily act to destroy her life in a conscious way? Or unlawful killing – was her death an act of murder or manslaughter? If you can't decide if any of these are true, you also have the option of returning an open verdict but this must be a last resort. You are dismissed.'

The judge stands and leaves the courtroom.

A wave of motion swells through the courtroom and gallery as everyone stands.

Alex is the last person to get to his feet.

Chapter 68

12.48.

Chloe leads our small group out from the back row of the gallery. We trail behind everyone else, but there's nothing to rush for. I look back at Andy. I don't know, but I guess that unless the verdict returns as unlawful killing, my evidence, and the police's concern that I may have been a party in Louise's death, will never come to a courtroom.

'Shall we walk into town and find somewhere to eat lunch?' Simon suggests.

'No. I want to stay here in case the jury come back quickly,' I say as Andy's hand lets go of mine. 'And I'd like to talk to Alex.'

Simon's and Chloe's heads turn and they throw me the same reproving look in the same moment.

I look away from them. Alex's blond head is a few metres ahead of us; he's surrounded by the people who clustered around him and his parents in the gallery.

My gaze turns to Andy, and I smile. 'Do you mind?' The question really asks if he minds if I don't introduce him. It's not the time, or the place, for introductions.

'Join us in the café afterwards,' Andy says.

My heart leaps into a sharp rhythm.

Andy's hand rests on my shoulder as we walk along the corridor, with Chloe and Simon ahead of us. When we are a few feet from the group surrounding Alex, I break free, Andy's hand slipping away. I glance over my shoulder. 'See you soon.'

Simon looks at me again. His parental look. He's angry with me.

But I must say something to Alex if I'm ever going to have a chance of being with the children again.

As Andy, Simon and Chloe walk away I'm left standing, unsure how to break into the group surrounding Alex.

'Hello, Helen. It was good of you to come and support Alex.'

I turn to face Mary. 'Hello. I wondered if I could speak to him?'

She smiles. 'Everyone wants to speak to him after that. I can't believe what that man said yesterday, that she was pushed. That's absurd. Alex half killed himself keeping her alive. I'm so glad they found someone who challenged that statement.'

She doesn't know it was me, and she doesn't seem to know about the pictures of me leaving Alex's.

'This must be awful for you all,' I say. 'How are the children?'

'They can't understand what this might mean for them and we've decided to only tell them what they need to know. I pray that the verdict will return as the truth, as suicide. I know Pat and Robert hate to think that, but ... it's what happened.'

'Mum.'

I turn and face Alex. He looks surprised. He hadn't realised it was me speaking with his mother, but now he looks at me – into me. In the way he did when I first met him, with a wary concern about how much he can trust me.

The recollection of the mistake we made is in his eyes and his skin colour's red.

'Hello. I just want to say ...' What? The words will not come. I want the children back. May I see the children? 'I ...' What? 'I hope the children are well and I hope when this is over you'll be able to get on with life. I ... and if you need me ...'

'Thank you. I need to wait and see what the verdict is before I can make any decisions about the future.' He looks beyond me, at his mother. Telling me he has nothing to say to me.

He and his mother walk on, past me.

Chapter 69

15.21.

'Hey.' One of the men who was sitting at the tables that Alex's supporters occupy walks across the room calling out to the others. 'The jury are coming back.'

My gaze reaches Simon, searching for the comfort that Simon always offers me.

But Simon isn't looking at me. He disapproves of me being here as much as Andy.

When we stand, Chloe threads her arm around mine, to walk with me. She's the only one that understands why I am here.

We sit in the same places at the back. My heart beats in heavy jumps as we stand for the judge. The jury walk in and settle themselves noisily. Everyone else is silent.

I grip Andy's knee as the judge asks, 'Have you agreed on a representative?'

A woman stands. 'I am the representative.'

'Have you reached a verdict?' the judge asks.

'We have.'

As Andy's hand rests over mine on his leg, I also clasp Chloe's hand with my left hand.

The judge looks at one of the administrative staff as if

ensuring they are ready, before looking back at the woman. 'Then please progress, and tell me your verdict on the cause of Mrs Louise Lovett's death.'

The woman looks across to the gallery, her gaze reaching Alex. Then she looks back at the judge with a slight motion of her lips before she speaks, a touch of a smile. 'From the evidence provided we conclude that Louise Lovett's death was suicide.' The last word is spoken in a firm loud tone that seems to repeat around the courtroom.

There is no cheer, no excitement. Louise is still dead. Gone. This verdict will not bring her back to her children. But now at least they can start to live without Louise destroying any chance of their happiness.

I let go of Chloe's hand, and turn to Andy. It's the same for me. Now I must learn to live again. 'Shall we go?' I can't do anything else, and there's nothing else for me to say to Alex.

'Yes.'

Simon looks around Andy, at me. I nod. He gives me a shallow smile.

Potentially as we walk through the door out of the courts, I am walking away from my last chance to see the children. I feel as though my heart is being clawed by a lion. Ripped. Shredded.

As we walk down the steps Andy catches a hold of the sleeve of Simon's jumper. 'Mate, I need to tell you something.' Andy's other hand is holding mine. He glances back at me, before looking at Simon, as Simon turns to listen.

I know what's coming.

'Helen told me that she believes she has that woman's heart, the heart of the woman who committed suicide. She moved to Bath to be near her family. She was stalking that man, watching those children.'

'No.' Simon's brow falls into a frown, his eyes focusing on me. I have seen that look of heartbreak before. Disappointment.

'Yes,' Andy answers. 'I have to work tomorrow, but I think she needs help, and I don't want to leave her alone. I think she should go back with you.'

'Lovett,' Chloe says, looking at me with eyes that say she has seen the light. 'Oh, my God. Helen ...' My name carries accusation. 'I knew I'd heard that name before. Louise Lovett was on your list.'

'What list?' Simon asks.

'She made a list of people who'd died the day before she had her operation.' Andy lets go of my hand, and runs his hand over his hair.

'I'm not ill,' I say, before the accusation comes.

'I think we need to decide that,' Simon answers. 'You can come home with me tonight. Chloe, you can stay with us if you want to. I'll take the day off work tomorrow and take you to see your old doctor.'

'I don't need to see a doctor.' My feet are fixing to the pavement, bolting down. I will not move a step. I am not having a bipolar episode.

'Andy, I want to go home with you.'

He smiles.

At least he is smiling, but it is a smile that offers platitudes, a smile that I would give to calm disgruntled children.

'Andy, I know you don't understand but I felt her spirit. I'm not ill.'

'God. Not that nonsense.' Simon groans on a breath.

'That truth,' I answer.

'I'll come with you,' Andy says, 'and stay the night. But you need to see a doctor to help you get better.'

'I'm not ill!'

Chapter 70

I've been crying on and off ever since we left the courtroom. I curled into Andy on the back seat of Simon's car and Andy held me tight, silently saying, I have you, I love you.

When we walked into the house the boys embraced my middle. It only reminded me that I'll never feel the girls hold me again.

Through dinner, it was difficult to swallow past the lump in my throat.

I am mourning.

Mourning because the children have gone.

Bipolar is like this – some days, and hours, are up and some down. But life is like this without bipolar sometimes, and Simon should know that. Bipolar is extreme. But this situation is extreme. And this evening all I want to do is curl up in bed and hug my knees.

'I need to go to bed. Today has exhausted me.' I stand and excuse myself from the others in the living room. The boys are asleep upstairs; everyone else is staring at an episode of *EastEnders* on the television.

My body is heavy with the weight of emotional fatigue as I

climb the stairs. Before I go to the spare room, I look into the twins' dark bedroom. From the light that stretches in from the landing, I can see the shapes of their bodies curled under their duvets.

I miss Hope, Rosie and Josh. I miss the smell of Hope when I lift her out of her cot. I miss the warmth of Rosie cuddled into my side when she's tired.

I breathe out as I walk to the room where Andy and I will spoon in the single bed.

I feel too tired to change into my pyjamas, but, knowing that I have to wear the same clothes tomorrow, I do before taking my toothbrush to the bathroom to clean my teeth.

'I don't know,' Andy says downstairs.

'I know,' Mim answers. 'I told you, Simon. I said she wasn't right after the operation.'

There's a loud sigh, which I know is Simon's enduring sigh.

They are talking about me.

I walk along the landing, trying not to make the floorboards underneath the carpet creak.

'I did warn her when she looked up dead people that it was abnormal. I didn't know she thought one of them was talking to her,' Chloe says.

Andy has told them everything.

My heart is pumping with a thrust that wants me to run down and address this. But instead I sit on the top step in my pyjamas and listen to the words drifting upstairs, my hands holding onto my knees.

'She's definitely not well,' Simon says.

I am well. My body rocks backwards and forwards as my hands slide from my knees to my ankles.

'Simon. I've been telling you. She's more than unwell, she's becoming dangerous again. She told Andy she moved to Bath to become involved in the lives of those children. What next? What if she'd taken a child? She'll end up in a prison. It's an obsession. She needs to go to hospital.'

No. I stand, holding the bannister, and walk down.

'She had sex with that man,' Mim says. 'Only days after she was married. She's ill.'

'Had sex with who?' Andy's voice has moved. Changed.

I run down the last few steps, my bare feet slipping on the carpet as my hand slides down the bannister.

'Alex Lovett, the father,' Mim's voice clarifies.

'Andy!' I don't want him to know that. Don't tell him that.

I will lose everything.

AN END
OR
ANOTHER BEGINNING?

Chapter 71

1 day after the inquest.

There's a smell that's individual to hospitals. Before I even open my eyes, I know where I am. The pillow crinkles when I move my head – bedding that has been washed with disinfectant.

The room is a cream, non-committing colour. But there are no machines. This isn't a room in a ward that is trying to keep me alive. This a room in a ward that has shut me away, and there's no one in here but me. But I hear others outside. Talking nonsense. Shouting over nothing.

They have put me away again and silenced my mind with drugs.

I am not mad. This is not an episode of manic behaviour.

'I am not ill!'

Chapter 72

1 year, 3 months, 2 weeks and 4 days after the inquest.

The sky is a clear azure blue, and the leaves on the trees are amber, gold and ruby-red against it. Perfect. It's not even cold today. Cool, but not cold. It's just a lovely autumn day to be out walking.

I look down into the pram; Joy is fast asleep. I tuck her little hand back under the thin blanket. It's not cold, but she is tiny and precious, and I don't want my daughter to become at all uncomfortable.

I probably have another hour of this beautiful and quiet walk before she wakes for another feed.

I stroke her cheek with the tip of my finger before my hand moves away. I can never resist the urge to touch her.

My heart is jubilant. It's been jubilant since the day she was born.

A smile plays on my lips, as it always does as I walk along the Regent's Park path. The path is lined by a bed full of flowers that are in their final flush, holding on until the first hard frost will come.

A few metres on, I can see children playing on the farthest edge of the lawn underneath a tree. They look as if they're gathering conkers.

One day Joy and I will gather conkers and thread strings through them.

'Helen?' A male voice reaches through the park, catching on the wind. 'Helen?'

I stop walking and look from one side to the other.

'Helen Arnold?'

There is a group of people gathered around a low branch. With photographic equipment around them. A man is waving a hand, at me.

He moves then, walking towards me.

I only know one man that it might be.

Blond curls catch the orange autumn sunlight.

'Hello,' he calls from a distance away. 'I thought it was you.'

My hand lifts to acknowledge him, but I don't shout back.

It's strange that Louise's death gave me life and then Alex's actions stole the new life I had made.

His actions took the children and Andy away from me.

Andy and I divorced six months ago. He hasn't been able to forgive me for a drunken error. I don't blame him. I blame me. I chose to let Alex do that.

'Hello,' he says again when he is only a few feet away. He's not clean-shaven but his beard and moustache are neatly tamed. He's wearing pale jeans that have no stain and a grey hooded sweatshirt.

His gaze is on the pushchair. 'Yours?' he says when he reaches me.

'Mine,' I confirm.

'Are you living in London with your husband now?'

'I am living in London, but I'm not married any more.'

Perhaps the tone of my voice stops him from asking why.

'I can't believe I've bumped into you,' he says. 'Rosie still talks about you. The nice Helen. The nice nanny.' His lips lift in an easy but shallow smile. There is no dark aura around him, his aura is autumn coloured – yellow, gold, orange and shining amber like the conkers.

A smile pulls at my lips as I see and hear Rosie say the words. But Rosie will have grown up a lot since I last saw her. Her voice and her manner will be different. 'Are the children well, and happy?'

'They are. Thank you.' His smile lifts suddenly, into a broad, wide, natural smile that I haven't seen formed by Alex's lips before. The smile falls away as quickly as it came. 'Are you busy? Are you on your way somewhere?'

'No. But I can't be out too long.' I look at Joy, as though the reason is obvious.

'If you can hang around for a few minutes, this shoot is nearly done and we could catch up over a coffee. If you don't mind waiting?'

This isn't the man I knew in Bath. 'I don't mind waiting.' But my heart is skipping. He might let me see the children again. I have Joy but I've never forgotten them, nor stopped loving them, despite doctors trying to convince me that the emotion I felt for them was part of a drug imbalance after the heart operation. That is what they said had caused my mood swings last year. They said it was the reason I thought I heard Louise.

Like Simon, Chloe, Andy and Mim, the doctors did not believe in a sixth sense.

There is another natural but shallower smile. 'I'll be as quick as I can. Rosie will be thrilled when I tell her I saw you in London. Don't go anywhere.' His eyebrows lift when he says the last words, to emphasise the request. Then he turns and jogs rather than walks back to where the other people are gathered.

My heart beats steadily, letting me know that it's there, pulsing, keeping me alive, as I watch the models, men and women, posing against the low branch.

It's barely ten minutes later, when he comes back towards me. 'Hello, again.' His arms lift and open. In the gesture I have seen him offer as a welcome to his children day after day.

'Hello, again,' I echo, unsure what else to say, as my arms lift to share the embrace. I don't know this Alex.

His arms wrap around my neck, as mine embrace his middle. We hold each other for an instant then break apart.

I think he's gained a little weight, although he still looks muscular.

'Where would you like to go? Do you know anywhere near here?'

'No.' Not that I can think of.

'I know a good small café in a street at the edge of the park. That way.' He lifts a hand to point. His other hand touches my waist to steer me.

'What's her name?' He looks at Joy as we begin walking and his hand slides away from my waist.

'Joy.' I glance back at the group of people in the middle of the lawn. 'Do they need you to pack up?'

He smiles with that sudden, but fleeting, broad smile. 'That's what I pay assistants for.'

'You sound different,' I say, and look so different.

'There's a counsellor who will take credit for that. It took several months of heart-bleeding and learning how to climb out of the dark place I was in at the point you worked for me.' His eyebrows lift a little. 'I probably look better too, and things look better to me.'

'Is that why the children are happier too?'

'Have they had counselling? Yes. But they are also seeing Louise's parents as well as mine, and they feel very loved. We have gradually built up the trust again, since the inquest.' His eyes tell me that he has remembered that I was there.

'I'm glad.'

'So am I. The children have a memory jar,' he continues, 'where we store every good memory that we have and then when one of us is missing Louise we pull out all the memories and share them. It makes us feel better and helps us to focus on the good things. One of the counsellors recommended it.'

'That's a lovely idea.'

'We'll go out that gate.' He points at an exit between the hedging. 'And you? I'm sorry to hear about your marriage.'

'I was very upset at the time, but I'm used to being on my own with Joy now.' I did not dare to take a pregnancy test until I'd missed four months, and by then Andy and I were no more. But I have Joy. My child. Andy's and my child, that is the record on her birth certificate and that is what she will grow up believing. I will not break Andy's heart for a second time. But as she grows there's no similarity to Andy appearing.

I haven't tested my theory – but I know the truth.

Alex's hand touches my waist again as people pass.

She has his hair. Joy's hair looks just like Hope's.

When we walk out of the gate, the touch falls away. 'I know how that feels,' he answers. 'I thought I deserved to be ripped apart with the pain of losing Louise. But now I know that I can and should carry on.'

'Your counsellor is good – that sounded very convincing.' My counsellors were just as good. I knew everything to say, and everything not to say.

My heartbeat pummels my ribs.

'The café is there.' He points across the road.

It has a quaint, old-fashioned bow window. A bell above the door rings when he holds it open for the pushchair. I look down at Joy but she's not woken.

'It's table service. Where do you want to sit?'

'In the corner over there. There's space for the pushchair by the wall.'

He beckons a waitress over before we sit down.

'What do you want?' He looks at me as she comes across, pad in hand.

'A decaffeinated flat white, please.'

Alex looks at the waitress. 'Just a black coffee for me,' he adds. 'Can I do anything?' Alex looks at me, and I realise he's asking if I want help with Joy.

'No. Thank you. I'll leave her in the pushchair unless she wakes up.' I sit down.

'Motherhood suits you,' he says. 'Is your ex-husband on the scene at all?'

'He is. He looks after her every other Saturday.'

I'm sure a blush darkens my skin. Joy is my last secret but one I'll take to my grave. She has my nose, mouth and ears. Just because she has blonde curls and almost blue eyes no one will be able to say she isn't Andy's without proof. I tell anyone who asks that my mother had blonde, curly hair.

His smile twitches. 'I don't think I could be a Saturday father. I'd want my full half-share.'

I guessed that. It's why there was never any doubt in my mind that she would be Andy's child.

Alex looks down at the pram. 'She looks like an angel.'

'She is. Do you have any pictures of the children on your phone? I would love to see how much they've grown.'

'Yes.'

Our coffees arrive as he hands the phone to me.

The children are beautiful. Hope has become the image of Rosie, and Rosie is fast becoming the image of her mother, and Josh looks more and more like the man he'll become as a young boy.

We talk about them, about Alex's photography, about Joy, and the conversation never breaks until there's a small gurgling sound from the pram. 'Oh.' I turn immediately, with the protective urge of motherhood, unbuckle the straps and lift her out of the pushchair. She drags her blanket with her.

When I look up, Alex is smiling at us.

The fair, fine little wisps of hair on her head are tangled. I stroke them flat as her sleepy eyes look to me with hope; knowing that food will come. I attract the attention of the waitress, reach for the bottle of breast milk that is in a cooling container in the back of the pram, take the bottle out and hold it up. 'Please can you warm this for me?'

I look over at Alex. He's watching us, with that broad smile fixed on his lips and it doesn't fall.

'Would you like another coffee?' he asks.

'Yes, please. There's no need for me to rush off now.'

He orders when the waitress returns with the bottle of warm milk. Then looks at me. 'I'm free for the afternoon. We can take Joy for a walk, if you'd like to?'

I'm enjoying his company. 'Yes. That would be nice.' I'm sure I blush but he's not looking at me. He's looking at Joy sucking thirstily from the bottle's teat.

His smile lifts and then falls away. 'I used to be the master of a bottle feed.' When he looks at me his eyes speak of images, memories, that he looks at within his head.

'Do you have a new nanny now?' I ask. I couldn't fulfil that role now; I will never leave Joy to the care of someone else.

'No,' he says when he turns back. 'I manage it, between school, afterschool clubs, nursery, my parents, Louise's parents and neighbours.'

'Sounds like fun.'

He smiles, watching Joy again.

'What happened to the woman in the basement?' I smile to soften the question.

'Gone. Gone before the inquest and never returned. She wasn't really me.'

'So does that mean you still look for women late at night?' I smile again as Joy's small hand rests over mine, holding the bottle with me. When I am breastfeeding her hand rests on my breast.

'That makes me sound like Jack the Ripper. No. My focus is on being a father. I discovered, I don't need sex to survive.'

I laugh. 'Was that a phrase learned on a counsellor's couch?' He looked like Jack the Ripper sometimes, with that dark aura around him.

'It was.'

The woman arrives with our second cups of coffee.

'There's a canal near here,' he says as the waitress leaves us. 'We could go for a walk along the canal path after this.'

'You know a lot about the area for a man who doesn't live in London.'

'I know it from the perspective of a photographer looking for sites to take pictures. It's called Little Venice.'

I smile. 'I know. I'm a Londoner.'

He looks down at the coffee in his cup, holding the handle. 'I felt guilty when you stopped working for me. What happened ...' He looks up. 'It wasn't fair on you. I was drunk.

I can't even remember ... I'm glad we've seen each other again, and that I have a chance to say sorry. I am sorry.'

'You said sorry at the time, and I'd drunk too much too. It wasn't just your fault, and perhaps it was even my idea.'

'Was it?' His forehead twitches, displaying wrinkles for a moment. 'Poor Hope and Rosie cried for weeks after you left.'

'I washed her mum's T-shirt; that's probably why.'

'She forgave you within forty-eight hours, and it did need washing. I could never have washed it, though.'

A smile tugs my lips as Joy lets the bottle's teat slide out of her mouth.

Hope and Rosie fill my mind's eye as I put the bottle down and move Joy, sitting her so I can rub her back.

The autumn sun is warm on my back as we walk along the canal path, serenaded by the leaves of the trees whispering as they sway in a breeze. One particularly strong gust of wind lifts dozens of helicopter-seeds off the top of a sycamore tree, and sends them spinning high up into the air. After a minute or two the seeds twirl down on top of the houseboats.

Most of the boats along here are moored, but the occasional motor of a canal barge disturbs the idyllic sense of escape from the city.

Joy is happily looking up at us and the passing trees. Her feet kicking under the thin blanket.

'Tell me about you. Your history. You know everything about me,' Alex says as we walk. He doesn't know about my life. He knows nothing beyond what was on my CV. I can tell him everything, nothing or anything.

I start at the beginning and tell him the truth about the hippy parents who deserted Simon and me. I tell him about my heart condition, and Dan, and the operation that changed my life.

I say that my childhood probably impacted on how much I was dependent on Dan's love. I invested all of myself and he didn't return the favour.

Alex likens that to his relationship with Louise. 'Only her illness had a cure.' A note of bitter regret slips into his voice.

I talk about Andy, about how I thought Andy was my fate, my one, that Dan and I separating, and my moving to Bath, had been for a reason. I do not mention my sixth sense, or why I really moved to Bath. I do tell him how hard it was to lose the job looking after the children, and then to lose Andy.

His arm comes around me and his hand squeezes my waist for a moment before falling away. It's a reassuring gesture that he might have used with the girls.

His hands slip into the back pockets of his jeans as we walk on, as though he thinks that the gesture was too forward and regrets the intimacy.

'I have something to confess,' I say.

He glances at me, his skin colouring a little pink, as though he's nervous of what he will hear.

'I have a condition called bipolar.'

His pale eyebrows lift. 'Really?'

'Yes. Do you know about it?'

'A little.'

I tell him everything about what it means for me, and he listens. He listens in a way that only Simon and Andy have listened to me before. No. He listens without judgement. Simon and Andy have judged my actions.

But then Alex has made bad decisions due to depression.

'Depression is not the same, I'm sure, but, believe me, I know how it feels to be emotionally ill.'

'Tell me about the good times you had with Louise, about the memories in your jar,' I say, to lighten the conversation.

He smiles, immediately, and talks about his childhood. He tells me about the car-park wall; they used to sit there and talk about being on top of the world.

It's not until the light starts to change and the temperature drops that I realise we have been walking and talking for a couple of hours. 'I have to take Joy home,' I say, when there's a break in the conversation.

His lips lift and fall, in a sort of smile. 'Yes. I ought to get back and get on with processing the pictures I took today. But it has been a lovely afternoon. I'm glad I saw you, Helen.'

'I agree.' It has been a very good afternoon.

He leans down and strokes his forefinger along Joy's cheek. 'And it's been a pleasure meeting you, little lady. You are a poppet.' She catches hold of his finger and plays with it. That natural smile that I have only known from him today appears. When she releases his finger, he shares that smile with me.

He hasn't seen himself in her, and if he can't see himself then no one else will.

I stop walking as we reach the path that will let us exit the canal.

'Do you want a hand down the steps with the pushchair?'

'Yes, please.' He moves in front of me to lift the front of the pushchair. Then, at the bottom of the steps, he puts the pushchair down, straightens and looks into me, his hands sliding into his back pockets.

'When does Joy go to her father next?'

'Andy has her tomorrow.'

'The children are with Louise's parents for the whole weekend. So, would you like to go out for dinner tomorrow evening?' The question is spoken in a tentative tone, but his smile is confident.

'I ...'

'I won't be offended if you say no.'

'Yes.' The word breathes through me. I haven't heard Louise speak since I left his house, but, today, I'm not sure who has just answered ...

Chapter 73

'I think half this stuff needs to go in the bin,' Chloe says as she cuts open another cardboard box.

'Or a charity shop,' I say.

We are opening the boxes that have been stored in Simon's garage since Dan and I split. I wasn't ready to go through them when I moved to Bath and I didn't care about them when I moved in with Andy.

When I moved into a flat with Joy that was only two rooms big, there wasn't the space to care about taking this historical baggage with me. But Simon has put his foot down this time, insisting I either move my boxes into Alex's with Joy and me, or get rid of them.

I look at the box that Chloe has opened that contains kitchen crockery. 'That can all go to a charity. Alex has all that stuff. There's nothing I want in there.'

I draw over a shoe box and pass it on to her as she moves the other box aside. The diamond on my finger catches the daylight that shines through the open garage door. I lift my hand, looking at the ring, and smile.

'Stop flashing that rock at me,' Chloe jokes.

I laugh. 'You're just jealous because John still hasn't asked you.'

'I don't know how much harder I can hint. While everyone you date falls on their knees.'

'I can't help that.' I laugh. I am the happiest I have been in my life. I have Joy, and Alex, and the children. His parents and Louise's parents. Everything. A complete family.

'This is full of hospital letters,' Chloe says, flicking through envelopes. 'Do you need to keep these?'

'I don't want those. I've had enough of hospitals for the rest of my life.'

'This is something different.' She pulls out a pastel-blue A5-size envelope.

I know what it is. I lean back, resting my bottom on my heels, as she does. I want to grab the envelope out of her hands, but I can't make it obvious that I know about it.

'It's a card from an organ donors' charity,' she says, looking at the franking. 'You received this over a year ago. You didn't tell me about it. Is it from the donor's family?'

'Put it away,' I say.

Her thumb slips under the leaf to tear the envelope open.

I grab it out of her hand. 'It's private. I didn't open it because I decided I didn't want to know, after what happened with Louise Lovett's family.'

I bend the envelope in half and press it into the back pocket of my jeans. 'Everything else in there can go on the bonfire.'

'Okay, tetchy.' She closes the box and moves it aside to take on the next pile to be sorted. 'I understand,' she snaps.

No, she doesn't. None of them do. I didn't open the letter at the time because I couldn't have stood to read nice words from Robert and Pat Dowling after the inquest.

The bonfire is still burning, flames licking high into the air, when it's time for Liam and Kevin to go to bed. They used the fire that's consuming the history of my life to melt marshmallows on sticks for s'mores after dinner.

Simon and Mim take the boys indoors.

I am out here alone, for the first time since Chloe left.

I pull the bent card out of my pocket and look at it.

My thumb slots into the hole that Chloe tore earlier and I tear the hole wider, ripping the envelope until the tear is wide enough to get the card out.

I throw the envelope into the flames.

There's a picture of white roses on the front of the card. A mass of white roses, like the flower bed in the Dowlings' front garden.

I glance at the house, at the back door, to check no one is coming before I open the card.

Thank you, so much for contacting us. The first words pop out at me as a small photo-booth picture drops onto the paving slab I'm standing on. *You have no idea how much it means to hear …* I bend to pick up the photograph as I read … *what this has done for you. Knowing that …*

I look down at the picture.

Oh, my God.

It's not a picture of Louise.

No.

It's the man with the ginger hair and thick beard.

I throw the card and the picture into the flames.

That's not true.

The fire blackens the edges of the picture and the card, the black creeping inwards.

Our son Rory are the last words to extinguish on the card.

His eyes are the last thing to disappear from his picture.

LOUISE

Chapter 74

The day of the fall.

He stops running as I lift my hand, but instead of stopping entirely he walks, slowly, towards me. His hands lift, palm up in conciliation.

'Don't come closer. Stay away.' He doesn't stop.

There are pictures in my mind, of our past, here, planning our futures. Developing dreams. His dreams have come true.

Mine ...

'Louise, get down.' The car door is left open behind him and the car is in the middle of the tarmac.

This is our marriage, the future we dreamed of together.

'I can't.' But I haven't found the courage to fall.

'Louise, listen to me. We can solve this. We'll get you back into a clinic.'

Where they will force tubes down my throat. No.

'Mummy?' Josh has climbed out of the car.

'Stay away,' I say to Alex again. 'Please.' I want to find the courage.

'I can't stay away, can I? You have children. You can't really think that they don't want you here. They love you. They need their mother. Get down, Louise.'

My head shakes. I can't imagine how to go on with life. How

to keep arguing every day. To keep fighting with food every day. To keep looking at the disappointment in their eyes. The children's and his. It's easier to imagine my skull breaking apart on the pavement beyond this wall. 'You're pushing me into doing this. I can't make you happy. I can't do anything right. You push and push at me.'

He takes another four steps. He's only a metre away.

'If I'm not here then I won't keep letting you all down.'

'You won't let us down if you get off the wall and we get you into a clinic.'

'I can't do it, Alex.' My head shakes and my fingers curl on the concrete wall; a fingernail breaks, weakened already by the lack of nutrition.

It hurts to sit here, the concrete wall cutting through my clothes and skin and into my bones. But it hurts to do everything – anything.

'I don't want you to go into a clinic for my sake.' Alex is walking closer. 'Not for me. For the children. They need you.'

He's too close. His anger scares me when he's close.

I see someone moving at the entrance of the stairwell behind him.

'They'd be better off without me!' A scream lifts my voice as I raise a hand, palm outward to keep him away. 'Then, you wouldn't shout at me and frighten them!' My words reverberate from the bare concrete walls around the car park. 'You push me away! You're never happy!'

He's one step away.

'Only because you never try to get better and they can't cope with any more of this!'

His hands brace my arms, as my hands press against his chest; my strength so much weaker than his.

His fingers curl about my arms and overlap his thumbs. He looks at that – at how small my arms are in his hold. Then he looks at my eyes – into my eyes. 'Tell me you will try harder to get better, for the children's sake?'

My head shakes, because I can't promise. He knows I can't promise.

He sighs and I think he is going to help me off the wall. 'Louise, I love you, but I need to let them be free. Let us all be free.'

His hold on my arms suddenly pushes me back and he lets go.

I'm falling. Screaming. I am falling. Alex pushed me.

My children!

THE END

Acknowledgements

This story has been on a significant development journey and without the support of the brilliant Charlotte Ledger and Emily Ruston in One More Chapter it would not be the story it has become. Thank you for all your guidance, encouragement and, most importantly, your belief in me.

Thank you also to my wonderful husband who has absolute confidence in me, for all his support in doing the day to day things so that I have time to write.